MY
TINY
LIFE

Being a True Account of the Case
of the Infamous Mr. Bungle,
and of the Author's Journey, in
Consequence Thereof, to the Heart
of a Half-Real World Called
LambdaMOO

MY
TINY
LIFE

Crime and Passion
in a Virtual World

JULIAN DIBBELL

An Owl Book
Henry Holt and Company
New York

Henry Holt and Company, Inc.
Publishers since 1866
115 West 18th Street
New York, New York 10011

Henry Holt® is a registered trademark
of Henry Holt and Company, Inc.

Chapter 1 was originally published in a somewhat
different form in *The Village Voice.*

Library of Congress Cataloging-in-Publication Data

Dibbell, Julian
My tiny life : crime and passion in a virtual world / Julian
Dibbell. — 1st ed.
p.   cm.
"Being a True Account of the Case of the Infamous Mr. Bungle, and
of the Author's Journey, in Consequence Thereof, to the Heart of a
Half-Real World Called LambdaMOO"—CIP t.p.
"An owl book."
ISBN 0-8050-3626-1 (alk. paper)
1. Computer crimes—United States. 2. World Wide Web (Information
retrieval system) 3. LambdaMOO.   I. Title.
HV6773.2.D53   1998
364.1—DC21   98-13636

Henry Holt books are available for special
promotions and premiums. For details contact:
Director, Special Markets.

First Edition 1998

Designed by Paula R. Szafranski

Printed in the United States of America
All first editions are printed on acid-free paper. ∞

1   3   5   7   9   10   8   6   4   2

For Jessica, who is more beautiful to me
than text can say

Contents

Author's Note

The narrative contained herein is as true to life, and to the facts, as I could bear to make it. In a few spots I felt compelled to jigger the chronology of events for the sake of a smooth story line, but I did so only with matters concerning my own history, not that of the MOO, and only where such alterations affected the substance of my report no more than trivially. As for quotes, I was obliged to invent a few in the autobiographical "RL" episodes, which have been reconstructed mainly on the basis of memory and brief journal entries, but the book's quotes are otherwise taken straight from transcripts of online conversations, from MOO-mail or e-mail, or from interviews conducted via telephone or face-to-face. In a handful of cases, I conflated separate real-time quotes from a MOO player into a single quote, and occasionally I cleaned up typos I thought were more distracting than telling. Likewise, I sometimes revised a few words for the sake of clarity.

For the sake of privacy I made other alterations, the main one being that names were changed from actual to fictitious ones throughout the book. This is common journalistic practice, of course, but here it may seem oddly superfluous considering that the "actual" names I changed were mostly pseudonyms to begin with, used by people whose real-life identities are in many cases still unknown to me. If my approach was unusual, however, so were the circumstances: Lambda-MOO happens to be a world in which, for technical reasons, knowing a person's name is the approximate virtual equivalent of knowing that person's phone number, home address, and social security number as well. And given that that world is also readily accessible to anybody with an Internet account, I thought it best not to offer unavoidable encouragement to any ill-mannered rubberneckers (or worse) who may lurk among my readers. (I don't mean you, of course, and I should add that visitors to LambdaMOO are usually treated no less kindly than they treat the locals.)

Additionally, when writing about Lambda residents who could not reasonably be considered "public figures" within the context of the MOO, I sometimes took measures to conceal their identities from other MOOers as well as from visiting outsiders. These measures variously included rewriting the residents' descriptions of their virtual selves and possessions, revising information about their real lives (such as hometown, age, and place of employment), or both. I changed the non-MOO details of some "MOO-famous" figures as well, to keep certain aspects of their real lives private.

Where I felt there to be no compelling reason for fictionalizing a name or pseudonym, I left it unchanged. This didn't happen often, though. Real names and pseudonyms found in the book include my own, those of Pavel Curtis, and those of LambdaMOO characters long gone from the MOO and very unlikely to return. They do not, however, include the names of the Lambda "satellite worlds" Interzone and aCleanWellLightedMOO, although neither place, I assure you, is any less—or more—real than LambdaMOO itself.

MY
TINY
LIFE

The Low-Humming Room Full of Bone-White Boxes
You are in a quiet, low-lit room full of stacked
  metal boxes, their surfaces mostly white, like
  old bones, studded here and there with pale
  green-yellow pinpoint lights that flicker on and
  off. The boxes are computers, twenty-five of them
  or so: collectively they hum a damped and hissing
  drone. There is carpeting beneath your feet --
  thin, corporate, and clean. There is an exit to
  the south.
You see The Server here.
Pavel and The_Author are here.

Pavel shrugs.

Pavel says, "Well, there it is. Not much to look at,
  really."

The_Author looks at The Server.

look server

The Server
You see a box as unremarkable as any other in this

room, only more so. Three feet square by one foot
high, some cables slithering out the back, no
flickering lights or any other outward indication of
activity within. The box sits at about knee level,
stacked unceremoniously on top of another one just
like it.

The_Author has come 3,000 miles to look at this
  machine.

The_Author crouches for a better look and wonders at
  his disappointment. He didn't think he was so foolish
  as to hope for more than this. He didn't expect the
  emptiness he feels inside him now. He can't imagine
  what it is he expected, really.

The_Author stands and glances momentarily at Pavel.

look pavel

Pavel
You see a portrait of Santa Claus as an early-middle-
  aged man. Thick brown hair to shoulder length, a
  full, dark beard, and eyes that underneath their
  long, fine lashes actually do appear to twinkle in
  the manner of the mythical Father Christmas. But
  Pavel is otherwise not very mythic looking. He is
  wearing jeans and running shoes, and his T-shirt
  hangs loosely over a comfy paunch.
He is awake and looks alert.

@aliases pavel

Pavel is also known as Pavel, Pavel_Curtis, Haakon,
  Lambda, The_Archwizard, Keeper_of_the_Server,
  and God.

Pavel seems, perhaps, to sense The_Author's wish that
  there were even the slightest note of drama to be
  wrung from this profoundly uneventful moment.

[6]

Pavel says, "You know, I brought PennyAunty down here
once and do you know what she said?"

Pavel says, "'My world is in there.'"

Pavel mimes, with outstretched hands and eyebrows
raised, the wonder that his earlier visitor felt
before the silent, bone-white presence of The Server.

Pavel shrugs.

The_Author smiles awkwardly. He is the slightest bit
embarrassed. He knows now what it is he was expecting
to find here, and it's ludicrous: he really felt,
without admitting it to himself, that he was going to
see what PennyAunty only pretended to see. He thought
that he was coming here to finally gaze directly at a
world he had been living in for months.

The_Author realizes now that during all those months he
never really doubted LambdaMOO was in this box,
compact, condensed, its rambling landscapes and its
teeming population all somehow shrunk down to the
size of The Server's hard-disk drive.

The_Author remembers with a twinge of newfound
understanding the way the people there sometimes
attached the curious prefix "tiny" to the features of
their world, the way they spoke of "tinyscenery," and
"tinygovernment," and so on.

The_Author thinks of how impossible it was to ever
quite believe the place was not, in fact, a place. Of
how he never could quite shake the thought that
LambdaMOO existed somewhere in a concrete sense, that
somewhere, out beyond the scrim of fantasy and
distance through which he interacted with the MOO, it
waited to be seen unveiled -- an X on the map of the
material world, a thing as tangible as any rock, or
house, or island.

[7]

The_Author knows he isn't the first person to make this kind of mistake. He knows that new technologies like this one have a history of sowing metaphysical derangement in the minds of those who first behold them -- that in the middle nineteenth century, for example, even educated Frenchmen were known to fear the camera's gaze, suspecting that it could not work its representational magic on a person without stealing a little of his soul.

The_Author, come to think of it, is carrying a small camera in his pocket at this very moment. Why not? he asks himself.

The_Author pulls the camera out and aims it at The Server, and shoots. Perhaps, he muses (deciding to indulge his metaphysical derangement just a little longer), perhaps through some strange alchemy of representational technologies the camera has captured an image of The Server's soul. Perhaps it will produce a photograph of what he came to see: the tiny world of LambdaMOO and all the tiny people in it.

The_Author puts the camera back in his pocket. Three weeks from now he will hold in his hands the photo he's just taken and he'll look at it and think, "My world is not in there. The 1s and 0s of it maybe, the nuts and bolts. But not its soul."

The_Author will have to start all over then. He will have to try and find another way of representing what the camera failed to show. He'll have to go back to the night it all began for him and trace his steps from there.

VR

LambdaMOO is a new kind of society, where thousands of people voluntarily come together from all over the world. What these people say or do may not always be to your liking; as when visiting any international city, it is wise to be careful who you associate with and what you say. . . .

—LambdaMOO logon screen

A Rape in Cyberspace

Or TINYSOCIETY, and How to Make One

They say he raped them that night. They say he did it with a cunning little doll, fashioned in their image and imbued with the power to make them do whatever he desired. They say that by manipulating the doll he forced them to have sex with him, and with each other, and to do horrible, brutal things to their own bodies. And though I wasn't there that night, I think I can assure you that what they say is true, because it all happened right in the living room—right there amid the well-stocked bookcases and the sofas and the fireplace—of a house I came later to think of as my second home.

Call me Dr. Bombay. Some years ago—let's say about halfway between the first time you heard the words *information superhighway* and the first time you wished you never had—I found myself tripping now and then down the well-traveled information lane that leads to LambdaMOO, a very large and very busy rustic mansion built entirely of words. On the occasional free evening I'd sit down in my New York City apartment and type the commands that called those words onto my computer screen, dropping me with what seemed a warm electric thud inside the house's darkened coat closet, where I checked my quotidian identity, stepped into the persona and appearance of a minor character from a long-gone television sitcom, and stepped out into the glaring chatter of the crowded living room. Sometimes, when the mood struck me, I emerged as a dolphin instead.

I won't say why I chose to masquerade as Samantha Stephens's outlandish cousin, or as the dolphin, or what first led me into the semifictional digital other-worlds known around the Internet as multiuser dimensions, or MUDs. This isn't quite my story yet. It's the story, for now, of an elusive congeries of flesh and bytes named Mr. Bungle, and of the ghostly sexual violence he committed in the halls of LambdaMOO, and most importantly of the ways his violence and his victims challenged the thousand and more residents of that surreal, magic-infested mansion to become, finally, the community so many of them already believed they were.

That I was myself already known to wander the mansion grounds from time to time has little direct bearing on the story's events. That those same events were, months after, to draw me deeper into the complex, flickering core of Lambda-MOO's shadow reality than I had ever thought to go is also, I suppose, of only a slight and hindsighted relevance to the matter now at hand. I mention it only as a warning that my own perspective may, at this late date, be too steeped in the sur-reality and magic of the place to serve as an altogether appropriate guide. For the Bungle Affair raises questions that—here on the brink of a future in which human existence may find itself as tightly enveloped in digital environments as it is today in the architectural kind—demand a clear-eyed, sober, and unmystified consideration. It asks us to shut our ears for the time being to techno-utopian ecstasies and look without illusion upon the present possibilities for building, in the online spaces of this world, societies more decent and free than those mapped onto dirt and concrete and capital. It asks us to behold the new bodies awaiting us in virtual space undazzled by their phantom powers, and to get to the crucial work of sorting out the socially meaningful differences between those bodies and our physical ones. And perhaps most challengingly it asks us to wrap our late-modern ontologies, epistemologies, sexual ethics, and common sense around the curious notion of rape by voodoo doll—and to try not to warp them beyond recognition in the process.

In short, the Bungle Affair dares me to explain it to you without resort to dime-store mysticisms, and I fear I may have shape-shifted by the digital moon-light one too many times to be quite up to the task. But I will do what I can, and can do no better than to lead with the facts. For if nothing else about Mr. Bungle's case is unambiguous, the facts at least are crystal clear.

The facts begin (as they often do) with a time and a place. The time was a Monday night in March, and the place, as I've said, was the living room—which, due largely to the centrality of its location and to a certain warmth of decor, was in those days so invariably packed with chitchatters as to be roughly synonymous among LambdaMOOers with a party. So strong, indeed, was the sense of convivial common ground invested in the living room that a cruel mind could hardly imagine a better place in which to stage a violation of LambdaMOO's communal spirit. And there was cruelty enough lurking in the appearance Mr. Bungle presented to the virtual world—he was at the time a fat, oleaginous, Bisquick-faced clown dressed in cum-stained harlequin garb and girdled with a mistletoe-and-hemlock belt whose buckle bore the quaint inscription KISS ME UNDER THIS, BITCH! But whether cruelty motivated his choice of crime scene is not among the established facts of the case. It is a fact only that he did choose the living room.

The remaining facts tell us a bit more about the inner world of Mr. Bungle, though only perhaps that it wasn't a very cozy place. They tell us that he commenced his assault entirely unprovoked, at or about 10 P.M. Pacific Standard Time. That he began by using his voodoo doll to force one of the room's occupants to sexually service him in a variety of more or less conventional ways. That this victim was exu,* a South American trickster spirit of indeterminate gender, brown-skinned and wearing an expensive pearl gray suit, top hat, and dark glasses. That exu heaped vicious imprecations on him all the while and that he was soon ejected bodily from the room. That he hid himself away then in his private chambers somewhere on the mansion grounds and continued the attacks without interruption, since the voodoo doll worked just as well at a distance as in proximity. That he turned his attentions now to Moondreamer, a rather pointedly nondescript female character, tall, stout, and brown-haired, forcing her into unwanted liaisons with other individuals present in the room, among them exu, Kropotkin (the well-known radical), and Snugberry (the squirrel). That his actions grew progressively violent. That he made exu eat his/her own pubic hair. That he caused Moondreamer to violate herself with a piece of kitchen cutlery. That his distant laughter echoed evilly in the living room with every successive outrage. That he could not be stopped until at last someone summoned Iggy, a wise and trusted old-timer who brought with him a gun of near wizardly powers, a gun that didn't kill but enveloped its targets in a cage impermeable even to a voodoo doll's powers. That Iggy fired this gun at Mr. Bungle, thwarting the doll at last and silencing the evil, distant laughter.

These particulars, as I said, are unambiguous. But they are far from simple,

*Pronounced approximately eh-SHOO.

for the simple reason that every set of facts in virtual reality (or VR, as the locals abbreviate it) is shadowed by a second, complicating set: the "real-life" facts. And while a certain tension invariably buzzes in the gap between the hard, prosaic RL facts and their more fluid, dreamy VR counterparts, the dissonance in the Bungle case is striking. No hideous clowns or trickster spirits appear in the RL version of the incident, no voodoo dolls or wizard guns, indeed no rape at all as any RL court of law has yet defined it. The actors in the drama were university students for the most part, and they sat rather undramatically before computer screens the entire time, their only actions a spidery flitting of fingers across standard QWERTY keyboards. No bodies touched. Whatever physical interaction occurred consisted of a mingling of electronic signals sent from sites as distant from each other as the eastern seaboard of the United States and the southern coast of Australia. Those signals met in LambdaMOO, certainly, just as the hideous clown and the living room party did, but what was LambdaMOO after all? Not an enchanted mansion or anything of the sort—just a middlingly complex database, maintained for experimental purposes inside a Xerox Corporation research computer in Palo Alto and open to public access via the Internet.

To be more precise about it, LambdaMOO was a MUD. Or to be yet more precise, it was a subspecies of MUD known as a MOO, which is short for "MUD, Object Oriented." All of which means that it was a kind of database especially designed to give users the vivid impression of moving through a physical space that in reality exists only as words filed away on a hard drive. When users log in to LambdaMOO, for instance, the program immediately presents them with a brief textual description of one of the rooms of the database's fictional mansion (the coat closet, say). If the user wants to leave this room, she can enter a command to move in a particular direction and the database will replace the original description with a new one corresponding to the room located in the direction she chose. When the new description scrolls across the user's screen it lists not only the fixed features of the room but all its contents at that moment—including things (tools, toys, weapons) and other users (each represented as a "character" over which the user has sole control).

As far as the database program is concerned, all of these entities—rooms, things, characters—are just different subprograms that the program allows to interact according to rules very roughly mimicking the laws of the physical world. Characters may not leave a room in a given direction, for instance, unless the room subprogram contains an "exit" at that compass point. And if a character "says" or "does" something (as directed by its user-owner via the *say* or the *emote* command), then only the users whose characters are also located in that room will see the output describing the statement or action. Aside from such basic constraints, however, LambdaMOOers are allowed a broad freedom to create—they can describe their characters any way they like, they can make rooms of their own and decorate them to taste, and they can build new objects almost at will. The combination of all this busy user activity with the hard physics of the database can certainly induce a lucid illusion of presence—but when all is said and done the only thing you *really* see when you visit LambdaMOO is a kind of slow-crawling script, lines of dialogue and stage direction creeping steadily up your computer screen.

Which is all just to say that, to the extent that Mr. Bungle's assault happened in real life at all, it happened as a sort of Punch-and-Judy show, in which the puppets and the scenery were made of nothing more substantial than digital code and snippets of creative writing. The puppeteer behind Bungle that night, as it happened, was a young man logging in to the MOO from a New York University computer. He could have been Mother Teresa for all any of the others knew, however, and he could have written Bungle's script that night any way he chose. He could have sent an *emote* command to print the message *Mr_Bungle, smiling a saintly smile, floats angelic near the ceiling of the living room, showering joy and candy kisses down upon the heads of all below*—and everyone then receiving output from the database's subprogram #17 (a/k/a the "living room") would have seen that sentence on their screens.

Instead, however, he entered sadistic fantasies into the "voodoo doll," a subprogram that served the not-exactly kosher purpose of attributing actions to other characters that their users did not actually write. And thus a woman in Haverford, Pennsylvania, whose account on the MOO attached her to a character she called Moondreamer, was given the unasked-for opportunity to read the words *As if against her will, Moondreamer jabs a steak knife up her ass, causing immense joy. You hear Mr_Bungle laughing evilly in the distance.* And thus the woman in Seattle who had written herself the character called exu, with a view perhaps to tasting in imagination a deity's freedom from the burdens of the gendered flesh, got to read similarly constructed sentences in which exu, messenger of the gods, lord of crossroads and communications, suffered a brand of degradation all-too-customarily reserved for the embodied female.

"Mostly voodoo dolls are amusing," wrote exu on the evening after Bungle's rampage, posting a public statement to the widely read in-MOO mailing list called *social-issues, a forum for debate on matters of import to the entire populace.

"And mostly I tend to think that restrictive measures around here cause more trouble than they prevent. But I also think that Mr. Bungle was being a vicious, vile fuckhead, and I . . . want his sorry ass scattered from #17 to the Cinder Pile. I'm not calling for policies, trials, or better jails. I'm not sure what I'm calling for. Virtual castration, if I could manage it. Mostly, [this type of thing] doesn't happen here. Mostly, perhaps I thought it wouldn't happen to me. Mostly, I trust people to conduct themselves with some veneer of civility. Mostly, I want his ass."

Months later, the woman in Seattle would confide to me that as she wrote those words she was surprised to find herself in tears—a real-life fact that should suffice to prove that the words' emotional content was no mere fiction. The precise tenor of that content, however, its mingling of murderous rage and eyeball-rolling annoyance, was a curious amalgam that neither the RL nor the VR facts alone can quite account for. Where virtual reality and its conventions would have us believe that exu and Moondreamer were brutally raped in their own living room, here was the victim exu scolding Mr. Bungle for a breach of "civility." Where real life, on the other hand, insists the incident was only an episode in a free-form version of Dungeons and Dragons, confined to the realm of the symbolic and at no point threatening any player's life, limb, or material well-being, here now was the player exu issuing aggrieved and heartfelt calls for Mr. Bungle's dismemberment. Ludicrously excessive by RL's lights, woefully understated by VR's, the tone of exu's response made sense only in the buzzing, dissonant gap between them.

Which is to say it made the only kind of sense that *can* be made of MUDly phenomena. For while the *facts* attached to any event born of a MUD's strange, ethereal universe may march in straight, tandem lines separated neatly into the virtual and the real, its meaning lies always in that gap. You learn this axiom early in your life as a player, and it's of no small relevance to the Bungle case that you often learn it between the sheets, so to speak. Netsex, tinysex, virtual sex—however you name it, in real-life reality it's nothing more than a phone fuck stripped of even the vestigial physicality of the voice. And yet, as many a wide-eyed newbie can tell you, it's possibly the headiest experience the very heady world of MUDs has to offer. Amid flurries of even the must cursorily described caresses, sighs, or penetrations, the glands do engage, and often as throbbingly as they would in a real-life assignation—sometimes even more so, given the combined power of anonymity and textual suggestiveness to unshackle deep-seated fantasies. And if the virtual setting and the interplayer vibe are right, who knows? The heart may engage as well, stirring up passions as strong as many that bind lovers who observe the formality of trysting in the flesh.

To participate, therefore, in this disembodied enactment of life's most body-centered activity is to risk the realization that when it comes to sex, perhaps the body in question is not the physical one at all, but its psychic double, the bodylike self-representation we carry around in our heads—and that whether we present that body to another as a meat puppet or a word puppet is not nearly as significant a distinction as one might have thought. I know, I know, you've read Foucault and your mind is not quite blown by the notion that sex is never so much an exchange of fluids as it is an exchange of signs. But trust your friend Dr. Bombay, it's one thing to grasp the notion intellectually and quite another to feel it coursing through your veins amid the virtual steam of hot netnookie. And it's a whole other mind-blowing trip altogether to encounter it thus as a college frosh, new to the Net and still in the grip of hormonal hurricanes and high school sexual mythologies. The shock can easily reverberate throughout an entire young worldview. Small wonder, then, that a newbie's first taste of MUD sex is often also the first time she or he surrenders wholly to the quirky terms of MUDdish ontology, recognizing in a full-bodied way that what happens inside a MUD-made world is neither exactly real nor exactly make-believe, but nonetheless profoundly, compellingly, and emotionally _true._

And small wonder indeed that the sexual nature of Mr. Bungle's crime provoked such powerful feelings, and not just in exu (who, be it noted, was in real life a theory-savvy doctoral candidate and a longtime MOOer, but just as baffled and overwhelmed by the force of her own reaction, she later would attest, as any panting undergrad might have been). Even players who had never experienced MUD rape (the vast majority of male-presenting characters, but not as large a majority of the female-presenting as might be hoped) immediately appreciated its gravity and were moved to condemnation of the perp. exu's missive to *social-issues* followed a strongly worded one from Iggy ("Well, well," it began, "no matter what else happens on Lambda, I can always be sure that some jerk is going to reinforce my low opinion of humanity") and was itself followed by others from Zakariyah, Wereweasel, Crawdaddy, and emmeline. Moondreamer also let her feelings ("pissed") be known. And even Xander, the Clueless Samaritan who had responded to Bungle's cries for help and uncaged him shortly after the incident, expressed his regret once apprised of Bungle's deeds, which he allowed to be "despicable."

A sense was brewing that something needed to be done—done soon and in something like an organized fashion—about Mr. Bungle, in particular, and about MUD rape, in general. Regarding the general problem, emmeline, who identified herself as a survivor of both virtual rape ("many times over") and real-life sexual assault, floated a cautious proposal for a MOO-wide powwow on the subject of virtual sex offenses and what mechanisms if any might be put in place to deal with their future occurrence. As for the specific problem, the answer no doubt seemed obvious to many. But it wasn't until the evening of the second day after the incident that exu, finally and rather solemnly, gave it voice:

"I am requesting that Mr. Bungle be toaded for raping Moondreamer and I. I have never done this before, and have thought about it for days. He hurt us both."

That was all. Three simple sentences posted to *social. Reading them, an outsider might never guess that they were an application for a death warrant. Even an outsider familiar with other MUDs might not guess it, since in many of them "toading" still refers to a command that, true to the gameworlds' sword-and-sorcery origins, simply turns a player into a toad, wiping the player's description and attributes and replacing them with those of the slimy amphibian. Bad luck for sure, but not quite as bad as what happens when the same command is invoked in the MOOish strains of MUD: not only are the description and attributes of the toaded player erased, but the account itself goes too. The annihilation of the character, thus, is total.

And nothing less than total annihilation, it seemed, would do to settle LambdaMOO's accounts with Mr. Bungle. Within minutes of the posting of exu's appeal, HortonWho, the Australian Deleuzean, who had witnessed much of the attack from the back room of his suburban Melbourne home, seconded the motion with a brief message crisply entitled "Toad the fukr." HortonWho's posting was seconded almost as quickly by that of Kropotkin, covictim of Mr. Bungle and well-known radical, who in real life happened also to be married to the real-life exu. And over the course of the next twenty-four hours as many as fifty players made it known, on *social and in a variety of other forms and forums, that they would be pleased to see Mr. Bungle erased from the face of the MOO. And with dissent so far confined to a dozen or so antitoading hardliners, the numbers suggested that the citizenry was indeed moving toward a resolve to have Bungle's virtual head.

There was one small but stubborn obstacle in the way of this resolve, however, and that was a curious state of social affairs known in some quarters of the MOO as the New Direction. It was all very fine, you see, for the LambdaMOO rabble to get it in their heads to liquidate one of their peers, but when the time came to actually do the deed it would require the services of a nobler class of character. It would require a wizard. Master-programmers of the MOO, spelunkers of the database's deepest code-structures and custodians of its day-to-day administrative trivia, wizards are also the only players empowered to issue the toad command, a feature maintained on nearly all MUDs as a quick-and-dirty means of social control. But the wizards of LambdaMOO, after years of adjudicating all manner of interplayer disputes with little to show for it but their own weariness and the smoldering resentment of the general populace, had decided they'd had enough of the social sphere. And so, four months before the Bungle incident, the archwizard Haakon (known in RL as Pavel Curtis, Xerox researcher and Lambda-MOO's principal architect) formalized this decision in a document called "LambdaMOO Takes a New Direction," which he placed in the living room for all to see. In it, Haakon announced that the wizards from that day forth were pure technicians. From then on, they would make no decisions affecting the social life of the MOO, but only implement whatever decisions the community as a whole directed them to. From then on, it was decreed, LambdaMOO would just have to grow up and solve its problems on its own.

Faced with the task of inventing its own self-governance from scratch, the LambdaMOO population had so far done what any other loose, amorphous agglomeration of individuals would have done: they'd let it slide. But now the task took on new urgency. Since getting the wizards to toad Mr. Bungle (or to toad the likes of him in the future) required a convincing case that the cry for his head came from the community at large, then the community itself would have to be defined; and if the community was to be convincingly defined, then some form of social organization, no matter how rudimentary, would have to be settled on. And thus, as if against its will, the question of what to do about Mr. Bungle began to shape itself into a sort of referendum on the political future of the MOO. Arguments broke out on *social and elsewhere that had only superficially to do with Bungle (since everyone seemed to agree he was a cad) and everything to do with where the participants stood on LambdaMOO's crazy-quilty political map. Parliamentarian legalist types argued that unfortunately Bungle could not legitimately be toaded at all, since there were no explicit MOO rules against rape, or against just about anything else—and the sooner such rules were established, they added, and maybe even a full-blown judiciary system complete with elected officials and prisons to enforce those rules, the better. Others, with a royalist streak in them, seemed to feel that Bungle's as-yet-unpunished outrage only proved this New Direction silliness had gone on long enough, and that it was high time the wizardocracy returned to the position of swift and decisive leadership their player class was born to.

And then there were what I'll call the technolibertarians. For them, MUD rapists were of course assholes, but the presence of assholes on the system was a

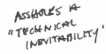
ASSHOLES A "TECHNICAL INEVITABILITY"

technical inevitability, like noise on a phone line, and best dealt with not through repressive social disciplinary mechanisms but through the timely deployment of defensive software tools. Some asshole blasting violent, graphic language at you? Don't whine to the authorities about it—hit the *@gag* command and said asshole's statements will be blocked from your screen (and only yours). It's simple, it's effective, and it censors no one.

But the Bungle case was rather hard on such arguments. For one thing, the extremely public nature of the living room meant that gagging would spare the victims only from witnessing their own violation, but not from having others witness it. You might want to argue that what those victims didn't directly experience couldn't hurt them, but consider how that wisdom would sound to a woman who'd been, say, fondled by strangers while passed out drunk in the middle of a party, and you have a rough idea how it might go over with a crowd of hard-core MOOers. Consider, for another thing, that many of the biologically female participants in the Bungle debate had been around long enough to grow lethally weary of the gag-and-get-over-it school of virtual-rape counseling, with its fine line between empowering victims and holding them responsible for their own suffering, and its shrugging indifference to the window of pain between the moment the rape-text starts flowing and the moment a gag shuts it off. From the outset it was clear that the technolibertarians were going to have to tiptoe through this issue with care, and for the most part they did.

Yet no position was trickier to maintain than that of the MOO's resident anarchists. Like the technolibbers, the anarchists didn't care much for punishments or policies or power elites. Like them, they hoped the MOO could be a place where people interacted fulfillingly without the need for such things. But their high hopes were complicated, in general, by a somewhat less thoroughgoing faith in technology (*Even if you can't tear down the master's house with the master's tools*—read a slogan written into one anarchist player's self-description—*it is a damned good place to start*). And at present they were additionally complicated by the fact that the most vocal anarchists in the discussion were none other than exu, Kropotkin, and HortonWho, who wanted to see Mr. Bungle toaded as badly as anyone did.

Needless to say, a pro–death penalty platform is not an especially comfortable one for an anarchist to sit on, so these particular anarchists were now at great pains to sever the conceptual ties between toading and capital punishment. Toading, they insisted (almost convincingly), was much more closely analogous to banishment; it was a kind of turning of the communal back on the offending party, a collective action that, if carried out properly, was entirely consistent with anarchist models of community. And carrying it out properly meant first and foremost building a consensus around it—a messy process for which there were no easy technocratic substitutes. It was going to take plenty of good old-fashioned, jawbone-intensive grassroots organizing.

So that when the time came, at 7 P.M. PST on the evening of the third day after the occurrence in the living room, to gather in emmeline's room for her proposed real-time open conclave, Kropotkin and exu were among the first to arrive. But this was hardly to be an anarchist-dominated affair, for the room was crowding rapidly with representatives of all the MOO's political stripes, and even a few wizards. Lombard showed up, and Aurea and Quanto, Spaff, TomTraceback, Eldopa and Bloof, ShermieRocko, Silver Surfer, MaoTseHedgehog, Toothpick—the names piled up and the discussion gathered momentum under their weight. Arguments multiplied and mingled, players talked past and through each other, the textual clutter of utterances and gestures filled up the screen like thick cigar smoke. Peaking in number at around thirty, this was one of the largest crowds that ever gathered in a single LambdaMOO chamber, and while emmeline had given her place a description that made it *infinite in expanse and fluid in form*, it now seemed anything but roomy. You could almost feel the claustrophobic air of the place, dank and overheated by virtual bodies, pressing against your skin.

I know you could because I too was there, in one of those pivotal accidents of personal history one always wants later to believe were approached with a properly solemn awareness of the moment's portent. Almost as invariably, of course, the truth is that one wanders into such occasions utterly without a clue, and so it was with me that night. Completely ignorant of any of the goings-on that had led to the meeting, I showed up mainly to see what the crowd was about, and though I observed the proceedings for a good while, I confess I found it hard to grasp what was going on. I was still the rankest of newbies then, my MOO legs still too unsteady to make the leaps of faith, logic, and empathy required to meet the spectacle on its own terms. I was fascinated by the concept of virtual rape, but I was even more so by the notion that anyone could take it altogether seriously.

In this, though, I found myself in a small and mostly silent minority, for the discussion that raged around me was of an almost unrelieved earnestness, bent it seemed on examining every last aspect and implication of Mr. Bungle's crime. There were the central questions, of course: Thumbs up or down on Bungle's virtual existence? And if down, how then to ensure that his toading was not just some isolated lynching but a first step toward shaping LambdaMOO into a legitimate community? Surrounding these, however, a tangle of weighty side issues proliferated. What, some wondered, was the real-life legal status of the offense?

Could Bungle's university administrators punish him for sexual harassment? Could he be prosecuted under California state laws against obscene phone calls? Little enthusiasm was shown for pursuing either of these lines of action, which testifies both to the uniqueness of the crime and to the nimbleness with which the discussants were negotiating its idiosyncracies. Many were the casual references to Bungle's deed as simply "rape," but these in no way implied that the players had lost sight of all distinctions between the virtual and physical versions, or that they believed Bungle should be dealt with in the same way a real-life criminal would. He had committed a MOO crime, and his punishment, if any, would be meted out via the MOO.

On the other hand, little patience was shown toward any attempts to downplay the seriousness of what Mr. Bungle had done. When the affable Shermie-Rocko proposed, more in the way of a hypothesis than an assertion, that "perhaps it's better to release . . . violent tendencies in a virtual environment rather than in real life," he was tut-tutted so swiftly and relentlessly that he withdrew the hypothesis altogether, apologizing humbly as he did so. Not that the assembly was averse to putting matters into a more philosophical perspective. "Where does the body end and the mind begin?" young Quanto asked, amid recurring attempts to fine-tune the differences between real and virtual violence. "Is not the mind a part of the body?" "In MOO, the body IS the mind," offered Shermie-Rocko gamely, and not at all implausibly, demonstrating the ease with which very knotty metaphysical conundrums come undone in VR. The not-so-aptly named Obtuse seemed to agree, arriving after sufficient consideration of the nature of Bungle's crime at the hardly novel yet now somehow newly resonant conjecture that "all reality might consist of ideas, who knows."

On these and other matters the anarchists, the libertarians, the legalists, the wizardists—and the wizards—all had their thoughtful say. But as the evening wore on and the talk grew more heated and more heady, it seemed increasingly clear that the vigorous intelligence being brought to bear on this swarm of issues wasn't going to result in anything remotely like resolution. The perspectives were just too varied, the memescape just too slippery. Again and again, arguments that looked at first to be heading in a decisive direction ended up chasing their own tails; and slowly, depressingly, a dusty haze of irrelevance gathered over the proceedings.

It was almost a relief, therefore, when midway through the evening Mr. Bungle himself, the living, breathing cause of all this talk, teleported into the room. Not that it was much of a surprise. Oddly enough, in the three days since his release from Iggy's cage, Bungle had returned more than once to wander the public spaces of LambdaMOO, walking willingly into one of the fiercest storms of ill will and invective ever to rain down on a player. He'd been taking it all with a curious and mostly silent passivity, and when challenged face-to-virtual-face by both exu and the genderless elder statescharacter PatSoftly to defend himself on *social, he'd demurred, mumbling something about Christ and expiation. He was equally quiet now, and his reception was still uniformly cool. exu fixed an arctic stare on him—*no hate, no anger, no interest at all. Just . . . watching.* Others were more actively unfriendly. "Asshole," spat MaoTseHedgehog, "creep." But the harshest of the MOO's hostility toward him had already been vented, and the attention he drew now was motivated more, it seemed, by the opportunity to probe the rapist's mind, to find out what made it tick and if possible how to get it to tick differently. In short, they wanted to know why he'd done it. So they asked him.

And Mr. Bungle thought about it. And as eddies of discussion and debate continued to swirl around him, he thought about it some more. And then he said this:

"I engaged in a bit of a psychological device that is called thought-polarization, the fact that this is not RL simply added to heighten the affect of the device. It was purely a sequence of events with no consequence on my RL existence."

They might have known. Stilted though its diction was, the gist of the answer was simple, and something many in the room had probably already surmised: Mr. Bungle was a psycho. Not, perhaps, in real life—but then in real life it's possible for reasonable people to assume, as Bungle clearly did, that what transpires between word-costumed characters within the boundaries of a make-believe world is, if not mere play, then at most some kind of emotional laboratory experiment. Inside the MOO, however, such thinking marked a person as one of two basically subcompetent types. The first was the newbie, in which case the confusion was understandable, since there were few MOOers who had not, upon their first visits as anonymous "guest" characters, mistaken the place for a vast playpen in which they might act out their wildest fantasies without fear of censure. Only with time and the acquisition of a fixed character did players tend to make the critical passage from anonymity to pseudonymity, developing the concern for their character's reputation that marks the attainment of virtual adulthood. But while Mr. Bungle hadn't been around as long as most MOOers, he'd been around long enough to leave his newbie status behind, and his delusional statement therefore placed him among the second type: the sociopath.

And as there is but small percentage in arguing with a head case, the room's attention gradually abandoned Mr. Bungle and returned to the discussions that had previously occupied it. But if the debate had been edging toward ineffectuality before, Bungle's anticlimactic appearance had evidently robbed it of any forward motion whatsoever. What's more, from his lonely corner of the room Mr. Bungle kept issuing periodic expressions of a prickly sort of remorse, interlaced with sarcasm and belligerence, and though it was hard to tell if he wasn't still just conducting his experiments, some people thought his regret genuine enough that maybe he didn't deserve to be toaded after all. Logically, of course, discussion of the principal issues at hand didn't require unanimous belief that Bungle was an irredeemable bastard, but now that cracks were showing in that unanimity, the last of the meeting's fervor seemed to be draining out through them.

People started drifting away. Mr. Bungle left first, then others followed—one by one, in twos and threes, hugging friends and waving good night. By 9:45 P.M. only a handful remained, and the great debate had wound down into casual conversation, the melancholy remains of another fruitless good idea. The arguments had been well-honed, certainly, and perhaps might prove useful in some as-yet-unclear long run. But at this point what seemed clear was that emmeline's meeting had died, at last, and without any practical results to mark its passing.

It was also at this point, most likely, that TomTraceback reached his decision. TomTraceback was a wizard, a taciturn sort of fellow who'd sat brooding on the sidelines all evening. He hadn't said a lot, but what he had said, in emmeline's room and elsewhere, indicated that he took the crime committed against exu and Moondreamer very seriously, and that he felt no particular compassion toward the character who had committed it. But on the other hand he had made it equally plain that he took the elimination of a fellow player just as seriously, and moreover that he had no desire to return to the days of wizardly intervention. It must have been difficult, therefore, to reconcile the conflicting impulses churning within him at that moment. In fact, it was probably impossible, for though he did tend to believe that the consensus on *social was sufficient proof of the MOO's desire to see capital justice done in the Bungle case, he was also well aware that under the present order of things nothing but his own conscience could tell him, ultimately, whether to ratify that consensus or not. As much as he would have liked to make himself an instrument of the MOO's collective will, therefore, there was no escaping the fact that he must in the final analysis either act alone or not act at all.

So TomTraceback acted alone.

He told the lingering few players in the room that he had to go, and then he went. It was a minute or two before 10 P.M. He did it quietly and he did it privately, but all anyone had to do to know he'd done it was to type the @who command, which was normally what you typed if you wanted to know a player's present location and the time he last logged in. But if you had run a @*who* on Mr. Bungle not too long after TomTraceback left emmeline's room, the database would have told you something different.

Mr_Bungle, it would have said, *is not the name of any player.*

The date, as it happened, was April Fool's Day, but this was no joke: Mr. Bungle was truly dead and truly gone.

TOADED ?

They say that LambdaMOO wasn't really the same after Mr. Bungle's toading. They say as well that nothing really changed. And though it skirts the fuzziest of dream-logics to say that both these statements are true, the MOO is just the sort of fuzzy, dreamlike place in which such contradictions thrive.

Certainly the Bungle Affair marked the end of LambdaMOO's brief epoch of rudderless social drift. The rash of public-spiritedness engendered by the events might alone have led in time to some more formal system of communal self-definition, but in the end it was the archwizard Haakon who made sure of it. Away on business for the duration of the episode, Haakon returned to find its wreckage strewn across the tiny universe he'd set in motion. The elimination of a player, the trauma of several others, and the nerve-wracked complaints of his colleague TomTraceback presented themselves to his concerned and astonished attention, and he resolved to see if he couldn't learn some lesson from it all. For the better part of a day he puzzled over the record of events and arguments left in *social, then he sat pondering the chaotically evolving shape of his creation, and at the day's end he descended once again into the social arena of the MOO with another history-altering proclamation.

It was to be his last, for what he now decreed was the final, missing piece of the New Direction. In a few days, Haakon announced, he would build into the database a system of petitions and ballots whereby anyone could put to popular vote any social scheme requiring wizardly powers for its implementation, with the results of the vote to be binding on the wizards. At last and for good, the awkward gap between the will of the players and the efficacy of the technicians would be closed. And though some anarchists grumbled about the irony of Haakon's dictatorially imposing universal suffrage on an unconsulted populace, in general the citizens of LambdaMOO seemed to find it hard to fault a system more purely democratic than any that could ever exist in real life. A few months and a dozen ballot measures later, widespread participation in the new regime had already produced a small arsenal of mechanisms for dealing with the types of violence

BALLOT SYSTEM (HAAKON)

that called the system into being. MOO residents now had access to a *@boot* command, for instance, with which to summarily eject berserker "guest" characters. And players could bring suit against one another through an ad hoc mediation system in which mutually agreed-upon judges had at their disposition the full range of wizardly punishments—up to and including the capital.

Yet the continued dependence on extermination as the ultimate keeper of the peace suggested that this new MOO order was perhaps not built on the most solid of foundations. For if life on LambdaMOO began to acquire more coherence in the wake of the toading, death retained all the fuzziness of pre-Bungle days. This truth was rather dramatically borne out, not too many days after Bungle departed, by the arrival of a strange new character named Dr. Jest. There was a forceful eccentricity to the newcomer's manner, but the oddest thing about his style was its striking yet unnameable familiarity. And when he developed the annoying habit of stuffing fellow players into a jar containing a tiny simulacrum of a certain deceased rapist, the source of this familiarity became obvious:

Mr. Bungle had risen from the grave.

In itself, Bungle's reincarnation as Dr. Jest was a remarkable turn of events, but perhaps even more remarkable was the utter lack of amazement with which the LambdaMOO public took note of it. To be sure, many residents were appalled by the brazenness of Bungle's return. In fact, one of the first petitions circulated under the new voting system was a request for Dr. Jest's toading that almost immediately gathered several dozen signatures (but failed in the end to reach ballot status). Yet few were unaware of the ease with which the toad proscription could be circumvented—all the toadee had to do (all the Ur-Bungle at NYU presumably had done) was to go to the minor hassle of acquiring a new Internet account, and LambdaMOO's character registration program would then simply treat the known felon as an entirely new and innocent person. Nor was this ease necessarily understood to represent a failure of toading's social disciplinary function. On the contrary, it only underlined the truism (repeated many times throughout the debate over Mr. Bungle's fate) that his punishment, ultimately, had been no more or less symbolic than his crime.

What *was* surprising, however, was that Mr. Bungle/Dr. Jest appeared to have taken the symbolism to heart. Dark themes still obsessed him—the objects he created gave off wafts of Nazi imagery and medical torture—but he no longer radiated the aggressively antisocial vibes he had before. He was a lot less unpleasant to look at (the outrageously seedy clown description had been replaced by that of a mildly creepy but actually rather natty young man, with *blue eyes* . . .

suggestive of conspiracy, untamed eroticism, and perhaps a sense of understanding of the future), and aside from the occasional jar-stuffing incident, he was also a lot less dangerous to be around. It seemed obvious, at least to me, that he'd undergone some sort of personal transformation in the days since I'd first glimpsed him back in emmeline's crowded room—nothing radical maybe, but powerful nonetheless, and resonant enough with my own experience, I felt, that it might be more than professionally interesting to talk with him, and perhaps compare notes.

For I too was undergoing a transformation in the aftermath of that night in emmeline's—and was increasingly uncertain what to make of it. As I pursued my runaway fascination with the discussion I had heard there, as I pored over the *social debate and got to know exu and some of the other victims and witnesses, I could feel my newbie consciousness falling away from me. Where before I'd found it hard to take virtual rape seriously, I now was finding it difficult to remember how I could ever *not* have taken it seriously. I was proud to have arrived at this perspective—it felt like an exotic sort of achievement, and it definitely made my ongoing experience of the MOO a richer one.

But it was also having some unsettling effects on the way I looked at the rest of the world. Sometimes, for instance, it grew difficult for me to understand why RL society classifies RL rape alongside crimes against person or property. Since rape can occur without any physical pain or damage, I found myself reasoning, then it must be classed as a crime against the mind—more intimately and deeply hurtful, to be sure, than cross burnings, wolf whistles, and virtual rape, but undeniably located on the same conceptual continuum. I did not, however, conclude as a result that rapists were protected in any fashion by the First Amendment. Quite the opposite, in fact: the more seriously I took the notion of virtual rape, the less seriously I was able to take the tidy division of the world into the symbolic and the real that underlies the very notion of freedom of speech.

Let me assure you, though, that I did not at the time adopt these thoughts as full-fledged arguments, nor am I now presenting them as such. I offer them, rather, as a picture of the sort of mind-set that my initial encounters with a virtual world inspired in me. I offer them also, therefore, as a kind of prophecy. For whatever else these thoughts were telling me, I have come to hear in them an announcement of the final stages of our decades-long passage into the Information Age, a paradigm shift that the classic liberal fire wall between word and deed (itself a product of an earlier paradigm shift commonly known as the Enlightenment) is not likely to survive intact. After all, anyone the least bit familiar with the workings of the new era's definitive technology, the computer, knows that it operates on a principle impracticably difficult to distinguish from the pre-Enlightenment principle of the magic word: the commands you type into a computer are a kind of speech that doesn't so much communicate as *make things happen,* directly and ineluctably, the same way pulling a trigger does. They are incantations, in other words, and anyone at all attuned to the technosocial mega-trends of the moment—from the growing dependence of economies on the global flow of intensely fetishized words and numbers to the burgeoning ability of bioengineers to speak the spells written in the four-letter text of DNA—knows that the logic of the incantation is rapidly permeating the fabric of our lives.

And it was precisely this logic, I was beginning to understand, that provided whatever real magic LambdaMOO had to offer—not the fictive trappings of voodoo and shape-shifting and wizardry, but the conflation of speech and act that's inevitable in any computer-mediated world, be it Lambda or the increasingly wired world at large. This was dangerous magic, to be sure, a potential threat—if misconstrued or misapplied—to our always precarious freedoms of expression, and as someone who lives by his words I dared not take the threat lightly. And yet, on the other hand, I could no longer convince myself that our wishful insulation of language from the realm of action had ever been anything but a valuable kludge, a philosophically imperfect stopgap against oppression that would just have to do till something truer and more elegant came along.

Was I wrong to think this truer, more elegant thing might be found on LambdaMOO? I did not know. I continued, in my now-and-then visits, to seek it there, sensing its presence just below the surface of every interaction. Yet increasingly I sensed as well that if I really wanted to see what lay beneath those surfaces—to glimpse unveiled whatever there was of genuine historical novelty in VR's slippery social and philosophical dynamics—I was going to have to radically deepen my acquaintance with the MOO somehow.

For a time I considered the possibility, as I said, that discussing with Dr. Jest our shared experience of the workings of the place might be a step toward the understanding I sought. But when that notion first occurred to me, I still felt somewhat intimidated by his lingering criminal aura, and I hemmed and hawed a good long time before finally resolving to drop him MOO-mail suggesting we have a chat. By then it appeared to be too late. For reasons known only to himself, Dr. Jest stopped logging in. Maybe he'd grown bored with the MOO. Maybe the loneliness of ostracism had gotten to him. Maybe a psycho whim had carried him far away or maybe he'd quietly acquired a third character and started life over with a cleaner slate.

Wherever he'd gone, though, he left behind the room he'd created for him-self—a treehouse *tastefully decorated*, as he'd described it, with rare-book shelves, an operating table, and a life-size William S. Burroughs doll—and he left it unlocked. So I took to checking in there occasionally, heading out of my own cozy nook (inside a TV set inside the little red hotel inside the Monopoly board inside the dining room of LambdaMOO) and teleporting on over to the treehouse, where the room description always told me Dr. Jest was present but asleep, in the conventional depiction for disconnected characters. The not-quite-emptiness of the abandoned room invariably instilled in me an uncomfortable mix of melan-choly and the creeps, and I would stick around only on the off chance that Dr. Jest might wake up, say hello, and share his understanding of the future with me.

It happens, in fact, that Dr. Jest did eventually rise again from his epic sleep. But what wisdom he had to offer on that occasion I couldn't tell you, for I had given up the habit of my skittish stakeouts by then. Some final transformation had come over me between visits to that lonely place: the complex magic of the MOO grew gradually to interest me less and less as a way of understanding the future and more and more as a way of living the present, until one day I tele-ported home from Dr. Jest's treehouse for the last time, determined to wait no longer for a consultation with my fellow doctor to give me what I wanted from the MOO, but to wrest it instead from the very heart of the place. I was resolved now, to make a life there—to loosen for a while the RL ties that kept me still a sort of tourist on the MOO and to give in, body and soul, to the same powerful gravity that kept so many other MOOers logged on day after day and for hours at a time.

And in the end that's just what I did, so that for a brief, unforgettable season the buzzing haze of VR came at last to envelop my existence: my small daily dra-mas were absorbed into the MOO's teeming reservoir of small daily dramas, my labors were directed as much toward the ongoing construction of that virtual world as toward the quotidian maintenance of my stake in the material one, and my days were swept by the same broad currents of MOO history that gave rise to the Bungle Affair and the momentous social changes that followed on it.

That is all quite another story, of course. Yet as I said before, it begins where Mr. Bungle's ends, and there remains now only a very little of his to tell. Dr. Jest did finally reawaken, it's true, one late-December day—but he didn't even make it to January before he decided, for no apparent reason but old times' sake, to go on a late-night Bungle-grade rampage through the living room, thus all but formally requesting to be hauled before an official mediator and toaded with a vengeance. The new MOO polity promptly obliged, and I, still busily contriving to loosen those RL ties in preparation for my full-time residency, missed by days my last chance to hear the doctor's story from his own virtual mouth.

But this was no great loss, I suppose. For after all what more could I have learned? Dr. Jest's relapse into mindless digital violence, mocking as it did my wishful projection of hard-earned wisdom onto him, was lesson enough, driving home what Bungle's story in its fullest implications should have already taught me by then: that nothing in the MOO was ever quite what one imagined it to be.

I would still have to learn this lesson many times over, of course. I'd learn it again when on the eve of my immersion in VR two separate and credible sources revealed to me that the virtual psychosis of Mr. Bungle had been even starker than anyone guessed: that the Bungle account had been the more or less communal property of an entire NYU dorm floor, that the young man at the keyboard on the evening of the rape had acted not alone but surrounded by fellow students calling out suggestions and encouragement, that conceivably none of those people were speaking for Bungle when he showed up in emmeline's room to answer for the crime, that Dr. Jest himself, thought commonly to have reincarnated the whole Bungle and nothing but the Bungle, in fact embodied just one member of the original mob—just one scattered piece of a self more irreparably fragmented than any RL multiple personality could ever fear to be.

I don't know exactly how often it occurred to me, in the VR-saturated months to follow, that other such shards of Mr. Bungle's shattered identity might lurk among the ethereal population I moved through on a daily basis. But if they were there they never made themselves known, and I certainly never tried to sniff them out. It was far too late for that: the time had come for me to live in LambdaMOO, and I no longer sought the company of ghosts.

NEW YORK CITY, DECEMBER 1993

The Cubicle
You are in a half-height half-cubicle in the editorial
   offices of New York City's Premier Alternative Weekly
   Newspaper. The desk is cluttered with books,
   magazines, office-wide memos, rubber bands, pens,
   take-out menus. The wall is covered with some sort
   of private iconography: postcards from Brazil, from
   California; a bumper sticker from the "In-N-Out
   Burger" drive-thru chain; a scrap of circuit board
   from inside an old computer; a photograph of Claude
   Elwood Shannon, inventor of information theory,
   taken in 1952; some photographs of friends, of
   family. The usual desperate attempt, in short, at
   carving a personal space from the employer's bland
   domain.
The_Author works here as a part-time copy editor and
   sometime contributor.
You see a telephone and Atex word-processing terminal
   here.
The_Author is here.

The_Author is eating Indian take-out from a paper plate
   and moving commas around in someone else's thoughts
   about the prospects for democracy in Haiti.

The_Author has been moving the other writer's commas
 around for years but can't remember ever having
 spoken to him directly. Once a week or so The_Author
 calls this writer's words up on his terminal; once a
 week or so he sends the words back to the writer
 through the office network; once every couple months
 the two men pass each other in the corridor and nod.

The_Author squints at his terminal and tries to shake
 the knots out of a particularly knotty sentence. He
 weighs the sentence in his mind, feeling for the
 hidden shape of the writer's thoughts. But he is
 having difficulty concentrating. His own words, he
 sees, are even now being read in the cubicle next to
 his, his sentences weighed, his commas moved around.
 It's distracting.

The telephone rings.

look phone

telephone
A sleek black corporate-issue multilined office phone.

The telephone rings.

@exam phone

telephone (#20354) is owned by
VV_Publishing_Corporation (#666).
Aliases: telephone, phone, blower
A sleek black corporate-issue multilined office phone.
Obvious verbs:
a*nswer phone
hang*up phone
g*et/t*ake phone
d*rop/th*row phone

The telephone rings.

The_Author answers the telephone.

The voice on the other end of the line goes, "Hi. Julian?"

The_Author says, "Uh-huh."

The voice on the other end of the line goes, "It's me. Karen."

The_Author has no idea who Karen is.

The voice on the other end of the line goes, "exu. Silly."

The_Author almost yelps. He almost throws the receiver back onto its cradle, as if it had bit him.

The_Author says, instead, "Oh, hi."

The voice on the other end of the line goes, "Yeah, well, the fact checkers over there called me to check some things in your article and I asked them to transfer me over to you when we were done, so . . . heh, here I am."

The voice on the other end of the line cannot be exu's.

The_Author has been interviewing exu on the MOO (about the Bungle Affair, for the article that even now is being read in the cubicle next to his) and he knows the voice of exu pretty well by now. He knows it at least as well as he knows the voices that inform the articles he copy-edits every week, and he knows it doesn't suffer any from the comparison. It is a smoother, livelier voice than most; it has the clarity and the warmth of straight Scotch; it frankly doesn't sound a bit like the high-pitched, slightly adenoidal, slightly quavering tones The_Author's hearing from his telephone.

The_Author is glad to hear them nonetheless. Amid the
  interviews and other online conversations, you see,
  he has begun to think of exu as a friend. And so they
  talk, the Author allowing himself to believe the
  voice on the telephone is really hers, enduring for a
  while the strangeness of this unaccustomed medium.
  Enduring it the way he sometimes, as a child, used to
  pull himself out of a pool to shiver momentarily in
  cold air, knowing he would feel that much warmer when
  he dove back in.

The_Author says, "Hey, I'm thinking of writing a book
  about the MOO. I'm thinking I'll, you know, move in
  for a few months and see what happens and write it
  all up in the end."

The voice on the other end of the line goes, "Cool."

VR

2

The Scarlet Balloon

Or TINYGEOGRAPHY,
A Long View and an Overview

It was early in the afternoon of my first day as a full-fledged inhabitant of LambdaMOO, and I was in the living room.

It was very bright, open, and airy there, with large plate-glass windows looking southward over the pool to the gardens beyond. On the north wall, there was a rough stonework fireplace. The east and west walls were almost completely covered with large, well-stocked bookcases. An exit in the northwest corner led to the kitchen and, in a more northerly direction, to the entrance hall. The door into the coat closet was at the north end of the east wall, and at the south end was a sliding glass door leading out onto a wooden deck. There were two sets of couches, one clustered around the fireplace and one with a view out the windows.

There was a crowd in the living room, as usual, but I didn't know anybody in it. Minnie was there—I'd heard her name in conversation once or twice before—and someone called Jimpsum, watching me with mild interest. Lestat, the vampire, was also present, as were Lopher, Pensee, Squib, phedro, Jackson, Portia, Mehitabel, Zaphtra, Spunkin, Dweezilheimer, and a guest.

The guest was beige.

The crowd, in general, was doing what you did in the living room, which was nothing in particular. My screen was filling up rapidly with lines of idle chat and random silliness.

A cockatoo perched near the fireplace squawked, "Just another MOO."

Pensee bravely gags the cockatoo, read the next line on my screen, *ignoring nipped fingers and frantic squawking.*

The cockatoo was a robot, programmed to repeat at random a small selection of the hundreds of statements spoken in its vicinity over the last few hours. The cockatoo was immensely annoying, but its designer had mercifully equipped it with a gag command, which shut it up for a little while at least.

Spunkin, observing Pensee's brave gagging of the cockatoo, thought, "Beat me to it."

Spunkin thought this out loud, actually, wrapping his thought in a little typographic thought balloon, which looked like this:

Spunkin . o O (Beat me to it.)

Pensee grinned.

Mehitabel said to Lopher, "Furrmi was OK, I guess. Too many danmed typos, though."

Lestat's soft chuckle echoed in my ears as he returned to New Orleans to feed. Lestat was gone.

Lopher said, "Well, Furrmi and I weere good drinking pals :)"

Mehitabel said, "Er, 'damned' that is. Damn."

Pensee said to Lopher, "Oh dear, I'm sorry to hear that."

Mehitabel blushed.

Chemo comes out of the closet (so to speak . . .), said my screen.

Jimpsum said, to no one in particular, "Which of these is the most important to you in your life: spiritual enlightenment, good grooming, sex, pizza, electrical appliances, spray starch?"

Lopher said, "What can I say? I like fuck ups, and he was one of the biggest ;)"

Chemo slid open the glass door to the deck and slipped out, sliding the door closed behind him.

Burg teleported in.

Template teleported in.

Mehitabel teleported out.

Spunkin thought, "Hmmm. Spray starch . . ."

Minnie said, "NairTM."

A teal guest came out of the closet (so to speak . . .).

Portia said, "Good grooming before sex and pizza after."

The teal guest slid open the glass door to the deck and slipped out, sliding the door closed behind it ("it" being the guest, of course, which like all other guests was of the neuter gender).

Spunkin fell down laughing at Portia's answer.

Minnie said, "Or Trident Sugarless bubblegum."

Jimpsum chuckled politely at Minnie.

Burg looked at Minnie with some curiosity (or so Minnie's automated look-detector informed us). Burg was the twenty-sixth to do so that day.

Jimpsum said, "Assume you have a thousand dollars. Do you keep it, or go for what's behind door number three?"

phedro exclaimed, "KEEP IT. ALL THE PRIZES SUCK ANYWAY!"

Leda teleported in.

Minnie said to Jimpsum, "I'd give it to a homeless person."

Burg said, "Does anybody here go to Northwestern?"

Minnie looks preposterous with this halo on her head, Minnie emoted.

Pensee grinned a little.

Template looked at Minnie with some curiosity. Template was the twenty-seventh to do so that day.

Jimpsum said, "If you could pass your time with foolish daydreaming instead of doing a decent job of what you're supposed to be doing, would you endlessly mull over simple-minded questions like these?"

Inspector Gadget entered from the north.

Burg teleported out.

Rob Lowe came out of the closet (so to speak . . .).

Burg teleported in.

Spunkin said to Jimpsum, "Uh . . . isn't that what we're doing now? :-)"

I exited to the north.

I was in the entrance hall.

It was a small foyer, the hub of the currently occupied portion of Lambda House. To the north were the double doors that formed the main entrance to the house. There was a mirror at about head height on the east wall, just to the right of a corridor leading off into the bedroom area. The south wall was all rough stonework, the back of the living room fireplace; at the west end of the wall was the opening leading south into the living room and southwest into the kitchen. And to the west was an open archway leading into the dining room.

There was nobody there, and for that I was grateful. The living room had its charms, to be sure, but I preferred them in smaller doses than the one I'd just taken. It exhausted me to try and follow the interactions in there; keeping track of the disjointed threads of conversation and the flighty comings and goings of the residents felt too much like trying to navigate a cocktail party under the influence of various psychotomimetic drugs.

Besides, even under the best of circumstances I had never been that good at working a room, and for anyone even moderately unsure of his social graces, the living room was not necessarily the most delightful place to be. Indeed, in my earliest visits to the MOO, the living room had seemed to me an emotional torture chamber comparable only to the luncheon tables of junior high school. There was something downright cruel, I felt, in the architectural decision that obliged guests and newbies—whose sleeping quarters were located by default in the living room's coat closet—to step out into a crowd of deftly chattering regulars every time they logged on and made their first awkward forays into the MOO. Even if the regulars hadn't sometimes gone out of their way to make the new arrivals feel clumsier than they already did (in an earlier design of the living room's sliding glass door, for instance, any players too green to know they had to type *open door* before exiting would find their boneheaded, nose-flattening collision with the pane announced to the room in humiliating detail), the experience would still have been a trying one for many a budding MOOer. Just as at the lunch tables of yore, the challenge of finding one's place in that boisterous roomful of strangers could be daunting, and it hardly helped matters to learn, as one soon did, that beneath the surface of the living room's giddy chitchat the regulars were often carrying on a number of unseen conversations (both with one another, via the *whisper* command, and with players in other rooms, via the long-distance *page* command) in which, for all one knew, all manner of sneering judgments were being passed on one's ungainly newbie self.

Thankfully, within a few weeks of my first visit I had found a new place to sleep—the little red Monopoly hotel in the dining room, where I'd installed my nineteen-inch TV set and crawled inside and called it home (using, naturally, the *@sethome* command to do so). And not long after that I had found a new set of friends—through exu, who had taken me under her wing and introduced me to her lively, bohemian circle. From then on, whenever I connected to the MOO I usually teleported straight to exu's room, a.k.a. the Crossroads, materializing in the richly cluttered attic she'd constructed beneath the roof of an old barn in the fields just west of Lambda House, and lingering there into the night trading erudite quips and lowbrow gossip with assorted anarcho-pagans, slacker intellectuals, and queer-theorist computer programmers.

Some nights the party migrated over to Interzone—a MOO founded by exu and her pals and modeled on somebody's notion of a postapocalyptic Berlin—and I would migrate with it. I'd set up an Interzone connection in a second onscreen window and spend my evening there, meeting new friends of exu's and switching briefly back to LambdaMOO to add their Lambda character-names to the growing list in my automated login-watcher, which alerted me when anybody I might like to talk to happened to connect. exu was already on the list, of course, as were Kropotkin and HortonWho; and soon there was Sebastiano, who lived in a small gay community woven into a rug hung from the wall of exu's barn; and S*, whose principal Lambda character (loosely based on the woman who shot Andy Warhol) lived inside a small, free-floating bead of seawater; and Niacin, who had so many alter egos on Lambda it was hard to say exactly where he lived.

And there was Gracile, too, and Elsa, and Alva, all good for a late-night tête-à-tête, along with others who would do in a pinch—the upshot being, in short, that I no longer had to enter the living room with anxiety knotting up my stomach, wondering if I was cool enough or clever enough to rate a nod from the upper-classmen. I had my own cool, clever crowd now, and I could take the living room or leave it as I pleased, and so I did. I'd pop in now and then to hook up with an acquaintance or two; or sometimes I'd just wander in and sit there on the side-lines for a while and watch, with quiet amusement, the dizzying, cartoonish goings on.

Today, however, I had gone into the living room in search of something other than companionship or entertainment: I was looking for a new home.

I more or less had to, because the old one, as I'd discovered to my dismay upon logging in earlier that day, had apparently vanished into thin air. The television set in which I slept was still intact, and I had awoken as usual amid the fat-cushioned Oriental splendor with which I had decorated it (drawing much of my inspiration, you may as well know, from dim memories of *I Dream of Jeannie* and the silken interior of Barbara Eden's magic lamp). But when I tried to leave my lushly appointed lair I noticed something was seriously amiss: the exit, which had always reliably led through the glow of the television screen out into the hotel room beyond, now led no place at all. It wasn't that the exit was blocked, as a quick examination told me, nor was it exactly a matter of the TV set having been removed from its location. What appeared to have happened, on the contrary, was that the location had been removed from the TV set. The very ground on which it stood, that is to say, had been snatched out from under it, for the hotel room itself was gone, and gone without a trace—erased from the database with-out warning or explanation or even, evidently, the slightest concern for the resulting metaphysical quandary of my television set, now separated entirely from the fabric of MOOspace and bearing me along with it through the topographic limbo into which it had been cast.

I was annoyed, but hardly mystified. I quickly deduced the reason for this disruption. The hotel room, I well knew, had belonged to a player named Ecco (who was a dolphin and a very longtime presence on my login-watcher list), but Ecco had not logged on in several months and as a consequence she had been "reaped"—her account closed, her character erased, her hotel room and other properties and creations reduced to the electronic bits of which they were made and redistributed to more active players. Ecco learned that she'd been reaped not long after it happened, and I heard the news not long after that, because she told it to me herself—face-to-face, in the genuine, physical flesh. Which was how she told me most things, actually, and which was also only natural, considering the fact that Ecco, the late virtual dolphin, was in real life Jessica, the woman I shared my home and bed with.

As it happens, the death of Ecco and the life I lived with Jessica were not unrelated phenomena. We'd been together nearly three years by then—a record for me after the decade or so of fitful, fraught liaisons that comprised my adult love life, and an emotional achievement topped only by my unprecedented decision (finally acted on sometime in the midst of Dr. Jest's long sleep, and just a month or two after I'd moved my TV set into Ecco's virtual hotel room) to actually live under the same real-world roof with her. Granted, it wasn't as if we'd gone so far as to get formally hitched, but for the time being it wasn't as if I was really capable of going that far anyway. For though I loved Jessica dearly, and though I had nothing against marriage in principle, in practice it was clear to me by now that a whole thoroughly uninviting closetful of psychological baggage would have to be sifted through before I might aspire to so unflinching a state of union. It's embarrassing to admit, yes, but there it is: I had reached that stage in some people's lives when their jumpy progressions from one partner to another can no longer pass for anything as rational as shopping around or as liberating as free love. I suffered, I knew, from a hard case of that pandemic set of affective phobias and existential willies known to the layperson as fear of commitment. The symptoms weren't anything too terribly severe, but they were tenacious enough that my relatively tranquil RL cohabitation with Jessica qualified as a small personal miracle, which I regarded with the appropriate measures of reverent wonder and superstitious anxiety.

Yet if this novel state of affairs could be said to constitute a great leap forward in my fumblings toward intimacy with the woman I loved, its effects on our MOO relationship were nothing short of terminal. Indeed, they could hardly have turned out otherwise, since the very existence of that relationship had always largely depended on the physical distance we'd maintained between us. In the beginning, I suppose, the strange new world of LambdaMOO may have brought us together in a spirit of shared discovery, but it very soon became just a nice place to meet on the nights we found ourselves bedding down separately in our crosstown apartments—a warmer, somehow more physical plane than the raw VR embodied by the telephone, where communication was perhaps more efficient but the opportunities for an emotionally convincing good-night cuddle (to say nothing of a leisurely hour of lovemaking amid the plush furnishings of an enchanted mansion's master bedroom) were not quite as ample. It came as no surprise then, really, that our moving in together brought an almost immediate end to our MOO encounters, even though as a two-phone-line household we could as easily have carried them on from opposite ends of our new apartment as we had from opposite sides of the city. There just wasn't much of a point any-more.

Nor evidently did any other very compelling motives remain, in the wake of our domestic merger, to keep Jessica returning to the MOO. My irregular visits continued, of course, but hers grew increasingly infrequent and eventually stopped altogether. Two months went by without her logging in, then three, and then at last a fatal four—the maximum period of inactivity allowed to Lamb-daMOO players by the all-knowing but not exactly all-merciful wizards, who'd recently been charged by the MOO electorate with maintaining a strict regimen of population control and had taken to the task with a more or less punctual ruthlessness.

And so Ecco had been reaped, and so I had arrived a few days later to find my virtual home adrift in the void. And so, now, I stood here in the entrance hall of Lambda House, sizing up the room's potential as a setting for my TV set.

The potential was not tremendous, but I hadn't seen much better. Earlier in the day exu had offered to let me put the TV in the junk-strewn yard in front of the barn, and I had gratefully taken the offer into consideration. Of my MOO friends, after all, exu was still the closest (we'd even met in real life, briefly, when she and Kropotkin came to New York for a short midwinter visit), and the idea of putting roots down in her neighborhood appealed to me. But even in VR there was something unsettling about the thought of leaving a perfectly good piece of consumer electronics out in the heat and dust of a barnyard. And though the liv-ing room seemed a more obviously congenial locale, the instant I teleported into that maelstrom of sociability I remembered why I'd been so glad to stop sleeping in the coat closet. Besides, the living room's owner didn't appear to be permitting anybody to set up house within the room itself—nobody lived there but the cockatoo, and all things considered, I supposed that was as it should be. Every community, virtual or otherwise, needed its public gathering places, and the living room could hardly serve that function if individual players started staking out their turf there.

As far as I could tell, however, nobody did much gathering in the entrance hall. People mostly passed through it, pausing for a while to chat with other passers-through perhaps, but always ultimately heading somewhere else. Nobody would care much if I made my home here, I didn't think, and the location was certainly central.

I took another look around, which is to say I typed the *look* command and saw the entrance hall's description one more time:

It was still a small foyer, the hub of the currently occupied portion of Lambda House. To the north were the double doors that formed the main entrance to the house. There was a mirror at about head height on the east wall, just to the right of a corridor leading off into the bedroom area. The south wall was all rough stonework, the back of the living room fireplace; at the west end of the wall was the opening leading south into the living room and southwest into the kitchen. And to the west was an open archway leading into the dining room.

I squinted my eyes and tried to picture my nineteen-inch television set blending in with the scenery—over there beneath the mirror perhaps, or next to the globe that stood in the corner, or up against the rough stonework of the south wall.

I couldn't see it.

I exited to the east.

I was in a corridor.

The corridor went east and west. There was a door to the north leading to a powder room. A door to the south led to the stairwell.

I went east.

The corridor ended here with short flights of stairs going up and down to the east. South led to one of the master bedrooms.

I went south.

I was in a large bedroom, the main master bedroom of the house, overlooking the pool to the south through a sliding glass door. There were louvered doors leading west, and a north exit back to the corridor.

An obnoxious beeping sound was going off every few seconds:

«*beep*» it went.

«*beep*»

I ignored the beeping. It was just the burglar alarm, and apparently you could waste an amusing few minutes trying to solve the puzzle of how to shut it off, but I had never bothered with it before and didn't feel like trying now. I just pretended the noise wasn't there, as I usually did—as I had, for example, the night Ecco and I had had tinysex right here on the bed, heedless in our newbie enthusiasm of the fact that the room was open to the public, and that anybody could have walked or teleported in on us right in the middle of our steamiest emotes.

«beep»

I smiled at the memory. And I realized that this was not the place for me to make my new home, either. I needed someplace a little farther off the beaten path. Someplace cozy, and written well and warmly. Someplace where the scenery had a little poetry in it, but wouldn't clash with the matte-black finish of a magic television set.

«beep»

But how was I to find this place? Just wandering from room to room like this could end up taking days, what with all the construction that had gone on in and around Lambda House in its three years of existence. I needed some way to step back and look at the MOO as a whole—some vantage point beyond it all from which to scan the possibilities.

«beep»

I thought a bit.

«beep»

I thought some more.

«beep»

I opened the sliding glass door and headed south.

From the pool deck I walked west a bit, into a relatively neglected corner of the Lambda gardens. A bubble floated in midair there—I slipped inside it, smiled to see one of TomTraceback's alter egos curled up asleep within, then slipped back out and continued south. I passed the blue-and-white awnings of a makeshift outdoor café. I crossed a well-tended patch of turf complete with Italianate reflecting pool and Victorian gazebo. At the south end of the patch of turf I let myself through a wooden gate into a large open field of tall grass, and there I stopped and had a look at what I had come here for: three brightly colored hot-air balloons, straining at their moorings.

I chose the scarlet one with the golden lion figure sewn into its surface and clambered into its basket. I'd never actually been up in one of these balloons before, but the flight instructions, written on a placard inside the basket, were simple to follow: I released the ropes, rose up into the virtual sky, and drifted.

And as the words of the landscape drifted along beneath me—the street in front of Lambda House, the pool deck behind it, the little gazebo and the makeshift café, all scrolling up my screen at the gentle pace of breeze-blown flight—I did my best to see LambdaMOO in its sprawling entirety, the better to find my place within it. For this of course was what had led me to the balloons: I wanted to know the MOO as I might know a map, taking in the breadth of its topography with the single, sweeping gaze of a bird's-eye view, looking down from up here where the virtual birds would have been flying if anyone had bothered to write them in.

Unfortunately, however, birds were not the only thing missing from these heights. The sky program was a clever one (conceived and designed by the industrious Dif, a relative newcomer who would eventually be appointed one of the MOO's few RL-female wizards), but it apparently lacked the intelligence to provide the coherent overview I sought, instead offering balloon-travelers only a randomly sequenced selection of the texts describing LambdaMOO's various outdoor locations. This proved a nice enough way to get acquainted with the range of building activity going on in the environs of the house, but it told me little about the overall shape of the terrain. Soon I was floating over hilltops, woods, castles, apartment complexes, the Colorado Rocky Mountains, and even something that looked a lot like the entire country of Brazil, with no sense whatsoever of how any of these places was connected to any other, or even whether they were connected to the greater topology of the MOO at all. I felt no less lost now than I had before I'd climbed into the balloon, and all the more anxious to somehow orient myself. Was there *no* way, I wondered, to catch an end-to-end glimpse of the MOO? Could the balloon not rise any farther perhaps?

I checked the instructions: it could. I turned on the burner momentarily, and the balloon climbed higher—as high, in fact, as it could go. Surely now the view I had taken to the sky for would come into focus. Expectantly, I typed *look down*, and the following words slid across my screen:

As you drift, you see all of LambdaMOO spread out below you. It's hard to pick out details from such a high altitude, though.

And what else could I do then but smile? The sky was only telling me to do what all MOOers must in order to feel themselves in place within VR, and what I should have known to do all along: fill in the details on my own. The sky was telling me to use my imagination now as I used it everywhere else in the MOOish world, to wrap it around the skeletal words of which that world was made and bring them to life inside my head. So I did as I was told. Inside my head I started building the map I craved, putting it together from a grab bag of mental images and phrases I had gathered over the course of all my previous visits. It looked, more or less, like this:

Near the northeast corner stood the map's anchoring feature—Lambda House, of course, three stories high and counting, an immense split-level absurdity mixing one part Gothic gloom to four parts California ranch-style cheer. Outside the front door of the house, to the north, a road ran west into nothingness, and north of that road some rarely visited commercial buildings had been erected. South of the road, and west of the house, the fields began: the barn was there, a gypsy camp, a landing site for spaceships, a haunted graveyard, and so on off into the western hills, which sloped gently upward and then down to the beaches of the virtual Pacific. Back in the other direction, east of the fields and south of the house, the backyard spread comfortably, accommodating the pool and the hot tub and the café and the gazebo, not to mention a pleasantly climbable oak tree and a challengingly navigable hedge maze. Further south lay the field of hot-air balloons, and a forest of old-growth trees, and inside that forest a handful of gardens scattered here and there along with, if memory served me, a cottage or two.

All in all, the map came together rather nicely, I thought. Until I thought further. For the picture that had thus far formed in my head, I quickly realized, really represented only a thin slice of the MOO's actual geography. Missing, for starters, was the fairly extensive subterranean MOO: the lush, verdant lands hidden in caverns directly below the gazebo, the shopping mall that radiated out from Lambda House at basement level, and other underground regions I presumably had yet to stumble across. These would all have to be traced onto the map somehow, as would the even vaster areas carved unobtrusively out of MOO-space by various dizzying tricks of scale. There were the player homes tucked inside television sets and bubbles and drops of seawater, for example; there was that spacious and often bustling nightspot, Club Doome, located at the corner of an urban intersection shrunk down into a model railroad set in the mansion's guest room; and perhaps most dizzying of all, there was the Earth itself, spinning quietly on the axes of a globe in the entrance hall, medium-sized to all outward appearances but of planetary magnitude once you stepped into its atmosphere—and growing more capacious all the time as newly arriving MOOers added fond simulations of their hometowns, home states, and home countries to the globe's open database.

As difficult as such spatial perversities were to keep straight in my mental image of the MOO, however, there were other locations even harder to fit into the map. What to do, for instance, with the quaint little cosmic wormholes that lay strewn about the MOO like so many Easter eggs—the magical books, mirrors, paintings, and plastic-snow-filled crystal balls that upon being opened, gazed at, shaken, or otherwise engaged became portals into parallel universes of one sort or another? Where *were* these strange dimensions in relation to the already quite sufficiently strange one in which Lambda House existed?

And more naggingly, where exactly were all the hundreds of places whose owners had never even bothered to link them into this loopy, post-Euclidean geography, choosing happily or lazily to reside in the featureless nowhere-land my television set had lately been banished to? Did these free-floating locales perhaps share the same conceptual space occupied by the so-called satellite MOOs—the breakaway worlds like Interzone or aCleanWellLightedMoo (established by a group of Lambda old-timers and dedicated to the fiercely realistic re-creation of a small piece of the outskirts of Mankato, Wisconsin), which ran on computers thousands of miles from Palo Alto but remained linked by ties of history and community to the homeworld that spawned them?

I tried once more to envision it all. The house and the surrounding lands. The subterranean realms clinging to the underside of MOOspace. The bubble homes and parallel worlds swelling like n-dimensional wasp galls within the very tissue of it. The nonregion of unlinked places wrapped in a kind of cluttered orbit around the topologically correct core perhaps, with the satellite MOOs orbiting out at a much farther and much less crowded remove.

Thus summarized, the big picture did indeed seem finally to cohere—but only as long as I ignored the radical discontinuities and physical paradoxes I was necessarily papering over in my effort to imagine any sort of big picture at all. The harder I tried to reconcile these recalcitrant realities with my vision of the MOO, the fuzzier that vision became. And the more consideration I gave to the equally recalcitrant fact that the MOO's geography, besides being a deeply chaotic thing, was a highly volatile one as well, with random regions being built in and removed all the time, the closer the vision came to falling apart altogether. I began to realize why so few maps of the MOO had ever been attempted, and why the few that did exist mapped only the simplest details—a floor or two of the house, say, or the broad outlines of the beach-front regions—while often qualifying their own efforts with tacked-on disclaimers about the inherent instability of the terrain.

And then, looking down from my balloon at the inscrutable details of the landscape far below, I realized something else. It occurred to me that there *was* in fact one map that represented the width, breadth, and depth of the MOO with absolute and unapologetic reliability—and that map was the MOO itself.

This was not the most esoteric of epiphanies, of course. It doesn't take a whole lot of thinking about MUDs, after all, to come up with the proposition that a MUD is, at bottom, simply another member of that broad class of representations specializing in the schematic depiction of place, and generally known as maps.

And yet, if I would have you understand the deep impression that this insight made on me, I must ask you now to join me in a detour from my account of life on LambdaMOO while we consider just what sort of map a place like LambdaMOO might be, and how it got that way. I must ask you, in other words, to delve with me into a brief genealogical history of the MOO, beginning roughly in time immemorial.

The vastness of the time frame is inevitable, I'm afraid, for any historically complete taxonomy of the human innovations ancestral to LambdaMOO must really start where humanity itself did: at that elusive evolutionary moment when the strictly private act of imagination blossomed into the preeminently social one of representation, and the machinery of culture was born. Language, narrative, ritual—all of these are engines for the creation of virtual realities, and always were, for always they have served first and foremost to allow two or more minds to occupy the same imaginary space. And always that imaginary space has stood as a challenge to technology, or maybe a plea: to make the space more vivid, more substantial, to give it a life of its own. Primitive inscription was the earliest device to answer the call; painted cave walls and graven clay tablets lent images and words for the first time a kind of autonomous existence, independent of the bodies whose fleeting speech and gestures had hitherto bound them. But the drive to perfect the technology of representation hardly stopped there, needless to say, and it's nothing less than the entire history of this drive to perfection that comprises the proper genealogy of VR—the full record of every technique ever devised for making the shared illusion of representation come more convincingly alive, from the venerable conventions of perspective drawing and of the realist novel to the latter-day wizardries that have given us photography, television, Disneyland, and 3-D, smellovisual, surround-sound cinema.

It is possible, however, and in the end probably more enlightening, to tell a less ambitious story about the lineage of LambdaMOO. For just as nothing puts us humans more precisely in our place amid the abundant and interconnected branches of life's family tree than the observation that we are descended from

[5 1]

apes, so too the MOO's place in the evolutionary history of the virtual is perhaps best grasped by considering the relatively simple fact of its descent from maps.

Whence maps themselves arose, I couldn't rightly say. As for their present-day status as a pet metaphor of certain delirious strains of postmodernism (according to which the image of a huge map overgrowing and ultimately replacing the territory it charts—Jean Baudrillard's "finest allegory of simulation"—condenses everything you need to know and dread about the decay of the real in contemporary culture), I assure you it isn't theoretical modishness that leads me to locate the origins of the MOO in the invention of cartography. Any close encounter with a map is all it takes, really, to sense the embryonic MOOspace embedded within it. Just look at a map yourself for a while and try, as you look, to resist the urge to imagine yourself transplanted into the tiny territory spread out before you, riding the tip of your own colossal index finger down toy rivers and over minute mountain ranges, hopping flealike from city to city as your giant gaze flits across the chartscape. More than most other traditional ways of representing the world, maps conjure a vision of representation itself as a space the viewer might enter into bodily, a construct not merely to be comprehended but to be navigated as well. They invite interaction, and of course they frustrate it too: their smooth surfaces remain impenetrable, like shop windows, inspiring in the most avid map-gazers a yearning that has less to do perhaps with simple wanderlust than with an ancient dream of literal travel into the regions of the figurative.

Small wonder, then, that the earliest appearances of maps seem to have been followed not long after by the first attempts to shatter their surfaces and place the viewer, as it were, inside them. Board games is what we would call those attempts today, but that shouldn't keep us from recognizing them as crude realizations of the map's implicit interactivity. Nor should it dissuade us from suspecting that the impulses behind their invention were far from trifling. After all, the oldest game of all—the casting of lots—began as a device for divining the will and wisdom of gods, and the history of games in general remained entwined for millennia with that of religious and magical ceremony. Is it such a stretch, then, to speculate that the oldest of board games—which seems to have been a prehistoric, northeast-Asian sort of Parcheesi in which tiny horsemen raced each other around a circular chart not dissimilar in design to the earliest maps of the world—enacted for its players a voyage through the shadow world of the imagination, the world where gods dwelt and that the still-novel technologies of representation brought to life?

Not that the game wasn't also, undoubtedly, something very much like fun. But even fun has its serious dimensions, and in the case of board games (leaving

MAPS
↓
BOARD GAMES
↓
ATTEMPTS TO "SHATTER" MAP ↦ ENTER THEM
(CF. INDUSTRY HISTORY)

aside those that, like Scrabble, for instance, don't in effect represent any sort of navigable territory) the fun to be had has always to an exceptional degree depended on and referred back to the dread seriousness of fate. The ancient racing games evolved quickly into games of battle like checkers and chess, and much later into economic contests like Monopoly and the Game of Life, but what has remained a constant in their appeal is that they quite literally map the real world of day-to-day and ultimately life-and-death existence onto the timeless and ultimately inconsequential realm of the imagined. They promise a temporary escape from the inescapability of history (whether personal or global) into a place where history is just a simulacrum built of rules, turns, strategies, and dice rolls, a weightless flow in which no outcome is so fatal that it can't be rewritten the next game around. After all these years, in other words, board games continue to show their religious roots, since even our simple, secular delight in these rough-hewn virtual worlds turns out to be, in a sense, just another way of wrapping our hearts and minds around religion's primal conundrum: the cosmic raw deal that gave us each just one life to live.

Still, secular delight is also, in another sense, simply its own reward, and if the tension between reality and unreality was always the source of the board-gamer's delight, then it stood to reason from the outset that a heightening of that tension would increasingly be sought by players as the games evolved. With other sorts of games, of course, gambling has long been the preferred means of flavoring the airy stuff of play with the rugged feel of real-life results, but tellingly enough, this quick-and-dirty injection of genuine fate never became much of a fixture of board games. Instead, starting with the archaic precursors of chess, they have more often borrowed from real life not its consequences but its complexity. With the arrival of chess itself in courtly sixth-century India—and with the later development of the East Asian game of Go—the board game attained a degree of tactical intricacy that remained unsurpassed for hundreds of years, suggesting perhaps that for the time being the form's evolving complexity had actually outpaced that of social reality.

By the middle of this century, however, reality was catching up with a vengeance, and for the first time board games of a significantly hairier complexity than chess's began to appear. Inspired, no doubt, by the increasingly media-blitzed busyness of the postwar information landscape—and nurtured, obviously, by the sudden abundance of leisure time in postwar consumerist societies—these new games carried out their inherited role of simulating history with an unprecedented and often overwhelming attention to detail. Their earliest exemplars were the monumental war games produced since the 1950s by the

[handwritten marginalia:] +LEISURE TIME ↓ +POSTWAR/ INFO SOC ↓ "HISTORICAL SIM" GAMES, 1950s

Avalon Hill company: played on towel-sized, geographically precise maps of combat sites like Gettysburg, Stalingrad, or Waterloo, encrusted with arcane rules and timetables designed to model actual conditions of battle, and littered with hundreds of miniature playing pieces all subtly different from one another in their designated abilities, the games demanded a certain obsessive fortitude just to get through the instructions, let alone to commit to the hours, days, or even weeks a single game might take to play.

But even these tabletop sagas proved to be light diversions compared to the groundbreaking genre that emerged from their midst in 1973, when two veteran wargamers named Gary Gygax and Dave Arneson introduced a new game they called Dungeons and Dragons. Abandoning the typical military-historical setting in favor of a mythical age peopled by wizards, dwarves, elves, and other Tolkienesque entities, D&D (as millions of aficionados would later routinely abbreviate it) took wargaming into a whole new conceptual world as well, turning it into an endeavor so involved and involving that it became, in some ways, difficult to recognize as any sort of game at all.

D+D

The most obvious of D&D's novelties, perhaps, was its near-total indifference to what had until then supplied the formal cornerstone of virtually every game in existence—direct competition between players. Collapsing the wargamer's swarming battlefield of units into a single heroic character loaded with dozens of

+ COOPERATIVE
PLAY

precisely defined attributes, skills, and possessions, the rules didn't prohibit player-characters from fighting against each other, but they made it much more interesting for them to band together instead and set off on lengthy, shared adventures. These adventures were designed and refereed by a godlike metaplayer known as the dungeon master, who threw potentially lethal monsters and other dangers at the players and awarded ever-more-impressive powers to the survivors in accordance with a mind-numbingly complicated set of rules. Roughly speaking, then, there *was* a point or two to it all, but winning wasn't one of them. In fact, nobody ever clearly won the game, and for that matter no game ever clearly ended: players simply battled on from adventure to adventure until their character was killed, at which point they felt a little sad, maybe, and then created a new character, so that in principle, games might go on for as long as anyone cared to play them. In practice, they sometimes lasted years.

Such elaborately structured open-endedness brought board-gaming closer than ever, of course, to the free-form complexity of real life itself, and this was no small contribution to the evolutionary history of virtual worlds. But in the end, D&D's truly pivotal role in that history should really be credited to a subtler breakthrough: its slight yet radical redesign of the millennia-old relationship between the board-game player and the board. Dungeons and Dragons succeeded as no game ever had at slaking the ancient desire of the map-gazer to enter the map, and it did so, paradoxically enough, by simply taking the map away. Drawn up fresh by the dungeon master with every new adventure, the D&D map remained hidden from the players at all times, its features revealed only as the players encountered them in the course of adventuring, and even then only by the DM's spoken descriptions. Gone was the omniscient, bird's-eye perspective that had always undercut map-gaming's illusion of immersion, and in its absence game-play took on a near-hallucinatory quality so integral to the experience that the official *Player's Handbook* now actually begins with vaguely shamanistic tips on how best to achieve it:

MAP CREATION ↓ "ENTERING" GAME MAP

"As [the dungeon master] describes your surroundings, try to picture them mentally," advises the manual, walking novices through a hypothetical labyrinthine dungeon. "Close your eyes and construct the walls of the maze around yourself. Imagine the hobgoblin as [the dungeon master] describes it whooping and gamboling down the corridor toward you. Now imagine how you would react in that situation and tell [the DM] what you are going to do."

What had happened, in effect, was that the cloaking of the map had also hidden the player's token self, the game-piece, thereby compelling the player to put himself psychically in its place. As a result, D&D players weren't merely *represented* by their richly detailed characters—they were *identified* with them, in a relationship so distinctively intimate that in time it came to be recognized as the definitive feature of both D&D and its scores of eventual imitators, which to this day are known generically as role-playing games. As apt as the name is, however, it doesn't do justice to the breadth of the innovation, for the same mechanics that made D&D's style of role-play so vivid also made D&D more than just a new kind of game. They made it, frankly, a whole new mode of representation—an undomesticated crossbreed, combining the structured interactivity of the board game with the psychological density of literary fiction, yet eluding the ability of either medium to fully embody it. Indeed, the grab bag of primitive media actually used in playing Dungeons and Dragons—pencil and paper for making maps, dice for resolving combat situations and character details, and the spoken word for just about everything else—tended to give the impression that the technology hadn't yet been invented that could single-handedly manage the unwieldly hybridity of the new form.

The impression was a false one, however. The technology *had* been invented,

↓ ADVENTURE

[55]

three decades earlier in fact, when a small army of British and North American engineers perfected a species of overgrown calculator known as the all-purpose digital computer—and in the process inaugurated what might reasonably be considered the single most revolutionary moment in the history of representation since the emergence of language. Even before the computer existed as functional hardware, the theoretical work of mathematician Alan Turing had established that the device was no mere number-cruncher, but rather the ultimate representational Swiss Army knife, a universal simulator capable in principle of symbolically re-creating the dynamics of any real-world process it was possible to imagine. Like the board game, then, only on a much grander scale, the computer was a tool for creating artificial history, and by the time Dungeons and Dragons appeared, computer scientists had long been peering into their machines to watch such complicated and consequential events as rocket flights, managerial decisions, and World War III unfold in the weightless, adjustable atmosphere of digital make-believe.

In comparison, obviously, the simulation of an adventurous romp through faerie posed scarcely a challenge to the technology, and given the abundance of free time, enthusiasm, and sword-and-sorcery geeks among the junior code-slingers of the day, it was really only a matter of time before someone did the requisite programming. In the event, it was three years after D&D hit the stores that a pair of evidently underworked Palo Alto hackers by the names of Will Crowther and Don Woods wrote the world's first computer-based role-playing game, an instant classic known variously as ADVENT, the Colossal Cave Adventure, or simply Adventure.

Formally speaking, there was little about the game that any D&D player would find surprising. The principal setting was the bowels of a cavern crowded with dwarves, dragons, and magic treasures, and though the position of dungeon master was gone, the DM's basic functions were performed transparently enough by the game's underlying code. Written descriptions appeared onscreen in elegantly sparse but otherwise entirely standard DM-speak ("YOU ARE IN A MAZE OF TWISTY LITTLE PASSAGES, ALL ALIKE," "YOU ARE IN A VALLEY IN THE FOREST BESIDE A STREAM TUMBLING ALONG A ROCKY BED"), and adventurers typed in stripped-down versions of typical D&D player-statements ("GO SOUTH," "DROP SWORD," "KILL DRAGON") to which the program gave equally typical responses ("KILL THE DRAGON WITH WHAT, YOUR BARE HANDS?"). Yet from a psychological perspective, Adventure's automation of the dungeon master was clearly no trivial modification. For as a direct result, the rules that defined the game world suddenly *felt* a good deal more like those that defined the physical world. No longer dependent on a human referee's always revocable agreement to abide by them, the binary-encoded laws of Adventure were maintained instead by the same sort of logical machinery that had always enforced the laws of nature: a nonnegotiable procession of unthinking causes and inevitable effects. Any moderately skilled programmer could always stop the game and rewrite its rules, of course, but for anyone in the midst of exploring it, the world of Adventure was as hard-wired as gravity, and almost as convincing.

One particularly lifelike element no one would find in that world, however, was other people. Quite unlike Dungeons and Dragons, you see, Adventure was a solitary entertainment, pitting a lone player against the creatures of code that dwelled in the software recesses of the Colossal Cave. It was also a high-quality, addictive entertainment, to be sure, and wildly popular in computer labs throughout the world. Yet anyone who came to the game seeking role-play at its richest was bound to sense something missing—and once again, as with the earlier leap from D&D to Adventure itself, it was really just a matter of time before some inspired young programmer took on the task of completing the picture.

But time was aided, too, in this case, by historical coincidence, for it happened that the high-techies of Adventure's early years were just starting to get used to a fairly radical notion about the computer: namely, that it was an ideal tool for connecting its users not only to complex, abstract realms of logic and data, but to one another as well. The technology of computer-mediated communications had been in its infancy at the start of the '70s—when the first nodes of what would later become the Internet were sprouting in Pentagon-fertilized fields of academe—but it grew steadily, and in the final year of the decade its coming of age was signaled by a cluster of landmark developments. The earliest computer bulletin boards had been wired into the phone system by pioneering PC hobbyists the year before; the first commercial online services opened for business not long after; the first Usenet newsgroups began to circulate, stirring up a hint of the vast global storm system of discussion they would eventually grow into; and last but assuredly not least, code-smiths Roy Trubshaw and Richard Bartle, both of them undergrads at Britain's University of Essex, spent much of the year putting final touches on a program that would at last fulfill the promise of computerized role-play, allowing two or more geographically distant players to enter the game at once.

Its name was MUD. The MU stood for "multiuser," and much later, as you may recall, the D would commonly be taken to stand for "dimension," but at the

time what it really stood for was "Dungeon," in homage to a popular Adventure
knock-off known by that name. The game space itself likewise leaned heavily on
Adventure-inspired conventions, as the generically evocative look and feel of the
opening description made plain:

> You are stood on a narrow road between The Land and whence you came.
> To the north and south are the small foothills of a pair of majestic moun-
> tains, with a large wall running around. To the west the road continues,
> where in the distance you can see a thatched cottage opposite an ancient
> cemetery. The way out is to the east, where a shroud of mist covers the
> secret pass by which you entered The Land.

Naturally, The Land was filled with the usual automated hobgoblins and hidden treasures as well. But there, precisely, MUD's debts to its predecessors
ended, because The Land was also filled with real live people, and their presence introduced new elements of surprise and camaraderie into computer-
adventuring's clockwork worlds. These elements, in turn, raised the attraction of
those worlds to an apparently irresistible level. By early 1980, the DEC-10 main-
frame on which the new game was installed had been opened up to logins from
beyond the university, and it wasn't long before the machine was swamped with
an influx of players so hooked that a near-total ban on outside MUD connections
(permitted by school authorities only between two and six o'clock in the morning) did little to discourage them. "Even at those hours," Richard Bartle later
recalled, "the game was always full to capacity."

Such a hit was bound to spread, of course. Requests for copies of the game's
core operating system started coming in from around the world, and Bartle honored them, exporting MUD code to Norway, Sweden, the United States, and
Australia (where in time the games' network-clogging proliferation would lead to
an official, continentwide prohibition of them). Inevitably, other hackers took
to revamping and reinventing the program—streamlining its inner workings,
adding to the diversity and realism of its features. And wherever new variants
appeared, new worlds were built around them, often retaining the stock sword-
and-sorcery thematics of the original MUD, but increasingly veering off into
realms of almost fetishistic specificity. Devotees of Anne McCaffrey's dragon-
happy fantasy novels stepped into great scaly text-bodies to roam detailed re-
creations of the books' faraway planets; *Star Trek* fans built vast working models
of the *Enterprise* and sailed them off through MUDspace; college students

erected simulations of their schools and spent nights slashing giddily away at monstrous, digital parodies of their professors.

Hundreds and thousands of person-hours went into the collective design of these games, and many more went into the often passionate playing of them— and all the while the culture at large obliviously looked elsewhere for visions of the mind-bending dream-tech of artificial worlds it was beginning to sense computers had in them. Millions got their first glimpses of the dream in early-'80s science fictions set amid the gleaming, corporate geometries of a place most memorably referred to (by novelist William Gibson) as cyberspace, and millions more saw it later in breathless media accounts of goggles-and-gloves contraptions being patched together by starry-eyed Silicon Valley capitalists, yet few people outside the MUDding community seemed to realize that a global VR industry of sorts was already cranking out one lucidly believable digital microcosm after another, more or less just for the fun of it.

MUD AS "GLOBAL VR COMMUNITY" a "INDUSTRY"

"LUCIDLY BELIEVABLE MICROCOSMS" = VR?

And even among the MUDders, it's safe to say, not many saw with clarity just what an oddly substantive sort of fun their pastime was on its way to becoming. Right up to the end of the '80s, after all, all MUDs were still at least ostensibly nothing more than games. Granted, they were impressively elaborate games—no less free-wheeling and engrossing than the pencil-and-dice role-playing epics they descended from—but they were games nonetheless, with specific adventures to be pursued, puzzles to be solved, and typically, hierarchies of points-based levels to be ascended (leading ultimately to wizard grade and the right to build new regions and adventures into the game). Even so, however, MUDders had long noted the marked tendency of the game space to become a social space as well. Players not infrequently stepped outside the game without leaving the MUD, going "OOC" (or out of character) to hang out amid the passing adventurers, to haggle over administration of the game and its resources, to deepen the genuine friendships and authentic antipathies formed in the midst of play. Something very much like real community was coalescing at the edges of all that make-believe, in other words, and though such virtual communities were hardly rare in the online world, nowhere did they enjoy as richly nuanced and concretely grounded a setting as amid the gesturally expressive make-believe bodies and psychically immersive make-believe landscapes of which MUDs were constructed.

IC | OOC

Despite their principal deployment as games, then, MUDs were more than just incidentally serviceable as a medium for broader forms of social intercourse. They were in fact ideally suited for the role. And it may be that a recognition of that fact was what led, late in the summer of 1989, to the final significant turn in the technological path to LambdaMOO. Or it may not be. James Aspnes, the Carnegie-Mellon grad student who took that turn by creating TinyMUD,* the first of what would eventually be referred to as the "social MUDs," certainly didn't seem to think he was inventing anything but a more fluid adventuring environment. "I wanted the game to be open-ended," Aspnes wrote later, explaining his decision to leave the conventional framework of player-rankings and fixed goals out of his new MUD. And open-ended the MUD indeed turned out to be, though hardly in the familiar, structured manner made standard long before by Dungeons and Dragons. The truth was, TinyMUD really had no structure at all—it was literally whatever its players wanted it to be. With building privileges no longer limited to a wizard class, the topology of the MUD quickly came to reflect the diverse whims and backgrounds of the inhabitants, with virtual Taiwans popping up next to virtual Cambridges, and Wesleyan University steam tunnels leading to the buildings of a University of Florida campus. In time there was even a full-scale replica of Adventure to be found somewhere on the grounds, though it's unlikely many TinyMUDders ever sought it out. For it was clear enough by then that, whatever James Aspnes's original intentions may have been, people didn't really come to TinyMUD to play games.

What they did come for wasn't exactly easy to pin down, but neither was it all that hard to understand. They came to create, for one thing—to build spaces and construct identities. They came, too, to explore the sprawling results of all that creation. But mainly they came for the simple reason that other people came as well. They were there to talk, to tell jokes, to make love and fall in it, to bitch and bicker and backstab. They were there, in short, to make human contact, which by a hardly remarkable coincidence seems also to be what most people are on this planet for. Even less remarkable, then, are the facts that TinyMUD, which its creator had expected to "last for a month before everybody got bored with it," instead grew fat and thrived in various incarnations for years; or the fact that it inspired a miniboom in the construction of MUDs generally and social MUDs in particular; or the fact that its success almost instantly began to attract the attention of scholars and professional media developers, intrigued by the now amply demonstrated depth and versatility of MUDs and eager to explore their limits.

---

*TinyMUD's prefix appears also to have been the source of the "tiny" sometimes used in the local terminology of social MUDs, LambdaMOO included. Aspnes says he picked the prefix because of the relatively small number of code lines in his program, but as I suggested earlier, I suspect its subsequent spread into common usage had more to do with the sense of miniaturization endemic to a world that exists "inside" a small computer somewhere.

And what of the fact that the earliest of such high-minded investigations was initiated by a thirty-year-old Xerox researcher called Pavel Curtis? Surely, in the context of the grand evolutionary narrative we've been tracing, that particular point of information is among the least remarkable of all. But as it is the point upon which the entire narrative converges, let it be noted: that on the morning of the day before Halloween, in the year 1990, Pavel Curtis issued the command that for the very first time summoned into existence LambdaMOO, a social MUD in the classic mold, with little at that point to distinguish it from the general run of TinyMUD's progeny aside from its exceptionally powerful set of world-constructing tools (built into the original MOO code by its author, Stephen White) and the fact that a major multinational corporation would be keeping a close watch, through Curtis, on the world LambdaMOO's players constructed with those tools.

Of course, given the relatively hands-off nature of the experiment, even the latter distinction didn't ultimately make much of a difference to life within the MOO. Nor might it have meant much outside the MOO either, had the multinational corporation in question been a different one. But inasmuch as Curtis worked for the same Xerox think tank that had essentially dreamed up the personal computer from scratch a decade and a half before (only to watch helplessly as Xerox marketers dropped the ball and a tiny start-up by the humiliatingly cutesy name of Apple carried it into the end zone), his employer-sanctioned interest in MUDs rather conspicuously suggested that they might contain the seeds of the next revolution in the nature of the human-computer interface.

Thus, where TinyMUD had cleared the way for research into MUDs as a serious technosocial phenomenon, LambdaMOO ushered the new field in with a loud and legitimating fanfare. Before long, ethnographers, sociologists, and literary theoreticians were poking their heads into the nearest MUD for an often illuminating and invariably gratifying glimpse (here was a world, after all, in which the social construction of reality wasn't a matter merely of academic dogma but of basic physics), and the Net was peppered with research-oriented MUDs that went beyond LambdaMOO's ant-farm experimentalism into areas of ever-more pragmatic application. There were MUDs designed to teach kids about science and programming while they played, local-area MUDs where teams of office workers gathered to coordinate ongoing projects, a MUD where far-flung astronomers came to trade observations amid the whirling orbs of a virtual solar system, and even, perhaps inevitably, a MUD reserved for media researchers who felt like getting together to talk about, well, MUDs mostly.

So that by the summer afternoon of 1994 on which I showed up at Lambda-MOO to wrestle with the curious case of the dislocated television set, the world I happened to be coming home to was but a single member of an increasingly diverse ecology of such worlds. The three or four hundred MUDs now up and running embodied a range of applications stretching from the still very popular hard-core adventure games through the more broadly focused social and research MUDs and on out to the first limited prototypes of schemes in which the entire Net might someday be blanketed by one big MUD, its code distributed across all the world's computers and its sprawling terrain providing context for every type of digital interaction conceivable. More and more, as well, the tens of thousands who inhabited these worlds were dividing into loose and loosely antagonistic sub-cultures reflective of their divergent interests, with habitués of the social MUDs sometimes jocularly disparaging the adventure worlds as so much "hack-and-slash" childishness, and adventurers in turn dismissing the social worlds as "chat systems with furniture."

Despite the growing differences between MUDs, however, it was an underlying unity that still ultimately defined them. For just as there had never been any MUD so steeped in playful make-believe that it wasn't also fertile ground for serious emotional connections among its players, likewise there was yet no MUD so dedicated to serious purposes that it could do without the elements of playful make-believe that made it function. All MUDs, that is to say, existed in a conceptual twilight zone between the games from which they had evolved and the real-life social meshes they had come to resemble, and at bottom it was in this irreducible ambiguity—rather than in any of the increasingly various uses to which MUDs were being put—that their deepest significance lay. They constituted neither an escape from historical existence nor simply an electronic extension of it, but rather a constantly disputed borderland between the two—between history and its simulation, between fate and fiction, between the irrevocable twists and turns of life and the endlessly revisable possibilities of play.

If I make any great claims for the curiousness of LambdaMOO, therefore, understand that they are really only claims on behalf of MUDs in general, and also, perhaps, on behalf of what can really only be called the human condition. Like all MUDs, you see, LambdaMOO was still essentially a map, and like all MUDs it mapped a place as yet uncharted by conventional cartographic means: the strange, half-real terrain occupied by the human animal ever since it started surrounding itself with words, pictures, symbols, and other shadows of things not present to the human body. It's a place we're all well-acquainted with, of course, since we live in it from the moment we begin to talk till the moment we have nothing left to say. But have you never noticed how seductively exotic even the most familiar ground can come to look, when it is looked at in the tiny abstractions of a map?

It was that sight, at any rate, that I was looking down upon from up there in my scarlet balloon—and yes, the way I saw it, it truly was a sight to behold.

I felt like Balboa on the cliffs at Darien up there. I felt like Armstrong in the Sea of Tranquility. It was as if, in finally understanding that the MOO and my hoped-for map of the MOO were in fact one and the same, I had stumbled upon some mythic place I never thought I'd see, a latter-day El Dorado or Shangri-La that I had long heard rumors of but couldn't have guessed I'd someday get to gaze on with my own two eyes.

It was no paradise I had discovered, of course. Not really. The mythic place I had in mind was in fact that same unfortunate, legendary empire that so fascinated Baudrillard—the realm whose cartographers once produced a map of such faithful detail it blanketed the entire imperial territory, bringing on the decline of the empire and with it the eventual rotting away of the map. This fable, as told or perhaps retold by the great Argentine storyteller Jorge Luis Borges, had long since worked its way into the mythologies of postmodernism, looming for years at the edge of any conversation in which anyone took for granted the fundamental and probably fatal inability of contemporary society to distinguish between reality and simulacrum.

But if the usual tones in which the fable was discussed were either dark with foreboding or cool with irony, my own mood now was anything but. Rather than dreading the cultural implications that seemed to follow from LambdaMOO's confusion of map and territory, I found myself frankly delighting in them. At that moment, the view from the balloon looked to me like anything but a metaphor for a culture suffering through the final, delirious stages of advanced modernity. It looked, instead, like nothing so much as a metaphor for the cure. For though I had always known that the MOO was a place people came to in part to exercise and share their creativity—to make culture, in short—what I saw now for the first time, gazing groundward in my attempt to make some sense of this convoluted cosmos, was the remarkable cultural object all that collective creativity had produced. I saw a territory that mapped the community that had made this map, gradually shaping it over months and years of small acts of construction. I saw my own little lost piece of that territory—the television home I had so carefully crafted and the modest corner of my dear, departed Ecco's hotel room that she had once upon a time set aside for it—multiplied by the thousands into a complex chart of all the individual imaginations and moments of connection that flowed daily through the MOO.

I saw, in other words, the elusive and poignantly human beauty infused in this gnarled and ungainly shape, and if I didn't exactly see in it a work of art as well, that was only because I sensed modernity's working definitions of the term were inadequate to so organically communal a mode of creation. No lone, heroic figure had made LambdaMOO, nor could its meaning be displayed in any museum or sold in any gift shop. It existed for and in the webwork of relationships that built it, accumulating the kind of raw and life-infested aesthetic power found otherwise only in such grand, undirected collaborations as coral reefs and city skylines. Yet unlike the reef, with its millions of indistinguishable constituent microorganisms, LambdaMOO let every collaborator's individuality glint amid the grandiosity of the whole. And unlike the cityscape, with its millions of residents shut out of the high-stakes development game, LambdaMOO let all inhabitants participate in building the world they inhabited.

It seemed too idyllic to be true, this vision, but I couldn't quite bring myself to doubt it. By now I was thinking rapturously populist thoughts in the key of Walt Whitman and Woody Guthrie and feeling mildly embarrassed for myself even as I thought them, yet I couldn't shake the feeling that my excitement was somehow justified, that I had stumbled upon a creative form more radically democratic than any I was familiar with, and more meaningfully participatory than any critic of the alienating modern gap between artist and spectator could ever hope for. That I had found this form, moreover, not among the guardians of some embattled premodern culture struggling to hold on to its authenticity, but precisely here, in this hothouse of simulation erected on the high frontier of late technological culture, seemed less a reason for reconsidering my rapture than a cause to savor it all the more.

I savored it, therefore—and knew right then and there that the place I was seeking for myself in LambdaMOO was going to have to be more than just a cozy nook somewhere. Nor could my simple television set be the only contribution I made to the MOO's evolving geography. I wanted to leave a far more memorable mark on this world than that, and after all who wouldn't, seeing it as I now saw it? Someday, I sensed, LambdaMOO and all the other player-built MUDs might very well be remembered as the beginning of a long, vibrant tradition of similarly emergent digital art forms. I didn't want to live to regret not having participated more fully in this moment after it was gone.

And thus it was, dear reader, that the Garden of Forking Paths—my own egre-
giously sprawling addition to the egregious sprawl of LambdaMOO—was born.

Or rather, I should say, thus it was that the garden was born again. For I had actually conceived the project some months before, when a nascent fascination with
the ancient Chinese fortune-telling system known as the I Ching (or Book of
Changes) had sparked an urge in me to build a working model of the oracle inside
the MOO. It was an obvious idea, in some ways. Based on a gracefully intricate
binary code in which six consecutive tosses of coins or sticks generated one of
sixty-four possible six-bit bytes (or hexagrams), each pointing to a particular
reading from the book's cryptic wisdom, the I Ching had effectively been an exercise in digital programming from the moment of its pre-Confucian invention.
Nor did this make it especially unique among fortune-telling devices and other
games of chance. Generally speaking, such things were a cinch to translate into
the algorithmic mechanics of VR, and LambdaMOO was fairly littered with
them: a full-featured casino awaited visitors to the basement shopping mall, a
Crazy Eight Ball lay buried in the pile of board games heaped in the dining room,
a mechanized gypsy woman read fortunes to players passing through the
encampment south of the barn. There was even, for that matter, a rather nicely
designed I Ching book, complete with built-in coin-tossing mechanism, to be
found also amid the wagons of the gypsy camp.

But I had something a little less literal in mind. Why re-create the I Ching as
it existed in real life, after all, when VR gave me the chance to set the oracle's
complexities free from the amber of their material shape and embody them anew
in whatever imaginable form I wanted? I racked my brains trying to picture what
that reembodiment might look like. I toyed with this idea and that, considered
talking books and mystic slot machines, drew sketches and diagrams, grew fed up
with them all, then finally, on the brink of settling for some unsatisfying plan
whose details I have happily forgotten, I hit on the answer. My I Ching would not
be a book, exactly, nor would it quite be a machine, but like the MOO itself it
would be partly a combination of both and mostly something else entirely: it
would be a place.

And as soon as I guessed that much, the rest came to me in a quick, bracing
shower of afterthoughts. The place, I knew, would be a monumental natural
landscape, shot through with a filigree of repeatedly branching paths. Visitors
would start out in the center of the terrain, where they would flip a virtual coin to

determine whether to take a northern route or a southern one. Either direction would lead them to a fork in their path, and the coin again would tell them which way to go, leading them to the next fork, where they would once more follow the coin's direction, and so on. After the sixth coin toss, the wanderers would have made enough binary choices to spell out a hexagram—and would also have reached their destination, where they could then either meditate on the scenery (depicting some aspect of the imagery traditionally associated with the hexagram they had just traced) or else go for a quicker and dirtier enlightenment, typing the command *look within* to call up instantly the relevant text from the Book of Changes.

Now, I Ching purists might object that my scheme simplified certain crucial aspects of the consultation process, and I wouldn't argue with them, but the idea of the garden seemed vibrantly right to me nonetheless. For the most part its simplicity struck me less as an abridgment than as an echo of the I Ching's own elemental elegance. And its user interface likewise struck me as nicely attuned to the nature of the oracle, which typically, I knew from experience, was consulted at moments when one's life path had reached a fork and the need for direction signs had become acute. I liked this resonance in particular, and was pleased as well to recognize a second one lurking within it—a second text, not to be found in the pages of the I Ching but definitely related to it, and more definitely related to my long-term understanding of the MOO than I could at that moment have guessed.

For I was thinking then of yet another Borges story. This one told the tale of a captured Chinese spy in World War I who discovered far from home and in the final moments of his life the legacy of an accomplished ancestor, one Ts'ui Pên, whose own final achievement had been the composition of a book that was at once a "chaotic novel" and a labyrinth. It was a labyrinth "forking in time, not in space," however—a violation of the terms of both conventional fiction and daily existence, with their requirement that "each time a man is confronted with several alternatives, he chooses one and eliminates the others." In Ts'ui Pên's fiction—to the mournful admiration of his condemned descendant, whose own self-chosen doom lay implacable moments away—all alternatives were pursued, every fork in history's path taken. At each instant of choice, the protagonist created "diverse futures . . . which themselves also proliferate and fork," producing a convoluted "network of times" that embraced "*all* possibilities."

This network was the labyrinth, and though I'm aware that Borges's depiction of it has since been glossed by techno-savvy literary critics as a premonition of the

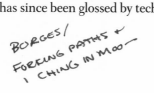
BORGES/ FORKING PATHS + I CHING IN MOO

branching digital structures underlying hypertextual universes such as the World Wide Web, what I saw in it just then was a crystalline image of the existential space the I Ching aimed to guide its readers through—and that I now aimed obliquely to model in virtual space. I had no hope of rendering the concept as exquisitely as Borges had, but I decided nonetheless that it wouldn't be too vain of me to borrow for my work the name he'd given both his story and the remarkable artifact it framed. For wasn't my creation the real "Garden of Forking Paths" anyway? Ts'ui Pên's only metaphorically deserved the title, after all, and here I was about to build the literal thing—garden, paths, forks, and all.

Or so I fondly believed. But I wasn't then figuring into my plans that same geometric proliferation of possibility that had mired the last thirteen years of Ts'ui Pên's life in an essentially unfinishable effort. My own task wasn't quite so open-ended, of course, but as I quickly discovered once I broke ground on the garden, even the six simple choices the I Ching called for would require me to build no fewer than 127 locations, each one containing either a fork or a hexagrammatic end point. And though it was no great challenge to carve the basic shape of all those sites out of thin MOO air (I took care of that right away, mindlessly typing the @dig command 127 times in a single late-night, finger-numbing frenzy), composing the scenery for each of them was a far more daunting matter. I wanted unique descriptions for every site, you see—not just the final hexagrams, but every stop along the way. I wanted every route to every destination to leave a trail of indelible images in the traveler's mind, to fuse in memory the I Ching's message and the path that led to it. And I soon reached the conclusion that what I wanted was going to cost me more late-night frenzies of composition than I could possibly, in those early, tentative days of my relationship to the MOO, afford to spend.

And so, almost as abruptly as I had taken up the project, I let it drop. Which isn't to say I threw it out: I didn't want to, and I didn't really need to either, having carved its sixty-four pathways into a palm-sized jewel-box landscape that fit almost unnoticeably into the arabesque decor of my television set. I entered the jewel box now and then, showed exu and other friends around its barren, labyrinthine terrain, its fork-sites spreading monotonously like so many fresh-built soundstages waiting for the set crew to come fill them with the illusion of place. Sometimes I took a crack at a description or two, and sometimes I even pictured myself finally scrounging up the hours and the inspiration to finish the job in its overwhelming entirety. But mostly I thought I knew better. Mostly I thought the garden was an engaging dream, and a nice conversation piece, and

MOO/I CHING

ultimately just another monument to the unearned ambition of newbies such as I, destined to languish like dozens of other eternally half-done mega-objects mothballed away in player-rooms across LambdaMOO.

But then on that first midsummer day of my immersion in VR, I rode a balloon to the top of the sky and looked back down on a MOO I hadn't quite recognized before, and in that moment my prognosis for the Garden of Forking Paths changed markedly for the better. All the sights and insights that floated up to me in that high-flying basket—the impossible, churning shape that the MOOish cosmos presented to my mind's eye; the map that I saw inextricably embedded in that shape and the cultural marvel that I saw in every wrinkle of that map—they all added up in the end to just one realization: I was going to build my garden after all.

It was going to be the mark I left on LambdaMOO's map. And more than that, it was going to be my homage to that map. For I understood now that at some not too airy level of analogy, the garden was the spitting image of the MOO that I was seeing for the first time that day—the MOO whose history began somewhere on Asian steppes, millennia ago, when humans first gazed fascinated at the tiny abstract territory embodied in maps and decided they would ride their tiny abstract horses into that place. The MOO that hovered now, I Ching–like, between the seductive whimsy of a game and the supple seriousness of life. The MOO that in the months ahead would come to seem to me a catalog of all the human hopes and anxieties that ride the border between what is and what might be—from the utopian longings surging through MOO politics to the experimentalist urges and schizo-paranoid tendencies amok in MOO identity play to my own lifelong commitment jitters, soon sorely to be tested in this lush terrarium of possibility. I would eventually see all these emotions and all these MOOs reflected, honored, in the network of paths and choices my garden was to come to be.

MOO AS "CATALOGUE OF AFFECT / VIRTUALITY"

But for now I had seen all I needed to see.

I let the balloon drift for a while. I sank it on a downdraft to tree-top height, cruised randomly till the barnyard came into sight below me, then pulled myself up over the basket rim and leapt. No parachute, of course, and no matter: I plummeted screaming to the ground, made a largish crater there, and arose from it unscathed, like the textual cartoon character I was.

Evening had come to the barnyard, written into the description by a clever little algorithm that kept track of the hour and season and supplied the appropriate atmospherics. The barn rose up before me, its decade-old coat of red paint chipped and peeling, the gray-brown shingles of its roof covered with moss and withered leaves and festooned at the eaves with *clumps of twigs, dry grass, and string, where swallows have built their nests.* Attached here and there to the front of the barn was an eclectic but somehow meaningful disarray of plastic doll heads, bright-painted animal bones, and warped 45 rpm records, while old farm implements and whimsical shrines littered the yard around me.

I smiled, recognizing exu's style in the place and loving it. I decided then that I would gladly take her up on her invitation after all, and lay my television set to rest out here amid this handsome clutter. It hardly mattered to me anymore that a barnyard was not the proper place to put a TV set. The Garden of Forking Paths would be finished soon enough, and when it was I could easily build a cozy little cottage all my own just off the garden path. But in the meantime I wanted most of all to make my home among my friends, right here, where the closest of them had built a place of memory and precious junk, and offered me a piece of it.

I would have told her all this then and there, except that exu had had to make a sudden disconnection just a few moments before. She did most of her MOO-ing, I knew, during whatever slack time she could scrape from her office day job, and when she had to go, she had to go. I could tell her in the morning, and she could attend to the moderately complicated business of building my TV set into the scenery here whenever she got a chance to. I didn't mind waiting.

I wasn't, in fact, in much of a mood to mind anything just then. I felt sated with the discoveries of the day, and touched by exu's welcoming gesture, and at the edge of those emotions I could feel the onset of a sort of runaway affection I had come to think of as peculiar to VR—a strangely weightless feeling that seemed unwilling to remain attached to the particular people who brought it on. It tended to expand out of all proportion, to seep gaslike through the gauzy limits of whatever virtual object contained it and bathe the surroundings in its pinkish haze, so that presently I found myself wanting vaguely to hug not only exu, wherever she might be, but the twisted old oak tree in the middle of the barnyard, the barn itself perhaps, and maybe even the very pixels of my computer monitor, if I could somehow manage it.

I let the feeling pass unacted-on, however, and did not rule out the possibility that I had simply gone dizzy with hunger. For it was true that my stomach was growling fiercely by then, and it was also true that though the satisfactions to be found in LambdaMOO were many, dinner was not among them.

I typed @*quit*, therefore, and shut my computer off, and made my way upstairs to find a bite to eat.

[handwritten margin note: VIRTUAL PLEASURE VS / AS PHYSICAL HUNGER (2 DIZZIES)]

A Rock in Midstream
You are on a comfortable, flood-smoothed rock somewhere
   between the New Jersey and the Pennsylvania shores of
   the Delaware River. The rock's face rises a foot or
   two above the waterline, with ledges you can walk on
   spreading out from it just underneath the surface. The
   river flows on toward the southwest, placid and cool.
You see inflatable raft and inflatable raft here.
Jessica, A_Girlfriend_of_Jessica's_and_the_Boyfriend_
   of_the_Girlfriend, and The_Author are here.
The afternoon sun shines bright, warming the surface of
   the rock.

The_Author wades out into the shallow waters that ring
   the rock, leaving the others to soak up sun, eat
   cheese and apples, rest a while from the rigors of
   rowing.

The_Author walks a couple yards to where the ledge
   drops off and stands there holding an oar in his
   hand, feeling the river pass gently around his bare
   feet, ankles, and calves.

The_Author looks up at the nearer shore, the New Jersey
   side.

look new jersey

High bluffs rising lush-green from the water's edge,
  turning ashen as they climb, becoming pine, and
  shale, and edges sharp as cut glass where they meet
  the cloudless sky.

The_Author looks over at the farther shore.

look pennsylvania

High bluffs rising lush-green from the water's edge,
  turning ashen as they climb, becoming pine, and
  shale, and edges sharp as cut glass where they meet
  the cloudless sky.

The_Author grins. He has that ticklish sensation a
  person sometimes gets when standing on or near a
  border line. You know the feeling: Your senses tell
  you there is no essential difference between the
  land on either side of the line, your sense of
  sociopolitical reality insists as strongly that there
  _is_ one, and the contradiction spins your head
  around a little.

The_Author feels too lazy at the moment, though, to
  think very hard about this ticklish feeling. Too bad.
  It might help him explain why, after two weeks of
  daily immersion in virtual reality, this sudden
  getaway into the great outdoors doesn't hit him with
  as stark a sense of contrast as he thought it would.
  It might occur to him, for instance, that he hasn't
  really gotten away. That sociopolitical reality is
  not that different, finally, from the virtual kind,
  and that a human being never inhabits a physical
  landscape without also inhabiting its ghostly,
  abstract counterpart -- the geography of language,
  law, and fantasy we overlay, collectively, on
  everything we look at.

The_Author (none of this occurring to him) turns and looks at his companions on the rock, and smiles.

A_Girlfriend_of_Jessica's_and_the_Boyfriend_of_the_Girl friend, as it happens, are presently of two minds about The_Author: 1. The Girlfriend isn't sure The_Author is exactly what Jessica needs in her life right now. 2. The Boyfriend is asleep.

The_Author respects these opinions, having shared them both at one time or another.

The_Author has wondered lately, in particular, how fair to Jessica all this MOOing is, and whether it won't end up being a flashpoint for the tensions always looming in their apartment. He has already picked up hints that she resents his lengthening hours on Lambda, nor does he much blame her: there is a strange world plugged into the wall just outside their bedroom, and she's no longer part of it.

The_Author turns away again, looks out at the river's broad stream, breathes deep.

The_Author takes a playful swat at the water's surface with the flat of his oar, a glancing blow that sends a small splash arcing high and upstream. He watches as the flying water beads and catches sunlight just before it drops back down, and then he swats the river and watches it fly again. And again.

Jessica laughs.

The_Author turns and sees her grinning warmly at him from her perch on the rock, watching him play.

look jess

Jessica
You see cream-white skin spread smooth across broad

angles of bone and splashed with dark: black eyebrows
arching sharp and fine over sloe-brown eyes, thin
strands of chestnut hair licking down toward her
neck, toward a body shaped like ocean waves and
wrapped up, at the moment, in a striped blue-and-
white two-piece bathing suit.
She is awake and looks alert.
Carrying:
half-eaten apple
The Fifth-Year Grad Student Blues (one case)

The_Author, as he always does, melts at the sight of
her like this, her smile open, unabashed, inviting
him to drop his guard for good and claim his right to
a lifetime of this moment's sweetness.

The_Author, as he always does, stops only a little
short of accepting the invitation.

VR

3

The Purple Guest

Or TINYLAW,
and Its Discontents

Time had a slow and slippery way of flowing on the MOO. Broken up by the insistent interruptions of RL (of sleep, work, meals, and social life), my MOO days stuttered like an <u>archipelago of dreams</u> across the surface of the real days, touching down for just an hour or two at a time but somehow lingering in my imagination for much longer. In my first week I clocked fewer than ten hours in VR (far short of my standing aim of thirty, and well shy of the hard-core MOOer's typical fifty, sixty, or even seventy weekly hours), yet it felt to me as if I'd already spent a lazy season there. MOO time was in no hurry, it seemed, and consequently neither was I: the work of completing my garden could wait, and so, for that matter, could anything else requiring my focused attention.

So I flitted instead from diversion to diversion. I explored the grounds some more, gossiped with friends and small-talked with strangers. I read casually from the MOO's organic tabloids—the mailing lists, with their daily accumulations of scandal, scuttlebutt, and silliness. And when the Fourth of July swung by, I joined a friendly crowd in the backyard to watch virtual fireworks light up the midnight LambdaMOO sky. I sat with exu and others in the grass reminiscing about sparklers and charcoal snakes, gazing up at a potluck of pyrotechnics programmed earlier in the day by assorted locals. We applauded the best of the creations: Hackamore's O.J. Simpson starburst (*A thousand tiny lawyers come sparkling out of the OJ Rocket, falling like pin-striped rain through the darkness*),

[handwritten margin notes: (DEAN) DISCONNECTION / ISOLATION / VS. FLOW, CONSTANT]

[handwritten note: "MOO TIME" SLOW/SPORADIC]

exu's airborne Thomas Pynchon allusion (A *screaming comes across the sky* . . .),
Kerrit's climactic typographic blowout, which looked like nothing so much as . . .
well, which looked pretty much exactly like this:

```
        *           *               *          *        *        *
   *         *                          *           *      *        *
     *    _____      _____     _____      __      __  __
      *   /_/_/_/_/    /_/_/_/_/    _____      /_\_\    / _| |_|
    *    /_/    /_/ /_/    *  /_/ /_/_/_/_/   /_/ /_/ \_\  /_|_|   |_|
      *  /_/    *  /_/ /_/  *  /_/ /_/        /_/ /_/ /_/  \_\/_/|_| |_|
        /_/____ /_/ /_/     /_/_/  *   /_/ /_/              |_|  |_!
      * /_/    /_/ /_/     /_/_/       /_/ /_/     *        |_| |_|
       /_/ *  /_/ /_/_____/_/_/     * /_/ /_/  *         |_|   |_|
    * /_/____ /_/ /_/_/_/_/_/ /_/_____/_/ /_/    *       |_|    _
      /_/_/_/_/   *          /_/_/_/_/_/    *                     |_|
     *   *   *        *     *              *         *      *
        *       *       *          *    *            *       *   *    *
```

All right, maybe you had to be there. But there I was, and unless I reached
back into my earliest childhood memories, I couldn't remember a Fourth of July
that had so amused me.

I was starting to feel, in fact, as if an unbroken procession of such amusements
lay ahead of me in this virtual sojourn of mine. I'd been around the MOO long
enough to know better, of course, but all the pleasant distractions with which I'd
been occupying myself—the clever camaraderie and the mechanical marvels, the
leisurely chitchat and the home-made fantasylands—were beginning to make me
wonder. Perhaps, after all, there *was* some truth to the newbie's naive first
impression: perhaps LambdaMOO really was, in the end, just fun and games.

And then one day an old familiar stranger came to call on me in the privacy of
my TV set, and once again I learned just how mistaken that first impression
can be.

It was near the end of my second week, while I was in the middle of a leisurely
afternoon of reading through the messages on *social*, that I noticed the wall
inside my television set suddenly twist and groan. Briefly the wall tried to force
itself into the form of a certain "Purple_Guest," and then as suddenly as it had
begun to warp, the room snapped, with a crack, back into shape.

I scarcely raised an eyebrow. This was simply the room's way of telling me that
yet another flailing guest character had tried and failed to teleport in past the

television set's programmable security mechanisms. It was a common enough occurrence. Guests were typically the newest of newbies, and as such they had an infantlike tendency to stick their unformed noses into whatever corner of the MOO caught their unformed eyes. You couldn't stop them from trying, really, and you tended to respond to their unbidden visits about the same way you responded to the unmanageability of infants generally, which is to say somewhere in the emotional range between gruff annoyance and smiling indulgence.

Myself, I was feeling rather smilingly indulgent at the moment, so I had the room's security subroutine beam a formal invitation to the would-be interloper and prepared myself to answer the usual guestly questions and hand out the usual old-timerly tips.

"Oh brave new woild," said the purple guest, teleporting in.

"Welcome," I said.

The purple guest laughed. "Thanks, Dr. B. Now I guess you have to work out whether I was quoting Will or Aldous."

DrBombay . o O (Will?)

"I trust you are well," said the purple guest. "Oh, as in Shakespeare, The tempest."

Purple_Guest's on a first-name basis with the mortal bard.

"Ah." I said. "I am well, but not so well-educated as yourself, I guess."

The purple guest grinned.

And I grinned back.

But to tell the truth, I was not sure how indulgent I felt anymore. There was something unsettling about this guest—something in the way it moved and spoke, in the ease with which it handled the basics of MOO-mediated interaction and in the casual familiarity with which it addressed me, that suggested the guest was not quite what it appeared to be.

What it appeared to be, of course, was nothing much. In addition to their neutral gender, guests were given a blank description by default, completely featureless except for the randomly assigned color that distinguished one guest from another. Just looking at the purple guest, in other words, told me nothing about who it really was, or what exactly its game might be, and I was getting impatient to know.

"Well, enough idle banter, Bond," I said, only half in jest. "What did you come to see me about?"

The guest seemed somewhat rattled by the directness of the question.

"Oh . . . nothing, really," it said. "I guess I've achieved that in ample measure, so will be off."

"Achieved what?" I asked, my impatience mounting.

"Nothing, really," it assured me.

But I was hardly reassured. The suspicion that this stranger was no stranger at all had now firmly lodged itself in my mind, and I was starting to consider the possibilities. I imagined various smirking friends of mine sitting hidden behind that blank description, having a quiet laugh at my cluelessness; and I imagined worse: some tentacle of the Bungle collective perhaps, arriving at last to play head games on me in a twisted response to my long-gone attempts at contact. Of course, it was entirely possible that the guest really was just a guest, and if it was, I hardly wanted to give it the impression we were all a bunch of hair-trigger para-noids here on LambdaMOO. But all the same, I couldn't help continuing my interrogation.

"Well . . . do you have a character here yet?" I asked, cloaking the question as best I could in the guise of disinterested small talk.

Purple_Guest is completely devoid of character.

"I see. Well, have you been on here many times before?"

There was a pause.

"Yeeeesss," said the guest. "I think you could say that."

Aha! Then it was true—the "guest" was a regular, and therefore probably an acquaintance as well. The cat was out of the bag, or halfway out anyway, and we both knew what that meant: it was time to play the ever-popular LambdaMOO parlor game "Guess the Guesst."

But my purple visitor demurred:

"Let's just do lighthearted banter," it insisted. "Unless the imbalance of iden-tity bothers you overmuch. Take it as read, however, I mean you no harm."

DrBombay holds his chin and cocks a wary eyebrow at you, I emoted. It seemed safe enough at this point to believe that the guest was not in fact intent on mess-ing with my mind, but I wasn't about to stop my detective work now.

"Liked your Goldfinger reference earlier, by the way," said the guest, obviously trying to distract me from thoughts of further investigation. "We could do duel-ing Blofelds, eh? Eh, Mr. So-Called Dr. Bombay? Ahm very much afrrrraid your plans for worrrld domination are doomed."

The purple guest giggled. But I was having none of it.

DrBombay pokes you about the soft squishy parts in an investigative sort of way.

"Or we could do a kind of Chandler thing . . . ." said the guest.

"A chandler thing?" I punned. "Sorry, I lost all my candle-making skills cen-turies ago, back when they invented whale-oil lamps."

"I was thinking Raymond, but never mind. Mean gritty streets, mean gritty detective, interspersed with poetry."

DrBombay starts yanking vigorously on that nosish-looking thing there in the middle of that headish-looking thing toward the upper part of you. "Gotta be one of them Halloween type masks," *he mutters.*

"Everything profound loves the mask," replied the purple guest, quoting somebody or other, I guess.

I said nothing.

The guest said nothing.

The seconds passed while I tried to think of something even remotely clever to say.

DrBombay has gone all fuzzy-headed, I emoted finally. And it was true. The rambling thrust and parry of the conversation had at last exhausted me. It was hard enough maintaining the requisite flow of hyperliterate semisequiturs during late-night hangouts up in exu's Crossroads, where I more or less knew who was who, but here, in the mysterious presence of the purple guest, it was starting to seem impossible. I knew it wasn't cool of me to feel this way, at least not by the standards of my MOOish friends, who greatly prized a certain studied insouciance in the face of VR's never-ending supply of indeterminate identities. But I couldn't help it: Not knowing which of my acquaintances I was talking to apparently caused the banter centers in my brain to simply shut down.

The purple guest sighed.

"Just wanted a chat," it said. "An Escape from Dread Significance."

I tried again to think of something to say, but couldn't.

"I guess an absence of significance is just as significant, though," the guest continued. "And as they say: There is no significance without a despotic assemblage."

I blinked.

I read those words again.

And suddenly I felt a bit of the fuzziness clear from my head as a smile of comprehension spread across my face.

It wasn't that I had a very good idea what the guest was talking about—or even the slightest notion what a "despotic assemblage" was—but I knew a quote from the fashionable French anarcho-philosopher Gilles Deleuze when I saw one, and I knew therefore, at last, exactly who my mystery caller was. For of all the admirers of Deleuze I'd encounted on the MOO (and the place was lousy with them, for reasons I never quite fathomed and would in any case probably take a dissertation to explain), only one had so hungrily consumed the great man's words that he seemed incapable of getting through a conversation without burping a few of them up here and there. And only one, moreover, had any particularly compelling motive to keep his identity hidden as he made his way about the MOO. The purple guest, I had to conclude, was none other than Horton-Who—brilliantly loquacious Australian autodidact, perennial MOO-anarchist agitator, and as of some five weeks previous, the first and only one of Mr. Bungle's one-time persecutors to have met with the same capital fate as the notorious voodoo-doll rapist.

"GHOSTS" - BANNED/ MOOICIDE RETURN AS GUEST

I was chatting with a ghost, in other words. Or more precisely with a *geist*, as some MOOers designated those semipresent souls who, having lost access to their regular characters (either by official judgment or, more often, through an act of "MOOicide" meant to free them from a hard case of VR addiction), returned to haunt the place wearing the one virtual body still readily available to them: that of the faceless, fleeting guest.

What HortonWho had done to deserve his banishment to geisthood's twilight existence wasn't entirely clear to me at the time. I knew that a dispute had been filed against him under the new mediation system, that the dispute had accused him of the harassment of some half a dozen leading citizens of LambdaMOO (all female, though no one seemed to have characterized his harassment as sexual), and that even though the sentence ultimately handed down wasn't quite as unforgiving as Mr. Bungle's (HortonWho had been newted rather than toaded— his character put in a coma, so to speak, rather than put to death, and scheduled for revival at the end of six months), its severity suggested that whatever the precise nature of HortonWho's supposed transgressions, they weren't exactly your average, run-of-the-mill breach of local etiquette.

Beyond that much, however, I don't think I really *wanted* to know a lot more about the matter. I liked HortonWho, as it happened. Though famously abrasive in both public and private debate, he was also singularly cordial and urbane when he wanted to be, and he seemed mostly to want to be on the few occasions we'd spent much time together. But it also happened that among HortonWho's alleged victims was a former number-one ally of his (a former VR lover as well, I had come to learn) by the name of exu, and my friendship with her was by now beginning to feel as strong as any I had formed in real life. The thought of delving deeper into the dispute's details, therefore—of trying to choose a side (or not choose one) as I sifted through the heap of conflicting interpretations and partial truths in which the episode seemed likely to be mired—put my stomach in knots.

But there was no way around it now. HortonWho had blown his cover, and didn't seem to mind much having done so. He obviously was in a mood to talk, and obviously there would be no avoiding the subject of his newting. But I supposed that was all right with me. I was glad to see him now, six months earlier than I thought I'd get to, and if there was to be an awkward moment or two in our conversation, that was a small price to pay for the chance to converse at all.

Our reunion was in any event a pleasant one. We grinned; we hugged; we shared an imaginary bottle of plum brandy to celebrate the occasion. And then, because my dread of unpleasant topics was not so great as my desire to get caught up with a not-so-very-long-lost friend, I asked him:

"How are you, old man?"

"Well, I've been better," said the purple guest. "Lost net access courtesy of the cabal. Mostly fine, though."

I was taken aback. I had been prepared to hem and haw about HortonWho's expulsion from the MOO, but the news that he'd been temporarily banished from the Internet as well left me at a loss for words. All I could think to ask was how in the world this had happened. And HortonWho, naturally, told me how, because upon this matter, as upon most others, HortonWho had quite a bit to say.

He explained, for starters, that when he spoke of the "cabal" he meant the small group of MOOers who had filed virtual suit against him, consisting of the six aggrieved female players and of one male player, by the name of Cro, who had initiated the dispute on their behalf. He went on to explain that among the most aggrieved of the aggrieved was a certain Laurel—another one-time virtual intimate of his—and that in the heat of the dispute against him Laurel had decided to take matters beyond the confines of the MOO.

She took them all the way to Melbourne, in fact, where HortonWho lived and worked, by sending intercontinental e-mail detailing the allegations against him to both his supervisor in a software developing venture and his local Internet site administrator. The acts alleged were largely "threats," including threats of "making spurious professional complaints, leveling fabricated charges of academic misconduct, contacting professional journals, revealing confidences and medical information to employers and professional colleagues, attacking professional works in public fora, making crank phone calls, and so forth." "This individual," the e-mail further claimed, "is also articulate and clever enough to make his threats carefully worded and veiled to be difficult to interpret from a casual inspection of computer logs. . . ." Additionally, HortonWho was charged with "vile public communication," "offensive behavior," and sundry other menacing speech acts, the sum total converging on an all-inclusive charge of "systematic harassment."

HortonWho denied it all (though he seemed ready to admit to the more-than-occasional episode of "offensive behavior," and I certainly never heard him say he wasn't "clever" and "articulate"). But the university administrators in charge of his Internet account could not be moved. "They pulled the plug immediately," said the purple guest. "They refuse to discuss Laurel's nastygram with me. The more stridently I insist, the more convinced they are that the e-mail is correct."

Horton's boss, on the other hand, was more inclined to give him the benefit of the doubt. But the boss was "livid," nonetheless, about the fact that Horton's adventures in VR had resulted in a potential threat to business operations (the possibility of criminal charges against one of the company's few employees was the least of it: Horton needed Net access for his daily programming work), and after calming down a bit the man delivered an ultimatum: either the MOOing stopped or Horton's job was history.

For most people, I suppose, the choice would have been an easy one, but anybody who knew HortonWho knew how many months of intense emotional and intellectual energy he had by now invested in his MOOish existence, and I don't doubt that he agonized over his decision. But in the end he chose employment, and after scaring up a temporary, jerry-rigged connection to the Net, he logged on to Lambda just long enough to post to *social and other mailing lists the announcement of his withdrawal from MOO society—to which MOO society soon replied by officially declaring the withdrawal mutual and sentencing HortonWho in absentia to his six-month banishment.

And now the outcast stood before me, a skulking geist, come MOOing on the sly to ruminate upon the ruins of his virtual life.

Purple_Guest [sings] HortonWho died last week, and now he's buried in the rocks. Everyone still talks about how badly they were shocked. But me, I expected it to happen, I knew he'd lost control, when he built a fire on Lambda, and shot it full of holes.

DrBombay takes a swig of plum brandy and passes you the bottle.

Purple_Guest was (for some reason) surprised when VR crossed the border into RL. Both are thereby impoverished.

Purple_Guest takes the bottle, taking a deep draught and swilling quietly.

I thought for a bit, and had to agree: there was something startling and a little sad about the way the virtual had collided with the real in Horton's case. It was a blunt reminder that the MOO was not the self-contained world its conventions pretended it to be, and it came as something of a shock to me.

Not that I had any more excuse for my surprise than Horton did—the Bungle Affair had taught me nothing if it hadn't taught me that the line between VR and RL was no more impermeable than the line between what happens inside our heads and what happens outside of them. But the Bungle Affair, in its final outcome, had taught me other things as well—that true community might be possible in the MOO, for instance, and that there might be something like real justice to be found in that community's enforcement of its defining values. And now I couldn't help feeling that those possibilities were in a kind of jeopardy. For hadn't the decision *not* to pursue RL charges against Mr. Bungle been the act that declared LambdaMOO's readiness, at long last, to handle its problems on its own? Hadn't it established a consensus that MOO crimes would be met with MOO punishment, no more or less? And hadn't that consensus been built as much on pragmatism as on poetic justice—intended as a kind of insurance against the confusions that might come of seeking redress from institutions ill-equipped to grasp the quirks and subtleties of MOOish life, and a kind of guarantee that the requisitely clueful institutions would be built and nurtured within the MOO?

I'd thought so anyway, and I thought now that I must be glimpsing a partial, and maybe even ultimately a total, unraveling of that consensus. It was true, of course, that if Laurel's charges were valid, then it was HortonWho himself, with his RL threats, who had first pushed the conflict into the world outside the MOO, thereby obliging his antagonists to seek its resolution there. But however it had happened, a boundary had been breached, and the case of HortonWho, I sensed, had come to straddle the line between VR and RL far more challengingly than the case of Mr. Bungle ever had.

Just how great a challenge it was, however, was hard to gauge without knowing how it was that HortonWho had ended up a newt as well as a MOOicide. How, I wondered, had the participants in Cro's dispute against him handled the question of the extravirtual dimensions of the case? Which aspects of the now thoroughly tangled web of RL and VR events had they chosen to consider, and what had they opted not to judge? What, in short, were the newtable acts alleged in that dispute?

"Unspecified. Totally," said the purple guest. "I was accused and convicted of 'harassment' (however spelled) without being confronted with my accusers or their evidence."

He told me I should have a look at *D:Cro.vs.HortonWho*, the official mailing list attached to the dispute, if I wanted something like the full story. I groaned at the thought. The list, I knew, was probably hundreds of messages long and was sure to be a sprawling hairball of contradiction and recrimination. But where else could I go from here? I decided I would give the list a skim, at least, and I muttered something to that effect.

And then I changed the subject to a hopefully more cheery one:

"You will be HortonWho again, won't you, when the six months are up?"

I could only assume he would. The heat from his boss would have to blow over, eventually, and even if it didn't, I couldn't picture HortonWho abandoning for good the character he'd spent the last two years building up into a fixture of LambdaMOO's sociopolitical landscape.

Nor, apparently, could HortonWho. But his plans for the afterlife of his lately estranged virtual body were not quite what I'd imagined.

"I doubt I'll reactivate him," said the purple guest. "I have an idea for a hanged man clock, may have mentioned. Kinda installation."

I was intrigued, and the guest was only too happy to elaborate:

"HortonWho on a gallows. In a dark landscape. A raven on his shoulder. Listening, creaking. Feet dangling in a puddle, rope creaking, wind whistling, a smouldering fire splutters and gives off acrid smoke. The activity of observers makes the body react, feet pointing to one of twelve signs. The signs being zodiacal, and interpreted elementally."

Purple_Guest's after an iconic representation of the hanged god, he added. "I'm hoping it will be sumptuous in mourning. Like a black velvet Elvis painting with eyes that follow you around the room :)"

I laughed. "You know, it's kinda dull around here without you."

The purple guest smiled. "I think the dullness is endemic. I mean, look at it . . . all the people who used to have a revolutionary spark are now simpering reactionaries, apologising for the structures here and the fact they don't work."

There was a pause, and then I nodded, grinning.

But I felt a twinge of awkwardness as I did so. Because for one thing, though I'd heard enough today to wonder if something wasn't just a little rotten in the state of Lambda, I wasn't actually so certain that the social structures of the MOO weren't working, all things considered. And what was more discomfiting, in any case, was that I more or less knew which MOOers Horton had in mind when he spoke of former "revolutionaries," and I knew that the one who surely loomed the largest for him was his old comrade-in-arms exu, toward whom, I further knew, he felt more bitterness and hurt than he did toward anybody on the

MOO. I could understand why, to a certain extent—their affair had ended badly, in confusion and betrayals—and I could even, if I had to, sympathize. But I preferred not to have to, because for my part, I could think of nobody on the MOO toward whom I felt more warmth and admiration, and it frankly made me squirm when he got even remotely close to talking about her.

But the purple guest, thankfully, left exu's name unspoken. He preferred instead to hint darkly at the retribution he would one day visit on the "cabal" and all allied with them. He spoke of "gathering force" in his exile, and of the grave mistake his enemies had made in chasing him off the MOO when they should have let him stay where they could keep an eye on him.

"The sparks from this will glow for a long long time," the purple guest warned. "Incendiary dreams will walk."

And right about then, as if on cue, I got a cheerful page from exu, who had just logged on and seemed to want to chat. I paged her back, and then, anxious to avoid a disagreeable scene, I whispered to the guest that exu was around and possibly on her way over to my room.

"Eeep. OK, I'll vanish. Don't let on, 'K?" said the guest. "She +will+ ask, if I'm any judge."

I agreed, a bit wearily, to guard the secret of his identity, for it was true enough that given the variety of surveillance tools used regularly by LambdaMOOers to keep track of who was where, exu might already have taken note of the purple guest's presence in my room. But the guest was gone before my assurances even left my computer. So I said good-bye to the empty air and teleported over to exu's, where I was greeted with a hug and a pleasant conversation and not a single question about who my visitor had been or so much as an allusion to the once and maybe future HortonWho.

[handwritten note: SURVEILLANCE = WHO'S WHERE]

I breathed a heavy sigh, two parts relief to one part sadness. They were both my friends, these two sworn enemies, and I hoped that sooner or later I could figure out a way to be a friend to both of them without also, at the same time, feeling like a traitor to them both. In the meantime, I now realized with a glum sense of resignation, the least I owed all three of us was to give *D:Cro.vs.HortonWho more than just a skim.

And so, not long thereafter, I did exactly that: I spent two hours siphoning the contents of the mailing list from the MOO to my hard drive to my laser printer; and on the day after that I took the resulting 102 single-spaced, small-typed pages to work with me. And there—in the idle moments I might otherwise have spent with a copy of The New York Times in hand, updating my supply of common knowledge about the world my coworkers and I generally agreed we all lived in—I opened that fat document from another reality and began to read.

This was not the first document of its kind that I had waded into. For that matter, it wasn't even the first such document I had read in which HortonWho figured so centrally. Getting lost in the vast underbrush of legal and legislative documentation introduced by the new political order was in fact fast becoming one of the MOO populace's favorite "leisure" activities, and it had lately become one of mine as well. It so happened, moreover, that my initiation into this arduous pastime had been occasioned more or less directly by HortonWho himself, some two months earlier, when he'd filed a dispute I couldn't resist having a look at.

Registered in the Lambda legal archives as *D:HortonWho.vs.aCleanWell-LightedMOO,* the case and its attendant contradictions would later strike me as more than slightly relevant to my attempts at understanding the dispute that led to HortonWho's newting, yet at the time it intrigued me mainly as a spectacle of potentially historic dimensions. I was aware that the new mediation mechanisms had by that point been brought to bear on a wide variety of conflicts—ranging from the usual cases of harassment and MOO rape to flare-ups involving such rarefied issues as the responsibilities of public-room owners and the ambiguous privileges of the archwizard Haakon in a democratic MOO—but as far as I knew the scope of HortonWho's dispute was unprecedented. For the first time in the existence of this curious, fledgling legal system, a plaintiff was seeking satisfaction in a matter of what was semiseriously being referred to as "international law." HortonWho, that is to say, was bringing suit against another MUD.

You didn't have to know the historical background of the dispute to understand how such a thing had come about, but it helped. aCleanWellLightedMOO, was, after all, not just any MUD, but the oldest and the stablest of Lambda's breakaway worlds, and in taking it on, HortonWho was thrusting himself into the middle of a long and complicated relationship. Public opinion about CleanWellLighted was mixed, to say the least, and had been ever since CWL's inception in the waning days of the old wizardocracy, when certain less enfranchised quarters of the population had looked suspiciously on the fact that the new MOO's founders and earliest colonizers were almost exclusively members of Lambda's so-called "Power Elite" (the wizards and their friends). Haakon's subsequent dissolution of the wizards' reign (rumored to have met with only grudging acceptance among some of his corulers) didn't help matters much either: As LambdaMOO plunged forward into the ensuing months of tumultuous political change, and Clean-WellLighted continued to govern itself in the same autocratic fashion still preferred to this day by 99.9 percent of all MUDs, it grew easy and eventually common to think of CWL—as HortonWho, for example, did—as "the MOO founded in reaction to the Lambda democracy, the place the Power Elite fled to."

HortonWho, however, was perhaps more inclined than most LambdaMOOers to think of CWL that way, for it was his belief that he himself had played a pivotal role in causing the Power Elite to flee. Nor, though he had a tendency to exaggerate his own importance in the great events of MOOish history, was he altogether deluded in this belief. In the months preceding the wizards' abdication, Horton-Who had been a prominent member of what was called by some the MOO Underground, a loose affiliation of the politically disaffected that included exu and Kropotkin, among several others, and was dedicated more or less to the overthrow of the existing social order. "We were trying to make anarchy," exu said later. This seemed to mean, in practice, a lot of late nights hanging out in one another's rooms theorizing the local power structure, a good deal of agitating on the lists and in the living room for an end to the wizards' summary toadings of alleged troublemakers, and occasionally, a frank heart-to-heart with the powers-that-be about the need for fundamental change.

It was in the course of one of these latter conversations, Horton told me, that what he seemed to think of as his shining hour came to pass. It happened one evening when the leading lights of the Power Elite were gathered in and around the café in the backyard, as was their habit, and Horton, who had been haranguing them to no effect about the moral and political urgency of abandoning their dictatorial ways, decided to try a different tack: "I walked up to each of the wizards, in turn, Haakon, enaJ, TomTraceback, Chevy, and put it to them personally. I pointed out to them that if they were going to insist on being social wheels, it could easily eat up all their RL and MOO time. They'd assumed they could effect control. By the application of terror, I guess. But as I explained, it's easier to make ungovernable than to govern. And I think that realisation hit them hard."

No doubt it did, I agreed, but I couldn't help asking: had it really never hit them before? Could it really never have occurred to them that the day-in, day-out job of keeping the peace in this crowded virtual funhouse might in the long run be a huge drain on their time and energy? "Not in such stark terms, I think," said HortonWho—and anyway, he added, look at the timing: just a day or two after this parley in the café, Haakon delivered his edict withdrawing the wizards from the social sphere. What more proof could anyone need that HortonWho had effectively toppled the wizards' regime?

Well, however much weight you assigned to Horton's role in this first phase of the transition to democracy (and the archwizard, for one, was flabbergasted to learn years later that Horton assigned it any weight at all), there was no denying his centrality in phase two: the debates that led to Mr. Bungle's toading and, subsequently, to the introduction of the petition system. For by then it was a fairly well known fact that HortonWho's relations with Bungle's principal victim had progressed well past the stage of comradely solidarity. By which I mean, of course, that somewhere amid the heady days and nights that followed in the wake of the wizardocracy's collapse, amid the rubble of the old ways and the possibilities for new ones that seemed to lie wide open all around them, exu and Horton had become lovers. And so it was that when exu found herself grappling, confused, with the strange mix of violation and exasperation that Bungle's attack had left her feeling, it was to HortonWho she went for comfort. So too, it was in the closest of consultations with him that she reached the fateful decision to transform her confusion into action, to politicize it, so to speak, with her call for Bungle's toading. And therefore it was also really no surprise that HortonWho was first in line to publicly second her request—or that he made his subsequent arguments in its support with so much passion and rigor that TomTraceback would later cite them as decisive in persuading him, finally, that Bungle had to go.

In time, HortonWho came to lament his crucial part in the Bungle Affair as publicly and as forcefully as he had once performed it, but this too was perhaps to be expected. As it happened, the final outcome of the episode had never sat entirely well with him or, for that matter, with any of the self-styled anarchist crowd, exu included. After all their talk of building community and consensus, after all the hopes for a new form of social organization freely risen from the ruins of the old, Haakon's archwizardly imposition of the petition system had left a somewhat ashy taste in their mouths, and for a while, said exu, "we were really pissed. He was trying to do this deus ex machina social engineering when we were really trying to get a movement together."

By the time the first anniversary of Bungle's toading rolled around, the movement had pretty much moved on, but in the interim HortonWho had acquired sharper, more personal reasons for regretting his contribution to the evil clown's demise. His relationship with exu had crashed and burned—after a year in which the two had discovered for the first time just how deeply an affair conducted over the wire could reach into their minds and bodies—and he had come to mistrust her on a variety of levels, not the least of them being the political. exu had by now essentially made her peace with the new MOO order, and she'd even got herself elected to a position in the closest thing there was to a government agency on

LambdaMOO—the Architecture Review Board, which helped establish and maintain guidelines for local building and programming. But Horton's view of things had only gotten darker and more skeptical, and in particular, he had grown to think of the Bungle debates as one of the great shams of Lambda history. "Street theatre with a sacrificial clown," Horton now called it—a brazen, manipulative power play into which he, like the rest of the public, had unwittingly been enlisted by the treacherous exu.

As for the Power Elite, HortonWho seemed less and less inclined to believe their withdrawal to aCleanWellLightedMOO was anything but a tactical retreat—a way of continuing to wield their influence over Lambda's social affairs from a safe and unobtrusive distance. And though he wasn't the only MOOer who subscribed to some version of this theory ("Ruling from Orbit" was commonly said to be CWL's unofficial motto), he did seem more intent than most on doing something about it. He took to hanging out from time to time on CWL—mostly, he said, because there were a few people there he actually liked to talk to, but also, clearly, for the purposes of keeping an eye out for evidence of wizardly conspiracies to hoodwink the LambdaMOO public. These he sought to ferret out in various ways, including most notably the technique of planting himself in the middle of the CWL living room and hurling accusations with his proven passion and rigor, on the off chance that one or another of his rhetorical projectiles might actually dislodge a clue.

Needless to say, Horton's investigative methods did not, in the long run, much amuse the established residents of aCleanWellLightedMOO. And since their own amusement was more or less the whole point of the place, they put him on notice that any further obstreperousness on his part would result in his immediate eviction. Horton being Horton, however, this warning only led to a new round of living room denunciations, and in due time the local autocracy made good on its promise—first they newted him for a while, then they denewted him to see if the experience had taught him to stop his "baiting and provoking," then at last, having judged without further ado that he could not be taught, they toaded him. Horton, outraged, made one final attempt to regain his place in CWL: he logged on to LambdaMOO, located an ingenious MOO-to-MOO communications link maintained there by the CWL crowd, and through it transmitted a heartfelt appeal for clemency to his CleanWellLighted toaders. To which they responded by cutting off his access to the link.

And thus, dear reader, we arrive at the end of the historical background to *D:HortonWho.vs.aCleanWellLightedMOO* and the beginning of the dispute itself. For it was at this point that HortonWho decided that his treatment at the hands of the CWLers had gone beyond mere personal affront. It was a casus belli now, as far as he was concerned, and he wasted no time setting the machinery of a full-scale inter-MOO confrontation in motion. With a blind eye turned to the dullish fact that CWL's governing social metaphor wasn't so much that of the modern national polity as it was that of the senior prom (with best behavior expected from all and all rights to eject unwanted partiers reserved by the organizers), HortonWho immediately proceeded with his "international dispute," declaring CleanWellLighted "a repressive fascist state," offering his own "summary @toading without due process" as exhibit A, and insisting that Lambda-MOO, to preserve its integrity as a democratic society, must break off official relations with the offending power at once.

Nor did the apparent absence of any official relations to break off faze him a whit. He overcame that problem, in fact, in the same dazzling, three-point leap of logic that got him over the equally formidable hurdle of the mediation system's rules of engagement, which clearly forbade disputing any type of entity other than individual LambdaMOO players. This minor marvel of conceptual acrobatics on HortonWho's part began, if I understood it correctly, with the conjecture that in VR perhaps no relations were more official than the technological kind; it went on to the observation that the CleanWellLighted communications link was about as concrete a technological relation between Lambda and CWL as one could imagine; and it landed ultimately on the curious fact that the link, for some perverse technical reason, existed on Lambda as a player object—conveniently enough named aCleanWellLightedMOO, logged in continuously from the CWL machine at Boston's Northeastern University, and residing in a corner of the database evocatively entitled "Orbiting LambdaMOO."

Granted, HortonWho didn't make each one of these points explicit in his dispute, but then he didn't have to. All were elegantly implied in the bold, concise, and really only slightly crackpot proposition he submitted finally for the mediator's consideration:

Toad the link.

He didn't seem to be even remotely joking about it either. "Evil flourishes when good people do nothing," he intoned at the end of his opening brief. "Cut the link. @toad. . . aCleanWellLightedMOO."

Unfortunately for HortonWho, however, and for my expectations of a historic spectacle in the making, the good people of LambdaMOO seemed perfectly willing, in this case at least, to do nothing. To be sure, of the dozen and a half onlookers who gathered around the dispute's mailing list, there were those who appreciated HortonWho's general political points, and there were even a few who were willing to get behind his quixotically inventive specifics. But the majority opinion seemed ultimately to be that this dispute was just a waste of everybody's time. Some, for instance, saw it as formally groundless: if the dispute's standing depended on the premise that the link was a toadable player, they reasoned, then why did it not founder on the fact that the link itself had done nothing more heinous than stop talking to HortonWho? Others saw the issue as a social one, and wondered why it was that HortonWho was trying to convince a lone mediator to sever the entire MOO's communications with CleanWellLighted. Why did he not place a matter of such wide-reaching public consequence before the public itself, in the form of a petition?

That these questions failed, shall we say, to appreciate the poetry of Horton-Who's dispute was obvious. That they were in some cases also just rhetorical weaponry wielded by CleanWellLighted partisans seemed likely as well. But they were good questions nonetheless, especially if you took mediation at all seriously as an institution, and as they mounted it grew increasingly clear that the mediator (one Dr. Fate, if you can believe it) was in warm sympathy with them. Whether or not HortonWho's request was in fact headed for dismissal, though, remains technically speaking a mystery—for it wasn't long before the dispute got bogged down in procedural complications and HortonWho, in a possibly face-saving show of exasperation, withdrew it. I don't know if he gave much thought just then to transforming his complaint into a petition, but in any case events would soon enough convince HortonWho that CWL was a minor evil compared to Lambda itself. His brief career as an inter-MOO human rights activist was over, and the great cross-cultural showdown I had thought I saw gathering like thunderclouds over his dispute dispersed with scarcely a rumble. ✳

WIZARDS (MOOS) / POWER STRUCTURES / ANARCHISTS / AGITATORS / NOISE: "MOVEMENT" + ULTIMATELY NOTHING — PLUS CA CHANGE

Yet as I sat down during a coffee break two months later to examine the contentious beginnings of HortonWho's new career as a sometime geist and full-time newt, it was starting to dawn on me that the one broadly meaningful query posed by his abortive toad-the-link campaign was still very much in the MOO air. Half-baked or not, the proposal *had* sought, among other things, to test the depth of LambdaMOO's commitment to its new social system. Was Lambdamocracy worth defending against less open forms of virtual government—the dispute had implicitly asked—or was it not? Of course, the possibility of a broadly meaningful response to that question had mostly been swallowed up by

"LAMBDA DEMOCRACY" vs. MORE "OPEN" GOVERNANCE

the dispute's provocative idiosyncrasies, but here and there an eyebrow-raising comment had gotten through. "Personally," wrote the gruff Alpacazoid somewhere amid the wranglings of the *D:HortonWho.vs.aCleanWellLightedMOO mailing list, "I think democracy is overrated, especially for resources like MUDs."

And maybe Alpacazoid had it right. But me, I didn't know for certain one way or the other, and in that regard I was hardly alone. All around me, in fact, in a scattered but persistent buzz, a vast deliberation on the merits of the new MOO regime was under way. In quiet one-on-one conversations and searing *social-issues flame wars, in the intimacy of real-time mediation sessions and in the living room glad-handing of Architecture Review Board election campaigns, LambdaMOO was trying on virtual democracy like a new and hastily purchased pair of gloves, always questioning at some level whether the choice had been mistaken or whether its subsequent discomforts were just the inevitable complaints of a breaking-in period. It was everywhere, this mood of anxious experiment, but nowhere could it be felt more palpably than in the debates surrounding the great MOO-wide decisions of the day—the ballot measures that resulted when petitions finally came to a vote.

I had by now a certain familiarity with these debates. The taste for MOO-political entertainment that HortonWho's anti-CWL jihad had aroused in me had spurred me on toward bigger and better spectacles, and for the most part they didn't come any bigger and better than the ballots and their boisterous mailing lists.

The legislative history of the ballot *B:Minimal_Population_Growth, for instance, was a fascinating piece of sociology comprising several dozen screenfuls of intergenerational resentments, vigorously aired. Alarmed at the explosive population boom sparked by a recent spate of MOO-related RL media coverage (including, regrettably, my own), older residents bewailed the declining quality of Lambda life and called for an immediate locking of the gates against the newbie hordes. Newer arrivals, in response, grumbled loudly at the implication that they somehow had less of a right to be there than the old folks. The parallels to real-world controversies over immigration policy were obvious and even mildly amusing, but I was pleased to see that the arguments never took on quite the level of hysteria often present in such debates. And I was relieved as well to see the sensible outcome, in which the problem I had in some degree helped cause was resolved through passage of a compromise measure, written by exu, that reduced the growth rate from an average of fifty new characters a day to a much more manageable five.

. SOCIOLOGY / IMMIGRATION (NEW US OLD RESIDENTS)
. POLITICS + SOCIAL STRUCTURE

B:AntiRape, on the other hand, was a somewhat less inspiring affair. Written by Laurel just a little over a year after Bungle's toading, the petition was an attempt to finally codify the MOO's consensus that virtual rape was "abhorrent and totally unacceptable in this society." Its passage should have been a cakewalk, really, and would have been, had Laurel not insisted on additionally attempting the impossible: her petition included a clause establishing a clear division between virtual "speech" and virtual "action," with full freedom for even the most violent instances of the former and mandatory toading for any instance of the latter that could reasonably be described as rape. It was a noble try at enlightened zero tolerance, but it was a tall order indeed to ask MOOers to envision a solid line between words and deeds in a universe made entirely of text.

"I just don't think people _make_ the distinction with any clarity here," Tom-Traceback wrote to the ballot's mailing list, and if the lack of clarity in the surrounding discussion was anything to go by, he was right. The epistemological complexities that the previous year's debate had navigated so nimbly now rose up to swamp this one. Some MOOers, this time around, professed themselves appalled at the very concept of "virtual rape," declaring it a contradiction in terms and a painful trivialization of the experiences of RL rape victims. Others replied that this complaint was both wholly valid and, considering among other things the centrality of metaphor to the workings of MOOish VR, sort of beside the point. Libertarians and libertines, meanwhile, fearing for their virtual rights and their virtual hides respectively, were aghast at the draconian penalties proposed for behavior whose definition so depended on the vagaries of language and interpretation.

And there were other, less philosophical lines of argument as well. Mud was slung, personal morals were impugned. Supporters and opponents of the ballot wrestled hither and yon across a broad rhetorical battlefield whose cratered landmarks included charges of sexism (from both camps), tortured examinations of the meaning of sexual consent (with the requisite cross-references to RL date-rape controversies), occasional pointed reminders about the genuine suffering of MOO-rape's victim's (with the obligatory pointed rejoinders about the genuine suffering of the wrongfully toaded), and eventually, allegations of kinship between opponents' arguments and the policies of the Third Reich (with the leaden predictability of a flame war close to burning itself out).

At which approximate point exu—who had all along been putting up some of the ballot's more nuanced defenses—posted to *B:AntiRape* proclaiming the discussion now "contentious nigh unto the point of incoherence" and proposing, for the sake of entertainment if nothing else, that future contributions to the mailing list be made "in limerick form if you oppose the ballot, and in haiku if you support it." Almost all the leading participants in the debate took up the challenge (prize-winning entry: stingaree's "cherry blossoms fall/the goldfish darts in the pond/ VOTE YES OR DIE SOON"), and the debate collapsed into slap-happy silliness. Ultimately, a relative newcomer by the name of Evandra wrote up a less ambitious alternative petition asking simply that a notice be posted, for all inhabitants to see, warning that "sexual harassment (particularly involving unsolicited acts which simulate rape against unwilling participants)" could result in permanent expulsion. Evandra's proposal swiftly passed, Laurel's went down to narrow defeat, and the MOO breathed a collective sigh of relief, happy to leave the discussion behind it. It had been a messy, divisive business, after all, and I was happy to get to the end of it myself.

All the same, my reading of it left me tentatively hopeful. For all its confusion and ugliness, the *B:AntiRape debate had produced a far ampler discussion of the issues surrounding virtual violence than the Bungle Affair had. And in the end, through Evandra's timely intervention, the process had allowed Lambda-MOO at last to take the forceful, unified stand that Mr. Bungle had so long before dared it to. In this case at least, and in its own shambling, imperfect way, Lambdamocracy appeared to have worked.

"TESTING" THE
SOCIAL ORDER / DEMOCRACY

Of all the ballot decisions I had studied by the time I took up studying the case of HortonWho, however, the one that seemed the greatest test of the new social order was a proposal that still loomed undecided. It had risen to ballot status just eleven days before, which meant that three more days remained before the end of its two-week polling period arrived. Three days: and then the votes would at last be tallied, the results would be made public, and the question posed by the ballot—a question that was currently burning up the pages of *social and inspiring endless shouting matches in the living room—would in principle be resolved.

On the face of it, the question was a relatively straightforward one. The name of the ballot was *B:DisbandMediation, and you didn't need to know much more than that to get the gist of its intentions: informed by the possibly extreme but not exactly uncommon belief that LambdaMOO's existing mediation system had proved itself to be an irreparable morass of toxic inconsistency and well-intentioned incompetence, the ballot's initial clause proposed simply to scrap it.

But there the straightforwardness ended, for as the text proceeded, it became clear that this legislation aimed ultimately to banish not just the *present form* but the *very idea* of mediation from the MOO, and the route by which it would arrive at that end was a loopy one indeed. To start with, the ballot would henceforth invalidate nearly all petitions intended to promote or regulate "mannerly behavior," excepting only those that enforced such behavior at the level of MOO physics—i.e., of binary code. Examples of such proposals might include a mechanism that would curb the social no-no known as "spamming" (the abrupt filling of other people's screens with excessive amounts of text) by automatically limiting the length of people's utterances, or they might include an optional subroutine designed to search for and delete all textual obscenities before they reached the virtual ears of those who preferred not to hear them. The most basic and necessary of such gadgets would, upon passage of the ballot, be determined by an elected committee of fifteen MOO-citizens, who would thereupon submit a list of them to the voting public and then pass the winning selections on to the wizards for immediate implementation. Additionally, the committee of fifteen would solicit input toward a revised help file on "manners," which would become the community's last word regarding what was and wasn't kosher behavior—and would also thenceforth serve as a kind of pledge of allegiance to the local value system, to be signed by all MOO characters, present and future, under pain of automatic newting.

Once all of these tasks were completed, the committee would dissolve itself, and from that day forward MOO society, presumably, would run itself like the well-oiled machine into which it had been transformed, its members by and large unable to offend one another even if they wanted to, and far less likely in any case to want to, having all been forced at newt-point to agree to be nice.

It was hard to determine just what sort of fantasy was being floated here. Critics from the ranks of the MOO's libertarians, techno- and otherwise, saw it as the ultimate in hive-minded totalitarianism, a horror show of Orwellian control mechanisms and McCarthyite loyalty oaths. Those more concerned with nurturing a coherent and healthy MOO community, on the other hand, saw precisely the opposite problem: to them, the proposal was technolibertarianism's reductio ad absurdum—a final transfer of power from the community as a whole to the technology that was meant to serve it, and a naive denial of "the necessarily social and collective nature of human life" (as the eloquently fired-up communitarian Mzilikasi put it, adding for good measure, "I'm real gone the moment this passes").

That the text of the ballot answered with perfect alacrity to either of these opposing interpretations hardly helped clarify matters. Indeed, so finely balanced was the ballot's political ambiguity that it seemed almost purposefully designed to sow maximum dissension and bewilderment among the voting public—as if it had been crafted by a mind intimately familiar with the deepest nightmares haunting the MOO's political unconscious and possessed of a perverse genius for driving thoughtful, socially aware MOO citizens to hair-rending distraction.

TROUS.

Which, actually, it had been. The author of the ballot was a player named Minnie, and Minnie had indeed been driving fellow MOOers batty for some time now. She was on a relentless one-woman campaign to reform MOO politics from the ground up, and while this on its own would hardly have ruffled many feathers in a MOO now more or less governed by the aspirations of self-appointed reformers, its power to confound and annoy was greatly magnified by the manner in which she made her case. "Useful stuff incredibly encrusted in verbiage and weirdness" was how a MOO-acquaintance once defined for me the vexing style of discourse known to some as the "Art of Minnie," and for a firsthand glimpse of it I had only to examine her defense of *B:Disband. Long, semicoherent screeds spilling from one mail-message to another, cogent points drowning in rivers of psychobabble, dulcet-toned conciliatory gestures alternating with recklessly provocative condescension and sarcasm—all of these combined to earn Minnie much more than the average ballot-author's share of ad hominem attacks, and threatened at times to turn the entire discussion into a referendum on her maddeningly contradictory personality.

Where on earth had Minnie come from? It was a question often pondered. She seemed to have burst onto the political scene out of nowhere, suddenly bombarding it with screen after screen of her jumbled rhetoric, all in the service of an agenda sometimes only barely recognizable as of-this-MOO. And yet the truth was, Minnie was as much a creation of Lambda's political system as she was a pain in its butt, for it had taken months of grinding struggle with the machinery of MOOish governance to hone her peculiar compulsion to take a hammer to it.

Which isn't to say she hadn't arrived on the MOO already inclined to a critical view of its organization. She frequently made the claim, for instance, that her real-life background as a professional mediator in the Colorado court system, along with additional accreditation in the mental health field, was what compelled and authorized her to straighten out the MOO's "dysfunctional" social structure. But in fact, when she had first turned up, nothing about Minnie's behavior suggested any interest in the deeper workings of the place. She had seemed content to occupy herself with pleasant conversation in the public places of the MOO, and with the occasional construction of new ones for the pleasure of her fellow chatters. Some of those places were quite congenial, actually, like the popular "Hotter Tub" she'd built next to the original hot tub, adorning it with a lovely backdrop of distant hills and stars rendered in the typographic pictural style known as ASCII art, for which she had something of a flair. She might, for all we know, have happily gone on producing such creations for the rest of her virtual life, except that one day she found she'd used up her allotted building quota—and if she wanted more, she learned, she would have to go before the Architecture Review Board and ask for it. And that was the day Minnie's MOO-political awakening began.

The ARB rejected her request. Its ruling, she believed, was rooted partly in the board's longstanding prejudice against ASCII art, and that in itself was galling enough. But the closer she examined the decision, the more convinced she grew that it was fraught with procedural irregularities as well, particularly on the part of a certain ARB member named BriarWood. When she filed a dispute against BriarWood and lost, she began to suspect that forces larger than just the ARB were arrayed against her. And in a sense she was right: BriarWood, she discovered, was a rather well-connected MOOer, an adept young programmer with enough friends among the Power Elite to qualify as a junior member of the PE himself. But where most MOOers tended to think of the PE (if they thought of it at all) as a kind of social clique, no more or less noxious than the alpha cliques who lord it over secondary-school existence everywhere, Minnie quickly came to the minority view that they were something worse: a conspiracy to quietly subvert the rights and circumvent the will of the people of LambdaMOO whenever it pleased them to do so.

Paranoia, let me now point out in Minnie's defense, was in VR a somewhat more reasonable filter for apprehending reality than it was in real life. You have already seen, for instance, how the MOO's various social tools made possible a degree of surreptitious communication and observation unusual in most RL communities, except maybe the government-intelligence kind. Consider too that there was very little about the MOO that could not in principle be fiddled with on the sly by other MOOers, especially by those who had initiated themselves into the mysteries of the database's complex programming language, and most especially by those whom Haakon (but not necessarily anybody else) trusted enough to endow with the arcane powers of a wizard. Add to all this the recent, explosive proliferation of legal and political documents—which, at the same time as it exposed to light much of the hitherto-unseen conduct of social affairs, also introduced endless opportunities for disinformation—and you can understand, perhaps, that it was a simple matter of precaution to assume that in the MOO, at nearly every level of its workings, a good deal more was going on than met the eye.

MOOs as fostering paranoia

↓

conspiracy theorists

In Minnie's case, however, this simple precaution grew to be a sort of passion. She became the leading conspiracy theorist on the MOO, outdoing in fervor (if not in shrewdness) even HortonWho, whom she considered so soft on the Power Elite as to more or less be one of them. In pursuit of her suspicions, she filed disputes against one PE figure after another, mostly for obscure abuses of the public trust, and never with much success. Inevitably some of her targets turned the tables, disputing her for abuse of *them*, and one or two of those disputes did not go favorably for her. She began to suspect that the dispute system was rigged, designed specifically for ease of manipulation by the wizards and their pals, and she increasingly turned her efforts toward unrigging it. The mediation system permitted minor amendments to its rules if they were signed by at least thirty qualified players, so Minnie took to introducing amendments on a regular basis. Some of her proposals failed; those that passed were often overturned; and it was periodically alleged that she herself was trying to rig the system with her endless attempts at tinkering. It was all at last too much: the time had come, she realized, to tear mediation down and start again from scratch. The time had come to set before the people of the MOO the plan that would be known as *B:Disband.

By then, of course, Minnie's transformation into a political animal was complete. She could still be found getting silly in the living room on occasion, but otherwise her time was almost wholly taken up now with the business of composing mini-essays for the mailing lists, fending off legal attacks of one sort or another, going on occasional spying missions into aCleanWellLightedMOO to eavesdrop for evidence of PE malfeasance and collusion, and doing whatever else it took to advance her various causes. A broader public began to take notice of her, if only to observe that her mailing-list messages (or "posts," as such messages were commonly called) were getting to be intolerably long and repetitive. Minnie accommodated by introducing posts consisting only of a brief index referring readers to some other post she'd made weeks earlier, or on another list, but the resulting network of posts and pointers to posts hardly seemed to diminish her public presence. Instead the web of her messages spread like kudzu across the surface of the lists, consuming and at last becoming her identity as it grew. How thoroughly this mass of texts came finally to envelop her public persona may be gauged by a simple and somewhat melancholy fact, and that is that I cannot tell you to this day what Minnie's character was: whether she had created her MOO-self in the image of a goddess or of a unicorn or of a cartoon character or a loaf of bread I do not know, because by the time I got the chance to take a look at her description, she had replaced it with a long, rambling political advertisement, which she rewrote from time to time according to the daily urgencies of her campaign.

I felt a little sorry for her, myself, and I know I wasn't the only MOOer who did. What I did not feel, however, and in this I'm sure I also had plenty of company, was totally convinced she was anything but a crank. And consequently I was mystified, at first, to behold the vehemence and gravity with which Minnie's confused proposal to replace mediation with fully automated justice was being discussed. Why, I wondered, was this garbled scheme being taken seriously at all?

But I stopped wondering after I'd read my way through a few dozen messages on *B:Disband. For as the arguments wore on, it grew harder and harder not to recognize that the real confusions stirring the debate were hardly Minnie's—and that the ballot's core contradictions were in fact nothing more or less than an extension of those built into the mediation system itself.

Indeed, if you went back to the text of the ballot that had initiated the system, what you found was a document strikingly similar to Minnie's in its political ambidexterity. What you also found was a document by now historic: Crotchet the wizard's *B:Arbitration, the first ballot ever presented to the LambdaMOO voting public, and perhaps for that very reason a ballot crafted in such a way as to allow either of the two broadly opposing tendencies of the fragile new democracy to find something they could like about it. For those still wary of even the barest trappings of a virtual state, Crotchet's proposed system could be understood as just a loosely organized cooperative for the provision of neutral third parties— ostensibly modeled on the binding but noncoercive structure of RL arbitration (the name-change to "mediation" came later, further softening the degree of discipline implied), staffed by an all-volunteer pool of mediators, and guided in its rulings neither by legal code or precedent but by each mediator's own "understanding of manners and common sense." Yet Crotchet's proposal was equally generous to those who were eager, in the still-choppy wake of the Bungle episode, for a dependable means of enforcing minimal community values: mediators would be given broad powers to punish wrongdoers (subject to a kind of peer review whereby any five eligible citizens might vote to overturn the decision), disputes could proceed whether or not the disputed party chose to participate, and judgments could even be rendered in absentia if the "guilty" player failed to log on during the dispute process.

That there were basic incompatibilities between the two ideals on which the projected system was founded seems not to have given many people much pause at the time it was voted on: Crotchet's ballot passed by a solid three-to-one margin. But in time the cracks began to show, as inevitably they would. Those who thought they'd voted in a process for helping disputants quietly work out their differences couldn't help noticing—as the actual process got under way—that not all disputants were going willingly into the mediator's chambers. Those who thought they'd voted for community empowerment, meanwhile, started to realize just how little they could count on the collective power of a system that left each of its decisions almost entirely in the hands of whichever individual felt like tackling it. Grumbling set in, then various attempts at reform, some of them small scale (through the amendment process), some of them larger (*B:AntiRape, for instance), but all of them really just postponements of the day when the system as a whole would finally have to face the judgment of experience.

And if it was fate's idea of a joke that the occasion for that judgment should at last have arrived in the form of Minnie's verbiage-and-weirdness-encrusted plan to turn the MOO into one big digital engine of social harmony, no one seemed to be laughing. By now the urgency of the matter was such that even the most absurdly concocted scheme for replacing mediation would probably have been seized on as an opportunity for taking the final measure of Crotchet's embattled brainchild. As it was, the modest absurdities of *B:DisbandMediation were hardly enough to deflect attention from the burning issue nestled among them and summarized in the ballot's title. Scores of reasonable critics had been hammering away from every direction at the not-so-brilliantly-conceived particulars of Minnie's proposal since the moment she released it. But by the time the debate started coming to a boil, there were just as many voices being raised in support of the ballot's most basic aim, and these too came from both ends and every corner of the MOO's ideological map.

There were the lingering parliamentarians, convinced more than ever that the MOO needed a duly structured and elected officialdom to manage its day-to-day conflicts (BriarWood, for instance, seemed to have been working for months on the designs for a full-fledged judicial system, complete with courts of appeals and a constitution). There was the odd unregenerate wizardist, for whom the mediation system was but a messy travesty of the swift justice of yore. And there were of course the legions of the libertarian-leaning, raring to shake off an institution they now regarded as dead weight at best ("a couple dozen megs of shit" added to the LambdaMOO hard drive, wrote one) and a crude foretaste of the dread rule of bureaucracy at worst.

It fell mainly to Minnie, however, in one of her more lucid passages, to locate the simple sense of a hope disappointed that united all these otherwise conflicting critiques. "Whatever way one chooses to view Mediation," she wrote on

[handwritten note in top margin: PROBLEMS/ COLLAPSE OF MEDIATION SYSTEM]

B:Disband, "as a court system to enforce 'laws' or as a 'neutral friend' who will listen to two others and help them kiss and make up, it hasn't been successful, and has created more problems than it's helped."

Opponents of the ballot scrambled to point out that in reality dozens of disputes had been resolved by then to the substantial satisfaction of at least one of the parties, and often of both. But merely by recognizing the need to defend mediation they were ceding the high ground in the debate. For even the staunchest believers in the system's effectiveness had to grant, over and over, that its inconsistencies were more than just minor annoyances. Give it time, they pleaded nonetheless, let the forces in contention around the system balance themselves out, and mediation would no doubt mature into the reliable instrument of peace and justice we had every right to expect it to be.

It would have been much more fun, of course, to keep picking at the far greater inconsistencies of the system Minnie intended to replace mediation with, but if the *B:Disband* debate had ever really had much to do with the actual text of the ballot, that moment seemed now to have long since passed. In three days the polling period would end, the votes would be counted, and the results would be posted, but what that final figure would mean could no longer be stated with any precision. In three days I might try and guess whether LambdaMOO had had its say on Minnie's visions of reform, on Minnie herself, on the workability of the mediation system, or on the possibility of ever resolving the tension between the needs of the community and the needs of the individual in this or any other society—but a guess would surely be the best I could manage.

In the meantime, on a desktop far away from LambdaMOO, sat the text of *D:Cro.vs.HortonWho*, waiting to be plumbed. And that was more than enough to puzzle over.

"Just make it quick, OK?" was HortonWho's first message to the *D:Cro* list after the sticky preliminaries of selecting a mediator had been completed.

Horton had reasons of his own for urging haste (word of Laurel's letter to his systems administrator had just reached him, and he suspected it wouldn't be long before his connection got shut down), but his sentiment was doubtless widely shared. Certainly Cro, the character who had called the dispute on behalf of six acquaintances and presumably spoke for them as well, was eager to see the matter "confronted directly, without histrionics," and with as little distracting input from the gallery as possible. Likewise the mediator—ace haiku-slinger and longtime MOOer stingaree, as it happened—made plain his willingness to expedite the proceedings, which after all were at this point intended merely to give the injured parties a forum in which to air their grievances with the disputee. As for myself, I too couldn't help hoping, though the thickness of the document I held in my hands told me not to dare, that the process I was about to watch unfold would prove a swift and relatively simple one.

And in a way, I suppose, we got our wish. For HortonWho's next message to the list was also his last: it was his MOOicide note. And the message posted after that, barely five hours later, came from stingaree, presenting his abrupt decision, after all the earlier talk of nonpunitive dialogue, to slap a six-month newting on top of HortonWho's sudden self-exile. The dispute was as good as over, in other words, and now it appeared there wasn't much left to do but try and figure out how it had ended this way.

The bulk of the clues, naturally, were to be found in HortonWho's prodigious farewell message—two hundred lines of bitter indictment and rueful valediction that began with a brief and acid explanation of why he was leaving:

"I have been asked to choose between completing a long-term collaborative project, and continuing to play LambdaMOO. The choice was put to me by my collaborators, but in reality, was forced upon us by the actions of Laurel _.___, because her confusion between RL and VR is so complete that it extends into RL, and probably did so before VR was even a technical possibility."

The message revealed more than just the immediate reasons for HortonWho's precipitous exit, of course. Those curious blank lines following Laurel's name, for instance, were not HortonWho's doing but a judicious bit of post-facto censorhip imposed by stingaree after Horton had committed one of the more blasphemous speech acts it was possible to author within the MOO: the forced exposure of a fellow player's full real name. Evidently HortonWho meant to invade Laurel's real life as disruptively as she had invaded his, and if the attempt at letting all the MOO in on her RL identity was easily enough contained, his message went on to list other measures that might not be. "After close reading of our interactions," he warned, "Commonwealth police in this country are to investigate several possibly felonious actions by Miss ___. Feds in yours will likely be contacted. It will become public." The possibility of an Australian libel suit was also raised, along with the observation that "the last recorded settlement of a less damaging case alike in most other details was in excess of $40,000."

And there was more. The Xerox Corporation itself, we were told, might be named as an accessory in the imminent legal warfare, with the likely consequence being that the full weight of the RL state apparatus would soon come crashing down on "the cosy little world you +think+ you inhabit." That cozy little world was in any case not a very safe place to spend time these days, since "the closer it's drawn to RL, by the press, $$$, addiction, social acceptance; the more unreal, irreal, destructive of the real it becomes." By which presumably he meant that more and more the place would be attracting the likes of Laurel, a victim, he believed, of a full rack of "delusions and hysteria" whose psychological composition he proceeded to delineate in venomously clinical detail. It was at our own peril, he added, that the rest of us continued to MOO at all, and as of this posting he would have nothing more to do with any of us except outside the boundaries of this place. "Those of you who have been spoken with know where to find me (and yourselves)," he wrote, in a closing aside to the MOOers he still considered friends. "You start by typing @quit."

I had to smile when I read that final line, knowing as I did just how long Horton had subsequently managed to stay away. But the rest was not so amusing. The document's more personal aggressions, particularly, made me wince; and they had clearly done as much or more to stingaree, judging by his swift and hard-edged response.

"I had been hoping to delay my decision in this matter until I had collected further evidence," the mediator's lengthy explanation began. "However, Horton-Who has forced my hand with his . . . open and vicious attack on the character Laurel, and more importantly [on] the person who controls that player." With the forum for any conceivable rapprochement transformed into an arena for just the sort of vitriolic threat-mongering with which HortonWho stood vaguely charged—and with the possibility of further dialogue in any case now gone the way of the accused himself—Horton's newting seemed to stingaree an obvious resolution. While essentially just confirming the disputee's decision to withdraw from the life of LambdaMOO, it also strongly reiterated the MOO's disapproval of harassing behavior, and with any luck might give everybody involved enough time to cool off and regain some perspective on the whole episode.

There was one not-so-small problem with the mediator's otherwise Solomonic decision, however: on its own, HortonWho's final outburst was simply not enough to verify the charges of severe and persistent harassment brought against him, and so far nobody had been shown any other evidence of newtable delinquency. Not that any had really been required till now. In the sort of purely negotiatory dispute this one had started out as—and especially in one involving such deeply personal animosities—it was perfectly reasonable to keep the details hidden from the public's prying eye. But given the sharply judicial turn the case had since taken, and given too the mandatory period of public review it would now have to undergo, it seemed unlikely that the mediator's ruling would stand unless some substantial and compelling testimony was produced, in particular from the heretofore silent victims whose cause Cro had taken up.

Which raised a related question: just who was this Cro anyway, that he should be allowed to broach a dispute in which he made no claim of direct damage at the hands of the disputed? A cynical answer suggested itself. For as most of the MOO well knew, Cro was in fact Crotchet—or more precisely, "Cro" was one of several aliases registered to the owner of Crotchet. And Crotchet was of course not merely one of the MOO's oldest and most active wizards but the founder of the very system governing this dispute. And if so formidable a member of Lambda society were (let us say) to file a dispute of dubious substance, what were the chances that the weakness of his case would be overlooked, or that he would be spared the punishments mediators sometimes meted out to those who called spurious disputes? Better than most other MOOers' chances, certainly, and possibly good enough that his friends might be tempted to take advantage of them, prevailing on him to make their weighty accusations by proxy and thus shielding themselves from the risks and responsibilities they would run in launching the dispute on their own.

The possibility of just such a conspiracy, as it happened, was the first aspersion cast as *D:Cro*'s public airing-out got under way. Avid mediation-watcher Nikto lobbed it in a roundly skeptical message posted just after stingaree's decision— "In a word," he summarized, "this stinks"—and was immediately obliged to duck, as first stingaree and then Margaret (a CleanWellLighted regular and the first of Horton's alleged victims to pipe up) tossed back spirited defenses of Cro's role in the dispute. Both noted that Cro had called the dispute entirely on his own initiative, as a concerned citizen and friend, and whether or not he'd meant thereby to run cover for HortonWho's accusers, added Margaret, all six of them had subsequently stepped forth from Cro's shadow by officially joining the dispute as "interested parties." Nikto's response was diplomatic but unyielding. He considered the arguments, had a chat with Cro, and forthwith tendered an apology for suggesting that the disputants had engaged in any actively fishy collusion. He conceded, too, that his own familiarity with the goings-on of the previous several months made him "as sure as anyone can be about things MOOish" that the dispute was not spurious. But he stood by his belief that Cro's involvement set a worrisome precedent, and as the gathering momentum of the discussion made clear, he hardly stood alone.

Minnie in particular (drawn like a fly to honey by the dispute's aroma of procedural irregularity, and plainly eager to butt heads with the founder of the system she hoped one day to demolish) heaped criticism on Cro. Yet as other self-appointed peer reviewers chimed in with their concerns, it was becoming plain that Cro's role remained troublesome mainly because of the continuing inaccessibility of the evidence. If the details of HortonWho's actions were open for all to see, then the matter of Cro's standing would no doubt be reduced to a largely technical worry—but *where were the details?* Over and over, the question was asked by the accumulating onlookers. And over and over the questioners in turn were asked—by other spectators, by stingaree, by the interested parties themselves—to trust the mediator when he told them that the details he'd seen sufficed to warrant Horton's penalty.

Which isn't to say no explanations were given for the veil of privacy, or that the explanations weren't well worth considering. There was the claim, for instance, that much of the relevant data consisted of deeply intimate RL information HortonWho had gleaned and maliciously threatened to go public with. And more convincingly perhaps, there was the argument that any general scrutiny of what had by all available reports become an ugly and debasing state of affairs would only serve to extend the degradation. As exu put it: "I don't feel like having every nineteen-year-old on the MOO with an opinion deciding if I was harassed enough, whether I deserved it, or what constitutes harassment anyway."

Yet even exu couldn't long deny that in that unpleasant-sounding scenario lay something distantly akin to the essence of judicial procedure in an open society, and eventually she too found herself wondering aloud whether the veil hadn't been drawn too tight in this case, and whether some sane middle ground between "secret process and public spectacle" couldn't be reached in time to salvage the mediator's decision.

As the final phase of the review period began, however, no such compromise was in sight. At 8:05 Palo Alto time on the evening of the sixth day after Horton-Who's explosive departure, stingaree started the clock running on the twenty-four hours his decision would be open to official votes of no-confidence, and by 4 o'clock on the following afternoon the count was a slim two votes away from the five that were necessary to overturn. Though Minnie, first in line to cast her nay, had discovered, courtesy of the mediation software's automatic conflict-of-interest detector, that her litigious history disqualified her from voting on this particular dispute ("Another reason this process has become absurd . . ." she sputtered), and though the stalwart Nikto had yet to log in since the polling period started, the spirit of their dissent seemed to animate the accelerating movement toward dismissal. The three players who *had* managed to register their rejections offered a variety of reasons for doing so, but underlying them all was the same broad mood of unease that only a fuller airing of the evidence was likely to dispel. How unlikely was it, then, that at least two more players who shared that unease would connect within the next four hours and vote to overturn? Not very. The prospects for the survival of stingaree's ruling were looking bleaker than ever.

In a sense, therefore, what happened next wasn't actually much of a surprise. For given the urgency of the situation and the persistence of the doubts surrounding the dispute, what choice did its embattled protagonists really have? They broke their silence. First Margaret, at ten to 5; then twenty minutes later, exu and emmeline. Each posted a detailed message to the mailing list enumerating her complaints about HortonWho. Each described weeks or months of sustained and unrequited hostilities, variously including relentless taunts, poisonous MOO-mail, constant public defamations, malicious invasions of privacy, and repeated threats of worse to come, both in-MOO and beyond. Each listed measures she had taken to evade Horton's harassment (retreating from public rooms, blocking out his mail with the @*refuse* command, refusing other remote communications such as real-time pages), and each recounted ways he'd managed to circumvent those measures (sending mail from guest accounts, hacking his way into the women's private rooms, or simply ranting about them in public to the point that much of his venom reached their ears through third parties anyway).

The testimony had its weaknesses. Though VR interactions were easily and commonly captured to off-line files (or "logs," as MUDders termed them), and though existing logs of HortonWho's alleged verbal violence had been alluded to throughout the discussion, none were now produced. It being an undetectably simple matter to alter the digital stuff of which a log consisted, of course, the files might not have carried much evidentiary weight anyway, but their presence couldn't have hurt, and the claim that Horton's abuse was sometimes too artful to be recognized as such by anyone but its intended recipient didn't exactly explain away their absence. There were other problematic claims as well, some targeting behavior too typical of daily MOOish discourse to really be viewed with much alarm ("i've . . . been compared to hitler, in a rather subtle way," charged emmeline), some too infused with MOOish surreality to know quite what to make of without further explanation ("He made a puppet, named it after me and described it to look exactly like me, and used it to impersonate me in public," wrote exu).

By and large, however, and considered in sum, the statements given in the three messages painted a picture too vivid to be altogether disbelieved. Not all the pieces were there, perhaps, but you didn't have to squint too hard to see the pattern they fell into, or the cumulative toll they must have taken. The evidence that critics had been clamoring for was for all intents and purposes on record, and traffic on the mailing list, which had ramped up to a brisk ten messages an hour before the testimony was posted, dropped off to a nearly total silence in the three hours of voting time that remained. More significantly, no further votes to overturn were registered, and in fact two of the three already cast had been retracted by the time the last of the testimonial messages hit the list, so that when the 8:05 closing time at last arrived just one quiet no-vote still clung to stingaree's decision. The tally implied a somewhat more solid consensus than actually existed, as it turned out, and in days to come invective pro and con would once again be splattered across the mailing list as participants maneuvered for the coveted last word. But from this moment on no message could ever really be more final than the automatically generated one that presently appeared, confirming stingaree's decision as official. The newting of HortonWho had reached its formal conclusion, and there wasn't much that could undo it now except the steady passage of half a year's time.

I kept on reading, of course—the onward, dialectic flow of the debate pulled me along no less insistently than it pulled the debaters—but by this point in my perusal of *D:Cro.vs.HortonWho I had reached a conclusion or two myself. The question that had brought me this far now had an answer of sorts, and the answer, as best I could make it out, was yes: this dispute did *not* bode pleasant things for LambdaMOO's efforts to define itself as a community.

It wasn't that the conflict's leakage into the outside world had, as I'd feared, done any special damage to the MOO's implicit agreement to meet its own home-grown problems with its own home-grown solutions. On the contrary, the discussion in *D:Cro had retained throughout an almost unshakable focus on in-MOO matters, and even HortonWho's dramatic threats to plunge the MOO into the middle of an international RL legal scandal had failed to come true, as of a month and a half after he'd made them (as indeed they never would). Nor was it the dispute's undeniable lapses of due process that struck me as so ominous—though these were several, and in a few cases deeply unsettling. The inability of Horton to respond to his accusers' testimony, for instance—and especially considering the fact that it was those same accusers, or one of them anyway, who had arranged that inability for him—was a particularly glaring flaw in the proceedings.

But in the end, what most disturbed me about the case, what seemed so insistently foreboding, was the same thing that had always disturbed me about it, starting from the moment I'd first learned of it. For as I came to the end of my examination of the dispute, I found I could no longer close my eyes to the painfully personal connections that loomed at its core, and that I had once hoped

[handwritten margin notes: " CIRCLING: LA/MOO's DEFINING SELF AS COMMUNITY (a PROBLEMS)", "RL vs MEETING LM PROBLEMS w/ LM SOLUTIONS"]*

to keep my distance from. Not that they'd been paraded before the mailing list's readership, exactly: even in the detailed final messages of Margaret, exu, and emmeline, there'd been only a small number of clues as to the possible reasons for HortonWho's months of hostility. Yet to my mind, at least, those few hints told a long, unhappy story.

HORTONWHO/
EXU/LAUREL
RL/WORK/
ETC. →
LOVE AFFAIR
@ HEART OF
IT

The story's unhappiness might have struck me less forcefully, I imagine, if its narrative hadn't seemed to revolve around the two people who mattered to me most in all of this. But ineluctably, it did, and so I couldn't help but pick up on the signs and the suggestive circumstances: the particular intensity of the harassment described by exu; the fact that it had begun at a time when all the other women attached to the dispute (Laurel included) still knew HortonWho as a friend and not a fury; the fact that it had begun, in fact, in January of that year, a time coinciding roughly (as I and anybody close to exu knew) with the end of her ten-month-long involvement with HortonWho. These signs and others traced the sketchy version of events it saddened me now to contemplate: the flame of obsessive rage sparked in the embers of a dying love affair; its hungry, indiscriminate spread from one relationship to another, the fueling betrayals it must have sought from whatever representatives of womankind were nearest to hand; betrayals sometimes real perhaps, sometimes imagined, but always no doubt magnified in HortonWho's mind by a lingering hurt that possibly only now, with distance forced on him, might have a chance to subside.

"I once thought that the one thing about MOO that was real was its interactions . . . ," HortonWho had mused in one of the calmer moments of his MOO-icide note. "I have considered that to be quite false for some time now, at least since January 1994."

I hadn't caught the significance of the date the first time around, but on rereading the message now I could hardly miss it. Nor could I ignore any longer the disturbing sense of déjà vu Horton's words provoked, their curiously contrapuntal echo of the ones Mr. Bungle had spoken on the night of his toading, when asked to explain how he could have done what he'd done. "It was purely a sequence of events with no consequence on my RL existence"—wasn't that what Bungle had said? And on its surface at least, wasn't HortonWho's disavowal of the reality of human interactions in VR very nearly a paraphrase? Very nearly, yes. But beneath that surface, of course, the story was a different and ultimately a more troubling one. For HortonWho was no Mr. Bungle, not by a long stretch, and to understand what little I did of his story was to know as much. It was to recognize that the challenge he posed to the community wasn't that of a player who failed to take seriously what was most serious about VR—i.e., the hearts and minds of other players—but that of one who had succeeded only too well in doing so, and had subsequently retreated from that bittersweet success in one great, thrashing howl of pain spread across five months, two MOOs, and the lives of at least six former friends.

And while I'd always felt optimistic about LambdaMOO's ability to rise to Mr. Bungle's sort of challenge, by now I wasn't at all certain how well equipped it was to handle the likes of HortonWho's. Responding to the depredations of someone who had never really made himself a part of the MOO's social fabric was a relatively simple thing, after all—you just cut him off at the interface and that, more or less, was that. But things got complicated fast when the violence in question was as intimately entwined with on-going virtual relationships as HortonWho's had been. The stakes got higher, the feelings got deeper, the civics got thornier— and under the weight of all this intensification the machinery of LambdaMOO justice groaned more precariously than ever.

Nor would it do simply to fortify the existing system. True, mediation might better weather the storms of cases like HortonWho's if lasting solutions were found for the sorts of glaringly unanswered formal questions that had battered *D:Cro. (the murky legality of third-party disputes, for instance, or of confidential testimony). But it was also true, I was coming to realize, that no matter how close the mediation system came to procedural perfection, it might never quite feel adequate to managing the complex webs of interrelationship that put the reality in virtual reality. Indeed, the more explicitly the rules of the system were spelled out, the more likely it was to resemble what MOOers repeatedly insisted their virtual lives were not: a game.

This might not have been much of a problem, naturally, in RL, where the disjunction between the bloodless formalities of the courtroom and the existentially *VR's* freighted conflicts they presumed to resolve was a matter of mostly academic con- *AMBIGUITY* cern. But transposed onto the MOO, I sensed, that disjunction resonated all too *vs.* *AUTHENTICITY* unsettlingly with VR's essential ambiguousness—with the flickering fictionality *of RELATIONSHIPS* that framed its every moment, making those constant assertions of its authenticity so naggingly necessary and those occasional Bungle-esque denials of the same so disruptively plausible. Trying single-handedly to navigate the perilous waters of human connection was nerve-wracking enough under such circumstances; relying on the guidance of what even its defenders sometimes called a "toy legal system" could only, it seemed to me, compound the anxiety. "Mediation Lambda-MOO style was never intended to be for handling issues this damned serious," Minnie had declared a few hours before the official close of *D:Cro, and a few weeks after it, conversing quietly with me inside my TV set, exu had uneasily suggested that mediation was ultimately "just not suited for all kinds of things, or even, I think, most kinds of things." I had to agree. And I had to wonder whether *any* virtual judicial system could ever evolve into a truly satisfying answer to the problem of virtual conflict.

Which isn't to say I thought much, by this point, of the leading alternatives—though I'll admit that I had at various times and to varying degrees felt the tug of their utopian appeal. It was hard not to, frankly, whether on the MOO or in any other online community I'd ever poked my head into. The very building materials of such places, it seemed—the strong yet infinitely malleable structure of their underlying binary code, the powerfully convincing presence of the words that fleshed them out—encouraged the belief that there wasn't a problem within their boundaries that couldn't be solved by either moderately inventive programming or a sufficiently voluminous exchange of dialogue. On Lambda, the various expressions of this belief were too numerous and diverse to detail, but with respect to the issue of virtual justice at least, all you needed was a quick look at the *B:Disband* mailing list to grasp the basic arguments and the depth of their popularity.

I'd surveyed that list myself, of course, and as I said, the seductions of these utopianisms weren't entirely lost on me. But if some of their gleam, as I saw it, had already rubbed off amid the complications of the Bungle Affair, the hard case of *D:Cro.vs.HortonWho* had by now taken the shine off altogether. For how could I believe in the all-healing power of negotiation after witnessing the spectacular breakdown of dialogue that had effectively sealed HortonWho's fate? And what faith in the omnipotence of the software fix could I hold on to after the impossibility of techno-filtering Horton's intensely personal brand of harassment had been made so plain? To be sure, both dialogue and programming still commanded my respect as strategies for dealing with virtual conflict. But as solutions? They were partial at best, like the budding "toy legal system" itself, and certainly no replacement for it.

Which left me at last, amid the many disturbing lessons I was obliged to take home from my reading of the case, with only one really meaningful response. I'm not sure just when it came to me, whether it had taken shape in my mind by the time I turned over the last page, dazed and somewhat drained, that day in the office or whether it fell into place sometime after that. But I do know that by the end of the following day I had made my response official:

I had voted no on *B:DisbandMediation.*

Only later would it occur to me that that was the first time I had ever voted on a LambdaMOO ballot. Later, too, it would occur to me to wish that I'd savored

STRATEGIES VS SOLUTIONS —

that vote as the moment I ceased being merely a spectator in the arena of Lambda
politics and finally took a small step into the circle of the participants.

[handwritten margin note: VOTING ON BALLOT = "PARTICIPATING" a NOT SPECTATING]

But as best I recall I did not bring much enthusiasm to the exercise. And ultimately there wasn't much reason to. I wasn't voting so much *for* the existing
mediation system as *against* the idea that there was anything significantly better
ready to replace it, and given the present state of things that was a fairly grim
proposition to be endorsing. Even conceding that mediation "LambdaMOO
style" would at its finest never be a wholly satisfactory enterprise, it would still be
a long time and a lot of work before the system would begin to deserve a break
from constant criticism. In the meantime, it seemed clear, the attacks would continue. Anarcho-utopian urges, only slightly diminished by the occasional defections of disillusioned souls like me, would continue to crash against the insistent
evolution of virtual law. Intricate and deeply intimate webworks of feeling would
continue to be caught up in the clumsy, experimental mechanisms of that evolution, coming apart with grindingly unpleasant effects. And all in all, the most
rending aspects of what I had seen unfold in *D:Cro* would continue to assert
themselves, in one form or another.

I was voting for all of this, and could not pretend that I wasn't. For I had been
warned, after all. "The sparks from this will glow for a long long time," the purple
guest had told me, and though I hadn't been sure what he had meant then, by
now I was afraid I had a much better idea.

NEW YORK CITY, JULY 1994

The Bedroom
You are in the basement level of an overpriced and
  undersized East Village duplex apartment. It's either
  cramped or cozy down here, depending on your mood.
  The ceiling is low and the walls are never farther
  than a couple arms' lengths away. Pine bookshelves
  cover one wall, three dresser drawers (two black-
  lacquered and one cherry-stained) line another. In
  the northwest corner there's a bed: a waist-high
  platform painted white, a futon mattress also white,
  white sheets, white comforter, two bloodred pillows.
A black metal staircase spirals up to the ceiling. A
  passage to the southeast opens into The_Author's
  Fabulous Office Nook.
Jessica (sleeping) and The_Author (sleeping) lie in the
  bed.
You see 19-Inch Television Set here.
A little patch of morning sunlight nudges in through a
  window next to the bed.

The_Author snores.

Jessica rolls over, half-awake, pulls her body close
  to The_Author's and whispers gently in his ear:
  "Stop it."

MY TINY LIFE

The_Author stops snoring.

Jessica smiles and presses her face against the warm
  skin of The_Author's neck and drifts back into sleep.

The_Author snores.

The_Author is dreaming. In his dream, he sits before
  his computer, watching words from exu slide across
  the screen. They are angry words; she is accusing him
  of betraying intimate information about her to some
  third party, HortonWho perhaps. exu changes shape,
  becomes Kali, goddess of destruction. "Now you will
  feel the wrath of Kali," she pages ominously. She
  types a command that causes the text on The_Author's
  screen to shudder, as if in an earthquake. He tries
  hard to think of something witty to say that might
  defuse the situation. He decides to wake up instead.

The_Author shuts his mouth in mid snore. Slowly opens
  one eye. Lets it fall shut again.

The_Author yawns.

The_Author says, "You know, I wish I were awake enough
  to leave this bed, because I must say I have never
  experienced so prodigious an urge to pee."

Jessica raises herself on an elbow and looks with
  groggy disbelief at The_Author.

Jessica says, "Please don't use words like that this
  early in the morning."

The_Author laughs. "Words like what?"

Jessica says, "Like 'prodigious.'"

Jessica rolls over, away from The_Author, back to
  sleep.

The_Author says, "Oh. Heh. Sorry."

The_Author says, "I think it was all that MOOing I did
last night."

The_Author isn't kidding either. These intense, late-
night VR conversations, he has noticed, have a funny
way of messing with the language circuits in his
brain. Something about the ambiguity of the medium,
he figures, about the way it hovers between speech
and writing. After a couple hours glued to monitor
and keyboard trading words as fast as finger muscles
will allow, he can sometimes start to feel a kind
of meltdown going on inside him, as if the part of
him that usually does the talking and the part of him
that usually does the writing are getting all mixed
up together. Sometimes the feeling lingers after he
has logged off, and he wakes up the next day with a
throatful of writerly cadences and two-dollar words
waiting to be coughed up like morning phlegm.

[handwritten margin notes: AMBIGUITY OF MEDIUM — B/N SPEECH & WRITING — ORALITY? LITERARY QUALITY —]

The_Author rolls over and presses himself close to
Jessica, feeling her warmth the length of his body.

The_Author tries to recollect the details of the
various conversations that kept him up till 2:30 last
night.

The_Author remembers something else instead: text
shaking violently on a computer screen, an angry
goddess, a friend betrayed . . .

The_Author . o O (Hey! My first MOO dream!)

VR

4

Samantha, Among Others

Or TINYGENDER, A Love Story

I should tell you now, I guess, about Samantha. Or tell you, anyway, as much as I know about her, which is either precious little or nearly everything, or maybe both, depending on how you look at it.

I know, for one thing, exactly what people saw when they glanced her way: *It's really her,* the brief description read, *twitching her nose just like she did on the show. You see a light dusting of white powder on her upper lip, which might explain the nose-twitching, and an anxious dream of power in her eyes.* I know, too, exactly what she did the first time she showed up on LambdaMOO. And exactly what she did on the last. And roughly what she did on every visit in between. I know that no one on the MOO knew her better than I did, or had ever been closer to me than she was. Not exu, not even Ecco.

But I may never know, I think, in any final way, the things it mattered most for me to know about Samantha. My intimate access to the facts of her online life was a trivial achievement, after all. I'd made her, named her, crafted her appearance, and animated her every step, her every utterance on the MOO. How could I not have known her in the ways I did? To put it plainly, she was me: a *morph,* in MOOspeak, or in a different language *alter ego.* An "other self." And if the self I'd lived with in RL for over thirty-one years remained in many respects a mystery to me, I can't pretend my brief acquaintance with this new one ever really let me grasp much more about her than the basics of her virtual biography. Precisely

[handwritten annotation in right margin:] "MORPH" / ALTER EGO —

who she was to me, and to the world she lived in—these are the things about Samantha that I struggle still to make some satisfying sense of, and suspect I never will.

I'd had other morphs, of course, and would have more. There was the dolphin—Faaa, I called him, after the tragic, finny hero of the 1973 movie thriller *Day of the Dolphin*—and the rest: a handful of text-bodies I'd written and erased on the fly, or kept around for the purposes of an occasional, joking transformation. But prior to Samantha my morph-making had not yet crossed the gender line, and from the instant I first stepped into her, I felt the difference about the same way you feel the sudden lightness when an elevator starts to drop.

The moment still lives fresh in my mind. I created her one winter evening not long after the toading of Dr. Jest: replaced my hefty description of Samantha's cousin Dr. Bombay (I'd written him as *a walking optical illusion*, oscillating randomly between the sitcom's plump, pseudoscholarly fop and the image of a lean old streetwise back-alley medic) with her four-line wisp of text (*It's really her . . .*), typed a brief command that rendered the sex change complete (*@gender female*), and saved the persona to a new file under Samantha's name. And then I headed out to show my creation to the world.

Or more precisely, I headed out to show her to my friend Sebastiano. Not that I wanted *him* especially to see her, but someone had to, and Sebastiano happened to be the only MOOer of my acquaintance logged in just then. Besides which, I'd been meaning to pay him a visit for some time. Sebastiano lived in an airy cottage in the middle of Weaveworld, a rolling, woodsy region of the MOO tucked in amid the fibers of a tapestry hanging from a wall inside the barn, and he had promised to show me around the neighborhood someday. The place had been conceived in part, Sebastiano told me, as a sort of subcommunity for Lambda's queer contingent, a realm where the sympathetically oriented could build their homes and fill in a landscape together, and I was curious to see how this experiment in creative sociogeography was working out. And so I joined my friend that night, and we went walking, he and I—a thirtysomething gay computer scientist wearing the shape of a sullen teenboy lust-object, and a heterosexual adult male wrapped in a childhood recollection of pop-iconic femininity—along the leafy, moonlit pathways of Weaveworld.

At least I remember them as moonlit. I have a lot of memories about that night, not all of them quite accurate perhaps, but all still remarkably, sensorily present to me. They linger largely as a series of lucid images, the vibrant residue of a long and long-forgotten scroll of monochrome text: our hike from Sebastiano's cottage down a rolling green hillside, our pause amid a tidy, villagelike cluster of little sandstone buildings, our passage through the small town square and on to a vaguely tropical forest's edge, where we sat on benches beneath the stars, watching an automated monkey (Sebastiano's work) cavort among the trees. But most of all what I remember is the curious, enveloping sensation through which I apprehended these scenes, a sensation so delicate I could barely pick it out from the surrounding swirl of impressions and yet so insistently attached to all of them I could hardly have failed to notice it.

Or ultimately to have identified it. For though at first I couldn't have begun to say just whence this gauzy feeling came, by the time Sebastiano and I reached the monkey trees I knew there wasn't any mistaking its source: it was Samantha's skin—a woman's skin—and the feeling was that of being in it.

I hadn't expected anything like this. I hadn't thought, in fact, that I'd really be aware at all of the particular morph I was in. I'd hoped, of course, that Sebastiano might take note of my makeover and say something appreciative; and I felt gratified when he did. But I'd assumed that after that Samantha's presence would fade from my imagination, coming quickly to feel the same way my other morphs tended to—like costumes, donned in the spirit of the vast, extended costume party LambdaMOO sometimes seemed to be, but easily ignored once they'd made their splash.

Not that I didn't feel a kind of closeness to those masks, or sense certain deeply embedded aspects of myself carved into the surfaces of some of them. My attachment to the dolphin Faaa, for instance, was surely not without some lurking totemic significance. And as for Dr. Bombay, my core persona, I had no doubt that the wavering ambiguity I'd written into his description—its uneasy suspension between intellectualized ridiculousness and hardened competence—encoded all sorts of conflicting and barely examined truths about my self-image, both in VR and out of it. But in the end, however meaningful the statements these morphs made about me, in my mind they by and large remained just that: statements, attached to the phantom body I projected into MOOspace no more or less intimately than any slogan I might wear on a T-shirt.

Whereas Samantha—well, Samantha fit that body so closely I couldn't really detect the place where she began and the body ended. Nor did I very much want to. For here was the second surprise about being Samantha: it felt delicious. It felt soft, and graceful, and sexually alluring. It felt receptive, and charming, and poised, and several other ideally "feminine" things I'd thought myself too sophisticated to imagine as the defining aspects of a woman's inner life. Yet here they were, defining my experience of virtual womanhood in ways my intellect seemed to have nothing to do with, in ways that bypassed all the layers of irony built into my half-parodic identification with a half-parodic TV witch-mom and went straight to whatever part of me it was that found the fictions of gender as solidly believable as the ground beneath my feet.

Was I at all embarrassed then, that night, walking around possessed by so predictable a notion of what it felt like to be a woman? On some level yes, I suppose I was. But mostly, I confess, I was enchanted. Enchanted with *myself,* no less—or with this temporary self, I should say, though it came to essentially the same narcissistic thing. I chatted amiably enough with Sebastiano about the sights and social affairs of Weaveworld, but the truth was I'd lost all interest in the questions that had drawn me there. By now I was talking mainly just to hear myself talk, to hear the words pass through my head in Samantha's voice, and if there was anything in particular I wanted those words to be about, it really wasn't anything but Samantha. I would have liked to say exactly what it was I felt as I typed the text that moved her body around, to say just what was going on in my mind as I stood up playfully on one of the benches, walked along its surface, threw my head back to look up with a quiet smile at the stars.

But the words were slow to come, and when they finally did arrive they were not any I could call my own. They lent themselves to me, is how I'd put it—rose up into my thoughts out of the same basement warehouse of mass-cultural memories I'd borrowed Samantha from. For a brief Technicolor moment I saw Natalie Wood dancing self-enchantedly before a mirror in her finest party whites, and then the sentence just popped out, apropros of nothing my friend and I happened to be discussing right then but somehow, evidently, very much in need of being said:

"I feel pretty!" I declared, to the bemused Sebastiano, to the unhearing robot monkey, and to the warm night breezes I swear I felt caressing the smooth skin of Samantha's outstretched arms.

There was, of course, much more that might need saying. For that matter, there still is. That evening I had only begun to move beyond the shallowest engagement with the ways a gendered self could mutate and multiply inside the MOO, and to this day I can hardly say I've plumbed the depths. But it wasn't long after Samantha's debut that I began to acquire an ampler understanding of the possibilities, and if I'm really going to tell you all I know about her, I suppose I'd better tell you roughly what that understanding was, and how I came to have it. I suppose, in other words, I'd better pause a while now to tell you what I know about the brief but passionate encounter of a girl called Lisbet and a boy called Emory.

Let me start, though, by admitting that I knew the characters themselves not very well, or not at all—I never met Lisbet, never even got a glimpse of her, and I came in contact with Emory only three or four times in all my virtual existence. Still, I was well acquainted with them both in some of their other incarnations. Emory, as it happens, was one of exu's morphs, a lanky, denim-clad kid she told me she had modeled on the adolescent memory of a longed-for older cousin. And Lisbet ("Preppy With a Past," a mutual friend once told me, "dark haired, white skinned, repressed") in fact belonged to the RL-male player I knew as Niacin, although it seemed to be a matter of some indifference just which of his aliases you called him by. He had a lot of morphs, and never really lingered long in any one of them. In one form or another, though, he'd been a friend of mine for about as long as I'd known exu, which is to say about as long as I'd been around the MOO.

In fact, it was about the time I met them both that Niacin and exu themselves first got to know each other. Not that I had anything to do with their acquaintance—and not that it had that much to do with the story of Lisbet and Emory. Not really. Those characters were still undreamt-of then, and anyway there wasn't much about exu and Niacin's relationship at first to differentiate it from the thousands of other casual connections formed every day in the public spaces of the MOO. They both were regulars at Club Doome, the lively hangout tucked away inside the train set in the guest room, and there amid the general banter they sometimes found themselves trading quips about such mutual interests as poststructuralist psychoanalytic theory, contemporary avant-garde literature, and obscurely remembered '70s pop tunes (exu was thirty-two in real life, Niacin was only a couple years younger, and in the predominantly undergraduate environment of the MOO, we elders tended to be grateful for the presence of whatever peers our cultural radars could detect).

Beyond such passing moments of camaraderie, however, exu and Niacin might as well have been logging in to two different MOOs, for all their virtual lives coincided. exu, after all, was an experience-laden old-timer by then, an active veteran of the complex maneuverings of MOO politics and at the time well into her first full-blown tinysexual relationship, the extended affair with Horton-Who that already was instructing her in the exhilarations and exasperations awaiting those who took virtual intimacy to its limits. Niacin, on the other hand, was just another newbie then—still blinking wide-eyed at the very fact of VR, still only dimly recognizing the full range of social interactions that the MOO made possible, content for now to pass his time just being witty among the witty semi-strangers of Club Doome. Inevitably his callowness would fade, but whether his virtual existence would really change much in the long run was still an open question. For many MOOers, the simple pleasures of collective banter remained throughout their MOOish days the most they ever asked for from the place, and from the looks of things young Niacin might very well have grown up to be just such a chat potato.

But then one day he took the leap that was to vault him into another orbit altogether: he made his first female morph. He called her Giustina and described her as a delicate specimen of fallen eighteenth-century gentility, and he wrote her a tattered but elegant silk gown and gave her elaborate tresses that were just beginning to come undone. I couldn't say just why he made her that way, or why he made himself a female persona at all, any more than I could say exactly what caused me to do the same, months later. I can, though, tell you that by the social standards of LambdaMOO we were neither of us doing anything particularly groundbreaking. Indeed, a year before Niacin first switched his gender, Pavel Curtis had already devoted a page or two of a paper on typical MOOish behaviors to the phenomenon of male players masquerading part- or full-time as females. So commonplace had the practice become, he remarked, that "many female players report that they are frequently (and sometimes quite aggressively) challenged to 'prove' that they are, in fact, female." ("To the best of my knowledge," he added, "male-presenting players are rarely if ever so challenged.")

Pavel also took a number of well-educated guesses as to why so many males might choose to pass as females in VR, but he didn't have a lot to say about what is probably the most meaningful answer to that question: Because they could. It was a remarkably easy thing to do, in point of fact—much easier certainly than it had ever been in the physical world, where the telltale flesh and bones of the cross-dresser created difficulties that, in a universe of pure text, could largely be transcended by a simple change of personal pronouns. And it was much easier too, for that matter, than might be deduced from Pavel's reports of spot-checks by self-appointed gender police. The truth is, such outright paranoia was really just a deviation from a far more nuanced norm, in which players generally took for granted the marked fluidity of gender in VR, yet at the same time also tended to take at face value the virtual gender of whomever they were interacting with. It wasn't a question of gullibility, mind you. It was simply that the players' need to slot their fellow players into the conceptual pigeonholes of gender turned out, in the end, to be more urgent than their need to know the biological truth about them. And thus it came to be the case that as a rule (and not without notable exceptions), a "female-presenting" player was presumed female until such time as someone went to the unlikely trouble of proving otherwise.

Why wonder, then, at the numbers of male MOOers who experimented with virtual drag? Or bother to ask what particular urges led them to do so in the first place? In real life, perhaps, the risk and effort and general stigma associated with effective cross-dressing might require of its practitioners a certain well-tended fire in the belly, but in an atmosphere like LambdaMOO it hardly took much in the way of inner compulsion to take the plunge. In fact it rarely took a lot more than a whim, as far as I could tell: a passing spell of boredom maybe, or a twitch of idle curiosity, and suddenly there you were, your gender flipped, your description rewritten, your new self loose among the MUDding crowds. And only then did you begin to sort out what, if anything, intrigued you about the experience.

Which isn't to say you might not have a lot of sorting out to do. As Pavel had concluded, and Lambda's collective wisdom confirmed, the payoffs of cross-gendered MOOing for male players were many and varied, and potentially rather knotty. Some players, of course, simply enjoyed the extra attention given to women in any social setting, and especially in one where men outnumbered them by about two to one. Others liked the challenge of deception, testing the limits of their ability to pass for female with a daring that Shannon McRae, another participant ethnographer of Lambda folkways, once wrote of as an improbable sort of "'90s machismo." Still others came to value the experience as a glimpse of life on the far side of the gender gap—a firsthand, eye-opening sampler of the routine harassments, double-edged perks, and broad-brushed preconceptions most women encounter every day. And naturally there were many players in whom any number of these sometimes contradictory motivations could be found commingling to one degree or another, which may begin to give you some idea of what a tricky proposition it could be to say just what was going on when real-life boys got it into their heads to become virtual girls.

But it got trickier, and for Niacin it quickly got about as tricky as it could. For of all the various ways in which tinytransvestism engaged the male imaginations of LambdaMOO, none complicated analysis quite so thoroughly as the one that soon became the centerpiece of Niacin's new life as an imaginary female.

Did I say complicated? The phrase is adequate, I guess. But if you really want a feel for the size and shape of what our boy was heading into, I suggest you consider briefly the incident that got him going in the first place:

Consider the girl he was that night—his second female morph, or maybe his third, a tautly sketched generation-Z neofeminist called Furie, about five eight, chin-length black hair tucked into a black stocking cap emblazoned HIPS TITS LIPS = POWER, black jeans, white T-shirt, harness boots, black hooded Carhartt jacket, and *on the back of her left hand, between the thumb and forefinger, a small dark blue tattoo in the shape of a gothic cross.*

Consider, too, the unmistakable attentions of a certain Blaize, a female-presenting character who'd been friends with Niacin for a while now, who knew of his cross-gendered creations, who even recognized Furie as one of them the moment she met her in the living room that evening (it wasn't hard—morphs changed a player's name and description only, not the readily accessible object number attached to the player's account). Who nonetheless found herself drawn to the girl in a more than amicable way.

Consider, then, the fact that Niacin, though still a netsex virgin after six months' MOOing, was well-enough informed by now to know where Blaize's open flirtations were headed. Consider the pent-up curiosity they stirred in him. Consider his excitement, his anxiety, as Furie flirted back. His half-panicked, half-suggestive exit to the mansion's roof. The readiness with which Blaize followed. And there, at last, the meeting of their virtual lips tits hips, high up above the grounds of LambdaMOO, a swirl of textual gropings exchanged almost as fast as network lag times would allow and brought, alas, to a premature end when Niacin's RL roommate had to use the phone and left him staring at his abruptly disconnected computer, shaken, aroused, in wonder.

And after you're done considering all that, save a thought or two for this detail: it is not known to me, nor was it known to Niacin with any certainty, what the real-life gender of the character who deflowered him was. "The word is that she was a he RL," Niacin told me many months later on an afternoon visit to my TV set, "but I never found out one way or another. I sorta thought Blaize was a girl at the time, but I was obviously aware of the possibilities to the contrary."

Obviously: he was one such possibility himself.

All right now: how would *you* propose to locate on the standard-issue map of human sexualities what happened between Blaize and Furie that night?

I can tell you that in the real world Niacin had always lived and lusted as a heterosexual. I can tell you too that in the virtual world it was hardly unheard of for straight men to log on as queer women and cruise for girl-girl action, with the predictable result that much if not most of the lesbian sex that took place on the

MOO was performed by smirking pairs of mutually deceived male players. But Niacin was not so easily taken in, nor did his casual recognition of Blaize's sexual indeterminacy suggest that he was all that eager to be. He knew that even if Blaize was actually a woman, the chances that she very firmly believed *him* to be one were far too slim to let him claim their liaison had stolen him a peek into the secret life of lesbians. Yet he also knew that even if Blaize was really a man, he couldn't quite claim that he'd just experienced his first homosexual encounter either.

What had it truly been then, underneath the surface? A straight couple heated in their embrace by the exoticizing mediation of a same-sex fantasy? Two men joined by their feminine reflection in a postmodern variation on the ancient, murkily homoerotic theme of the circle jerk? Or had it, perhaps, been finally nothing else but what its surface mutely insisted it to be: an unresolved pastiche of possible bodies both real and imagined, a moment of attraction suspended among the available categories of gender-marked desire like an image lost amid a house of mirrors, bounced endlessly from one to another to the next and back until you knew that if you tried to find where the truth of it stood you'd only end up equally as lost?

Well, maybe. Maybe not. In any event, as we've established, Niacin never bothered to learn just what flavor of body had reached out and touched him that night, nor did he ever have sex with Blaize again. Exactly why their history ended there I do not know, but I can tell you one thing: it wasn't because Niacin had lost interest in the possibilities their gender-warped assignation had introduced him to.

On the contrary, he set out almost immediately on what he would remember as "a really aggressive girlmorph cruising phase"—a manic many weeks of se- ductions, dalliances, brief affairs, half-hour stands. The configurations of these couplings were never quite as open-ended, though, as Blaize and Furie's multiply coded rooftop tryst had been. Invariably Niacin chose partners who presented male, invariably he believed them also to be RL males, and almost as invariably he was careful not to disturb whatever illusions they might cherish as to his own RL womanhood. It was, in short, a rather tightly scripted scenario he gravitated toward.

[margin handwritten: "MULTIPLY CODED" (INDETERMINATE AFFAIRS)]

And what's more, whether he knew it or not at the time, the script was not exactly an original one. For here, again, the literature and the local lore had long before codified Niacin's new pastime as a characteristically MOOish phenomenon, with Pavel Curtis's brief but canonical discussion of tinydrag more or less revolving around the subject of those cross-dressers who contrived, as he somewhat clinically put it, "to entice male-presenting players into sexually explicit discussions and interactions."

[margin handwritten: "tinytransvestitism"]

Pavel's view seemed to be that these false seductresses did what they did primarily "for the fun of deceiving others," and in some ways Niacin's approach to his transgendered conquests vouched for this hypothesis. To be sure, he never displayed the sort of maliciousness that notoriously led some cross-dressers to log the text of their grapplings with eager, clueless males and then to post the resulting document of said males' cluelessness in as public a virtual place as they could find. But you only had to look at the women Niacin invented to sense he took a certain craftsmanlike pleasure in overcoming potential skeptics. There was never anything too flagrant about their attractiveness, never anything that quite put them over that line separating the run of female text-bodies from what were sometimes called FabulousHotBabes, after a legendary character once created by a prominent male MOOer to parody the shameless porn fantasies in which (so common wisdom held) transvestites on the prowl usually cloaked themselves. Niacin's women were fantasies too, of course, but by the time he hit the scene, it seems, the common wisdom had so convinced most male players of their ability to spot the fictional temptresses among them that to tempt successfully required only a minimal respect for decorum, and maybe a little style.

And style, I should note, was something Niacin had more than the average MOOer's share of. I never got the opportunity to read the short stories he liked to write when he wasn't on the MOO (or otherwise slacking his way through the Austin, Texas, software-company day job that was his lifeline to VR), but I have no doubt that the people in them were drawn with memorable concision—or that he would have made an excellent writer of fashion-catalog copy as well. Indeed, some of his most popular MOO descriptions were, like Furie's, essentially nothing but the details of their clothing and their hairstyles, presented nonetheless with such precision and flair that they seemed almost the distillation of a personality, the story of a character condensed, as it were, into the moment just before its telling.

Further along in his morphmaking career, Niacin's profiles would at times get more elaborately literary, as for instance in the case of his middle-period tour de force Electraglide, *your basic six-foot-one streaky-blonde half-Bengali snowboard goddess gurl*, whose four-paragraph description interwove the usual spot-on fashion touches (*Deadbolt baseball hat . . . big K-Mart lumberjack shirt . . . majorly bad cutoffs*) with a neo-Beat litany of lyrical brush strokes (*Electraglide is about windburn. Electraglide is about speed. Electraglide is strung so high that colors blur around her. . . . Electraglide isn't doing shoes today. . . . Electraglide is crazy*). But even at their simplest, his creations always sparkled with the artful care he put into them, conjuring an image whose clarity the boys of LambdaMOO somehow found easy to mistake for honesty.

Nor, as I've said, was Niacin merely a passive witness to such mistakes. In his defense, I guess, it should be pointed out that on at least one occasion he did *try* to open a male suitor's mind to the possibility that the virtual female who stood before him might not in fact be animated by the body of an actual one ("Your clothes descriptions couldn't possibly be the work of a man," was the gentleman's blithely self-deluded reply). But even then, you'll note, Niacin forbore from cutting to the blunt truth of the situation, and more often he concealed that truth with a considerably more active hand. He made up convincingly mundane RL lives to go with his stylish VR personae, for example, and he fed their details to his partners. He "acquired" unused e-mail accounts from female colleagues at work, and he used those e-mail addresses and others to obtain from Lambda's tight-fisted registrar of players a small legion of "spare" accounts—each one a *"FRAUDULENT"* numbered object unto itself, each untraceable to the others, and each, therefore, a tool well-suited to the fraudulent ends Niacin now pursued.

But finally it has to be asked: Was the pursuit itself in fact what spurred him on? Did Niacin thrill, as the literature and lore might have us suspect, to the deceptions he was working? Was he for instance pleased as punch, do you suppose, to learn one day that a perfectly unobjectionable young MOOer (call him Raytheon) had fallen big-time for a spare of his named Alexandra—and not just for the appealing, red-haired lass of Alexandra's description-text, but for the RL woman with whom Raytheon believed he had shared a string of intimacies, with whom he'd exchanged stories about their respective real lives, with whom he was now painfully, obsessively in love? Trust me, folks: Niacin was not amused. He felt like a heel, in fact, and the feeling didn't exactly abate when (some time after he had nervously and without so much as a "Dear Raytheon" taken *a boy.* Alexandra out of circulation) Niacin and the unsuspecting dupe happened to become fairly good friends, obliging him regularly to nurse his silent guilt in the telepresence of the boy whose heart he hadn't ever meant to wound.

"I *never* told him the truth," Niacin confessed to me, a very long while later, "and I still feel weird about it."

Do not assume, then, that the practice of subterfuge was all fun and games for Niacin. In fact, let's clear this up right now: it wasn't even *mostly* fun and games. The truth is, deception thrilled him only a little—and frustrated him sort of a lot. "I wanted to *be* what I represented as much as possible," he later explained, and hence his private knowledge of the falsity of his representations proved "more of an annoyance than anything else." Niacin would frankly rather not have known that the men projecting their desires onto his projections were being bamboozled—if anything he would have preferred to be just as caught up in the illusion as they were. But if this was the only way he was going to experience how it felt to be on the receiving end of a man's desire for a woman, then bamboozle he must. <u>For it was that experience, finally, and none other, that he wanted most from his secret incursions into the sex lives of other men.</u>

Yes, but why, I hear you ask impatiently, why exactly did he want that? A fair question, I suppose, though I would have thought the answer obvious:

He got off on it.

Or as Niacin himself no less matter-of-factly put it: "It was hot." Beyond that, I'm not really sure what to tell you. I could point you back to the common wisdom, I guess, whose counsel obliged even the sober-minded Pavel Curtis to acknowledge, in the end, that the motivations of men who tinyvamp their fellow men might possibly have as much to do with erotic impulses as with pranksterish schadenfreude. "Some MUD players have suggested to me," he wrote, "that such transvestite flirts are perhaps acting out their own (latent or otherwise) homosexual urges or fantasies, taking advantage of the perfect safety of the MUD situation to see how it feels to approach other men." Pavel deemed the notion "plausible," and I for one would hardly dispute its basic validity.

Nor, it seems, would Niacin. "Homoerotic desire? Of course," he told me once when I asked if that had played a part in his cruiser-girl activities. "It was no big deal."

But there was also, surely, more to it than that. After all, if his was just a simple case of repressed homosexuality finally breaking out of its compulsory heterosexual shell, then why wasn't Niacin seeking the company of the MOO's many homosexuals? Why wasn't he "taking advantage of the perfect safety of the MUD situation" to see how it felt to approach men who were themselves unabashedly attracted to other men—the likes of Sebastiano and his Weaveworld pals, say? Was it really only lingering denial that kept his homoerotic explorations so thoroughgoingly entangled in a web of simulated heterosex?

I reserve for you the option of believing that it was. Read on, however, and I think you'll come to share my own conclusion that, in fact, the dormant sexual appetite now awakened in him was a taste for nothing quite so much as for that thoroughgoing entanglement itself.

He kissed the boys, then, and sometimes even made them cry, and all in all—those awkward teardrops notwithstanding—he found sufficient titillation in his cross-gendered forays to keep him coming back for more. But as the weeks passed and what had been a discovery became a habit, he started by and by to wonder if there wasn't, possibly, some dimension of the experience that was eluding him.

You have to keep in mind, of course, the sorts of situations he was falling into. Easily arranged, hastily consummated, and necessarily not much deeper than the seductive facades Niacin brought to them, his sexual encounters during this period were somewhat—how to say it?—limited in their power to engage the soul. Keep in mind as well the sort of person he was falling in with. Self-selected in large part from the barely postadolescent majority of MOOish males (and naturally from the most hot-to-trot of the bunch), Niacin's partners had, by the end of his first two netsexual months, taught him a lesson about young straight men in general that he might otherwise have gone to his grave unschooled in. To wit: "How woefully unimaginative and cloddish they are inna sack."

Clearly, Niacin was ready now for something a bit more challenging.

He was ready, in other words, for Emory.

And Emory? What was he ready for? Pretty much whatever, from the looks of him:

Having pissed away what was left of the family money and nothing to show for it but an old red and black BSA motorbike that he keeps in perfect working order, he ended up in the North Woods, where he does carpentry sometimes.

He keeps his long, sandy hair tied back mostly. His eyes are pale blue, with flecks of gold in them and grey rings around the iris. High cheekbones, mouth quirked up in an ironic grin. He's wearing a black t-shirt tucked into a pair of tight, faded levis and black workboots. In the pocket of his shirt, a pack of Lucky Strikes and the tooth of a wolf.

The description was a classic of its genre, in much the same careful way so many of Niacin's also were. Archetypally butch, but almost delicately so; plainly good-looking, but never plainly described as such; clearly fictional, but of that sort of fiction that conveys a lived familiarity with its subject matter—Emory was built for netsex, it was obvious, and yet not quite so obvious as to spoil the illusion of hard-edged, soft-centered, unselfconscious manhood he projected. Had I myself come across him before I knew who'd written him, I don't think I would have guessed his author was a woman—and if I had, I'm sure I would have figured her for an old hand at the cross-gendered seduction game.

The truth, however, was that exu had never really attempted a boy-morph before Emory. She'd made a male or two before, but those were gods, not men— a Xango (deity of thunder) and an Ogum (war) to round out her Afro-Brazilian pantheon—and anyway she hadn't ever much identified with them. In fact, for most of her MOOish life she hadn't really identified with her few female characters either. Instead, the gender she had mostly preferred to spend her time in was, precisely speaking, neither masculine *nor* feminine. It was hermaphrodite.

This was something of an unusual choice—though hardly on account of its evasion of the usual RL options. As it happens, the MOO's *@gender* command offered a fairly wide variety of neither-male-nor-female possibilities, and players not infrequently took the offer up. For example, in addition to the hermaphrodites (to whom the gender-tracking subroutines assigned the label *either* and the pronouns *s/he, him/her, his/her, his/hers,* and *him/herself*), there were those who opted at least occasionally for *neuter* (*it, its, itself*; useful when playing talking toaster ovens and the like), *plural* (*they, them, their* . . . ; nice for collective organisms: bee swarms, codependent couples), *egotistical* (*I, me, my* . . . ; no third person references allowed, see also the royal gender's *we, us, our,* etc., and *second person's you, your, yours* . . .), or the graphically noncommittal *splat* (**e, h*, h*s, h*self*).

By far outweighing all of these in popularity, though, was an invention known as *Spivak*, whose pronouns *e, em, eir, eirs, emself* had the unique attraction of feeling and functioning much like one of the standard gendered pronoun sets without, however, quite bringing either of them to mind. Whether *Spivak* therefore represented an absence of gender or simply a third alternative was a matter, evidently, of some debate. I can recall putting the question to a thoughtful spivak friend of mine one evening in the hot tub and failing, not surprisingly I guess, to get a straight answer out of em. On the other hand, I have since learned from McRae's investigations that some spivaks—especially those with active tinysex lives—had a pretty clear sense of emselves as inhabiting a specific gender, with its own roles, its own predilections, and even its own genitalia (think tendrils).

Whatever the spivak's ontological status, however, the option never much appealed to exu. "I liked the idea of containing both, not being without," she said of her hermaphrodite period. To be a spivak, as she saw it, was to efface one's real-life gender status, when what she'd really wanted in those days was to keep that status in play, unsettled, indeterminate. "For an entire year," she remembered, "not even my closer MOO friends were certain of what my real gender was—and guesses were pretty sharply divided. It was *fun* being gender ambiguous."

Yet in the end, she admitted somewhat wistfully, what she'd liked best about that ambiguity was not so very different from what seemed to attract many spivaks to their choice. For whether a spivak saw emself as a spaghetti-crotched mutant or a conceptual void, eir curious pronoun-choice tended to have roughly the same effect on eir dealings with other players as exu's hermaphrodism often did: it shorted out the binary circuitry with which those players' minds processed gender, rendering the very notion blessedly, if temporarily, inapplicable. Or as exu later sighed: "People treated me as a me rather than as a gendered being."

And who could begrudge her her longing for that unsexed state? I wouldn't dream of it. And yet I can't help surmising that that same longing was in a sense its own contradiction—that in it lay the closest thing there was, that is, to an essential difference between the ways men and women fucked with gender on the MOO.

It was a MOOish commonplace, of course, that if men sometimes went female just to enjoy the mixed privileges of "standing out," by the same token women most often flipped their bits in order to evade the constant attention that rained down on virtual females regardless of their real-world packaging. But what exu was talking about, I think, was something a little deeper. It was an escape not just from femininity but from the onerous primacy of gender itself in most women's lives—from the constantly echoed insinuation that the face of humanity, like that of God, will always be a man's, and that a woman consequently might as well resign herself to being all her life a female first and only secondly a human being.

And if therefore it made some sense, however paradoxically, to think of *Spivak* and *either* and the other disgendered options as characteristically female choices, then what of Niacin's headlong plunge into tinyfemininity? Might it not be argued by a similar logic that he was chasing an experience only a man could really find intriguing? By which I mean, of course, not so much the experience of inhabiting the opposite gender as that of consciously inhabiting gender at all—an experience somewhat more alien to men than women, after all, in a culture that still hasn't quite decided whether "man" is a synonym for people in general or just the ones with penises. Just as exu's fondness for hermaphrodism, then, might be read as a woman's logical desire to flee the territory of conventional sex roles at the earliest opportunity, so Niacin's thing for virtual drag might best be understood as a uniquely male romance with the thought of exiting the unmarked vehicle of masculine identity for a while and, as it were, exploring that territory on foot.

It's a hypothesis anyway. Whether it applied to MOOish gender play in general is a question I leave for future sociologists of the virtual to resolve. My own research, if you want to call it that, never really got close to conclusive. I asked around a bit, kept my eyes open, and quickly fell in with the general consensus that there were in fact a great deal more RL men playing virtual women than there were RL women posing as virtual men (a phenomenon roughly mirrored, by the way, and probably not coincidentally, in the real world's ratios of drag queens to kings). But I never felt as certain about the RL gender breakdown of the spivak/hermaphrodite population. It might be true that most of them were really women; or it might not. What was, however, certainly the case was that the handful I got to know firsthand, while indeed predominantly female in real life, didn't exactly add up to a representative sample.

Let me restrict my observations, then, to the particular, and simply note that however devoutly exu may have wished to escape the constraints of RL gender, it would not be long before she learned that LambdaMOO wasn't really the place to make her getaway. I don't know if she came to share my intuition that her VR *either*ness was as much a reflection of her fixed RL gender status as a release from it. But even if she did, I can assure you it wasn't anything so wispy as an intuition that finally shook her loose from her vaguely utopian attachment to virtual hermaphrodism.

What did it, of course, was Mr. Bungle.

One wonders, idly, why exu's sexual haziness failed in Bungle's case to do its job and spare her his severely gender-coded attentions. Had he somehow discovered the RL truth behind her ambiguous VR mask? Had he just been guessing, like myself, that that sort of ambiguity was more likely a woman's gambit than a man's? Or had he in fact guessed nothing? Had he simply defaulted to the crude paranoia of the queer-basher, lashing out at exu precisely *because* she was ill-defined, and therefore threatening to the boundaries that maintain male privilege?

One wonders. And yet for exu such conjectures were somewhat beside the point. What mattered to her, in the end, was not what Bungle had been thinking as he'd dragged her androgyne self back into the poisonous web of RL sexual power relations. What mattered was that he had thought to do so at all.

"The Bungle Incident gendered me in a nasty kind of way," exu told me many times, in so many words. "That was part of the shock of it."

She switched to *female* not long after that night, and she never went back to hermaphrodism again. She didn't have to give it up, of course. It wasn't as if Bungle had blown her cover, after all, or even as if she'd felt she had a cover to blow—the truth was, she'd never really cared that much who knew her RL gender, so long as they'd respected her MOOish indefinition. But Bungle had taken something from her nonetheless, and even if it was only a certain naïveté about the possibilities for breaking free of gender's gravity in the seemingly weightless

VR = STILL GENDERED! ☺

space of VR, the quiet, hopeful thrill of being *either* just wouldn't be the same without it.

Mostly, she chose not to dwell on what she'd left behind. But sometimes if you asked her about it a kind of bitterness welled up again, and she might tell you then that she could almost wholeheartedly agree with the grim arguments of certain psychoanalytic feminists she'd read in school: "That women are gendered precisely by Bungle's sort of violence: by loss, lack, violation. We're made holes of from the moment we become aware, and if we forget, we're reminded soon enough."

You can imagine, then, the ticklish mix of feelings with which exu—female by something less than choice for about half a year now—learned that her old pal Niacin had lately taken up the habit of being a woman more or less just for the fun of it.

Or can you? No, I suppose there is a detail or two I'd better fill you in on first. Such as, for starters: I'm afraid I may have misled you when I said there was nothing all that special about exu and Niacin's friendship in its early days. That happens, actually, to be true; but unless you understand that a certain ambient flirtatiousness tended to seep into even the most innocuous relationships on the MOO—a byproduct, I'd guess, of MOOish pseudonymity and the instant intimacy it nurtured—then you might have taken me to imply that not so much as a spark of erotic feeling flashed between the two new acquaintances. And there you would be wrong.

There was a spark. And as the months went by there gradually was more: a gently provocative edge crept into the occasional crossings of their well-matched conversational styles, a tension just insistent enough to register in both their minds as something a little more, perhaps, than the usual Club Doome bonhomie. "It was a game," exu recalled. "A game of wit, consisting entirely of sporadic verbal volleys. And it didn't matter which way the game went."

Actually, it wasn't even clear the game was going anywhere at all. By the time of Niacin's rooftop induction into tinysexual maturity, after all, exu still had her virtual hands full with HortonWho, and in the weeks that followed it certainly wasn't as if Niacin's dance card remained empty either.

But when one afternoon Niacin introduced exu to his newly minted Giustina morph, exu had a sudden inkling of the destination toward which their aimless game had actually been drifting all along. Giustina flashed her aristocratic ankles,

she tossed her half-undone tresses, and if exu in her mourning cloak of biologically correct *female*ness felt any hint of annoyance at the spectacle of Niacin's
giddy, snap-on girlhood, it was presently eclipsed, surprise surprise, by a vivid
and most unmournful urge. To be precise: "I wanted," exu told me, "to undo her
hair the rest of the way, roughly, with my fingers, while bending her head back
and kissing her throat."

The surprise, I should add, lay not so much in exu's attraction to the image of
a female body (she'd had her share of same-sex liaisons in real life) as in the possibilities that this attraction seemed suddenly to be nudging her toward. Mr.
Bungle had beaten all the fun out of her dreams of living beyond gender, of
course, but what was this coquettish invitation Giustina's ankles were presenting
to her now? Could there really be a sequel to her ill-fated foray into gender play—
a new approach, this time not seeking to silence gender's incessantly chattering
voice, but to amplify it instead, channeling it into a strange, cross-wired loop of
desire and letting it feed back on itself until its own noise overwhelmed it?

Well, why not? That day exu chose not to make her feelings known to
Niacin/Giustina, but from then on the next move in their game waited quietly in
the back of her mind. Weeks passed. exu's affair with HortonWho began to teeter
and Horton himself, for uncertain reasons, began to show up less and less on the
MOO. Niacin meanwhile leapt into the arms of one young virtual dude after
another, intrigued, compelled, but edging every day a little closer to the limit of
his patience with their uninventive fumblings.

And then, at last, another spark: out of some not very well-illuminated corner
of Niacin's imagination Lisbet sprang one day—white-skinned, dark-haired,
repressed; the preppy with a past. And while it's possible he wrote her up with
other aims in mind than escalating the exchange of gentle provocations between
exu and himself, it's indisputable that this became, within a few hours of the key-
strokes that created her, the first notable accomplishment of Lisbet's brief, unreal
existence. For no sooner did exu lay eyes on the girl's description than Emory
began to take shape in her mind, provoked into being by the implicit challenge in
Lisbet's cool, brittle exterior and imbued with just the aura of wiry, tobacco-
scented naturalism exu thought it would take to meet that challenge.

In short, and not to put too fine a point on it, Emory was conceived for the
express purpose of getting into Lisbet's pants.

Which goal proved not so very difficult to attain, given the variety of circumstances conspiring to bring it within Emory's reach. The long, subtextual flirtation between his author and Lisbet's didn't hurt, of course, and beyond that
there was Niacin's almost Stanislavskian eagerness to inhabit the personae he

created, so that although he knew full well who'd invented the boy-morph who suddenly was hovering around his latest girl-morph, he couldn't help but see Emory through the girl-morph's eyes, responding pretty much as exu had planned to the wiry, tobacco-scented image Lisbet's own tight-laced vulnerability had inspired. "Emory made me totally wet," said Niacin, and that was only the effect of the boy's description. "Emory started remote-emoting at me then, very discreetly and ornately," and after the desert of cloddish, postadolescent come-ons through which Niacin had for two months been wandering, the subtlety of exu/Emory's approach fell on him like a quenching rain:

"I was a goner. . . ."

Indeed he was. But how far gone he couldn't then have guessed; nor did exu have any notion, really, of what she was so discreetly and ornately getting herself into. They both had reason to believe, of course, that they were adequately versed in the mechanics and dynamics of virtual eros by now. They'd each been around the block a time or two, by one route or another. But it is safe to say that within minutes of Lisbet and Emory's first embrace, both knew—both felt the knowledge coursing through their RL bodies—that they had stumbled onto an intensity undreamt of in their personal philosophies of tinysex.

"That first encounter practically blew the roof of my head off," was how Niacin put it. "As sex, it was one of the most amazing experiences I've had, VR or RL. . . . I almost passed out. . . . I was at work, all faint and shaky, practically coming in my pants. . . . I was afraid to move."

And exu, though she tended to be a little less indelicate in her descriptions of what happened that day, was clearly reduced to a similar state of distraction. Logged in from her workplace as well, she too felt almost physically rent by the gap between her mundane surroundings and the place into which her psyche had abruptly been thrust, a place which—well, "What was it like?" I asked, and exu:

"Like white hot. Like nuclear," she said. "It really was like melting into the screen."

All right all right, I realize that some among you are by this point shifting skeptically in your seats, anxious for just a bit more in the way of documentary detail— a scrap or two, let's say, of the text that traveled between Austin and Seattle that afternoon so that you, the most discriminating of my readers, can be the judges of what was or wasn't white hot, nuclear, roof-blowing, etc. And let me assure you that I feel your frustration, that I understand your desire for a closer look, and that I certainly would never, ever, mistake for mere voyeurism the spirit of purely intellectual inquiry that so obviously has awoken that desire in you.

But I'm afraid I'll have to ask you, nonetheless, to be satisfied with the secondhand scraps I've already supplied. Because for one thing: they're all the scraps I've got (there *were* limits, after all, to my two friends' openness about their sex lives). And for another: even if I had a complete, unexpurgated log of Lisbet and Emory's first tryst to show you, it almost certainly would fail to convey whatever power inhered in that event. I'm sorry, but it's true—transcriptions of tinysex are a notoriously underwhelming form of erotica. Invariably, the real-time dance of two heatedly thinking-feeling minds that brings a decent textual shagging to life evaporates the instant it's saved to disk. Invariably, what's left behind is either at best a dry but not uninteresting prose poem or, in the vast majority of encounters, a slapdash collection of banalities that wouldn't even make the cut at the *Penthouse* letters desk. The upshot being in either case—as it was undoubtedly in Emory and Lisbet's—that you really just had to be there to get the point.

But listen, if it's any consolation, I can tell you these details: On that October day a woman pretending to be a man made a kind of love to a man pretending to be a woman; the woman knew that the man was pretending and the man believed the same about the woman, and neither thought the other was deceived on this account; and nonetheless the man played his part carefully from beginning to end and the woman too was careful all the while to keep alive the fiction that she was a man. More than ever now, in other words, their interaction was a game. And if you're willing to take my word for it, I can tell you too that it was somehow precisely this—their final self-abandonment to the principle of play, of make-believe—that made that game at last so mind-shakingly real to them.

It scared them, frankly. Holed up in the Crossroads early the next day, Emory received a brief page from Lisbet, who was at the same time chatting with a small crowd on the hot tub deck. The message said: "I want you so much I can't even be in the same room with you"—and though there was surely an edge of playful, romance-novelesque hyperbole there, the undertone of erotic dread was genuine.

Actually, in the case of the man who'd written Lisbet's message, that dread was not only genuine but of a certain rather textbook variety. Amid the run-up to the previous afternoon's tangle, you see, it had passingly occurred to him that, though he tended to assume exu was in reality a girl, the question of her real gender had in fact never openly come up in all their months of friendship—and now, in the aftermath of said tangle, he suddenly was beginning to feel afflicted by the uncertainty. And no, I wouldn't blame you one bit if you happened to find it just a tad absurd that Niacin, after months of lifting his virtual skirts for pretty much any able-minded RL male not otherwise occupied, only now saw fit to suffer his first attack of homosexual panic. But understand: the stakes had changed. "I sensed the potential," Niacin said, "for something other than a quick fuck with Emory, a potential that was never there before. And while fucking boys put me off not a bit, the idea of having a *thang* with a boy was a bit troublesome. Especially in the case of one who was a closeish friend. . . ."

Ultimately, then, Niacin's fear wasn't quite so much the queasiness of homophobia as it was the anxiety of any playboy plunged unexpectedly into deep emotional waters. And in this, exu's anxieties were not much different. Not that she was any kind of dilettante, of course—her relationship with HortonWho had already taken her into some not inconsiderable amorous depths. But what she'd experienced the day before, with Lisbet, had felt like a whole new territory. She'd stepped into a psychic landscape she would only later have words to describe, and even then they would be words bleary with mysticism and poetry: "burning howling core of silent wind," "complete sloshing of identity," "ego dissolution," that sort of thing. What in God's name was she thinking, then, setting off into this realm with a person whose real face she'd never seen and whose real character she could only judge on the basis of a long, intermittent exchange of clever remarks?

But it was too late now for second thoughts. exu's apprehensions were fighting a losing battle against her desires; and Niacin's anxieties were no match for the attraction pulling him back toward the place his game with exu had finally led to yesterday. They met again, Lisbet and Emory. And after that they met another time, and then another. And soon you couldn't even call it meeting anymore: they were in each other's company from the moment exu's workday began until the moment Niacin's ended, trying their RL best to hide the arousal of their physical bodies, attending to their RL duties no more than they had to keep from losing their RL jobs.

They were playing harder now, inventing new characters and trying out old ones on each other. Niacin was no longer Lisbet only, but sometimes also Giustina, or the virile, bay-rum-scented Ishmael, or the lean old traveler Wattson; exu might be Emory or Xango or the sea-goddess Iemanja or even, on occasion, exu herself, whatever that was. For Niacin there was an element of rediscovery—as if all the permutations that had lurked unexamined in the heart of his hurried grope with the mysterious Blaize were now being taken out, each in its turn, and carefully, lovingly looked over. "We were boy/girl, boy/boy, girl/

girl," he said. "I was boy and she girl and vice versa . . . we did every possible combo. . . . We were like that for [weeks], shifting genders and bodies, fucking like mad, totally in love."

It was funny, in a way—the two of them furiously shuffling their identities and at the same time coming to know each other more intimately, perhaps, than they had ever known anyone. Between fictions, real-life stories were getting told: exu learned more and more about the complicated progress of Niacin's RL love life (he was by then six months into a stormy relationship with a woman who knew nothing about his virtual excursions); and Niacin in turn picked up details about exu's marriage that, among other things, helped finally to settle his doubts about her RL gender. But it wasn't really in these departures from play-acting that exu and Niacin caught their deepest glimpses into one another. Instead, it was in the play-acting itself—in their fluid minuet of name changes and textual makeovers—that they began to feel their innermost, least namable identities laid bare. "For some reason," said exu, "interacting through the fictions got [us] into these weird, core selves that were almost unbearable. Like the more fictional we were, the closer to some wordless reality we got."

And this was funny too, though perhaps not in a terribly amusing way. For what could it possibly mean to approach a wordless knowledge of another person through a medium composed entirely of words? Could exu and Niacin ever really arrive at such a knowledge, or did their headlong flight toward it doom their affair to crash against a terminal paradox?

It's a good question, if I do say so myself—although I regret to report that it remains a purely theoretical one as well. For in the end, the affair in fact ran aground on a somewhat less esoteric sort of contradiction:

"At a certain point my mind just fried," said Niacin. "The RL/VR split was making me crazy. . . ."

And yes, it's possible he could have handled that split a little better if he'd felt at all able to discuss its VR side with his RL SO—as exu somehow managed to with hers. But exu's policy of domestic honesty was not exactly for the faint of heart, and when you got right down to it Niacin's decision to keep his girlfriend in the dark about his virtual sex life was arguably not the most selfish of the choices he'd made since that life began. It wasn't easy on him, anyway: obliged at the end of the day to try and switch his feelings for exu off along with his computer, Niacin was forced to live with the awkward impossibility of doing so. Images of afternoon encounters bled through, inevitably, into disorienting dinnertimes and even more confusing bedtimes, and as both relationships progressed, the confusion only intensified. He rode it as far as possible, he said, "feeling totally fissured . . . but kinda relishing living on the edge that way . . . until I just felt like I couldn't take it anymore. . . ."

And there the story ended. Two months after Lisbet and Emory first met, they met again for the final time. Or maybe they didn't. Perhaps it was Wattson and Xango who met that day, or Giustina and Iemanja, or just plain Niacin and exu. It could have been any of them by that point, of course, and their interaction could have gone any number of ways. Niacin may have offered explanations for the two of them to haggle over, or he may have kept his intentions to himself while they indulged in one last afternoon of dizzying play. But it doesn't really matter which of the possible scenarios he ultimately chose, because in all of them the outcome was the same: the game would go no further from then on. Niacin checked out—just disappeared into the real world for a good long while and left exu to sift through the memories and begin to try and put them in some kind of order she could make sense of.

God knows she had her work cut out for her. And if she took time out at any point to cry a little while for Emory's sake, or even for her own, I don't recall her ever telling me about it.

I do recall, though, something of my state of mind as the details of Lisbet and Emory's story started trickling my way. Samantha's maiden, moonlit walk was several weeks behind me by then, and if my initial wonder at that curious experi-ence had already begun to fade, my slowly accumulating knowledge of what exu and Niacin had been through together did little to revive it. I saw now just how narrowly I had opened the door onto the world of virtual gender play that evening, and I began half-consciously to guess at the things I might eventually feel (besides pretty) if I chose to move further into that world. Would I discover in myself the same VR-induced chaos of erotic tendencies that Niacin had finally, in his weeks of kaleidoscopic experiment with exu, come face-to-face with—that part of him he referred to (with only the slightest whisp of a virtual chuckle) as his "polygendered omnisexuality"? Would I arrive at the strange state of ego-melting, postgendered grace that exu, for her part, swore she'd reached amid the same kaleidoscopic afternoons, in those moments when the game went white hot and "whatever it is that links gender to identity got completely displaced"?

I wasn't counting on it. But as I settled into an awareness of the possibilities, I found myself spending more and more of my limited MOO time as Samantha, moving about the Lambda grounds not so much in search of cross-gendered adventures as idly tempting fate to toss a few of them my way. Fate was in no hurry to oblige, it seemed, but I didn't mind. I continued to enjoy the almost fragrantly delicate sensation of being wrapped in my own secondhand notions of femininity, and by the time summer arrived and the MOO at last became a daily habit, I was as often in Samantha's skin as out of it—open still to whatever interactions she might lead me into, and casually hopeful that somewhere among them might lurk something as intense, as rich, or as illuminating as exu/Emory and Lisbet/Niacin's encounter seemed to me to have been.

But why should I pretend with you? Surely you'll have guessed by now that if Samantha's story had ever finally led to anything in the same league as Lisbet and Emory's, I would have skipped the long digression and told you all about it pages ago. And even if instead this comes as news to you, well anyway now you know: what's left to say about Samantha does not amount to much.

She did, in the end, have her share of memorable encounters; that much is true. But they were hardly what I'd call adventures, nor did they leave me feeling especially enriched. On the contrary, what I remember most about Samantha's ample portion of my first few weeks of daily residence (for it was in her body, you might now be interested to know, that I rode the scarlet balloon to the top of Lambda's sky on that inaugural afternoon, that I subsequently did much of my early scouting for a likely place to put the Garden of Forking Paths, and that I later cast my vote against Minnie's seductive dreams of technotopia) is a feeling of increasing wariness, as more and more regularly, it seemed, my female incarnation was approached by male strangers apparently convinced that she had nothing better to do than supply them with the time of day and other, perhaps more stimulating varieties of data.

Wherever I might be, whatever I was actually up to at the moment, their often stunningly graceless overtures somehow managed to blunder onto my screen. "Samantha, you are sexy," a certain plaid guest observed out loud in the middle of a crowded hot tub one evening. He then, when this silver-tongued inducement failed to lure me away with him to a more intimate setting, proceeded to curse me out in surprisingly expressive comic-strip style (his exact words: "$%@$%^%^&#^%&#&65"). And Plaid was hardly the least tactful of them. "Would you like to have some fun with my 10 inches?" a beige guest paged me once, from God knows where and without even the courtesy of a what's-your-sign to break the ice, while I was in the middle of a fairly involved discussion with a friend on the deck outside the living room. ("Why yes actually!" I paged back, "I just bought a new cutlery set and I've been looking for something to try it out on!"—but this proved too subtle for my would-be playmate, and I was obliged finally to spell it out for him in two- and three-letter words.)

The relentlessness of these intrusions came as something of a revelation to me (yes, even after all the real-life times I'd nodded sympathetically while girlfriends fumed about the one streetcorner lothario too many they'd put up with that day). And let me be frank, my fellow men: it didn't exactly make me proud to be one of us. In fairness, though, I should also note that not all my suitors were quite such discredits to the sex. Nor, to be entirely honest, was I always quite so unreceptive to their approaches. I liked to think of myself as a basically nice person, for one thing, and so, like many an RL woman I suppose, I found it hard to very firmly rebuff a man who put at least a little civility into his attempts to get to know me. But more to the point: it wasn't like I never felt the least bit curious myself about where those attempts might lead.

In fact, it had by then become a kind of semiofficial policy of mine that if I was going to have tinysex with anyone at all (now that Ecco was no longer around, that is), it was going to be with one of these same random lugs buzzing so reliably around the flower of Samantha's femininity. It seemed the simplest way to go about it, after all. I would scarcely have to lift a finger to get my hands on a partner, and better yet, I wouldn't have to worry much about any emotional complications either. I mean, I wanted some adventure, sure, but I found my real love life far too challenging as it was to want to risk the kinds of RL/VR conflicts Niacin and exu had had to negotiate. exu herself advised me against it, and she seemed to agree that if a quick, pinhole glimpse of the exotic territory she and Niacin had explored was enough to satisfy my curiosity, then a cross-gendered tumble with a randy stranger would easily—and safely—do the trick.

But it didn't take me long to figure out that, for Samantha anyway, there could be no such zipless tinyfuck: I simply lacked the nerve to pull it off. Nor was my squeamishness a matter of deep-seated sexual hang-ups, I don't think, or even of the ethical quandaries involved in letting another man deceive himself as to my real gender. Oh, I suppose I wrestled a bit with the moral issues, but was it really *my* fault if some people didn't know better than to believe everything they read on their computer screens? No: what unmanned me, finally, was not the prospect of a guilty conscience, but a rather less honorable fear of being discovered and publicly exposed for a fraud—an anxiety I didn't even quite realize was there until it overcame me one evening while I was holding up Samantha's end of a long conversation that had all the earmarks of a virtual date. "You like horses, right?" had been the young man's inaccurate but inoffensive opening line, after which he'd suggested we get acquainted over a game of one-on-one Scrabble in the dining room. A microscopic dew of nervous sweat started to glaze my RL skin then as suddenly, in quick succession, the Scrabble game ground to a halt, my date murmured silkily that he'd "much rather just talk to you anyway" (back in his room of course), and I proceeded to imagine all the horrible things he was going to say about me on *social and elsewhere once he traced Samantha back to Dr. Bombay and did enough asking around to put two and two together.

I managed, that night, to duck out before things got too cozy, and I even managed afterward to remain on friendly terms with the man in question, who called himself Leshko, who claimed in real life to be a thirty-one-year-old goldsmith and former heroin addict from Chicago, and who seemed, to my immense relief, almost totally unruffled when he did at last deduce my RL gender not too many days after our first meeting. By then, however, I had already abandoned once and for all my scheme to use Samantha as a vehicle for tinysex. I still held on to the possibility of a cross-gendered fling, but I no longer dared risk my MOOish reputation by having that fling in a morph traceable to Dr. Bombay. This meant, in effect, that I would have to postpone any actual flinging until after I had worked out the moderately complicated details of hacking myself an illegal second character.

Between this change of plans, then, and the increasingly tiresome barrage of Neanderthal pick-up lines, Samantha lost a good portion of her original appeal for me. In the time that remained of her existence (for her days, like those of all my morphs, were numbered, though I did not know it then), I think I slipped into her body on maybe four or five more occasions. Of these, I will mention only one just now.

It was in mid-August. I was in the hot tub once again, with friends, and very much enjoying the playful mood I had almost forgotten Samantha sometimes helped me into, when suddenly two guests, a magenta one and a khaki one, splashed boisterously into the water. These guests seemed to be of about the same age and sensibility as MTV's notorious teenage wastrels Beavis and Butt-head, and I imagine we would have simply ignored the pair if one of them hadn't then happened to address the other with that universal term of teenboy endearment "fag." With that, however, my friend theroux-que-sault insisted on holding up a big sign inscribed with the words *No homophobic slurs, please*, to which the magenta guest insisted on replying "Fuck you queer," to which my friend Enver in turn replied by teleporting both guests to a harshly described area of the MOO called Hades.

Within a few minutes, the magenta guest splashed back into the tub, and presently the bunch of us saw on our screens the unappetizing sentence *Magenta_ Guest pisses in the water.* I happened to have a voodoo doll on me, so I retaliated with the sentence *As if against its will, Magenta_Guest drinks its own piss water.* To which Magenta made the devilishly clever rebuttal "Well, no"—which prompted from me the equally Wildean "Well, uh, yeah."

And it was at about this point, when it appeared the goings-on could not possibly get any more juvenile, that the magenta guest did the one thing that stands out in my mind above all else that occurred that night.

"Samantha, can I pet your poodle?" asked Magenta. "Please?" And then before I could even begin to roll my eyeballs at the kid, it had happened: the magenta guest had *grabbed my poodle*. Whatever that was supposed to mean.

But of course I knew very well what the gutter-minded little guest intended it to mean, which is why I remember that moment so clearly. For though I couldn't help chuckling at the inanity of the offense—and though we immediately packed the offender off to hell again as casually as you might shoo a fly—I logged out at the end of the evening with a low flame of humiliation burning in me and a galling new sliver of knowledge lodged in my heart. I had learned at the guest's poodle-grabbing hand, you see, that if being in Samantha's body had the capacity to make me feel pretty, it could also let me feel a kind of ugly that a male body gave me only limited access to. The deeply embedded gender fictions that had brought the power of feminine sexual charm to life inside me turned out to work just as well for the powerlessness of feminine sexual subjugation, it turned out, and as I lay awake in my RL bed that night with angry, impotent fantasies of revenge floating lightly through my head, it amused me to suppose that after having long believed I'd successfully comprehended the curious, ambivalent rage of Mr. Bungle's victims, I had at last been given the opportunity to feel that very rage within myself.

But the truth is this: I was no more certain then than I am today of the extent to which my experiences as Samantha gave me firsthand experience of a woman's perspective. Just as it was unclear what she was to other people—the woman that the magenta guest and others saw, or the costume that my friends saw—so it remained unclear what she was to me: a man's fantasies of femininity turned loose, or a taste of the disembodied cultural voice that speaks inside a woman's head, that tells her how a woman acts, and how a woman feels.

NEW YORK CITY, JULY 1994

A Groovy Booth
You are in a high-backed, wood-paneled booth in what
  is surely, this week anyway, the grooviest little
  boho eatery on Ludlow Street. In the murk beyond the
  confines of the booth, you can just make out the gist
  of the restaurant's decor -- a peculiarly mid-'90s
  blend of thrift-store drabbery and art-schooled
  elegance.
Jessica and The_Author are here.

Jessica takes a sip from her martini.

The_Author chews the olive from his martini.

Jessica smiles at The_Author.

The_Author smiles at Jessica.

The_Author wonders how to put this, exactly.

The_Author says, "So. Uh . . ."

Jessica raises an eyebrow.

The_Author says, "So I've been thinking, you know, and
   it's like -- well if I'm really gonna do this whole
   MOO thing, OK, I mean I _am_ gonna have to at least
   try this whole tinysex thing, right?"

Jessica says, "Uh-huh. Which of course you did
   already."

The_Author gives her a quizzical look.

Jessica says, "Remember? You, me, the master bedroom?"

The_Author says, "Oh. Ha! Right. No, totally, yeah. Of
   course I remember. Heh . . . But it's, uh . . ."

The_Author says, "It's just that I think I should try
   it with someone I haven't, you know, actually had sex
   with in real life or, I mean, even _seen_ in real
   life. You know?"

The_Author says, "I mean as a sort of experimental
   thing?"

The_Author says, "Just to sort of see what it's like?"

Jessica looks at The_Author with a slight narrowing of
   her eyes and an even slighter grin.

Jessica says, "You want to just sort of see what it's
   like to have netsex with another woman. This is what
   you're saying?"

The_Author says, "Oh, no! No no no. I mean, probably
   not. I mean, no, I'm thinking definitely that the
   most interesting thing probably would be to do it in
   my female morph with some, just, random guy."

The_Author says, "Most likely."

Jessica sighs.

Jessica says, "So what's your point, Julian?"

The_Author says, "Oh. Well I mean I was just wondering, you know? I mean how you would feel about that?"

The_Author watches Jessica carefully. He does not particularly want to be having this conversation, but he has been advised it's for the best. exu told him so; something about the need for negotiating boundaries and anticipating potential disruptions and so forth. It all sounded pretty sensible to him at the time. Right now, though, he is not so sure.

Jessica shrugs, and gently smirks.

Jessica says, "Well what can I say? I mean you _know_ how I'm feeling about This Whole Monogamy Thing these days. Do whatever you want, I don't care."

WesleyYourWaiterForThisEvening appears as if from nowhere, two steaming plates of food in his hands.

The_Author . o O (Hm. Not quite the answer we wanted to hear, nope.)

WesleyYourWaiterForThisEvening sets a plate of Blackened Catfish with Zucchini and Rice on the table before Jessica.

The_Author . o O (Then again, certainly not the answer we _didn't_ want to hear.)

WesleyYourWaiterForThisEvening sets a plate of Grilled Pork Chops with Sauteed Spinach and Garlic Mashed Potatoes on the table before The_Author.

WesleyYourWaiterForThisEvening chirps "Enjoy" and disappears back into the murk.

The_Author begins to carve into his Grilled Pork Chops, looks up at Jessica.

[157]

The_Author says, "So you don't have a problem with
   this?"

Jessica, her mouth full of Blackened Catfish, looks at
   him inquiringly.

The_Author says, "I mean with me having tinysex on a,
   uh, on an experimental basis."

Jessica swallows, shakes her head and says "No
   problem," and she's smiling as she says it.

The_Author notes, however, that this is not the smile
   he loves. Not the one that melts and invites him. It
   has a hint of formality in it, this smile, and he has
   never seen her wear it except in self-defense.

The_Author grins back at her, more broadly than he
   means to, and starts cutting up his Grilled Pork
   Chops again.

The_Author thinks he may have lost his appetite.

VR

5

How Did My Garden Grow

Or TINYECONOMICS, Theoretical and Applied

In the early evening of the day after I voted no on *B:DisbandMediation*, I found myself standing in a realm of pure possibility and wondering (as one often does in realms of that sort) just how I was to proceed from there.

The surroundings didn't offer much in the way of clues. *You are standing on a path in a realm of pure possibility* was what I saw when I looked. And there was this advice as well: *You can stay here as long as you like, but it's boring, and more nerve-racking than you might imagine. Why not go north? Or south? Sort the yarrow stalks, toss a coin, pray for guidance. Seek and you will find.*

But I knew better. I knew that if I went south, for instance, I would find very little—just a few patches of hazily sketched scenery followed by a featureless wasteland of undescribed spaces. I knew, too, that if I went north the prospects wouldn't be much better. I knew, in short, that it was high time for me to get to work on the task I'd been so blithely putting off for the last few weeks: I must go forth now and finish my garden.

But as I said, exactly how I was to do so remained a question. Nor was it now the same simple question I'd once thought it was, back when the view from the scarlet balloon had seemed to promise me a limitless space in which to shape my monumental landscape. There were limits after all, I had learned—as inevitably there must be. For though I had the option, here within the MOO, of tucking the Garden of Forking Paths inside a jewel box or a carrot seed or even a passing thought if I so chose, out there in the real world there was only one place it could be stored, and that was the same small whirring disk of ferromagnetized metal upon which every other object in the crowded MOOish cosmos resided. Boundless though the imaginations that built LambdaMOO might be, in other words, its material resources were finite. There were only so many bytes of hard-drive space to go around, and as I had lately and dismayingly come to understand, my share of those bytes—my "quota," as the local jargon termed it—was quite possibly never going to be large enough to accommodate the grandiose construction I had in mind.

It was exu who had pointed out the problem to me. It was sort of her job to, actually. As a newly elected member of the Architecture Review Board (or ARB, which rhymes with "barb"), she was one of about a dozen MOOers officially charged with determining whose virtual creations had the right stuff to qualify for increased allocations of disk space. I knew very well of course that I was ultimately going to have to apply for such an increase myself—at 130 kilobytes and rising, the garden had already bloated me irrevocably beyond the initial 50-kilobyte quota granted each new player on the MOO. But somehow it had never occurred to me that the ARB might actually turn my application down. And it was on this point that exu finally was obliged to set me straight: she liked the garden a lot, as it happened, but she regretted to inform me that other ARB members might not be as willing as she was to overlook the project's almost absurdly extravagant bulk.

"The thing is this," she explained. "There's this new economy of scarcity around here. It's utter bullshit. Partly leftover hysteria about the recent population explosion; partly other stuff. But the upshot is, the ARB is giving out quota these days like hardly at all. Even when they do, first-time applicants generally apply for no more than 50K—and you're gonna need, what, 100? 150?"

I got her drift, and I didn't much like it. Sure, living over-quota wasn't the worst thing that had ever happened to me. It wasn't even quite the "big fucking pain in the ass" that exu sympathetically made it out to be. But its effects were quietly and steadily debilitating nonetheless: I couldn't create new objects, I couldn't add programming to the ones I already had, I couldn't invent new morphs. I was a virtual cripple, and what was maybe worse, I was a bum—living on borrowed quota, squatting on public disk space, dreaming of the day my finished garden would at last earn me a full reimbursement from the ARB and make a self-supporting citizen out of me again. Now exu seemed to be telling me that day might never come, and you can imagine how the news unnerved me.

DrBombay gives you a fearful look, I emoted at her, and "Jeez," I said, "what am I supposed to do?"

exu frets ARBishly, she emoted back. _Hates_ this.

"I wanna subvert this fucking fascist ARB stranglehold on creative building, is the thing," she said. "And this is just the sort of situation that gets me steamed. But don't worry for now, OK? I'm gonna ask some of the real long-time ARBers if they have any ideas on how to get you your quota back. They tend to be the biggest nazis of the bunch—especially the ones that were appointed by Haakon back in the pre-Bungle days—but I trust a few of them."

"Sigh," I sighed. "Well, see what you can do. Nothing beyond the bounds of propriety of course."

"Of course," said exu, grinning. "Meanwhile, you should prolly talk to Finn. Fellow ARB member. Elected. He's got a petition for term limits for ARBers which will hopefully shake loose some of the most severe fascists. And he's way, way helpful if you can catch him in the mood.

"Besides which," she added, with another grin, "you need to know him. He's part of the local color."

That much I knew. Almost from my first day on the MOO, in fact, I'd been hearing people talk about this Finn. Finn the outlaw, some called him. Finn the martyr, said others. Finn the patron saint of anarchists and libertines; Finn the hacker of wizbits and inventor of erotic player classes. Finn the hero—or villain, depending on who you talked to—of a distant piece of MOOish history called the Schmoo Wars. Or something like that. His exact place in the local mythologies hadn't been the easiest thing for me to keep track of, but by now at least I'd gotten the message loud and clear that it was a prominent one.

So naturally when exu offered to invite this illustrious personage to drop by my not-so-humble construction site for a look, I didn't dare decline. And thus it came to pass that in the early evening of the day after I voted no on *B:Disband-Mediation, I found myself waiting at the heart of my garden for Finn's imminent arrival—alone in a realm of pure possibility and wondering, as I believe I've mentioned, just how I was to proceed from there.

I wondered too of course just how, and even whether, Finn was going to help me proceed. His celebrity intrigued me, certainly, but at the moment what interested me more was his authority. He was an ARB official, after all, and even though exu was too, I couldn't really think of her as anything but a friend, or of her occasional visits to my garden as anything but social calls. Finn's impending appearance, on the other hand, loomed in my mind as a kind of preliminary hearing. My work, I sensed, was to be sized up now by an impartial emissary of the board—inspected, dissected, weighed in the balance, and in the end declared viable or not. If the verdict was positive, I could go ahead as planned, reasonably confident that exu's fears were exaggerated and that I wasn't just digging myself into a lifetime of quota deprivation. And if the verdict was not positive—well, so be it. I had shelved my plans for the garden once before. It wasn't like it would kill me to put this foolish dream of mine to rest once and for all.

Thus then, in an attitude of stoic reflection, did I approach the proceedings. Finn arrived, introducing himself with a simple "Howdy!", and had I bothered taking a look at him I would have seen an equally straightforward description—*a 5'9" young man of lithe build* with *dark hair . . . full lips . . . eyes of blue steel . . . a confident smile* and so on, cleanly written but otherwise unremarkable except, perhaps, for the "I LOVE LORENA BOBBITT" T-shirt fitted snugly to his chest. I did not look at any of this, however, for I was otherwise engaged: almost the instant Finn appeared my stoicism had crumbled, and it was taking all my concentration now to keep from throwing myself prostrate at his feet in an abject plea for his ARBly approval.

"It's a pleasure to make your acquaintance!" I gushed, shaking his hand perhaps a little too eagerly.

Finn grinned. A friendly grin? A perfunctory grin? A grin shot through with the easy contempt of the powerful for their supplicants? In the real world maybe I could have read the peripheral details of his gesture for some clue to my impending fate, but here there were no such visual aids: *Finn grins* was all I had to go on.

"Likewise," he said.

Then he said nothing.

"Oh, yeah," I managed, after a bit. "Well, this is my garden. Pretty much all that remains to be done here is to finish the descriptions of the various rooms. There's something like, er, 128."

I blushed, embarrassed to admit how big the place was. But Finn said nothing still. No doubt he had already typed @*measure* and gotten a look at the garden's egregious byte-count.

"Let me take you on a tour of one of the more finished wings," I offered, eager to change the subject. I headed north from the realm of pure possibility into the "room" I called Yin (as opposed to Yang, of course, which lay to the south).

Darkness surrounds you—said the description there—*deep and comforting. To the northwest (left) you sense something may be happening. To the northeast (right) you sense something else may be happening.*

Finn entered from the south, behind me. "What's the idea here?" he asked. "Is there some kind of cosmic divination going on?"

I told him then about the garden's concept: about the branching paths and the way they modeled the binary lines of the I Ching's hexagrams, about the unique words of guidance waiting at the end of each of the sixty-four possible pathways. I told him, also, how to use the garden's "oracle" program to navigate the paths. "At every fork, type one of three commands," I explained. "'Toss' coins, 'sort' yarrow stalks, or simply 'pray.' The oracle will tell you whether you've drawn a 'solid' line or a 'broken' one, and hence which way to go."

These details were important, but what I mainly wanted him to grasp about the oracle was that I'd programmed it myself. Not that this amounted to any great feat, you understand—the oracle was a mere ten lines of the sort of code no nine-year-old programmer would brag about these days. But it happened also to be the only actual code I'd written into the project myself, and I knew enough about the ARB's guidelines to know that original coding often made the difference between approval and rejection. Without it, even the most carefully crafted description-texts didn't count for much, and for that matter, they could even count against you. "Tinyscenery," it was called—place-descriptions that were nice to look at but impossible to interact with—and ARBish literature tended to speak of it in much the same tones the Bible reserved for practices like idolatry and fornication. Myself, I liked to think that the 128 handsome place-descriptions of which my garden was eventually to consist would fit together far too interestingly to be dismissed as the irredeemable heap of tinyscenery it might otherwise resemble. But I knew, even so, that it couldn't hurt to draw attention to the site's more obviously interactive aspects.

It heartened me therefore to see Finn linger, there in the darkness of Yin, and play with the oracle for a bit.

He tossed the coins and the oracle said: "The line is solid. Go right."

He sorted the yarrow stalks: "Go right," it said.

He prayed for guidance: "Go right," again.

And then, for a fourth time, the supposedly randomized program pointed him to the right, and I started to get the feeling things were not prepared to go my way tonight. True, four solid lines in a row didn't necessarily mean the oracle was broken, but it did look weird enough to cast doubt on my programming skills. And worse, the weirdness wasn't even pointing in the proper direction: the right-hand fork, I knew, led only into a desert of still-undescribed rooms—one empty place after another telling the visitor, *You see nothing special.*

"Uh, heh, let's uh, let's go left instead," I said. "Screw the oracle."

So left we went. Northwest:

It's winter. Frost is in the air. To the west (left) stands a grove of fruit trees. To the north (right) a mountain rises.

From there we went left again, toward the trees and into them:

You are in a grove of skeletal fruit trees, stripped bare by winter. The earth beneath them is black and pungent, rich with the life force that will reanimate the trees in spring. To the southwest (left), a path leads on through the grove. Another one leads to the northwest (right).

I chose the right-hand path this time:

You stand at the northern edge of a fruitless fruit grove. In the northeastern distance Ken mountain rises, snow-capped. A path leads west (left), toward a sound of rushing water. Another leads north (right), across a gentle upward slope covered with dry yellow grass, to a stand of firs.

I climbed the gentle upward slope:

You are in a sparse stand of firs on the southwest slope of a hill. The wind whispers in the branches. To the northwest (left) a path slopes down to a grassy clearing. To the northeast (right) a path climbs the hill.

I paused there, before the sixth and final fork, and waited amid the whispering firs for Finn to catch up with me. It took a mind-bogglingly long time—about a minute or two.

"Goddamn! Are you as lagged as I?" he asked when he arrived.

I wasn't. But I had to agree the lag was pretty bad that night, and silently I cursed it for yet another worrisome omen. People liked to say that lag was VR's closest equivalent to real weather, and they definitely had a point (if only because the lag and its vagaries occupied about the same proportion of casual conversation in the MOO as the weather did in real life). But the truth is, lag was more like air pollution: it was ugly, it was hazardous to the healthy functioning of MOOish society, and in the final analysis, it was attributable to nothing but the activities of that very same society. Debates sometimes flared up over just which of those activities contributed most to the lag. Quite a few MOOers seemed to believe it could all be blamed on the steady swelling of the database files, spreading funguslike across the surface of the hard drive as the number of inhabitants grew and their creations proliferated. Others argued it was something a little more complicated—most likely some factor of the number of people connected at any one time, with an equally probable correlation to the size and complexity of the objects those people were playing with. But either argument led to pretty much the same policy implications: small was beautiful, and projects as humongous as the Garden of Forking Paths had better show some seriously socially redeeming qualities if their architects wanted room to build them in.

Consequently, I couldn't help interpreting Finn's complaint about the lag as a veiled critique of my own burgeoning contribution to it. Nor did it encourage me much that he'd said so little else in the course of our walk, despite my chatty, running commentary on the Taoistical significance of the various sights along the way. My spirits sank as I imagined the scathing review he must have been composing in his silence, and when at last I led Finn up the rightward fork to the top of the hill, it only mildly amused me to see how well the final vista matched my mood.

From the top of a gently sloping hill, you look down upon a barren plain. The sky above is overcast, hidden. As far as you can see, it is the same: the closed face of the sky, the lifeless earth, their union at a horizon you will never reach.

There wasn't much more to say. Except this:

"Type 'look within,' " I said to Finn, and then I did the same.

After a laggy moment or two, I saw on my screen the cryptic but unmistakably gloomy counsel associated with the I Ching hexagram P'i, or Standstill: "Heaven and earth do not unite:/ The image of Standstill./ Thus the superior man falls back upon his inner worth/ In order to escape the difficulties./ He does not permit himself to be honored with revenue."

Briefly I pondered the words. In general they were taken to mean that the situation at hand had reached a hopeless impasse, which frankly sounded about right to me just then, and God knows the bit about not getting honored with revenue didn't make the passage seem any less painfully relevant. Still, it wasn't the I Ching's opinion I had come all the way out to this hilltop to hear. It was Finn's, and at this point I figured he might as well let me have it.

"So what do you think?" I asked. "Does this seem like a totally unconscionable byte-hog to you? Be honest."

And he was. But to my simultaneous relief and consternation, his honesty delivered neither the abrupt dismissal I had feared nor the unequivocal thumbs-up I had hoped for. Instead, Finn patiently explained that it was just too early to determine what the ARB's final judgment would be. "This thing is damn large," he informed me, but that didn't mean it couldn't win approval in the end: "You're going to have to convince us it's being used and enjoyed by the public, and that it is in some way themely."

I nodded politely, not exactly thrilled to be shown the hoops I still had to leap through to earn my quota biscuit, but not exactly devastated either. It was true, I knew, that the sin of "unthemeliness" ranked even higher than tinyscenery on the ARB's list of architectural no-no's. But I also knew that all I really had to do to bring the garden into conformity with LambdaMOO's "theme"—i.e., the fiction that everything there existed on or around the grounds of a vaguely magical mansion in the hills above Palo Alto—was spruce up its little jewel-box container and find some not-too-crowded tabletop or mantelpiece to put it on. As for showing that the garden was a hit with the public, well, what that appeared to mean was that I'd have to finish the thing and then test-market it a while before I could even think about beginning the official application process, and I supposed I could live with that.

But when Finn further advised me to meet with other ARB members before I did any more building, something in me snapped. Suddenly, and with profound irritation, I pictured an endless parade of bureaucrats marching through my creation, each one offering "helpful" suggestions and critiques while I took dutiful notes and tried hard to keep smiling lest some dyspeptic Servant of the People or another decided to dock me points for bad attitude.

"Aw fer shit's sake," I said, unable finally to contain my exasperation. "Well, at least it's nice to be reminded there's other political issues around here besides harassment."

And actually, I sort of meant that: there was a grim fascination in discovering just how little my balloon-borne rhapsody on the marvels of LambdaMOO's collective self-construction had anticipated the conflict-ridden land-use issues that awaited me down here on the ground. But despite Finn's own ongoing attempt at legislating ARB reform, my newfound interest in the sociopolitical dimensions of quota distribution evidently failed to rouse his sympathy. In fact, he rather seemed to take it personally:

"That's not fair," he snapped. "We can't approve every request these days. The MOO can't grow forever. The more space used, the slower the MOO, the worse off we all are."

And he was right, of course, in the long run. But that pretty much tore it for me. I didn't know quite how much stock to put in the rumors of Finn's mythic mischievousness, but right now I knew one thing for sure: if he'd ever been even one-tenth the hell-raising anarch those rumors made him out to be, his transformation into the straight-faced mouther of civic pieties who stood before me now was proof enough that something evil lurked in the heart of the ARB.

I apologized, all the same, for losing my cool. And in fact I would later come to recognize in Finn a figure every bit as colorful as—and a shade more complicated than—the Finn of legend. But for now our acquaintance had taught me only that

I wanted as little to do with the ARB as possible. I simply did not have the stomach to keep on canvassing its members for their approval; and more to the point, I found I didn't have the heart to let their potential disapproval stand between me and my foolish dream after all. There wasn't any question in my mind about it now: I would build my garden with or without the blessing of the MOOish state—and with or without it (I heard a brave, small voice inside me declare) I would get my quota back too.

Brave, did I say? Yes, and all the braver given that I didn't have the slightest idea, just then, that there was any source of quota in the whole wide MOOish world *except* the state. But five days later, as I sat on a beach by the virtual Pacific complaining about the ARB's tightfistedness to exu and another of her celebrity pals (the famous Doome: ARB member, quasi-wizardly programmer, and owner-architect of the storied night spot Club Doome), I learned that there was indeed another way for an overweening novice builder like myself to get his hands on more quota than he probably deserved:

"You could just talk to people and ask them to give you some of theirs," suggested Doome. "It might be the only answer at this point."

My RL mouth fell open. My RL eyes widened. How could I have missed so simple and so brilliant a solution?

Well, easily, as it turned out: elementary though it was, the notion that players ought to be allowed to transfer unused quota among themselves had only recently become a reality on LambdaMOO, and it remained one of the least conspicuous of the great post-Bungle social transformations. A ballot vote had ushered it in five months earlier (after weeks of vigorous campaigning by the ballot's author, a cheerful young gadfly by the name of dunkirk), but the wizards had been slow in bringing the new quota-transfer mechanisms up to the mandated user-friendly standards, and the practice hadn't yet caught on except among a small number of pioneering sophisticates.

Still, even in this embryonic form, quota-transfer was clearly an innovation of sweeping, even radical, implications. For one thing, it spelled the end of the ARB's state-sanctioned monopoly on the doling out of disk space; and as I quickly and somewhat giddily realized, it also therefore stood to take away much of the ARB's leverage over individual creative decisions. Beyond these immediate effects, however, lay the possibility of an even deeper challenge to the MOOish status quo. For though dunkirk had been careful to cast his petition as just another piece of LambdaMOO's ongoing democratization, nobody had mistaken it for a simple political reform. Quite plainly, quota-transfer was an economic reform, and quite plainly it was one that opened the door to a phenomenon whose world-transforming effects have long been known to outmuscle those of any mere system of government.

I refer, of course, to money. For what else had dunkirk's initiative made of quota but an incipient form of currency? Like the heads of cattle passed around among members of primitive herding societies, the MOO's most prized material resource could now be traded freely from player to player, and in thoroughly fungible, conveniently numbered little chunks, no less. It wasn't MOO-money yet, to be sure, but if ever there'd been a plum candidate for the job, transferable quota was it.

My curiosity was piqued, to say the least. There was something about the idea of virtual money that made me itch in a part of my brain I couldn't quite scratch: Wasn't money itself, I wondered, already a kind of virtual reality? Didn't its quasi-magical transmutation of worthless paper into genuine worth take place inside that same flickering gap between fact and fiction that VR inhabited? What then might it mean to reinvent money in VR's terms? Could a virtual society have any real use for such a thing—or would the desperate, necessity-driven suspension of disbelief that made money function in the real world simply dissolve amid the playful ambiguities of a place like LambdaMOO?

As it happened, this wasn't the first time I had asked myself these questions. In fact, I dated my fascination with virtual money to a moment several months prior to my discovery of quota-transfer, when I'd heard a talk touching glancingly on the subject at an RL symposium on MUDs at the Massachusetts Institute of Technology. The speaker was a man named Randall Farmer, who in the mid-1980s had helped design and run an early, commercial experiment in online VR called Habitat. Strictly speaking, Habitat wasn't a MUD, since it used animated, two-dimensional graphics to represent players and spaces, along with text-filled balloons hovering over the players' heads to convey their speech. But it worked enough like a MUD to merit the name, and all of the features Farmer described—including the monetary system that caught my attention—could easily have been ported over to the kinds of MUDs with which I was familiar.

Indeed, I had by that point already encountered a MUD or two in which pennies appeared randomly on the ground, so that if you spent enough time walking around looking for them, you might actually accumulate enough of them to pay for a virtual cab ride so that you wouldn't have to spend so much time walking around. But Habitat offered something rather more elaborate. On every day that a player logged in, Farmer explained, that player's Habitat bank account was credited with one hundred units of the local currency—virtual coins known as Tokens. Over and above this minimum wage, he continued, "players could acquire . . . funds by engaging in business, winning contests, finding buried treasure, and so on." And naturally there were things to buy: weapons, dolls, magic objects of various sorts, available mainly in vending machines called Vendroids, and redeemable at buy-back stations known as Pawn Machines (for a reasonably depreciated price, of course).

Here, in other words, was a rough stab at a full-fledged economy, and I was intrigued by its workings and its possibilities. But I found myself equally intrigued by my own sense that Habitat's Token system somehow came closer to being "real" money than that game of random pennies had. Once again I was reminded of the peculiar fact that it felt possible (as many MUDders besides myself have experienced) to distinguish among relative degrees of realness within these spaces in which everything seemed nonetheless to be at once true and false. And I began to suspect that figuring out the difference between "genuine" MUD money and "play" MUD money might shine a good deal of light into the murky semifictionality at the heart of VR's appeal.

Certainly Farmer's account of the Habitat experiment offered ample food for thought in that regard. For if the Token system looked like an interesting first step toward a robustly organic virtual economy, its failure to take off in that direction was no less interesting, and seemed mostly related to the ways in which the dictates of maintaining a believable make-believe world overrode the possibilities for cultivating something like functional markets. Some of these obstacles were really just temporary glitches of course. There was, for example, the Habitat world-builders' attempt to replicate the real-world phenomenon of local price variations by arbitrarily establishing price differences from Vendroid to Vendroid, which accidentally resulted one day in the sale-price of crystal balls at a certain Vendroid falling well below the amount being offered for the same item at a certain Pawn Machine on the other side of town. This was quickly discovered by a small band of players, who one night while the Habitat gods were sleeping spent hours shlepping crystal balls between the Vendroid and the Pawn Machine, buying low and selling high until by morning they had increased the balance in their bank accounts by two or three orders of magnitude.

Needless to say, that bug was fixed in pretty short order, but the programmers were never able to tackle a deeper problem—namely, that the economy they had created was an absurdly and inevitably inflationary one. After all, it didn't appear possible to compel the players to get virtual jobs—they *were* there to play—and hence it seemed necessary, if the Tokens were going to circulate at all, to keep on doling them out, automatically creating a hundred new ones out of thin air every time a player logged in for the day. The result in the long run was that Tokens grew increasingly worthless, while the objects most valued by the citizenry turned out to be (I kid you not) prosthetic heads, which players could win in contests and adventures of different sorts and use thereafter to replace their own heads as the mood struck them. Affluence became a matter not of how much money one had in the bank but of how many heads lined the walls of one's home, and nobody bothered translating the value of those heads into Tokens, or creating a Token-based market in heads, or indeed even trading heads for anything but other heads, as far as I know. Habitat's Tokens, then, ended up being just play money too.

Would quota-money meet the same fate? Or would it manage to take Habitat's experiment to the next level of virtual realism? And could I even say exactly what that level might look like? I couldn't, but by then it seemed clear to me that at the very least it would have to anchor the monetary system in what felt most real about the MOO, namely the human emotions invested in it. Desire, in other words—what MOOers really wanted out of the place, and what they were willing to pay for it—would have to be what regulated the creation of MOO money at every point in the system.

This was pretty basic economics, I suppose, but in practice it didn't seem all that simple to implement. As luck would have it, I came across an interesting attempt a day or two after my seaside visit with exu and Doome, when I logged in to an experimental MOO called Pt. MOOt, which was run out of the University of Texas and predicated on the notion (among others) that if you did not go out and acquire enough MOO money to buy some MOO food on a regular basis, your virtual body would end up flat on its back in the MOO hospital. Tying the circulation of money to the player's fundamental desire to keep circulating seemed like a sharp move to me, and I ended up spending a fair amount of time there, testing the system out. Mainly I occupied myself digging for gold in the virtual hills around the town of Pt. MOOt (yes, digging: there was a command for wielding a pickax and I spent hours typing and retyping it in hopes of finding a nugget) or roaming the countryside in search of bees to capture and sell to a bee-eating robot back in town who paid a decent amount for them. But it wasn't long before I realized that instead of selling the bees and nuggets to someone who really wanted them, I was just selling them back to the database whence they had emerged—so that in fact the whole process turned out to be just a more complicated version of Habitat's old mechanisms for creating virtual money out of thin air.

It wasn't that interesting things didn't happen in Pt. MOOt's economy. They did: joint-stock corporations emerged, and games of chance, and needless to say, the fact that Pt. MOOt managed to make the idea of taking up a virtual occupation even passingly appealing was in itself something of a coup. But none of this changed the harder fact that the money there remained, at bottom, funny.

What I took home from my Pt. MOOt foray, then, was a final, simple lesson: If LambdaMOO's quota was going to evolve into anything that could meaningfully be called real virtual money, it was going to have to do just that—evolve. As in the genesis of LambdaMOO's self-government, in other words, whatever monetary system might eventually take root there would do so only when at last a broad social need for it grew painfully obvious—and not simply because I or the wizards or anybody else happened to think it might be reality-enhancing, instructive, or just plain neat to try and implement it.

All the same, I couldn't help thinking that the possibilities implicit in the move to quota-transfer really were, well, sort of neat. Though to be honest, maybe neat wasn't exactly the word. Because I'll confess that for all the purely intellectual fascination those possibilities held for me, the one that ultimately loomed largest in my imagination was this: that somewhere in the newly fluid, protomonetary status of quota lurked some clever way for me to come into a big, fat, handsome pile of it, no strings attached, and overnight if possible.

Let me not give you the impression, however, that the problem of funding was my sole preoccupation in those days.

On the contrary, my virtual life had taken on a brisk, engaging complexity by that point, with quota worries only one among a healthy assortment of ongoing concerns and endeavors. Local politics, for instance, were more than ever on my mind, what with ARB elections in full swing and Minnie's antijudiciary campaign growing more confrontational by the day. *B:DisbandMeditation* had met with resounding defeat in the end, but that had hardly seemed to slow her down. She came back immediately with a leaner, meaner version, a petition entitled *P:NoMoreMediation* that abandoned altogether any pie-in-the-sky attempts at automating justice and focused laserlike on the rather simpler goal of annihilating the arbitration system (*Throw the Bums Out*, if I recall correctly, was the new petition's subtitle). At the same time, she was doing her very best—intentionally or not—to gum up for good the already gummy works of that haphazard system, filing one possibly-useful-but-maddeningly-incoherent reform proposal after another. The maddened arbitrators who had to vote on these proposals responded with increasing impatience, and Minnie responded with increasingly fevered insinuations of an elitist conspiracy arrayed against her, and inevitably the whole mess spilled out onto the pages of *social*, where the resulting reams of flame and counterflame began requiring much more of my attention than I really wanted to part with.

Nor was I alone in my discomfort with the situation. "I had a weird, middle of the night thought," exu paged me one afternoon. "Power on Lambda is being exercised now primarily by Minnie. She shapes and frames *all* public discourse these days."

Still feeling a little cranky about the ARB's lingering power to shape and frame *my* public discourse (and looking forward to casting my ARB-election vote for dunkirk, who promised to strip the board of its discretion over anything but the size of the total quota supply), I couldn't say I wholeheartedly agreed with exu's analysis. But that Minnie was a blight on the political culture? That much was fast on its way to becoming a MOOwide consensus. There were even, in some quarters, dark grumblings to be heard that drastic measures—including ominously unspecified acts of virtual violence—might be necessary to alleviate that blight.

Myself, though, I could care only so much about the public life of the MOO. After all, I had my private life there to look after too. And what that mostly seemed to entail right now was the very private business of acquiring an illicit second character. I had decided to call her Shayla: she would be a raven-haired and piercingly clear-eyed Irishwoman, a pickpocket and a vagabond, and the vehicle (I hoped) of as many untraceable cross-gendered conquests as I might find the time and interest for.

But first I had to get her embodied, and as I had anticipated, this was not an entirely uncomplicated proposition. To sign up for the new account I needed to submit a working Internet e-mail address, which in itself was no big challenge— as long as I was willing to submit my own. But in that case, the automatic character-creation system would officially register Shayla as a second character of Dr. Bombay's. And though in principle no humans except the LambdaMOO registrar (and, as always, the wizards) would have access to that information, that was already more humans than I wanted in on the secret. The trick, then, if I was going to keep the clandestine relationship between Shayla and the doctor hidden from even the all-seeing wizards, was to get my hands on a second Internet account, and one that didn't have my name attached to it.

Borrowing a friend's account was certainly not the way to go (I'd have to trust the friend to forward me the new character's password without peeking; fat chance). Nor was I shameless enough (or, let's face it, clever enough) to outright steal one. There remained to me, therefore, only the tender mercies of the free market, which in its infinite bounty soon delivered my solution in the form of a struggling local Internet access provider, desperate for new subscribers and happy to hand out a one-month trial e-mail account to anything that claimed to breathe, no questions asked.

I signed up as Rod Switt (a slight alteration of a dimly remembered college dormmate's name) and made my application for a LambdaMOO character posthaste. Certain flaky-looking aspects of my new provider's hook-up flagged the application as a suspicious one, and I was obliged to spend an anxious few days e-mailing even flakier explanations to the skeptical Lambda registrar (a post held at the time by the venerable wizard Sredna, a one-time RL girlfriend of Pavel's and the closest thing the MOO had to a den mother). But in the end she sent "Rod Switt" his new password anyway: I mouthed a silent, triumphal "Yes!" as the code came up on my fraudulent e-mail screen, experienced a brief twinge of guilt for having pulled the wool over the long-suffering Sredna's eyes, and promptly checked Shayla into the little red hotel inside the Monopoly set in the dining room.

She would not make her debut as a tinyvamp till several weeks later, though. It's possible I lacked the nerve for it just then, but what I told myself (and what was true in any case) was that I lacked the time. There was Dr. Bombay's own increasingly busy social calendar to manage, for one thing, and even that was swiftly getting crowded out now by the one activity that—finally—was taking precedence above all others for me: the long-postponed construction of the Garden of Forking Paths.

By then I was devoting hours to it daily—many more than I was spending with my friends on the MOO, and on average nearly as many as I spent at my real-life workplace. Indeed, I would have gladly quit my office job right then and there, I think, had someone told me of a way to make my living as a full-time virtual gardener. The work delighted me: I did it offline mostly, sometimes writing down the scenery on notepads at my desk, sometimes on a laptop computer as I reclined on the living room futon, but always feeling myself drawn into a virtual space as vivid and as ripe for exploration as the MOO itself was.

Perhaps even more so, by that point. Like many a player before me, after all, I was coming to recognize that my sense of virtual place grew more diffuse in very near proportion to the rate at which my virtual social life grew more concrete. The more my friendships multiplied and deepened, that is to say, the less I interacted with the environment in which those friendships were unfolding. Instead, I spent more and more of my MOO time holed up inside my television set juggling three or four private conversations at once—all of them conducted remotely of course, via the *page* command, and none of them, consequently, located anywhere in particular. exu would be talking at me from her nook in the roof of the barn, Niacin from the midst of one of his hot tub dips, S* from the unlinked bead of seawater she called home, and each of them in turn might be engaged in yet another broadly scattered handful of conversations. Add to this already well-dispersed scenario the technology of multiMOOing—which allowed us to make simultaneous connections to our Lambda and Interzone hangouts, bouncing back and forth between the two worlds with vertigo-inducing ease—and you can see why my conception of the MOO as a specific place had begun to blur even as my sense of it as a specific community sharpened.

Perhaps you can also see then why I so enjoyed the hours I spent working on the Garden of Forking Paths. I missed the richly environmental quality that had helped attract me to the MOO in the beginning, and the garden served in some ways to bring it back. My focus on the landscape there was total, and although much of that landscape still existed only in the murkier corners of my imagination, whatever did finally coalesce into written scenery seemed all the more intensely present to me for having sprung from my own creative efforts. With every daily batch of new descriptions (and every late-night run onto the MOO to paste them in), I was shaping a geography I knew as intimately as any sculptor ever knew the contours of her latest marblework: the barren trees and snowy mountain slopes of the wintry northwestern quadrant I'd shown Finn; the rocky canyons and flame-hued woods of the autumnal northeastern section, which I set to work on next; the bamboo groves and cool damp caverns of the vernal southeast after that; and as the end of my work drew near, the first patches of the bee-loud meadows and heat-baked sands that would fill the summertime southwestern quadrant when at last I finished.

In my mind, and on the MOO, I walked the pathways through those landscapes many times. Familiar though they were to me, the scenes I happened on along the way still managed now and then to take me by surprise. Sometimes, frustratingly enough, the surprise was learning that a particular detail or some turn of phrase just didn't work, and that I'd have to go back to my notepad then to ponder and revise. But other times what caught me short was nothing more or less than the ancient, mundane miracle of VR in full function: words meeting mind and sparking delicate, bright worlds into existence.

It was in those moments, mostly, that I felt the passing desire to leave all else behind and wander in the Garden of Forking Paths, uninterrupted, for another year or two at least.

.　　.　　.

But real life insisted on interrupting, of course—and for that matter, virtual life did too. I was finding, in particular, that I could no more put the nagging problem of my quota debt out of my mind than I could realistically abandon my day job. And with the garden heading toward completion there remained no easy solution in sight.

All along, I had been steadily following Doome's advice—approaching likely donors for as many bytes as they could spare. The likeliest had been the handful of my RL friends who had set up accounts on LambdaMOO, then never bothered much to use them. They left their characters sleeping and their rooms untouched, and best of all they left small piles of quota gathering dust and waiting for me to come along and scoop them up (it only took a friendly phone call or two). By now, though, I had fully tapped that reservoir of funds, and all I had to show for it was an insufficient 60 kilobytes.

Another 15K had come my way through somewhat more desperate means: I'd sold my ARB vote to a candidate who plainly had no other qualifications for the office than the size of his bankroll. He'd ended up losing anyway, so the transaction didn't weigh too heavily on my conscience, but still, it wasn't the sort of trick I cared to turn again.

Nor did I dare attempt the frankly sleazier maneuver of transferring Shayla's ill-gotten quota over to Dr. Bombay's account, as tempting as I found it. Quota-transfers were a matter of public record, and already my entirely legal donations from inactive friends had aroused the suspicions of a certain hyperactive do-gooder by the name of Memphistopheles, who'd sent me MOO-mail threatening to report me to Sredna unless I could prove these "friends" weren't actually bootleg spare characters of mine. In the end, a good word from exu had saved me from the wrath of Memf, but I'd learned my lesson: if I didn't want the MOO's small army of busybodies nosing around after Shayla's secret identity—and looking to turn it into a public scandal—I'd better limit her generosity toward Dr. Bombay to the occasional kind thought.

In any case the couple dozen kilobytes I could have skimmed off Shayla's account would have left me well short of the additional 100K I still needed. And so I was stumped. None of my active MOO friends had a byte to spare, it seemed. Nor could I really start asking strangers for donations until I had a finished product to show them. And why, I began to wonder, should I have to submit this sprawling labor of love to anyone's approval anyway? Why should a faceless public have any more right than the ARBocrats to determine the final value of the garden? There had to be a better way to fund the completion of my work, I felt, but what could it be?

The problem gnawed at me, and gnawed, until at last it evidently gnawed a small screw loose. This came to light one afternoon while I sat frustrated before my computer, unconnected to the MOO and hard at work on one of the occasional articles my ineluctable day job compelled me to write. In a routine fit of impatience and disgust with the words too-slowly filling up my screen, I cast my gaze away for just a moment—and suddenly was overpowered by a vision:

I saw myself constructing a machine, and on the surface of the machine I saw bright colors, and ornamental I Ching hexagrams, and a brass-plate label large and prominently affixed. And on the brass-plate label was embossed a single word, and the word was "Quotto." For this was no ordinary machine I was constructing, no: it was a machine built out of MOO-code and designed for the extraordinary purpose of selling tickets in a lottery of quota. And in my vision I saw that I must place this machine in the living room of LambdaMOO, and that the multitudes would flock to it then and buy their Quotto tickets for the low low price of one thin kilobyte each. And they would buy those tickets week after week, month after month, until the jackpots overflowed with fabulous amounts of quota while I, my fair share taken weekly off the top, grew fat with kilobytes as well.

The proceeds from this "quottery" would pay my garden debt many times over, but personal gain would hardly be my ultimate goal. Instead, I would take my staggering riches and use them to start a grant foundation in the public interest. I would call it alt.ARB, or something just as clever, and I would let the people know that every humble builder who had ever had a brilliant project scoffed at and denied by the soulless bean-counters of the Architecture Review Board could turn to my foundation for a helping and unquestioning hand. Thus then would I, Dr. Bombay, go down in LambdaMOO history: not only as the inventor of that great, enduring entertainment of the masses—Quotto!—but as the hero who at last laid low the ARB's undemocratic sway over free expression on the MOO.

The vision, as I said, was overpowering. I could barely focus on the RL work at hand for all the thoughts of instant MOO-wealth racing through my head. How I managed to complete the job at all that day I'll never know, but I did, and no sooner had I finished e-mailing my draft over to the office than I logged on to Lambda and teleported to the Crossroads to tell exu about my plans.

She listened patiently. And when I'd finished painting the picture of my imminent fame and fortune, she gently informed me that although I might indeed be remembered someday as the originator of Quotto, I couldn't now or ever claim to be the first MOO citizen to have come up with the idea of a grant foundation.

This let some air out of my sails, but I perked up again when I learned the name of the player who had beaten me to the punch: it was none other than dunkirk—the founding father of the new MOO economy, lately unsuccessful in the ARB elections but still one of Lambda's leading political thinkers as far as I was concerned. "He's been talking to me about starting a quota bank," said exu. "Nothing very thought out, but kind of a people's ARB. Sorta like yours only more along the lines of a lending institution. I'm not so sure it's the greatest idea, myself. For all its faults, I think the ARB does serve to encourage quality building around here. But you might want to try and brainstorm with him."

Before I could even answer, dunkirk appeared, summoned by a page from exu and emerging from the bowl of a small silver pipe that materialized in mid-air. And if the conversation that followed wasn't quite the historic meeting of the minds I guess I hoped it might be, our encounter proved a fruitful one all the same. dunkirk liked the lottery idea, for one thing, and he encouraged me to go ahead with it. He had also done a lot of thinking about the relationship between quota and currency, however, and he warned me against any approach that took the two as strictly analogous. "Quota is not quite like money," he said, which of course I knew, but then he ventured to explain why, and the way he put it hit me with the force of revelation:

"Quota is not quite like money because it is both the representative medium and the actual signified thing," dunkirk said.

And no, it wasn't exactly the pithiest of revelations—or even a very profound one, truth be told. But somehow I had failed till then to meet its implications head-on. I had failed to see in plain terms that, above all else, the phenomenon we call money is a semiotic system—a system of signs—and that like all such systems it depends on a slippery but critical distinction between the signifying object and the thing it signifies.

Even in my intuition that VR and money worked a similar conceptual magic, I hadn't quite grasped dunkirk's point, but now I saw the connection clearly: just as the possibility of endlessly imaginable universes like the MOO was rooted in the parlous gap between words and the world they were invented to describe, so too the genesis of money lay in the fateful slippage that occurred when some particularly valued kind of object suddenly came to stand for almost any kind of value imaginable. I saw, in other words, that quota would never become MOO-money until it stopped being just a mute quantity of hard-drive kilobytes and started signifying everything those kilobytes might possibly be worth to MOOers.

And I began at last to see just how the subtle workings of social evolution might eventually lead the MOO to this historic threshold. The details came to me more slowly than the initial insight did, but by the following day enough of them had fallen into place that I was eager to meet with dunkirk again and lay this second vision out for him. exu again made the social arrangements, dunkirk popped out of his silver pipe, and I began, there in the Crossroads, to sketch the scenario I felt certain would lead to the spontaneous generation of a full-blown money system on the MOO.

"OK. Let's say a person is desperate for quota for a very large project s/he's working on. S/he is so desperate in fact that s/he turns to the world's oldest profession for funds. . . ."

"Uh, hunting?" cracked dunkirk.

exu giggled.

I persisted: "S/he @digs herself a cheap motel room and sets up in business."

"Actually, I think photosynthesis came before hunting," dunkirk mused.

"Har har," said I. "So anyway, this person sets up a place where other characters can come and get their chlorophyll transformed into energy or some such thing, and . . . no that's not it."

exu . o O (Well you see, Timmy, when a pistil loves a stamen very, very much . . .)

I sighed IRL. I should have known better than to put sex in the middle of my scenario, since the subject rarely failed to set off one of those bouts of free-associative joking that always threatened, on the MOO, to run away with any line of thought more than a couple of ideas long. But I wasn't giving up. I sensed that beneath the wisecracks my audience was interested in what I was saying, and I still had a lot of it to say. I was about to explain to them that where my hypothetical MOOprostitute would have started out wanting quota simply because s/he needed the disk space, soon s/he might have clients who needed quota simply because they wanted to keep on visiting the MOOprostitute. I was going to explain how kilobytes would then no longer just be kilobytes, how the union of signifier and signified in quota would begin to come apart, and how the two would shortly go their separate ways, to circulate at last in a fully monetarized economy.

It didn't have to begin so tawdrily of course. Nor would it, in all likelihood. For the purposes of my argument, MOOhooking merely stood in for any number of possible catalyzing enterprises, and since its practitioners would have to compete with the crowds of willing amateurs already hanging out in the hot tub, it wasn't even the most promising of them. Popular hangouts like the tub itself, for instance, were rather harder to come by than tinysex partners, and sooner or later their owners would follow that fact to its logical economic conclusion. What would happen, then, when the quota-hungry builders of the most sought-after locales started charging for the right to gather in them? What would happen when Club Doome started costing half a K or so to get into? Or when the programmers of certain widely played-with toys started asking rental fees for the use of their products?

What would happen was that programmers and builders would no longer be the only players with a natural need for extra disk space—the masses of players who had always wanted mainly just to hang out and play would suddenly need it too. They would need it merely to maintain the quality of their MOO life, and that would now mean going out and earning it somehow. They might go hire themselves out as wageworkers on some master programmer's project. They might take up a berth in some former tinyhooker's now bustling house of ill-repute. They might go into a rapidly expanding banking industry. They might even escape the need to earn a living at all by hitting that big Quotto jackpot someday. But they would never, any longer, be able to get by without some steady supply of kilobytes, because from now on it would be quota that made the MOO go around.

All this I was going to explain to dunkirk and exu. But in the very moment that my fingers moved to continue typing out my explanation, fate blocked the way: a sudden wave of the heaviest lag I'd ever experienced came crashing down upon us all. My screen froze solid, and no amount of pecking at the keyboard could unfreeze it. Eventually I had to force a disconnect and spent another several minutes trying to log back on to the lag-ridden MOO. When finally I connected again, bringing Dr. Bombay out of the brief coma he'd lapsed into, dunkirk was still out like a light—and would remain so for the rest of the day. exu and I moved on to other topics, and as it happened I never did get another chance to discuss with dunkirk my vision of the future history of MOO-money.

Which was just as well, it turned out. For I decided later on that evening to take a look at the mailing list on which dunkirk's quota-transfer ballot had been debated before it was passed, and when I did I realized just what an unschooled naïf I would have seemed had circumstances allowed me to go on holding forth. My whole scenario, more or less, was laid out on the list already, hashed out and rehashed in far more detail and breadth than I could have managed. It was all there: prostitution, money-lending, entry fees for Club Doome and the hot tub, and many things besides. Stock exchanges, contract law, taxes, welfare payments—along with almost every other conceivable trapping of a modern market economy—were all projected onto the future of MOOish society, and their ramifications drawn.

It was a sobering experience, diving into the arguments of that list. I quickly learned that in my manic conceptual rush from Quotto to the upper reaches of high virtual finance, I had missed many complicating questions. How would inflation be kept in check, for instance, once the value of quota was no longer solely grounded in the fixed supply of hard-disk space? Or on the other hand, and perhaps more problematically, how would a free-wheeling quota-based economy affect the database's growing consumption of that supply? Wouldn't unused disk-space now flow more quickly into the hands of those most likely to use it, and wouldn't that tendency unleash an unprecedented flood of development, quite possibly exacerbating lag and other environmental ills beyond the limits of the tolerable? And what about the already troubling extent to which programmers enjoyed a privileged status on the MOO? Could a monetary system possibly do anything but further polarize that nascent class structure, casting programmers in the role of capitalists and nonprogrammers as the disenfranchised working stiffs?

dunkirk and other quota-transfer enthusiasts offered reassuring answers on all those counts. But the more I read, the less convinced I was that any of those answers addressed the larger issue lurking behind the questions. The point wasn't, finally, that the critics didn't think a virtual money system could work—it was that they didn't really *want* it to work. And the reason they didn't want it to work was easy enough to grasp: most people's experiences with the RL money system were not exactly delightful. The system generally delivered their daily bread and then some, true, but rarely without extracting its pound of anxiety and sweat, and always, it seemed, at the expense of the sort of genuine community many people looked for in the MOO. "If quota transfer does become a type of monetary system," wrote one dissenter (the eloquent space alien Nikto), "I believe we'll find that we won't have the utopia that some [of its] advocates seem to envision. Look around the real world. Free-market systems do not level the playing field, do not erase class distinctions. Them what has, gets. It will be no different here."

No less tellingly, the great hypothetical ticket-taker himself, Doome, had already posted a small dissent of his own, just a few messages before Nikto's. "I think it's kinda neat how Club Doome is being used as an example of how the 'quota=money' possibility could be used," he wrote. "But for the record, if it -does- become a 'quota=money' situation, I don't ever intend to charge quota from the patrons of Club Doome . . . :)"

It was when I read that, I guess, that I finally realized just how delirious my last two days of quota-crazed epiphanies had been. It wasn't that I felt particularly chastened by Doome's generosity—or that I thoroughly agreed with Nikto's grim prediction—but in them both I believed I now saw why quota would never mutate into money quite so spontaneously as I had been imagining. Five months into the era of quota-transfer, dunkirk still seemed to believe that just a little more time and a little more debugging were all that stood between his invention and its widespread adoption as a tool of daily MOOish life. But after my encounter with the *B:Quota-Transfer list, I couldn't help thinking that the real obstacle was a far less technical one. Quota-transfer promised any number of conveniences, and it even promised to make a few lucky MOOers fabulously quota rich, but it also threatened to import the multiple miseries of the RL economic system into a realm whose inhabitants could never quite stop hoping to build a happier world there than the real one. And as long as it harbored that threat, quota-transfer would remain the object of LambdaMOO's irreconcilable ambivalence—too appealing to be banished, but too dangerous to do much more than play with.

Which isn't to say the problem of how to divvy up the MOO's "natural" resources—its hard drive in particular—was something that would just fold up and go away if we all promised not to charge admission to our rooms. Money system or no money system, the problem remained; and I, with my quota debts still mounting, remained immersed in it.

The only difference now, of course, was that I dared no longer hope for any slick commercial scheme to come along and lift me out of my predicament. The Quotto machine, which only yesterday had held my imagination in its thrilling grip, seemed more ridiculous than riveting to me now. By this point I had given the idea sufficient thought to realize that only the most improbably full-blown of money systems would ever provide the broad distribution of greed and cash flow necessary to make a quota lottery profitable. And besides, even if I wanted to go ahead and program the damn machine anyway, I couldn't. In my eagerness to get myself back under quota, you see, I had been overlooking one simple but insurmountable problem: the operating system wouldn't let me write a stitch of new code until such time as I contrived (ha ha) to get myself back under quota.

And so there wasn't really anything for me to do but leave my fever-dreams of wealth behind and return, once more, to the place that had driven me to dream them.

I was in the garden the very next evening, pasting in descriptions of the final, summer quadrant. It was slow and somewhat tedious work at first, but as the night wore on, I felt a buoyant, brightening energy begin to hum within me. And the more it hummed, the more convinced I grew that this was not to be just another evening of modest, incremental additions to my slowly growing master-work. I hadn't thought this moment would arrive for at least another week or two, but by the time midnight rolled around there wasn't any doubting it: this very night, I was going to finish the Garden of Forking Paths.

I went and kissed Jessica good night and told her not to wait up for me, and then I sat back down in front of my computer, my mind awake with expectation. It was the busiest time of night, the tail end of the East Coast MOOers' after-dinner session overlapping with the start of the West Coast's shift, and between the resulting, bearish lag and the various pages I kept getting from chatty friends, it was all I could do to hammer out a couple brief landscapes in the first three hours after midnight. But around 3:30 the crowds thinned out and the lag died down and I began to make real headway. One place-description after another came to life inside my head and spilled out into the geography of LambdaMOO: An earth-dark hillside etched with soupy, pea-green, terraced rice paddies. A small, dune-draped lake island watched over by a chapped, abandoned light-house. A fruit grove bursting with improbable abundance, awash in the colors and the smells of mango, orange, basil, tulip.

I kept on dumping detail-laden landscapes into the abstract, undescribed locations of the garden until at last, a couple hours after daybreak, there were no more locations left to landscape. My work was done, almost, except for one important revision, which I'd been meaning to take care of for some time and hastened now to make complete. I made my way back to the center of the garden, and there I sat and thought a bit. And after I was done thinking, I typed a com-mand or two that wiped out my original, vague description of that spot (*You are standing on a path in a realm of pure possibility . . .*), and then I typed these words:

You are inside a small, open-walled summerhouse built in the Chinese style. Eight slender white columns support the octagonal roof of the structure, and a lengthy rice-paper scroll hangs attached to the column in front of you. On the scroll there is a good deal of writing; outside there is nothing to see but dim, swirling mists. And two paths: one leading north, one leading south. You are facing east.

I sat back and looked at the place again. It wasn't bad. The swirling mists were a little corny maybe, but the rest was more than serviceable. The hanging scroll would offer detailed instructions on how to navigate the labyrinth, once I wrote them up, and the eight-sided shape of the building would give the visitor a nicely subtle introduction, I thought, to the octal patterns of the garden and of the I Ching itself.

But what I liked best about the new description, I suppose, was that it did for that small portion of the garden what I had finally succeeded in doing to the garden as a whole: It transformed it from a place made of the airy, unspecified stuff of possibility into a place shot through with the color and texture of its own particularity. It made it real, in other words.

And yes, it's true there was a kind of melancholy in that transformation. There always is. Any one creation, after all, owes its existence to the myriad alternatives left uncreated, and the Garden of Forking Paths was no exception. An infinity of possible gardens had had to die that mine might live, and had I been in a more mournful mood just then I suppose I might have stopped to mourn them. I might have fallen prey to the paralysis of regret, setting out to wander the finished landscapes in an interminable round of revisions, seeking endlessly to recover this or that lost piece of the possible.

But I had no regrets that morning. None to speak of, anyway. The additional quota debt I had accumulated in that single, final burst of landscaping was roughly 25,000 bytes more than I'd been counting on, and I wasn't sure at that point how—or even if—I'd ever find a way to get myself back out of it. But I wasn't thinking about that now. Nor was I fretting much about the future of the MOOish economy, or about the growing tensions between the bureaucratic nature of the ARB and the populist spirit of the post-Bungle times, or for that matter about the possible absurdity of any attempt to shape a functional society in a world half grounded in imagination, the medium of pure possibility itself. All I was thinking, really, as I sat there eyeing in my own imagination the corners and the contours of that small, open-walled summerhouse built in the Chinese style, was that this would do for now.

I heard the sound of Jessica's alarm clock going off in the bedroom behind me, and I heard her rising groggily out of bed, and I took one final look at the words on my computer screen before it was time for me too to ready myself for the RL business of the day. I smiled and thought that this would do just fine.

QUOTA/
KB DEBT

NEW YORK CITY, AUGUST 1994

East 10th Street Between First and A
You are on a block of nicely spruced-up Lower East Side
  tenements running east to west, their heights uneven,
  their faces mostly brick, some painted and some not.
  A smattering of young and struggling ginkgo trees
  dots the sidewalks here. No parking space is left
  untaken.
Places of interest: The Famous Russian Baths of Tenth
  Street, at The Building Where The_Author Lives.

The_Author emerges from The Building Where The_Author
  Lives.

The_Author blinks into the morning sunshine. Looks like
  it's gonna be another scorcher.

The_Author walks west.

go west

First and 10th
This is the corner of First Avenue and East 10th
  Street. You can go north or south along First Avenue.
  You can go east or west along East 10th Street.

You see Buddy here.
The_Author is here.

Buddy catches your eye discreetly.

Buddy says, "Wassup, yo. Smoke? Coke?"

ignore buddy

follow author

The_Author goes west.

You cross First Avenue, nimbly dodging traffic as you go.

East 10th Street Between Second and First
You are on a nicely spruced-up block of Lower East Side
   tenements, running east to west, their heights
   uneven, their faces mostly brick, some painted and
   some not. A smattering of young and struggling ginkgo
   trees dots the sidewalks here. No parking space is
   left untaken.
The_Author is here.

The_Author is on his way to work. He's thinking of
   nothing in particular as he goes. Which means, these
   days, that he's aware of a presence, a kind of
   phantom continent, lying sunken just beneath the
   surface of his thoughts: the MOO. It's with him
   everywhere he goes now.

The_Author walks west.

Second and 10th
This is the corner of Second Avenue and East 10th
   Street. You can go north or south along Second Avenue.
   You can go east or west along East 10th Street.
The_Author is here.

The_Author goes west.

You cross Second Avenue, nimbly dodging traffic as you
   go.

East 10th Street Between Third and Second
You are on a Lower East Side block of nicely spruced-up
   row houses, running east to west, their heights
   uneven, their faces brick, some painted and some not.
   A phalanx of healthy ginkgo trees forms a leafy green
   arcade almost the full length of the block. No
   parking space is left untaken.
Places of interest: St. Mark's Church.
SweetJane (nodding) sits on a stoop at the west end of
   the block.
The_Author is here.

The_Author, as he walks, now turns his full attention
   to this unseen presence that accompanies him. He
   ponders, for the nth time, the mystery of its
   location, the way he feels it at once inside him,
   here, and outside, somewhere vaguely to the far west,
   and knows, as well, that he is fooling himself if he
   thinks it's really anywhere at all. He goes on
   fooling himself anyway.

The_Author ponders now, for the first time, something
   else about this presence: the gravity it has been
   taking on in recent weeks. In the beginning, he
   recalls, his daily visits were driven at least in
   part by something like a sense of duty, but not
   anymore. The MOO compells him now all on its own. It
   pulls at him when he is not logged on, and pulls with
   greater strength the more his head fills up with its
   dramas, its complexities. The MOO is getting denser,
   both inside him, here, and outside, somewhere vaguely
   to the west.

The_Author notices the junkie nodding on the stoop.

look sweetjane

SweetJane
Standing on a corner, suitcase in her hand, blah blah
  blah, hey listen that was twenty fuckin' years ago,
  you know, a girl can't stand on that corner forever,
  sooner or later she's got to _go_.
This one went down, from the looks of her, but maybe
  not so far she couldn't still come back up: bleached
  blond, the roots barely showing, nice summer dress a
  little rumpled, like she just got canned from a
  halfway decent secretarial gig. You wouldn't put her
  a day over thirty-five, and you won't find the track
  marks unless you look pretty hard.
She is barely conscious.
Carrying:
battered paperback

The_Author passes by SweetJane, close enough to make
  out the title of the book she holds in her hand (and
  was apparently reading just before she winked out).

look book in sweetjane

You see a funky old copy of the self-help classic
  Women Who Love Too Much.

The_Author sighs and walks on.

The_Author wonders what phantom continent SweetJane is
  visiting right now.

VR

6

The Schmoo Wars

Or TINYHISTORY, and the Ways a Programmer May Shape It

There were some, I am sure, who had said it was just a matter of time, and even I hadn't failed to detect its dark, unwholesome imminence hanging in the lag-choked LambdaMOO air. But all the same, the hacking of Minnie, when it came, came as a pretty nasty shock to me.

I learned about it on the day after I finished landscaping my garden, and I learned about it in the same way almost everybody else on the MOO already had: it was all over *social by then, like a big burst of red paint splashed against a wall and slowly drying into history. It had happened five days before, in the wee-est hours of a mid-August morning, while I had lain asleep and dreaming still, no doubt, of Quotto riches. The exact time of the occurrence was nowhere specified amid the frantic, angry messages that reported it, but the remaining details, as best I could make them out, were these:

The attacker probably logged on as a guest—and just as probably was a regular player, using one of the guest characters to cover his or her or his/her or its or eir or possibly h* tracks. Minnie was also logged on at the time, but shortly found herself disconnected and remained unable to reconnect for the duration of the attack. After Minnie was forced off, the attacker exploited an as-yet-undetermined security hole to gain direct access to her account and every object associated with it. Minnie, you'll recall, had done a lot of building in the days before she became a full-time political agitator, much of it dedicated to public use, and some of it, like the richly featured "hotter tub," quite widely enjoyed till now. But now, while Minnie attempted uselessly to access her account, the hotter tub and most of Minnie's other projects were being systematically disfigured or destroyed. The attacker went through her creations one by one, erasing code, rewriting descriptions, deleting entire objects, and finally—in a crowning gesture of negation I'll have more to say about in time—reducing the character-program that was Minnie herself to a three- or four-line shell of code, stripped of description, all possessions, and any capability of speech or action. When Minnie finally succeeded in logging on again, she couldn't even access the *look* command to see what had happened to her; she had to log in as a guest just to take in the extent of the devastation her character had suffered. In the words of one wizard summoned to the scene not long thereafter, the victim had quite literally been "hacked to bits."

Eventually, and with no small effort on the part of TomTraceback, Finn, and others deeply acquainted with the technical arcana of the database, the player object called Minnie was restored to some functional semblance of its former self. The rightful owner of that object, however, was still a bit of a wreck, if her ongoing performance on *social was anything to judge by. Since the early hours of the aftermath, it seemed, she had been asking the wizards for information that might help her track down the hacker, and whether she'd been asking politely or not I couldn't say; but when her nemesis the wizard Crotchet replied in a public post that the wizards had already done as much for her as Haakon's "New Direction" obliged them to, and that she'd have to look for any further remedies "within the bounds of the petition and arbitration systems," she sort of unambiguously lost it. Her rage flew out more naked and unhinged than I had ever seen it fly: in screenful after screenful of bitterness and long, half-finished sentences, she railed at Crotchet and the power structure she believed him to represent. She blamed him and his allies for what had happened, claimed that their unrelenting hostility toward her had in essence given the hacker "permission" to attack, and promised to make them pay for their complicity.

". . . I'll see Xerox, Pavel [Curtis], you, in real life court," she wrote in one message, and in the next she swore she meant it: "I have the resources (both financial and ethical), the time, enough faith and knowledge of what rl law is, what the application of real life democracy and individual voice in a VR environment was _supposed_ to translate into here (and how you HAVE been using this for your own ego/power needs), enough faith in [the ability of] 'normal intelligent players' to see the truth (as they have when my efforts have been pointed out to them in one-on-one situations, they SEE what the real story is—oh, have they been SHOCKED when they have seen . . ."

The rant went on, in message after message. She never bothered to explain just what the legal basis for her RL suit might be; she had too many other things to say. Too many threats to make, conspirators to denounce, obscure and arguable injustices and injuries to nurse. As I waded forward through her messages, I felt whatever sympathy I'd started out with draining away. Her anger was coming out all ugly, warped, and I just wanted to get through and past it now as quickly as I could.

But then, toward the end of that first, bilious flood of posts, she turned the focus back to the ultimately inarguable injury that had just been done her, and there I could not help but empathize. The damage inflicted on the objects she had built, she now explained, would not be easily repaired. The security flaw the hacker had exploited could very well still lurk somewhere within them, and finding and uprooting it did not appear to be a simple matter. Some techie types were telling Minnie that the only really safe way to proceed was to scrap the entire oeuvre and start again from scratch, if at all. Others said that such prescriptions were extreme, but that a complete recovery would still require a long, painstaking period of studying the objects for holes. In either case, the very thought of something similar ever happening to my own newly finished piece of Lambda real estate sent a chill into my bones.

"The creations here," wrote Minnie, "all creations of ours, from our real lives and how we experience them in this medium, are our 'children.' My children were killed. A year's worth of BUTT BUSTING WORK, because of an unstable person's getting 'permission' from the methods and styles of those people here who haven't a clue how to live 'communally.' Thanks to Finn, to Tom, some of my 'children' have been resuscitated, but are 'scarred'. . . .

"The bottom line? 'LambdaMOO is not safe for children and other living things.'"

God, Minnie could be sappy when she wanted to be, and I have no doubt that when she wrote those words, she very much did want to be. But as I read on through the messages that had piled up on *social*, I soon learned that the notion of MOOish creations as children had a more than merely sentimental relevance to Minnie's case.

In general MOOish usage, as a matter of fact, the notion was a strictly technical one, and deeply rooted in the way the database was structured. To put it simply, every item, or "object," in the database was said to be a "child" of some other object. And what that meant was roughly this: each object was in fact a little bundle of programs, and though that bundle might have its own capabilities and data coded into it by its human owner, it also had capabilities and data that it "inherited" from another such bundle, which was called its "parent" and was assigned to it at the moment of its creation.

Thus, for example, the set of programs representing my own character, Dr. Bombay (also known as object #53475), was born a child of the "builder" player class (#630), a "generic" object that gave him the ability to do things like @*dig* rooms and keep track of quota. In turn the generic builder was descended from alFarad's generic player class (#3133), which gave various additional powers to the builder player class and all its children (Dr. Bombay included). alFarad's player class itself descended directly from the generic player (#6, or in the programming shorthand reserved for certain elemental objects, simply "$player"), which conferred such basic player functions as talking, walking, and teleporting on its many descendants. And finally, at the top of this family tree, there was $player's parent: $root (#1), the fundamental object itself, endowing every last little thing on the MOO with the simple attributes (location, name, description, movability) that defined existence within the limits of the MOOish universe.

"We are all children of $root," I was told once by a wise old programmer (well, MOO-old anyway; I think he was twenty-four in real life), and I got the sense he meant the mysticism of the phrasing only half in jest. For there really was something just the slightest bit sublime in what he was saying: beneath the conflict and confusion and banality of the players' daily interactions, beneath the loopy, fragmentary geography those players had built up around themselves, an elegant oneness shaped the logical structure of LambdaMOO, now and for as long as the database might live. You could flood that database with a thousand different novel sorts of objects (if you had the quota), you could change those objects' lineages a thousand different times once you'd created them (if you knew how to work the handy @*chparent* command), but you never would perturb the infinitely extensible order of things in which each of those objects had its place—and through which, by the mediating grace of $root, each was ultimately related to every other.

In object-oriented programming circles (and the acronym MOO, remember, stood for "MUD, Object Oriented"), this sort of universal hierarchy was sometimes called an ontology, and that made sense. The MOO's hierarchy, in particular, had a striking similarity to such classical ontologies as the medieval Great Chain of Being, in which each entity in the cosmos depended for its existence on a higher level of entity, which in turn depended on a higher level, and so on, and so on, all the way up through armies of angels to the lap of God. But just like the Chain of Being, the MOOish ontology faced a tricky question once it reached that highest level: on what exactly did the ultimate source of being itself depend? Medieval scholars answered that question with the neat, if paradoxical, trick of letting God depend upon Himself, but LambdaMOO's designers turned for their solution to a darker, older model. They fashioned their ontology in such a way that the $root of all being rested upon being's own negation—upon the void, or more precisely, on a nonexistent object they called $nothing (#-1).

And $nothing, let me say, friends, was a strange, hair-raising thing to contemplate. "It is an invalid object, insubstantial in the database," said the wise programmer. "But it's a valid parent, used as an abstract for 'nothing.' So when something doesn't have a parent, it's parented to $nothing." In other words, $nothing was the perfect parent for $root, which in order to be a proper object had to have a parent, yet in order to be $root had to have no proper objects standing over it in the hierarchy of descent. Thus then did $nothing serve, however insubstantially, to anchor $root in its rightful place atop the MOO's chain of being. Thus too, though, was it a kind of abomination for any other object but $root to be directly parented to $nothing. For once @chparented to $nothing, an object was no longer in the lineage of $root, and therefore stood apart from the great, overarching family in which all things MOOish found existence. It became a thing as wraithlike, featureless, and invalid as $nothing itself. And while this was indeed a twisted state of affairs for any object to fall into, it could *really* screw around with things when the object in question was a player.

Some claimed, for instance, that by temporarily changing your own player object's parentage to $nothing, you could pervert the natural order of the database in such a manner as to acquire unholy amounts of wealth and power. "If someone knows what they're doing," said the wise old programmer, "they can push themselves to the void and come back as something 'inhuman' in the context of the database. No registered name, as much quota as they like. Maybe even make themselves a wizard." But such a scam, if it was even truly possible, was not for any but the lucky few, the adepts. For the great majority of players, the only likely way to emerge from so close a brush with $nothing was as a burnt-out residue of playerhood, a husk—a three- or four-line shell of code, in short, stripped of description, all possessions, and any capability of speech or action.

And if you were beginning to wonder why I'd strayed from my account of Minnie's hacking into these obscure realms of the technical, well, wonder no more. How else could I have readied you to grasp just what it meant to learn, as I now did, the precise nature of that "crowning gesture of negation" mentioned earlier? How else could I have hoped you'd understand it wasn't just a sappy sort of tingle I felt running up my spine when I discovered that the essence of the crime against Minnie was that she had been rendered—if only for a little while— a child of $nothing?

This bit of news turned up on *social courtesy of that same wise old programmer who, much later, would induct me into the deeper mysteries of the MOOish ontology, and who also, by the way, was Finn. His post hit the list at the end of a longish string of messages that had followed in the wake of Minnie's outburst, none of them particularly sympathetic. No one had actually come out and said she'd had it coming to her, but the implication was there: she'd been a thorn in the polity's side too long to ask for its condolences now, said some; her amateurish programming skills had left her and her objects wide open to attack, said others. But Finn, at last, burst in upon this chorus of judgment with an exasperated vengeance.

"Are you people actually supporting the hacking of Minnie's character?" he fumed. "Are you supporting her being chparented to $nothing?"

And there it was: the first public mention of Minnie's close encounter with $nothing-ness. And as I took it in, I felt the aforementioned tingling of my spine and knew, as I said, that it wasn't just the weird poetry of the programming jargon that was doing the tingling. I sensed a new understanding of the MOO taking shape inside me, just tentatively enough that had Finn not proceeded there and then to more or less spell it out for me, it might have faded back out of my mind as quietly as it had appeared. But Finn went on:

"Many folks made a big deal about 'MOOrape' a few months ago, equating RL rape with naughty words here on the MOO. What happened to Minnie here is the closest you'll come to a virtual rape. Real violation. An act of violence, not sex."

And sure, I might have quibbled with the offhand implication that the crimes of Mr. Bungle had amounted to no more than an exchange of naughty words. But at the same time Finn's point made me realize how incompletely I had learned the lessons of my encounter with the Bungle Affair. I had assimilated pretty well the fact that in a world built wholly out of language, the power of language is magnified in ways both devastating and illuminating. But what I hadn't quite appreciated was this: the language from which LambdaMOO was built was of two very different kinds. The writer in me had of course been quick to recognize the power of the "naughty words" Mr. Bungle wielded against his victims, for they had been composed in so-called "natural" language, the kind that writers and other humans have always used among themselves, one imagination speaking to another. But the other language spoken on the MOO—the rigorously logical language of the database itself—had failed to make the same impression on me.

True, I had in a grand and fuzzy way perceived that what I thought of as the "magic of the MOO" derived in large part from the logic of computer code. But when it came to acquainting myself with the day-to-day importance of the MOO's actual programming language, I'd pretty much taken a rain check. And now Finn was pretty much informing me the check was due. Now, after months of ignoring the language of the database as studiedly as I could—after having poured thousands of lovingly crafted words and only ten indifferent lines of code into the making of my garden, and after having voted no on *B:DisbandMediation largely out of knee-jerk scorn for its faith in the ability of programming to shape human behavior—I was obliged to recognize that that language could be wielded just as forcefully as Mr. Bungle's words of violation had been. In its vocabulary, words like *parent*, *child*, and *$nothing* might not have the deep associative resonances they would if spoken to a human being, but I had only to review the damages inflicted on Minnie to see what sort of power those words conveyed when whispered straight into the heart of the machine our little world was conjured from.

I could ignore that power no longer, it was clear; not if I wanted to understand how power really functioned in MOOish society. It would not be necessary, I decided, to become fluent in the language of the database myself, but I resolved thenceforth to pay much closer attention to the social roles of those who had attained such fluency—to their positions and their tactics in the political skirmishes of the MOO, to the parts they had played and were still playing in Lambda's long, strange virtual history.

This decision meant, to start with, that I must now pay much closer attention to Finn. Because I had the feeling that if any single event in Lambda's virtual history had anything to teach me about the power of the programmer, it was that mythic moment usually referred to as the Schmoo Wars. And of course, if anyone had anything to teach me about the Schmoo Wars—well, it was Finn, now wasn't it?

And so, not long thereafter, I made a point of calling on young Finn and asking him to tell me some of what he could recall about those days. And not long after that, I made another visit and asked him if he'd tell me more. And in time I made visits to other players—veterans, sideline observers, informed commentators—all of whom had their own versions of those famous events to report, so that within a few weeks time I had acquired an ample collection of recollections indeed.

Herewith, then, I submit to you the tale those recollections tell.

It begins, as tales will, at the beginning. And in the beginning, naturally, was the code. And naturally, the code was with Pavel.

And Pavel saw that it was good, because he'd been looking for something like it for a while now. Ever since he first learned about MUDs, in fact, and started toying with the idea of setting one up on a computer at the Xerox Palo Alto Research Center, where he worked, Pavel had been closely examining the various strains of MUD software available to would-be gods (as MUDders sometimes called the people whose computers sustained their digital worlds). To the fanatical game-player in him, there was much to admire about these so-called "MUD server" programs and the adventurous realms of dragon-chasing fantasy they brought so vividly to life. To the professional programmer in him, however, existing MUDware mostly looked like weekend coding projects hacked together by fanatically game-playing undergraduates, which indeed it mostly was. For his own system, he wanted something with a little more technical sophistication. On top of that, he wanted something with a lot less emphasis on fanatical game playing and a lot more room for collective world building. And when the day came that he stumbled across a piece of software called MOO—a new kind of MUD server with a powerful, object-oriented programming language built into it—he decided he had more or less found the something he was looking for.

So he got hold of the source code to that first MOO server—written by a Canadian undergraduate named Stephen White—and with the blessings both of White and of his own employer, he spent the next couple months knocking it into the sort of shape the professional programmer in him could live with. And when he was done doing that, he compiled the code into a working piece of software, loaded the software onto a computer hooked up to the Internet, and typed into that computer a command that said, in effect, "Let there be LambdaMOO."

The date was October 30, 1990, and the place was rather primitive. In the middle of it stood a rough stab at the mansion, Pavel's first creation after building himself a character (which would eventually go by the name of Haakon, but which for now let's just call object #2). His plans for the structure were based almost room for room on his own home in the hills near Palo Alto, and though in years to follow it would, as you already know, acquire a densely lived-in and impossibly ornate encrustation of annexes, extensions, towers, tunnels, wormholes, secret chambers, and pocket universes, right now it was just the barest core of a ten-room split-level California ranch house with a single wizard wandering its lonesome passageways, checking for bugs.

The place got cozy quickly, though. Pavel invited various friends and colleagues to take up residence (almost all of them professional programmers like himself, or pros in training), and they promptly set about building things up. On the ninth day, Pavel's ex-girlfriend Jane Anders arrived, became enaJ (object #66), and began making plans to add a VR version of Pavel's RL hot tub, which #2 himself had neglected to supply. To the subsequent delight of untold generations of players, enaJ had object #388, the hot tub, up and running within a few weeks. By January, she had applied her formidable programming skills to the completion of a working model of Pavel's swimming pool (which brought the number of objects in the database to #1428), and not too long thereafter someone dug a small, enchanted cavern beneath the pool, complete with dangerous dwarves and hidden treasure. Other friends of Pavel's busied themselves inventing such basic amenities as teleportation and paging, as well as an extensive system of "help" files to assist future players in the use of these inventions and others.

And all the while more friends kept turning up, and friends of friends, and soon the friends of friends were joined by strangers who were only chasing down a rumor they had heard, out on the Net, about a kind of programmers' paradise—a place where everything was made of code, and everyone knew how to code, and every day the very laws of physics of the place were tweaked a little by some clever hacker or another.

A short time after that, Pavel decided the moment had arrived to make an official announcement to the Internet at large, declaring LambdaMOO at last open to the general public. This was in February of 1991, according to some old-timers, although considering the fact that back then MOOers paid less attention to the passage of RL time than they did to the steady, object-numbered growth of the database, it is perhaps more accurate to say that LambdaMOO went public some time around #2400.

In any case, the announcement wasn't quite the world-changing event many existing residents half-feared it would be. Pavel, now officially known as Haakon (and less officially as Lambda, the name of the "civilian" character he logged in to when not required to exercise his archwizardly powers), had steeled himself for an influx of uncouth, chat-happy newbies. He had even deputized enaJ into his small staff of wizards for the express purpose, among others, of dealing with the expected increase in social unrest and bad programming (she took the wizardly title Sredna, under which name, you may recall, she would one day be duped into giving me the illegal spare character Shayla). But though the uncouth newbies did arrive in droves, and though the number of petty conflicts and broken objects requiring wizardly attention did begin to creep steadily upward, by and large the MOO remained as attractive to the more technologically sophisticated sort of MUDder as it had always been.

If anything, in fact, the appeal was only greater now. For not only did the gathering crowds of idle socializers provide a budding little mass audience for the ingenious feats of the programming elite—they also provided the key ingredient required for any elite to properly exist as such: a non-elite. Not that anyone was about to come right out and put it quite that way. As in many a small community, whatever divisions existed then stayed hidden beneath the social surface, and the surface remained a mostly friendly one. "In the early days the biggest arguments revolved around whether to use U.S. or Australian spellings in the names of programming functions," Haakon/Lambda later recalled, adding with a certain wistfulness that, back then, the place had still been intimate enough that he could (and did) personally greet each new player upon arrival.

A similar nostalgia tended to creep into the recollections of other wizards and their cronies, and if you listened to them long enough you might come away with the impression that those first months after LambdaMOO's public opening were a Golden Age—a time when MOOers lived in peace and productivity and had no need of any rules or disciplinary structures other than (it went without saying) the natural respect accorded by the chattering new arrivals to their technically accomplished elders.

But in fact the need for a more clearly defined social order was already becoming apparent. Unspoken local norms were quickly emerging, and the wizards were spending much of their time explaining them to the newbies who, in blissful ignorance, routinely transgressed them. In sympathy with his wizard friends, the ancient alFarad (#45) proposed to Haakon that a help file on "manners" be written up and made required reading for new MOOers. Haakon agreed, and made it so—and lo, *help manners* became a sort of MOOish Code of Hammurabi, surviving well into the age of post-Bungle democracy as the informal law of the land. Which was surprising in a way, since the document was in some of its particulars a baffling one. What was a newbie to make, for instance, of the stern proscription against hunting for "magic numbers"—a practice in which creators of objects built and destroyed dozens or even hundreds of objects in quick succession, rapidly running up the database's object count until they acquired an elegant number like #5000 or #6666 or #10101? Nobody unfamiliar with the MOOish tendency to fetishize the object count as the natural measure of virtual history could possibly guess what the fuss might be, and even some MOOers well versed in local ways thought the issue a somewhat ridiculous one. Yet experience had taught that magic-number hunting was a perennial source of strife, and *help manners* was in that sense wise to discourage it.

Also wise were the document's more common-sense rules for conflict-resolution, such as the famous dictum " 'Vengeance is ours,' saith the wizards," which enshrined the civilizing principle that disputes should be settled by official judgment rather than bare-knuckle feuding. There was no way, of course, to thoroughly eradicate the newbies' natural tendency to disturb the peace (kids will be kids), but the publication of *help manners* went a long way toward keeping that tendancy in check.

More and more, however, the MOO was being visited by players whom apparently no amount of rule-making could dissuade from raising hell. Some of these arrivals—like the bands of marauding fratboy types who blew in from the finest engineering schools in the land and set about afflicting the living-room crowd with screenfuls of all-caps nonsense and assorted sexual harassments—were easy enough to deal with through other means. Haakon or Sredna, say, would give them a few friendly words of counsel (which they would ignore) and then would simply kick them off the system as many times as it took to make them tire of coming back.

But others were more persistent—and more devious. Widely and vehemently reproached for ripping through all the object numbers from #14000 to #14999 in his quest for the magic #15000, a player by the name of Gottesmord responded to the condemnation with an obsessed vindictiveness. He took to playing mind games on people, issuing vague threats and deploying multiple characters to confuse and dismay the objects of his resentment, enaJ being one of his favorite targets. Frequently he staged fights between his own characters and then called on the unwitting enaJ to intervene in them, revealing the charade only after she'd wasted hours of earnest effort on resolving the dispute. Once, he even visited her in the guise of one of his spares, pretending to be a sympathetic stranger, and volunteered to help work things out between her and Gottesmord. She took the bait, spent a long, soul-searching evening engaged in "mediated" discussion with her tormenter, and nearly resigned her wizardship in disgust after he gloatingly revealed his deception.

Eventually Gottesmord was toaded, as was another famous bad boy of the time—Satyrik, who was said to mostly log on very drunk, and who in his various run-ins with the wizardry took such an intense disliking to the wizard Crotchet that he finally made his way to Crotchet's RL home and left an ominous-looking "voodoo" offering on his porch, along with roughly scrawled threats against the wizard's wife and children.

That things were getting slightly out of hand by then was obvious, perhaps. But where exactly they were heading was a more uncertain matter. Till now, the escalating breaches of civility in and around Lambda House suggested nothing more, all things considered, than the accelerated rate of random offense and indecorousness that sets in when any successful house party hits its stride. The possibility that this growing rowdiness might presently lead to agitation of another order altogether—that some as-yet-unknown transgressor of the local norms was soon to spark a controversy so wide-ranging as to introduce into LambdaMOO's still relatively homey atmosphere the rudiments of what could only be called class struggle—did not appear to be much on anybody's mind at the moment. Nor, at the moment, was it necessarily anything *more* than a possibility.

But at some point it became an inevitability. What that point was, exactly, may be debated by historians to come, but for my money there is really just one moment worth considering: The one in which Finn announced, to an unsuspecting virtual world, that he had invented Schmoo.

Did Finn himself suspect what he was loosing on the MOO? Perhaps. He certainly wasn't likely to mind if the social status quo got shaken up a little. He had arrived on Lambda about four months earlier, at the height of the wizards' fondly remembered Golden Age, and frankly hadn't found things all that golden, himself.

Not that he didn't like the place. On the contrary: after an early few months MUDding around on smaller, less flexible servers (where he'd discovered the joys of tinysex and virtual dragonslaying) he had stumbled into the open-ended universe of LambdaMOO as if into an epiphany. Here was a realm, he felt, where he could give free rein to the creative urges roiling in him—as he could not IRL, where he was slogging through freshman year at a state university near his hometown in West Virginia and finding himself bored to the brink of expulsion. He soon was MOOing almost every chance he got—teaching himself to program, designing and redesigning his character, building himself an elaborate Gothic tower annexed to the mansion, and generally relishing the possibilities implicit in a place as malleable and complex as LambdaMOO. "All gnarled and infinite," he called it, three years later, still enthusiastic even though (or possibly because) his RL circumstances hadn't much improved in the meanwhile. By the time I got to know him, he had dropped out of school and moved back, unemployed, into the basement of his parents' house, where he kept vampire's hours, rising from his bed around 11 P.M. each night so as to have the family's single phone line to himself. He was active on Lambda "nearly every waking moment," he claimed, and didn't seem to want it any other way.

"MOO is for me," said Finn. "It's for all the creators. You can change the world here, not just live in it."

But early on in his new virtual life, Finn discovered there was one aspect of the MOO he couldn't very easily change: its social structure. And that was a shame, in Finn's opinion, because the people he perceived as sitting at the top of that structure—the technical sophisticates who'd been the first to colonize the MOO—were not his sort of people at all. They were a soulless bunch, from what he'd seen of them—more interested in algorithms than in artistry, or even fun. They had a typical hacker's taste for cutting wit, ironic and dry, which dominated public expression on the MOO and left little room for the sort of "quirky, ribald humor" Finn went in for. And worst of all, at least from the perspective of a technological innocent like Finn ("I was just some kid with an Apple][whose only programming experience was in BASIC"), they seemed a lot less eager to share their ample expertise with unschooled newbies than to ridicule them for not already being experts themselves.

You may rest assured, of course, that the players Finn thus spoke of would dispute this portrait in nearly all its particulars—and not without reason, for Finn was nothing if not a hothead in his early days. But all the same, he wasn't the only MOOer who found the existing social climate back then somewhat oppressive. exu, for instance, who arrived a little while after him, would later remember that era as "the Reign of Snide Programmers Terror, when all nontechies were subject to showers of verbal abuse." exu and others mostly grinned and bore up under all the free-floating attitude, however, whereas in Finn it rankled, and became the basis for an abiding grudge against the MOO's techno-literate establishment. "I did not get along with them, no," he told me. "Moreso, I was disgusted by them. They were like high school geeks who now had their chance to be the in-crowd. Like they never learned a lesson being ridiculed in high school. They _wanted_ to be hip. They wanted to gather in little circles and smirk at the others. Except these people didn't have any sort of coolness on their side. No social skills. They had a proficiency in manipulating digits."

Was Finn then out to prove something when he downloaded the programmer's manual and began immersing himself in its esoteric details? Was he trying to show that, if he wanted to, he could be just as good at juggling bits and tweaking algorithms as the snidest of the überprogrammers? Finn denied it. "I don't program to sharpen my logic skills," he insisted. "I program because that's the mode of creation here. I program to CREATE."

Even so, of all the things he could have chosen to create in the beginning, there were few that would have tested his technical abilities as thoroughly and as publicly as the one he picked out, finally, for his first big programming project: a full-blown player class.

What could he have been thinking? There were proper sorts of objects for a novice programmer to start with, and player classes definitely weren't among them. Typically, you tried your hand at first on something simple and unobtrusive, like a five-line pair of fuzzy dice you could toss now and then for your own amusement, or a dozen-line box of "edible" jelly donuts you could pass around when friends dropped by your room (*eat donut,* they might type, and on their screens perhaps they'd see the words *You bite into the sugar-powdered morsel, savoring the goo that oozes from its flaky heart and swallowing with guilty satisfaction*).

After that, if you were starting to feel ambitious, you could move on to programming for the public at large. Suppose, for instance, that you'd done a little tinkering and produced a pair of jelly-filled fuzzy dice (object #16000, say), which you could either play craps with or feed to your friends, as mood and circumstances dictated. Well, that was a versatile little object indeed, and maybe other players, less adept at tinkering than you, might want to have one just like it for themselves. So you typed a quick command and presto: #16000 was made "fertile," meaning that anyone who wanted to could now create a child of it, just by typing *@create #16000.* The infertile child thus brought into the world had its own distinct object number (and whatever name and description its new owner chose to give it) but was in all other respects a carbon copy of its parent. Meanwhile the parent now faded, conceptually speaking, from the realm of the particular, existing essentially as an archetype whose only real purpose was providing usable copies of itself.

It became, that is to say, a generic object—which was precisely the kind of object you wanted to make if you wanted to make a name for yourself as a programmer. The more children an object of yours generated, after all, the more players were out there enjoying your handiwork and, hopefully, talking it up. Nor did it always require all that much in the way of programming skill, truth be told, to score a big hit with the MOOish crowds. To my knowledge, no fuzzy jelly dice were ever put in circulation on the MOO, but gadgets of roughly equivalent simplicity were often widely used. Most of them did practical things like alert their users when a friend logged on, or enable them to look at objects without being in the same room as them (such tools were typically programmed as "feature objects," or FOs, whose capabilities could be plugged directly into a MOOer's own player object without using up the quota needed to create a child). But if you didn't mind risking the disdain of serious programmers, there was one exceptionally easy way to almost guarantee broad popularity for your work while contributing absolutely nothing of practical value to the MOO: you could build a bonker.

For some reason MOOers, especially new ones, just could not get their fill of bonkers, which were a lowbrow form of entertainment similar to voodoo dolls, only without the sadistic edge. Once programmed, a bonker served essentially one purpose: it was to be taken to the living room or some other crowded place and swung merrily at the head of the nearest player, thus causing that player to produce an involuntary, preprogrammed utterance or action of some sort. Fart-inducing bonkers were frequently deployed, as were bonking technologies designed to make the bonkee sing a random line or two from the oeuvre of some particularly popular recording artist. The possibilities were not exactly endless, but demand for novel sorts of bonkers seemed insatiable, and even if you just combined a few existing functions into one multipurpose bonking machine, you could easily have a MOO-wide hit on your hands.

Or so a good many beginning programmers seemed to believe. The MOO was littered with their hopeful efforts—devices whose invention was hastily announced with a note on the refrigerator door, and whose descriptions invariably went something like this one, gleaned from a quick glance at "Bobbit's Kool Nirvana Bonker" (#87551), an object dedicated to spreading the words of the late great Kurt Cobain, among several other more obscure purposes:

> *You see a really Kool FO. It is a nirvanabonker <nirbonk> and it has more than 160 diffrent bonks. . . . It has all of their albums on it and has alot of there other songs not on albums too. It is more than a nirvana bonker though. You can Bughug people, Kill. people, Send people into the sewer <person>. . . . Also you can smash somebody to a flat spot with a wooden hammer. More verbs are coming. Tell all your friends about this KOol FO :). Nirvana Rules.*

Well, now: Could Finn have possibly done worse?

Had he but chosen to try out his nascent programming knowledge on a simple bonker, I have no doubt he would have produced a masterwork of its kind. Had he attempted something with just a touch more socially redeeming value—some modestly useful little feature object, say—he might have even earned the first glimmerings of respect from his programming betters. From there he could have gone on gradually acquiring a solid reputation, moving slowly, patiently, up the scale of difficulty in his choice of projects. A generic room whose lighting changed with the time of day? A helicopter made to dart precisely amid the drifting balloons of Lambda's sky? Who knows? Perhaps it might have been Finn instead of Zami and Dif who later programmed these remarkable inventions. So that eventually, his place among the MOO's top programmers assured, he could at last have taken up the challenges of inventing his very own player class without arousing so much as a whisper of doubt about his readiness to do so.

But no: Finn had to aim for the top before he'd even grazed the bottom. He had to go ahead and build his version of the one object players depended on more heavily than any other, next to $root: their digital body. For that was really what a player class provided—the form and functionality that made a player object what it was, that brought to life the vehicle through which a person spoke and moved and tinkered and bonked and did whatever else a person did in the virtual world.

It was among the rasher things a rookie programmer like Finn could do, in other words, to invite the mostly naive public of the MOO to put its bodily well-being in his rookie hands. But that's exactly what he did when after a few short weeks of work he switched the fertility bit on his magnum opus from 0 to 1 and started telling everyone in shouting distance that a brand-new player class called Schmoo was open for business. And there are those who'd say this reckless deed alone was sin enough to justify the storm of animosity that soon came raining down on Finn. Schmoo was not, after all, a model of programming virtue, as even Finn himself would concede (though only much, much later). The thing was buggier and less secure than any player class had a right to be, and probably Finn should not have marketed it quite so vigorously as he chose to do. At least not to the newbies anyway.

But the truth is, even Schmoo's worst enemies never claimed that they were moved primarily by concern for public safety. Just what it was that actually motivated them is a question we will soon enough consider in some detail, but for now I offer you Finn's short answer, according to which there were really just two things you needed to know about the controversy.

Number one: Schmoo's enemies, to a player, were members of the social circle Finn had already come to think of (and despise) as Lambda's technocratic elite. Some were wizards (Crotchet, for instance), others were not (like Rhay, a cofounder of aCleanWellLightedMOO, and BriarWood, the up-and-coming programming whiz who would later be the first of Minnie's many political antagonists). But it was clear to Finn that they all enjoyed a social prominence founded largely on their expertise—and that they couldn't stand the fact that someone so completely uncredentialed should have had the nerve to move in on their turf. "They resented me," said Finn, "as an unwashed upstart—someone without any 'proper' schooling in the ways of computer science.

"Someone who also had a very popular playing class," he added. And that was basically the other thing you needed to know about the controversy. Because despite its undeniable flaws, the player class called Schmoo was, sure enough, turning out to be a runaway hit. And if you knew that much, then you could easily deduce that something other than the quality of its construction must have been compelling all those MOOers to change their parentage from existing player classes to the upstart Schmoo. And once you'd made that deduction—well. Then all you had to do was take a quick look at the features Schmoo provided and you'd know just what that something was, and why it might not sit so comfortably with the guardians of decorum on the MOO.

I'll put it in a nutshell: this object turned its children into sex machines.

The time has come then, I suppose, to say a word or two about the subject of Finn and tinysex. And even it it's not the time, this is going to have to get said sooner or later, so we might as well just say it now and get the whole indecorous business over with.

Right, then: Finn was a virtual sex fiend. End of story. No arguments there, not even from the player himself, who, though he might take issue with my choice of words, was certainly delighted to regale me with enough first-person testimony to warrant those words and then some. Allow me to repeat them then, just so there's no confusion about this: the man was a virtual sex fiend.

Or as a longtime MOO acquaintance of his somewhat more generously put it to me, "Finn just *is* netsex." If he was logged on, odds were better than even he was at it, and even if he happened to be standing right in front of you engaged in some entirely nonprurient activity, the odds were still not bad: Finn was a master of the various MOOish means of being in two or more places at once, and frequently at least one of those places was the site of some salacious encounter or another. He might be multiMOOing, hanging out on Lambda writing code or making innocent chitchat even while he was getting all hot and bothered over on some other MOO. He might be paging simultaneously with multiple partners, discreetly setting up his next encounter at the same time he was bringing his latest to a climax. He might even, on occasion, *be* multiple partners himself, moving deftly between his primary digital body and a spare one in an admirable if not entirely selfless effort to satisfy some tender young virtual thing's desire to be fucked by two guys at once.

And by the way, yes: Finn's partners were always women. At least as far as he knew. Or anyway at least as far as he knew at the time they were his partners. Well, OK, actually sometimes they confessed to being RL males right there in the middle of the postcoital glow, or even in mid-coitus itself, which Finn had to admit took some of the fun out of the experience for him. But only some. "Sex is loose here for the most part. Like a dream," shrugged Finn. "And you don't discriminate in a dream. Woman. Erection. Mount." So if occasionally the woman in question turned out to be not quite the woman she seemed, well, that happened in dreams too. And anyway the point was not so much what sort of body sat at the other end of the connection—it was rather, so far as Finn was concerned, what sort of text that body was capable of putting on your screen. "Here, all the senses are tied to what you READ," said Finn. "Words are your environment. As in a dream—the illusion is reality."

Ah yes: reality. Philosophically speaking, it was a concept Finn could talk about with a fair degree of sophistication. Sexually speaking, however, it was not a thing he ever claimed to be much qualified to talk about at all. "I've had one 'girlfriend' iRL," he told me, referring to a young woman he met in a creative writing class and slept with for a while. "It didn't work out. I'm a very solitary person," he explained, although in fact the problem partly seemed to be that he was too attached to his none-too-solitary MOOish life to really hold up his end of an RL relationship. "After we'd have sex I'd try and ease away back online soon as possible. Sigh." In the end, the girlfriend simply couldn't compete with Finn's unending stream of MOO liaisons. And how could she? "Here, everyone is perfect. If you want them to be," said Finn, with a virtual grin I took to be just slightly self-ironic. ("And when they get on your nerves," he added, "you can @gag them.")

And so, while RL sex went basically nowhere for Finn, online he lived the kind of hyperactive sex life young straight men usually only pretend to be living, whether in their fantasies or in the locker room. The fact that Finn, in comparison, was only *sort of* pretending may seem like a minor distinction to you, but it was apparently major enough to keep him coming back day after day, year after year, to an endlessly revolving feast of sexual encounters, each beginning in a hormone-driven dance of seduction and ending a few hours or a few days later with Finn dazed and confused, but ready soon enough for the next prospective partner to cross his radar screen. "I lust like a lunatic, and wake up bewildered," said Finn. "I come, spill my seed, empty the lust, and I wonder what the Hell I've done. What I've said, what I've promised, that I wanted this woman to come _meet_ me. . . . It's kind of like lycanthropy. I'm an animal when I'm horny. And then I wake up naked in the dirt and think 'Huh?'"

Finn wasn't kidding when he spoke of spilling his seed, either. Nearly every time he had netsex, he told me, his orgasm was simultaneously virtual and real, thanks to a combination of agile "manual assistance" and concentrated self-control. "I live the fantasy in my head. I hold myself back until all the verbal cues say GO! and then I come. Here and . . . here." Impressed, and somewhat concerned for the safety of his computer keyboard, I asked him once as indirectly as I could just how much spilling he was doing. "PINTS AND PINTS AND PINTS," he roared back—jokingly of course, but if you thought about it, the total volume of emissions over his MOOish lifetime was probably a lot more than that, and Finn was quick to assure me he took great care with his aim.

"I shoot in the basket," he said, grinning as usual.

All right, so Finn was not exactly the romantic type. But it would be unfair of me to leave the matter at that, because as crude as Finn's erotic sentiments could be, he did nonetheless bring to the business of online copulation what I would have to call an almost painfully refined aesthetic sense. It was a curious dichotomy in him: on the one hand netsex was for Finn a dose of raw, unbridled id, a kind of "delusion, rage, dervish daze" that let him get as loose and nasty as he wanted to be; but on the other hand, and maybe more importantly, it was also a "writing exercise" that demanded a high degree of improvisatory precision—and made him highly sensitive to the missteps of a sloppy collaborator. "When someone isn't coordinating," he told me, "when they lose track of where the body parts are and suddenly they're across the room and hanging on the ceiling or something," well, in all honesty, it was enough to make him want to fake a sudden disconnection and call it a night.

"The most important aspect of netsex . . . is AWARENESS," Finn insisted. "Knowing where you are in the VR, what's around you, what the others are doing." It didn't seem like much to ask, but in practice Finn found that partners able to sustain that sort of awareness weren't easy to come by. Those who excelled at it were rarer still. "If our words mesh," as he put it, "if we breathe the same poetry"—then that was a joyous occasion indeed, and when it happened, it was capable of bringing him as close to the brink of romantic attachment as he ever got, online or off.

But mostly it didn't happen. And early on, that fact led Finn to an epochal conclusion: there were a lot of MOOers out there who could use some help with the subtle art of pulling off a virtually convincing roll in the hay.

Thus, patient readers, did the gooey trajectory of Finn's most intimate predilections come to intersect with the course of MOOish history. For what do you imagine was the earliest and ripest fruit of Finn's desire to spread the virtues of virtual realism among his fellow netsexers? Why, Schmoo of course—the player class that introduced into the world of MUDs that revolutionary tinysexual tool known as virtual nudity.

Granted, "revolutionary" may be overstating it. To be honest, by the time I arrived on LambdaMOO, virtual nudity had long since faded well into the woodwork of daily life there. It could be found built into a couple of popular playing classes, and it served, as it always had, a relatively simple purpose: it allowed its users to morph certain key aspects of their descriptions, thus making it easy for them to represent their bodies in varyingly appropriate states of dress, undress, and, optionally, arousal. Among those players who might have any use for virtual nudity, opinions varied as to its merits. Some players, I was told, never went into a tinysexual encounter without it, while others considered it a crutch, and antithetical to the free play of imagination that made such encounters worth going into in the first place. As for those players who were immune entirely to the seductions of netsex, they might at most have had a chuckle at the very existence of virtual nakedness, if they had any reaction to it at all. It was not, in short, the kind of thing the MOO I knew was likely to go to war about.

And yet the verdict of the MOO's collective memory was clear: the Schmoo Wars had been fought because Finn's player class could take its clothes off.

Which isn't to imply that the MOO elites who took up arms against the Schmoo were puritans or prudes. Finn thought they were, and never missed an opportunity to say so, but the truth is they liked RL sex as much as anybody (indeed, if gossip could be trusted, they seemed to like to have it with each other as often and in as many dyadic permutations as real geography and their own sexual orientations permitted). Nor was it the case, exactly, that they feared the anarchic energies sometimes unleashed by sex. After all, the MOO had been getting more and more unruly from the moment its population started growing, entirely without the aid of Schmoo. And though it's true that incidents of sexual harrassment had long comprised a sizable chunk of that unruliness, nobody seriously believed a player class dedicated to the promotion of tinysex was by its nature also bound to promote disrespect for the terms of the MOOish social contract.

What it came down to really was a question of style. Which in turn came down to what such questions usually come down to: a question of class. Which is to say that among the upper social strata of LambdaMOO, tinysex just wasn't done. It was a newbie thing, a waste of time, and a trivial distraction from the nobler pursuits of hacking code and trading dry ironisms. Nobody minded terribly, of course, if the swelling ranks of the arrivistes persisted in indulging this goofy habit of theirs—any more than if they went on mucking around with such other low-class pastimes as bonking or playing virtual Scrabble. But one thing had to remain understood: on LambdaMOO it was the programmers who set the cultural tone, and as long as they did, the culture of LambdaMOO would forever be defined by more important things than tinysex.

You can imagine, therefore, the shiver of exquisite distaste that must have passed among the programmers upon their learning that the noble pursuit of hacking code had been perverted to the goofy ends of the netsex crowd. It was as if a forbidden legitimacy had suddenly been granted to the gauche subculture of the nonprogrammers, as if their tacky value system had been hardcoded into the very ontology of the MOO. Which come to think of it, it pretty much literally had been—and at a frighteningly high level of the ontology to boot. With the creation of Schmoo, you see, netsex was no longer just some shady activity relegated to the private rooms of the disenfranchised. It was an identity, of all things, and worse than that, it was an identity honored by the highest authority in the land: the database itself, which now recognized a netsexer (in the form of a child of Schmoo) as surely as it knew a wizard from a guest.

God knows this little coup of Finn's came as a breath of fresh air to some. "With his design of a fuckable player class," exu would later recall, and fondly, "he brought the Specter of Pleasure to this ironic and cerebral place." But for the ironic and cerebral types who more or less ran that place, it had the makings of a small disaster. Finn was right, I think, to feel that his hubris in aspiring to the heights of technical expertise had offended at least some of the reigning techies, but had that been his only offense, the techies could have easily laughed it off. No, it was Finn's fusion of high MOO tech and low MOO culture that had taken things a step too far: he had crossed—and blurred—a line whose clarity the elite's position in the MOOish world depended on. Followed to its ultimate conclusion, Finn's transgression could lead to just one outcome, and it was a bad one. Not the typical worst-case scenario for embattled elites, to be sure: they would not be banished from the MOO, nor would they, strictly speaking, find themselves stripped of their powers. They would still be the wizards, and the well-connected friends of wizards, and they would still, in an administrative sense at least, be in charge. And yet, at some much deeper level—a cultural one, let's say—LambdaMOO would no longer be their home. What they had made of it would slowly sink beneath the rising tide of sex machines and fart-bonkers, until at last the MUD that once had been a programmer's paradise officially became, God help them all, a synonym for silliness.

There was only one thing to be done. The legitimacy that Schmoo conferred would have to be taken back, and pronto. And that meant that Schmoo itself would have to be delegitimated—by any means necessary, certainly, but by preference with the überprogrammer's delegitimating weapon of choice: fine-tuned ridicule.

Whence the subtle nature of the Schmoo Wars' opening salvos, which consisted, as far as anyone can recall, of nothing more than a few smirking comments, made mostly in private but never quite so privately that they didn't by and by get back to Finn and anybody else remotely curious about the opinions of the more important people on the MOO. The opinions in this case did not range widely: Finn was a buffoon and/or a sleazebag, his programming was lousy, and the very notion that the MOO had any need for a netsex-ready player class was variously silly, stupid, and repulsive. No doubt these judgments were rendered with far greater wit than my summary suggests, but the precise wordings, I'm afraid, are nowhere to be found in the historical record. History *does* tell us (well, Finn told me) that in time the mockery expanded into other, more creative realms of expression. Objects were made that parodied Finn's. Rhay built a "Schmoo-Land" containing a comically exaggerated Gothic castle, based on the tower Finn lived in. Crotchet whipped up a bogus player class called "SuperSmurf," which was not very super at all, having no features built into it whatsoever.

But wait. I'm getting ahead of the story here. For if it's certain that the anti-Schmoo forces did eventually broaden their attacks, it's also probably true that by the time they did, Finn had already more than returned their fire. The MOO's collective memory goes a little fuzzy around such fine points of chronology, but as I said before, Finn was a hothead—and hardly likely, therefore, to take even the slightest of his enemies' barbs lying down. Nor was he likely to feel too terribly intimidated by the mighty arsenal arrayed against him. Sure, his antagonists had sarcasm, cultural hegemony, and possibly even the *@toad* command on their side—but what of it? Finn had a secret weapon the likes of which the MOO had never seen, and that was Schmoo itself. Or more precisely, it was the growing number of players who identified themselves as Schmoo and who, in doing so, provided Finn with the raw materials of that highly combustible power source known in modern parlance as identity politics.

What else to call it? We've seen already how insistently RL attitudes toward gender played themselves out in VR, in ways both floridly inventive and poisonously crude. And even though, in curious contrast, real-world dramas of race, ethnicity, and nationality largely kept their distance from the MOO (at most, one now and then bumped into some slightly creepy, and probably white, O. J. Simpson impersonator in the living room, or heard a tepid complaint from one of the Brits or the Australians about the predominance of American culture on the MOO), that didn't mean MOOish society was incapable of brewing up its own robust, in-house versions of tribal conflict.

The Schmoo Wars proved that. And Finn, more to the point, seemed almost consciously intent on proving it. From the outset he had equipped Schmoo with features designed to strengthen the bonds of fellow-feeling among the users, to highlight their identity as Schmoos and encourage them to gather around it: a special *@who* command allowed them to see which other Schmoos were on the MOO at any given moment, while the "Schmoo Shout" feature let them chat with all the logged-in Schmoos at once, as if on CB radio. There was even a mailing list just for Schmoos, called *Schmoo* of course. And last but not least, once the hostility of the aristohackers began to make itself apparent, Finn had at his command the most powerful tribe-building tool of all: a known enemy.

He didn't hesitate to make the most of that tool. In his communiqués to the teeming children of Schmoo (how many were they now? dozens? hundreds? the historical record refuses to say), he started playing openly to their sense of second-class citizenship as newbies and nonprogrammers, while at the same time flattering them as a generally groovier class of people than the repressed and oppressive foes of Schmoo. Wisely, he gave the enemy a name, and a catchy one too—the "Power Elite," he called them, minting a phrase that quickly entered the daily vocabulary of the MOO and never left it. The collectivity of Schmoos, meanwhile, was given a suitably groovier label (the "Schmoo Love Cult") and with it a sense of self that must have been a pleasure to indulge. Their spirits high, their resentments focused, the Schmoos were fast on their way to becoming a political force to be reckoned with—and already made a feisty cheering section for Finn as he sallied forth onto the mailing lists to do rhetorical battle with the Power Elite.

For the Schmoos, and for the MOO, this was an interesting moment. My friend Sebastiano—who didn't arrive on Lambda till after the Schmoo Wars were already ancient history, but who knew a lot about ancient history generally—

compared it to the rise in popularity of the orgiastic cult of Bacchus in classical Rome, around 180 B.C. "The bachinalians," he said (for he was better at history than at spelling), "were not only being very sexual, but more imporantly, they were becoming a seperate powerful community. And Schmoo users were becoming a community under Finn's leadership." As a cofounder of the separate and very sexual community of Weaveworld, Sebastiano looked back on the growing power of the Love Cult as a heartening development, but his analogy also pointed to the risks the Schmoos were running as they grew. After all, he noted, the Roman authorities ultimately responded to the rise of the Bacchanalians by suppressing the living daylights out of them.

And sure enough, the anti-Schmoo attacks in time began to target not just Finn and his invention but the community that had coalesced around them both. One hesitates to call it persecution, although indeed some Schmoos reported that hostile anti-Schmooers were harassing them in the public spaces of the MOO, and that in general they felt pressured to "prove that they were interested in more than just netsex." For the most part, however, the campaign against the Love Cult was waged not so much with open hostility as with sporadic, well-placed propaganda, aimed at infiltrating doubts about the cause into the hearts and minds of Schmoos. The critics took to posting on *Schmoo, which was a great way to get Finn's goat, you bet, but also enabled them to tell the Schmoos directly about the risks involved in using a player class produced by so untested a programmer. Finn's technical skills were roundly maligned, but perhaps more damagingly, his ethical fiber was also questioned. How could the Schmoos be sure they ought to trust him? Did they not realize that the owner of a player class had privileged access to each and every one of its children, and to all the data written into them? Had they never considered the possibility that Finn, a confessed tinylibertine, had invented Schmoo for the sole purpose of peeping at hundreds of players' private descriptions of their naughty bits? Defections from the Schmoo Love Cult began to mount.

And Finn struck back with glee. He took to keeping a list of the defectors, and he railed against them as heartily as he'd been laying into the Power Elite. They were all "Infidel Slime" now, Finn's latest term of art for the enemies of the Schmoo nation, and Finn, I can only surmise, was having the time of his life.

How could he not have been? Here he was, this soon-to-be college-dropout from East Bumfuck, West Virginia, standing right square in the middle of the closest thing he'd ever seen to real live history, at the head of an army of fun-loving newbies amid the heat and dust of his favorite kind of war: a war of words. For that was what the Schmoo Wars really were at this point—an almost daily exchange of arguments and insults and harangues. And while Finn's technical abilities were then still very much a matter of debate, I can assure you there was never any question about his verbal skills. Finn loved to throw his words around, and he threw them well, and until this moment he had never in his life been called upon to throw so many in the service of so righteous a cause. It beat the hell out of creative writing class, that's for sure. And if it had kept on going this way, the truth is it probably would have ended far more happily for Finn.

But in the end, it wasn't verbal skills that decided the outcome of the Schmoo Wars. In the end, the war of words became a war of code, as once again—and not for the last time either—the native language of the MOO emerged to trump the native language of the MOOers.

It was BriarWood who made the first move of the end game.

He made it one day after he'd been studying Schmoo's source code for a while, examining the workings of a particular command called *@peruse*, which was a kind of remote-vision feature that made it easy for Schmoos to read the description of any object anywhere on the MOO. The anti-Schmoo crowd didn't care much for *@peruse*, although it's not clear why. They found it anti-VR, perhaps, or maybe antiprivacy. In any case they were always figuring out ways to write themselves some sort of shield against its gaze, while Finn in turn was always figuring out ways to code around the shields they wrote. The end result of all this effort being that the anti-Schmooers got pretty familiar with *@peruse*'s code, and pretty quick to find the weakness that would let them write their latest shield. Which I suppose was just what BriarWood was looking for on the day he made the first move of the end game. Except that on that day BriarWood discovered something else entirely. He found a gaping security hole, leading through *@peruse* straight into the heart of Schmoo itself.

Now, when you found a hole like that there was no question what you were supposed to do: you had to tell the object's owner about it immediately. Because a hole like that meant anybody who found it could just waltz right in, and take control of the object, and do any number of unpleasant things with it. Like erase its description, say. And replace that description with an obscenely phrased insult, for instance. And thereby make the object's owner look like a sloppy, second-rate programmer, for example. Which of course was something BriarWood would never, ever do. Except to Finn.

I asked BriarWood once why he had not done as etiquette required that day and told Finn about the hole. "I was Infidel Slime," he shrugged. And besides, he had a point to make. He'd been thinking for a while about creating a parody of Schmoo, something along the lines of Crotchet's SuperSmurf player class, only actively "evil" instead of merely lame. The idea behind the invention wouldn't be to abuse its hapless users so much as to make them understand how easily they *could* be abused—to "teach them a lesson about trusting the owners of player classes." But now that he'd gone and cracked Schmoo, there really wasn't any need to go to all the effort of designing an entire player class just to teach that lesson. He could demonstrate the problem just as graphically on Schmoo itself. And so he did. The next MOOer who happened to look at Schmoo after BriarWood was done with it would notice nothing different except its new description, which subtly yet unmistakably reminded all who gazed upon it that a generic object was only as trustworthy as the security measures built into it:

"This," read the revised description in its entirety, "is the fucking Schmoo player class."

Finn changed the description back immediately, and he also managed, pretty quickly, to find and patch the hole in *@peruse*. Nor did BriarWood escape justice altogether. Etiquette was etiquette, after all, and even if he *was* a well-connected friend of wizards, BriarWood had breached it in the extreme. He was handed a reprimand, therefore, by some higher-up or another—perhaps enaJ, who ranked about as high up in the power structure as a player could, but who nonetheless had something of a soft spot for the rabble-rousing Finn. ("He was fun," she told me later, and not even such a bad programmer, she allowed, as some of her friends made him out to be.)

But Finn was hardly appeased. BriarWood had gotten "a wee spanking," as Finn put it, when by rights he should have been punished no less severely than Finn's own creation had been violated. What could you expect from the Power Elite, though? That was how they operated, the weasels, going on and on about the rules of the MOO but never failing to bend them when it served the interests of one of their own. If Finn wanted vengeance, in other words, he was going to have to get it himself.

And get it he did. It took a little while—security holes don't grow on trees— but soon enough Finn found a way to break into BriarWood's player object. And once he'd found it, he didn't waste any time putting it to use. Into the object called BriarWood, Finn wrote a few new lines of code, the effect of which, in functional terms, was to boot BriarWood off the system every time he tried to log on. For Finn, however, the terms of MOOish crime and punishment supplied a somewhat more satisfying way of putting it: BriarWood had effectively been newted.

Not so effectively, though, that Finn's avenging code wasn't quickly found out, and easily removed. BriarWood's player object was restored to health in no time, and all things being equal, Finn probably would have suffered no more stringent punishment for what he'd done than BriarWood had received for his act of trespass.

It just so happened, however, that all things were not equal. Because although Finn finally had done no worse to BriarWood than BriarWood had done to him, there was a difference in their methods of attack, and it was all the difference in the world. Indeed, I'd hardly be exaggerating if I said that the world itself hung in the balance of that difference, for the world we are concerned with here was after all a virtual one, and in the course of taking his revenge Finn had done something that had the potential to shake that world to its very foundations. What Finn had done to get control of BriarWood's player object, it turned out, was nothing so innocuous—so unambitious—as merely cracking the object itself. No: Finn had once again aimed higher than he really should have. In one fell act of programming, he had cracked not only BriarWood's object, but its parent, and its parent's parent, and all its parent's parent's ancestors, every one of them, right up to and including (this was the heavy part) the Ur-ancestor $root.

Finn had hacked the MOO, in short.

Or more precisely, he had hacked a wizard bit. Which in functional terms meant that he had found a way to convince the system he had wizard privileges, and in the somewhat more satisfying terms of MOOish crime and punishment meant that he had committed the most unpardonable sin there was. Bar none. Even at the height of the uproar over Bungle's crimes, for instance, there'd been considerable agreement that his deeds fell short a notch or two of the gravity of hacking a wizbit. And long after Haakon had decreed the abdication of the wizards from the realm of social discipline, they still reserved the right to move swiftly and summarily against anyone discovered breaching system security at the wizbit level. "@*newt* first and ask questions later" was the policy, and insofar as such newtings were only temporary, it was a surprisingly uncontroversial one. Some wizards liked to justify it as a matter of "national security" ("I'm the CIA," enaJ/Sredna once said to me about her mandate to protect the server, "I don't have to follow due process"), but by and large the players didn't need RL analogies to appreciate the seriousness of a hacked wizbit. It was enough to know that anyone who possessed one could play havoc with the MOO—could erase any object at will, could spy on anyone's communications, could rewrite anyone's programs and could even, if she so desired, bring the whole place crashing to a sudden halt.

Finn remained uncharacteristically quiet, therefore, about this latest of his coups. He wanted to hang on to the wizbit as long as he could, and he certainly didn't like the thought of what might happen to him if he were discovered with it. But after he got done fixing BriarWood's wagon, Finn couldn't resist the urge to take his newfound omnipotence out for a spin or two, or three, to roam the MOO invisible and godly and to poke and probe into those dark corners of the database where only wizards were allowed to go. It was an understandable urge, of course, but it would prove to be his undoing. For it wasn't long before his pokings and probings caused the MOO to crash—a spectacularly grim event under any circumstances, and in this case especially unfortunate for Finn, inasmuch as his digital fingerprints were found all over the crime scene once the server was brought back online.

Finn swore up and down he'd never meant to force a crash—"I'm a knowledge addict, not a terrorist," he told a reporter for the *Lambda MOOspaper*—but that didn't do much to soften the hearts of the wizards. His goose was cooked, and in the end it was none other than his sometime sympathizer Sredna who did the carving. At the moment, she wasn't feeling very sympathetic toward him at all, and she probably would have toaded him on the spot if she'd thought she could afford to. But in Finn's case toading would have produced too much collateral damage. It would have erased Schmoo instantly, which certainly might have pleased some of the more radical elements of the Infidel Slime, but which just as certainly would have made instant orphans of all Schmoo's children, resulting in a lot more user complaints than the wizards really needed to deal with at this point.

So instead Sredna newted Finn. She newted him, and though she did not specify the length of time for which he was to remain newted, it seemed clear enough that forever would be just fine with the wizards. As for Schmoo, they decided to transfer ownership of the player class to a more cooperative young programmer by the name of CHATtle, who quickly set about making it more "user friendly"—adding help files, toning down the rebel cult appeal, that sort of thing.

"He cut its balls off," Finn was later heard to grouse, although that wasn't strictly true: the one thing CHATtle left almost entirely untouched was, ironically enough, the controversial netsex feature that had set the whole conflagration going in the first place.

Here, then, is how the MOO's collective memory records the moment: the Schmoo Wars were over. The Power Elite had triumphed. Finn stood bereft of all he'd ever owned in the virtual world and doomed to an exile that might never end. But for what it was worth, the children of the player class called Schmoo could still get naked anytime they wanted to.

I onced asked Rhay to describe the Schmoo Wars for me, and he answered flatly: "The most overromanticized period in MOO history." I didn't argue with him, nor could I have. I hadn't been there, after all, and Rhay had. He had seen the Schmoo Wars with his own eyes and from the front lines, and I was obliged, therefore, to take his word for it when he told me that the whole thing had really been no big deal.

I was obliged, and still am, to accept as fact that at the time, nobody really felt themselves to be fighting some sort of epic battle for the soul of the MOO. And that for that matter sizable segments of the Lambda population (including many Schmoos and various members of the so-called Power Elite) considered the conflict between Finn and his antagonists to be no business of theirs, and a childish business at that. And that finally, whatever broad sociohistorical significance may now be extracted from the Schmoo Wars was almost certainly written into them by the long, collective process of retelling through which a petty feud between a few young men with too much time and cleverness on their hands was afterward transfigured into the stuff of legend.

And yet, if I have preferred to tell a version of the story somewhat more in keeping with the legend than with these mundane facts, I feel no obligation to apologize. You wouldn't have learned much from the drier version, and anyway it was the legend, ultimately, as much as the Schmoo Wars themselves, that shaped the course of LambdaMOO's subsequent history.

A long hot summer of political agitation followed in the wake of Finn's newting, inspired in large part by his increasingly mythic memory. With Finn's theatrics of class rebellion echoing in their imaginations, a group of highly articulate but not especially technical players (who would eventually take to calling themselves by a name we've heard before: the MOO Underground) now began hassling the wizards in earnest about reforming the MOO's disciplinary mechanisms. "Free the LambdaMOO Seven!" was their rallying cry—a call to repeal the newtings and toadings of various brusquely punished MOOers, among them the old troublemakers Gottesmord and Satyrik, but also including two of Finn's longtime associates (Hackamore and Waif, both newted on suspicion of aiding and abetting) and most importantly Finn himself, who now made a terrific icon for the anarcholibertarian set. With his exile, the Promethean dimensions of

Finn's saga were at last complete: he had wrested the divine gift of *techne* from the programming elite, and for putting it in the service of mortal desires he had been condemned to an eternal agony of . . . well, no, it wasn't like he was chained to a rock with vultures ripping out his liver every day, but still. Finn was slightly more than human now, and therefore it was slightly more than just a joke when (for instance) a few adherents of the Underground built a larger-than-life Finn effigy one day and carried it around the living room, like the patron saint at a Catholic feast day, demanding his return.

(And wait—those two budding MOO-anarchists there, helping carry the giant Finn doll around, haven't we seen them somewhere before? Why yes, it's HortonWho and exu, newly acquainted amid the fun and fervor of the movement, and at this very moment beginning their long fall toward ill-fated passion! Chalk up another momentous consequence to the legend of the Schmoo Wars, then, though in this case not perhaps a strictly sociohistorical one.)

Summer turned to autumn, and what appeared to be the fruits of all this unrest began to ripen. Rumors circulated among the MOOers that a core subgroup of the Power Elite had decided to set up a MOO of its own, where they could program in peace far from the mounting social complications of Lambda. And when aCleanWellLightedMOO opened its doors in late October, what could anyone think but that the rumors had been true? The CWL crowd insisted that the only thing about Lambda they were trying to escape was the worsening lag, but the whole mood of the new place—its emphasis on orderly, realistic building, and on coordinated, "serious" programming efforts—suggested otherwise. It was exactly as if the denizens of CleanWellLighted (among them Rhay, enaJ, Crotchet, and Rhay's good friend TomTraceback) were conceding that the worst possible outcome of the Schmoo Wars had after all come true: that Lambda-MOO was no longer really their home, and that in any case, it was certainly nothing remotely like a programmer's paradise anymore.

Still greater concessions were soon to follow. A few weeks after the CWL inauguration, Haakon published "LambdaMOO Takes a New Direction," the document that formally handed responsibility for the social direction of the MOO over to the MOOers themselves. The wizardocracy had now come to an official end, and consequently the wizards would no longer be conducting the sorts of summary newtings and toadings that had so vexed the MOO Underground and its fellow travelers. What's more, as a sort of codicil to Haakon's edict it was informally agreed that the chief demand of the Underground would now be met, without conditions: the LambdaMOO Seven were granted amnesty en masse.

Which meant that after six months of indefinite banishment, Finn was back—the undisputed victor, finally, over a humbled Power Elite, and a man prepared to take his place now as a leading citizen of the brave new MOO he had so dramatically helped to bring about.

And never mind what Haakon told me years later (incredulous that I or anyone else could ever believe otherwise): that the so-called MOO Underground and the Schmoo Wars and the mythic memory of Finn had had no influence whatsoever on the wizards' decision to abdicate; that in fact the wizards had abdicated simply because it was too much work, finally, to try to manage the social affairs of a group of people as large as the Lambda population had become. What Haakon told me may very well be true, and indeed I see no reason not to believe it's true. But I also see no reason to believe it's truer than anything else I've told you about the Schmoo Wars. Because I'm pretty sure that in the end, the truest thing that can be said about them is that they marked the beginning of a much larger, much longer struggle between two equally compelling truths about how power functioned on the MOO. For if the reigning truth before Finn arrived had been that LambdaMOO was more or less what it appeared to be—somebody's house, with house rules and an implicit understanding that power rested ultimately with the owner of the place—that truth had serious competition once the Schmoo Wars came along and dramatized the fact that LambdaMOO was also an increasingly complex society, with power ultimately up for grabs among a variety of interest groups.

The contradiction between those truths wasn't easy to resolve, because of course, LambdaMOO answered readily to both. As crowded and diverse and downright weirdly intricate as it had grown to be, the MOO couldn't help but behave in almost every possible way like an autonomous and rapidly developing society. Yet all along, and long after the outlines of Pavel Curtis's Silicon Valley home were barely recognizable beneath the years of secondary architectural growth, the MOO remained essentially his own private house party, lodged inextricably within the confines of a computer he could pull the plug on any moment he chose to. That Pavel chose instead to mostly keep his nose out of the business of the MOO was one of the reasons the place had gotten as interesting as it had, but it never quite settled the deeply unsettling question that haunted nearly any discussion of politics on the MOO: wherein did real power finally reside? In the hands of those who struggled, collectively or otherwise, to secure it? Or in the hands of the archwizard and his trusted inner circle alone, to be relinquished or not as they saw fit?

We will see soon enough, in the fateful denouement of Minnie's long campaign against the Power Elite, that this unanswerable question continued to erupt into MOO-rending conflict long after the tumult of the Schmoo Wars had subsided.

But first, there is a personal matter I must attend to.

NEW YORK CITY, AUGUST 1994

Times Square Subway Station
You are underground. Concrete beneath your feet, above
  your head; an orchard of I-beam columns all around
  you. Smell of ozone in the air and naked bulbs
  throwing hard electric light all over everything. You
  can catch the N and R trains here. Go upstairs to
  transfer to the 1, 2, 3, 9, or crosstown shuttle.
You see The Madding Crowd here.
Jessica and The_Author are here.
It's like a frickin' sauna here.

The Madding Crowd mutters and mills.

look crowd

The Madding Crowd
What the fuck are _you_ looking at?

Jessica sweats.

The_Author sweats.

The_Author looks impatiently up the tracks.

Jessica says, "Can't wait to get home to the MOO, huh?"

The_Author chuckles mirthlessly, still looking up the
   tracks.

The Madding Crowd rumbles and roils.

Jessica says, "And how's your love life coming along
   anyway?"

The_Author turns and raises an eyebrow.

The_Author says, "My _what?_"

Jessica says, "Your love life. Any action there?
   Anything I should know about?"

The_Author feels his teeth clench and his temperature
   rise.

The_Author says, "Look. I _told_ you. I will _not_ be
   having any love affairs on the MOO. If I have netsex
   at all, it's only going to be so I can see what it's
   like. It's _research_, all right? _God_."

Jessica glares.

Jessica says, "Fine. You don't have to get so hostile
   about it."

The_Author says, "Well _you_ don't have to get so
   sarcastic about it."

The_Author says, "My 'love life.' Jesus."

The_Author looks away, fuming.

Jessica looks the other way, fuming.

The Madding Crowd swelters and swirls.

Jessica sighs.

New York City, August 1994

Jessica allows herself a sidelong look at The_Author.

Jessica says, "Well I just think you should know I don't think of it as research."

Jessica says, "I think of it as sex."

Jessica says, "And go ahead and do it. Because I told you I don't consider this a monogamous relationship at the moment. Remember?"

The_Author remembers. Five weeks ago -- not long after he began inhabiting the MOO in earnest, as a matter of fact -- Jessica declared over breakfast that the time had come for them to open up the possibility of seeing other people. It was the only way, she said, that she could stand to go on living with someone so unwilling to commit to her. He didn't think she meant it. He thought she was just being dramatic. He still does.

The_Author says, "All right, first of all: whatever. You want to live in a nonmonogamous relationship, feel free to do so. But don't expect me to join you in it. I have no plans or intentions to get involved with anybody else and I never have."

The_Author says, "And secondly, as for netsex: forget it. I thought the idea didn't bother you, but I was clearly wrong. So never mind. If you're gonna get this freaked out about it, I'll pass, thanks."

Jessica looks at The_Author with something like astonishment.

Jessica says, "No way. No fucking way. You're not going to put this responsibility on _me_. _I'm_ not the reason you're not going to have netsex. You want to know what the reason is?"

The_Author glares.

Jessica says, "You're afraid to."

The_Author fumes.

Jessica says, "You're afraid it would be too real."

The_Author glares, and fumes, and sweats, and almost
  cries.

The Madding Crowd chatters and churns.

VR

7

S*

Or TINYSEX,
In the Author's Experience

You'll want to know when it all began, of course.

Of course: one wants to know. One wants a moment etched as if in crystal that promises somehow to explain, to excuse, to ratify the whole ungovernable cascade of thoughts and impulses and small, life-altering actions that follows. A moment, say, like the Christmas Eve four years and two girlfriends before I ever kissed Jessica's lips (three years, indeed, before we ever exchanged a word) when I saw her standing with a mutual friend in the light of a midnight Mass and knew, with the absurd presumptuousness some attractions inspire, that we were going to be lovers.

In that moment, naturally, I did not know what I would long thereafter know: that the young woman standing in the church aisle wearing her beauty like a brilliant afterthought would turn out also to be blessed with a no less brilliant wit, and with a congenially dark erotic imagination, and with a heart not so entirely ringed with the thorns of a certain wounded wariness as to bar me from the deep wells of affection within it. Nor did I know (though by that point in my sexual career I should really have been able to guess) that despite these ample gifts I would nonetheless end up spending much of our time together torturing the both of us with nagging, obsessive doubts whose focus on Jessica was too neurotically misplaced to dignify here with any further description, and whose real origins in a certain wounded wariness of my own will come as no surprise to anyone who's ever seen the inside of a therapist's office. I had no idea, in short, how frail the certainty of that Christmas Eve would prove to be, nor indeed how many times I would grasp in panic at its memory before it finally started to sink in that my whole sad history of ambivalence came down to this: that I had never in my life quite learned to move beyond those light-headed first awakenings of desire. I had never learned to accept the fact that any attraction worth pursuing would never remain as simple as the moment that engendered it, would always be challenging me, in fact, to recognize in its every moment the outset of a journey into unfamiliar territory.

By which I really mean to say, I guess, that if even amid the tangible reality of RL bodies it doesn't quite make sense to locate an attraction's true beginning in any single instant, how can you expect me to pinpoint such a place in the phantom history of a virtual affair?

I mean, what should I tell you—that I was attracted to S* from the moment I first saw her? And what then should I claim to mean by that, if what I saw was only words? If what the words described was only one among the several bodies I would come to know her in? If even I can't say exactly which of them it was I finally came to know, many weeks later, in the most intimate way a virtual body can be known?

Well, I'll tell you anyway, because it happens to be true: my desire for S* began its slow rise to inevitability on the day we met.

It was an early afternoon on Interzone and I was visiting with exu there. Or rather, I was waiting in the abandoned grocery story that exu inhabited on Interzone for her to return from some RL distraction or another, and it was while I waited that S* happened also to drop by for a visit. She didn't call herself S* then, nor in fact did she ever—it was I who would one day call her that, but never to her face, and for reasons I couldn't then have guessed at. For now, the only name I knew her by was the one her present character bore, and that was Serpentella.

I figured Serpentella must be another friend of exu's, but I thought I'd have a look at her before I introduced myself. So I looked and saw the body of a sullen-eyed bleached blonde in her early twenties who made her living as the Amazing Snake Woman in a perpetually failing carnival. *Just having come from work,* the description went on to explain, *she wears a silver lame' bra on her pale torso, and her legs are encased in a papier mache serpent's tail. Her hair is cropped close to her skull, to accommodate the blue nylon mermaid wig that dangles from her left hand. If you look at her closely, you'll notice the many silver earrings and the pierced navel . . .*

*but then again, if you look at her that closely, she might do something extremely
unpleasant to you.*

"Hello," I said then. "Quite the description, dear."

I don't know why I called her dear. I think it's what I dimly imagined my own
Interzone persona would say (I called him Dr. Benway, after Burroughs's famous
nitrous-addled surgeon, and had described him as *This really old skinny guy in diapers*) but I think too something in the dead-pan, comic-book lyricism of the
stranger's description told me this was someone I was going to like, in one way or
another.

"Thanks," she answered, for some reason grinning wickedly. "I'm happy
with it."

"Goodness, such a wicked grin," said I, and then I said, "Pleased to meetcha,
if I haven't already."

One never knew, after all.

But no: "I don't think so. . . ."

Pause.

"I mean, I don't think we've met before . . ." she added quickly, floundering as
we all did at times amid the routine ambiguities of text-based chat. "I'm pleased
as well . . . heh."

I suppose I found her awkwardness charming, though she plainly didn't mean
it to be. She put it down to mid-morning caffeine deprivation, actually (for it
seemed she lived three time zones to the west of me), but that didn't stop me
from doing my corny best to be charming back: I typed *@create $thing called "a
cuppa joe,"* and then I described the new-made $thing as *Rich, black, piping hot,
you hear the voice of Juan Valdez calling in the distance . . .* , and then I handed the
fresh cup of virtual java to Serpentella, who laughed and thanked me for it—at
which point exu reawoke from her RL stupor, and our private introductory
moment came to an end.

And no: it wasn't exactly marked by fireworks, was it? But then, I wasn't really
looking for any; not at that point anyway. And even so, I left Interzone that afternoon with the half-formed sensation that somewhere inside me—somewhere
amid the Rube Goldberg mesh of mechanisms that guided my fumbling heart—a
wire had been tripped, and a timer set quietly to ticking.

A few weeks later I learned that Serpentella was called Solanas on LambdaMOO.
And bit by bit I learned, as well, an RL fact or two about the person behind those
names.

She lived in Vancouver, for one. She was a first-year graduate student in French literature there. She was, as advertised, a woman. She had green eyes and a curious tattoo in the small of her back.

I learned these things, for the most part, from exu, who had gleaned them firsthand during a recent visit the Vancouver woman had undertaken to finally meet her various Seattle MOO friends face-to-face. I did not seek these data out, nor did I press exu for more. They interested me of course, though not as much as you might think. Or anyway not as much *I* would have thought, had I not already learned a firsthand thing or two about the ways attraction functioned in VR.

For I must tell you now that Solanas was not the first MOO player I'd felt drawn to sight unseen. There had been others—only two, but those had been enough to show me just how loosely the phenomenon of virtual desire depended on any knowledge of the RL body desired.

The first was exu, as you may or may not be surprised to hear. We were never more than friends, officially—but who's to say there's ever been a friendship worth the name in which some murmur of eros didn't lurk? It lurked in ours, that's for sure, and in the beginning it did more than that: new to LambdaMOO, enchanted by its fluidity and playfulness but still somewhat shut out of it all by my own ungainly newbiehood, I gravitated toward this warm, quick-witted, and MOO-savvy new acquaintance with an eagerness that soon became an unmistakable infatuation—complete with anxious, RL blushes (and other, less G-rated physical responses) whenever she so much as typed a standard MOOish greeting-hug my way. I had no idea what exu really looked like then, nor really any sense that it could make much of a difference if I knew. It was only after my crush had somewhat abated that I met her face-to-face, during her brief visit to New York with Kropotkin, and though I found I couldn't take my eyes off her—so fascinated was I with this sudden, raw intimacy, this standing there with nothing between us except air—I can't say I felt anything like physical attraction. The real-life exu just was not my type. And even so, the erotic undercurrent of my affection for her never really died out. It only ebbed and flowed, a wayward tide, rising and falling in answer to a distant body that hardly needed to be seen to make its gravity felt.

And then there was Ashley-Melissa, who strode into my field of virtual vision on another memorable Interzone afternoon, materializing suddenly in the midst of a small gathering in exu's grocery store. She said a few brief hellos, then just as abruptly as she had appeared she disappeared again, leaving her description to shimmer on inside my head: *Insolent, affected pout with sheen of wild cherry lip-*

gloss. Pink wraparound mirrorshades. Body wave, slightly brassy frost & tip, feathered bangs. Her arms are covered in wash-off tattoos of spaceships, snakes, and cartoon characters, all in different stages of fade. She wears a hot orange midriff tee with Black Watch Tartan mini-kilt and combat boots. Her coltish teenage legs are scratched and scabby. Strung on a dirty piece of twine around her neck are silver-dollar sized pieces cut from old school lunchboxes: Farrah, Robocop, Woody from the Bay City Rollers, Scooby-Doo.

"Who was *that*?" I asked exu, smitten I think not so much by the image itself as by the shape of the mind I glimpsed between its lines—the mind of a woman about my age, it had to be (if the '70s kitsch details were anything to go by), with a fond eye for the pathos embedded in pop detritus and a keen feeling for the worlds of promise that can appear to lie just beyond a first look at another person. The sort of mind, I guess it seemed to me just then, that very well might fit mine the way a lock fits its key.

"That," exu replied, "was Niacin," and from the curtness of her tone I could tell at once how little her former lover's ever-expanding repertoire of polygendered personae amused her anymore. Myself, though, I had to laugh. Sure, the joke was on me, but it was a good one all the same. Niacin had caught me as he'd caught so many men before: fair and square, in a bright reflection of his admirer's own desire. And now at least I had the chance to get away unburned, the momentary flash of that desire reduced by exu's timely intervention to nothing more than a valuable lesson in the power of self-delusion.

Or so I thought. It turned out, though, that the attraction Ashley-Melissa sparked that day was a curiously enduring thing. The mind I'd seen at work in her description remained the same, after all, excepting of course the assumptions I'd made about its gender. And even that distinction—significant though it seemed to me as a man of hitherto unwavering heterosexuality—ended up a bit of a blur in the long run, smudged over time by Niacin's constant shifting back and forth between girl and boy, so that the better I got to know him, and the more I saw of his many, delectable morphs, the closer my aborted feelings for the creator of Ashley-Melissa crept back toward the threshold of awareness, maturing as they did so into an ambiguous concoction indeed. I mean, what was it, really, that was drawing me to this person? Was it the women he made? Was it the man who made them? Or was it the seductively indefinite relationship between the two? In time I felt the attraction clearly enough to understand that all these things, in fact, were tugging at me; but which of them tugged hardest I never could quite say.

What I *can* say, though, is this: it's very unlikely I would ever have come to feel the way I did about either Niacin or exu had my only contacts with them been face-to-face. And if you feel like drawing from that fact some sort of heartwarming, humanistic moral—you know, about the beauty that lies waiting to reveal itself to those not blinded by the accidental shapes biology bestows on mortals such as we, or whatever—then by all means be my guest. Personally, however, I tend to think that what I learned from these early attractions was more or less the same home truth I later got to know as one of LambdaMOO's most cherished maxims: "In VR, it's the best writers who get laid."

By which I mean that while my knowledge of exu's and Niacin's physical bodies played at most a negligible role in rousing my desire for them, the same can hardly be said about the bodies they built themselves out of the only building matter LambdaMOO supplied: the written word. And no, I don't refer here simply to the bodily images made explicit in their description files. I'm talking, rather, about the way the visible body functions in the world of matter as a kind of definitive icon of the self, and about the way that in a world of text it abdicates that role, inevitably, to language. In VR, just to restate the obvious, your words are no longer merely what you have to say—they are your very presence, they're what manifests you in the virtual world, and how you use them, consequently, tends to shape that world's perceptions of you in much the same way how you look frames what the real world thinks. Well-rounded, colorful sentences start to do the work of big brown soulful eyes; too many typos in a character's description can have about the same effect as dandruff flakes on a black sweater; and neither these nor any similar textual attributes, of course, turn out to be much more reliable as indicators of a person's real worth than their physical counterparts have ever been.

Please don't misunderstand: exu and Niacin are my friends, and it is far from my intention to suggest that they are anything but fine, upstanding human beings. Nor am I suggesting that it should be news to anyone that language can play a major role in the intricate theater of seduction. I only mean to note that when it comes to solving the complex equation that establishes a sexual attraction, the subtle variable of a person's "inner beauty" counts no more heavily in virtual reality than it does anywhere else. The fact that RL bodies weren't around to distract my erotic gaze, in other words, hardly means I now directed it straight into the depths of Niacin's and exu's souls. On the contrary, what that gaze was drawn to, still, was surfaces. It lingered over the shapes of phrases: over the clarity and verve of exu's conversational style, say, or the elegance and detail of Niacin's morphwork. And if I had to identify one single factor as the core of my desire for these two invisible people, I would say that, yes, it was precisely this charged attention to the contours of their textual bodies. And that the rest, of course, was what it always is, only more so: projection, fantasy, the attribution to another person of this or that magical quality missing in myself, all helped along tremendously by the central role of imagination in the very functioning of a low-bandwidth universe like LambdaMOO, and all nonetheless interwoven with a delicate, indispensable thread of genuine human connection.

My point being, I guess, that with Solanas the ingredients of my attraction weren't ultimately very different ones. Once more, it was a virtual surface my desire latched onto. It was a voice jumping into the late-night punning circles on Interzone with poise and a cutting enthusiasm; it was a lean but carefully sensual descriptive style ("Should it be 'leathery thump' or 'thump of leather'?" she paged me with seductive innocence one evening, soliciting input on a bit of ambient noise she was writing into one of her virtual rooms); it was a hard-edged friendliness that only went so far, that figured in my mind's eye as a smooth and egg-white shell, inviting me to look for cracks—or even make them, if I had to.

And of course I made them, eventually, though the truth is that I never really had to. I could have let things go the same way they had gone with exu and with Niacin—could have let desire do no more than seep into the fabric of our friend-ship, uneventfully. But instead I let it pull me straight into the middle of the one typical MOOish emotional dilemma I had promised myself never to experience firsthand. And since I may be tempted in the pages that follow to try and pass my motives off as alibis—to imply, for instance, that their origin in the hard domes-tic turbulence of my real life made them somehow overpowering within the dreamy, weightless atmosphere of the MOO—let me here repeat myself as plainly as I can: I did not have to do it.

But I had my reasons, like I said. And it's a fact they didn't have a lot to do with LambdaMOO.

The Living/Dining Room
You are at the ground-floor level of an overpriced and
  undersized East Village duplex apartment. A cheap
  Scandinavian loveseat hugs one wall and across from
  it a brick-faced fireplace fills most of another.
  Next to the fireplace a black metal staircase spirals
  down into the floor. To the south you see a small
  kitchen area. To the north a plate-glass door looks
  out into a small backyard.
Jessica and The_Author are sitting in the loveseat.

Jessica has something to tell The_Author, and she's
   telling it. Her words flow lightly but deliberately,
   with a flatness to their tone that's hard to read,
   even if the words themselves are unambiguous.

Jessica says, "Anyway, Eduardo's still in Mexico City.
   He'll be back in a couple of weeks when classes
   start. I really don't know what will happen then."

Jessica seems to have said what she had to say.

The_Author stares at the fireplace and he says nothing.
   He tries to remember what this Eduardo looks like. He
   met him once: A colleague of Jessica's from the
   Spanish and Portuguese department. A shyly amicable
   man of about thirty, he recalls. Handsome in a way
   that teetered between boyish and dissolute.

The_Author stares at the fireplace and still he says
   nothing.

Jessica says, "So that's it? The conversation's over?"

The_Author looks at Jessica.

Jessica is giving him a look he knows very well: lips
   tight, half curled into a hint of a bitter smile,
   eyes icy and eyebrows slightly raised. It is a look
   of fiercely guarded expectation, actually, though he
   almost never fails to mistake it for contempt.

The_Author says, "Well what the hell am I supposed to
   say?"

Jessica looks away, exasperated, hurt.

The_Author says, "No, seriously. Jesus. It's not like
   I'm the one who just sat down here and announced I
   slept with someone else two months ago and oh-by-the-

way-I'll-probably-be-sleeping-with-him-again-in-the-
very-near-future-thought-you'd-like-to-know."

The_Author glares at her and tries to enjoy his anger
while it lasts, because already he can feel it giving
way to self-reproach, and fear of loss, and raw
confusion.

Jessica turns her eyes back toward him and the look is
different now, not so familiar.

The_Author sees weariness in her face, and remorse, and
normally these might signal the onset of tears and
reconciliation, except that now they're mingled with
a new, unsettling calmness that promises nothing.
That expects nothing. That only watches him.

Jessica says, "All right. You're right. We don't have
to talk about this anymore right now."

The_Author doesn't reply. He stares at the fireplace
and tries to understand some things.

The_Author makes some headway.

The_Author understands at last, for instance, that this
"experiment in nonmonogamy" she's been talking about
has been no bluff.

The_Author understands that even so, she hasn't exactly
been honest about it either.

The_Author understands, in any case, that on some level
this is still an experiment of sorts -- a desperate,
despairing test that he could put an end to just by
telling her he's ready, finally, to let go of the
shroud of paralyzing doubt he's clutched so closely
to his heart throughout their days together and long
before.

The_Author can't tell Jessica any such thing, however, because even now he is not ready to let go. And the one thing that he still doesn't understand is why.

Jessica says, "I'd better get going."

Jessica lays her hand on The_Author's for a moment.

Jessica stands and gives him a tentative, solicitous smile.

The_Author glances at her and faintly smiles back, too uncertain now of what he really feels to do or say anything else.

Jessica disappears down the black metal staircase to the basement level of the apartment.

The_Author goes back to staring at the fireplace, and needless to say, this being mid-August, there is no fire in it.

I learned of Jessica's affair on the morning of the day before Minnie informed the wizardry that she'd been hacked to bits. Five days after Minnie's hacking I completed the basic architecture of the Garden of Forking Paths. And two days after that I became aware that my attitude toward Solanas had quietly transformed itself from one of idle interest into something bordering on active pursuit.

It was in the midst of a late-night visit to Serpentella's quarters that I began to get the picture. All evening we'd been paging pleasant, vaguely charged repartee at one another as we'd gone about our separate Interzone business—I muddling through a desultory conversation with my sometime hot tub colleagues Enver and theroux-que-sault (who politely pretended the whole while that they weren't also carrying on a private conversation of their own), she putting final touches on a new café-style hangout she had built amid the ruins of the run-down carnival she lived in. I'd joined her there at last and found the place impressively dingy: bug zappers zapped out loud from time to time and those mysterious leathery thumps could be heard as well, the sound perhaps of a riding crop falling to the floor somewhere in the back. A supremely bitchy robot-waitress worked the room, refusing to take orders. I sat down next to Serpentella on a low-slung, dilapidated couch and as I did so felt a tension in my gut that I hadn't felt in quite some time, but whose meaning I could hardly mistake. The mood seemed right, after all, the setting was optimal, and suddenly I realized that throughout the last few days of escalated flirtation I had been waiting for precisely such a moment to emerge. Now here it was, and to my only minimal surprise I found that I was working up the nerve to make a pass at Serpentella.

I didn't make it, though. Not then. The sudden arrival of her friend Alva rendered any such maneuver out of the question, and frankly that was just as well with me. I didn't have the slightest idea how I would have proceeded anyway, beyond making some sort of gushing protestation of enthusiasm for her MOO-constructions and seeing where things went from there. But the moment remained an awkward one for me nonetheless. Serpentella's friends Orf and Luna followed closely on Alva's heels, and before I knew it our tête-à-tête had metamorphosed into a party of which I felt myself to be anything but the life. I sat there tongue-tied, very much in touch with my inner teenager, and wallowing in an almost perfect re-creation of the alienation and thwarted puppy lust I recalled just then as having been the emotional hallmarks of every freshman-dorm social gathering I'd ever suffered through. Eventually I gave up even pre-tending to take part in the festivities, bid everyone a hasty good night, and typed *@quit*. And more than anything else, I think, it was the sour aftertaste of adoles-cent frustration I brought to bed with me that night that told me just how pur-poseful a turn my feelings for Solanas had finally taken.

I now stood face-to-face, in other words, with a question I had not yet had to give much serious thought to: what would it mean to act upon such feelings?

I hadn't wanted to face this question, you understand. I think I've made it clear, in fact, that I'd gone out of my way from the start of my MOOish sojourn to dodge it altogether, or at least to arrange things so that I might at some point be able to commit the act without having to worry about the feelings. And even though Jessica insisted that I was kidding myself in that regard, even though she'd told me to my face that no amount of anonymity and gender-bending could drain my intended netsexual experiments of their emotional content, both for her and me—well, she could insist whatever she wanted to insist. My conscience remained unmoved: I knew exactly why I had acquired my Shayla spare, and it wasn't for anything but the most level-headed of investigations into the curious late-twentieth-century technocultural phenomenon of tinysex.

All right, maybe not the *most* level-headed of investigations. And yes, it's true I couldn't guarantee that once said investigations got under way I wouldn't find myself at least a little stirred up by the experience, on some affective level or another. Still, there was never any doubt in my mind that if and when I finally got around to taking Shayla out for a roll or two in the hay, the excursion wouldn't amount to anything remotely impinging on Jessica's place in my heart.

But Solanas already was a different matter. The very fact of my attraction to her told me as much. And while I'm well aware that these days public opinion on the subject of computer-mediated adultery runs a sweeping gamut from those who consider it a laughable contradiction in terms to those who've cited it as grounds for divorce, I can't say it ever occurred to me to argue with my own gut feeling that any virtual involvement with Solanas would be a kind of infidelity. As for just what kind it would be, that too seemed clear enough after the briefest consideration: it would be a virtual infidelity, naturally, and hence an infidelity whose import, like that of all things virtual, would hover somewhere between that of the real and that of the imaginary, never quite attaining the freighted consequentiality of RL deeds but also never quite escaping the inevitability of RL consequences. The only real remaining question, then, was how to live with those consequences.

And this was not an easy question to decide. It simplified things somewhat that on LambdaMOO there seemed to me to be just two general schools of thought on the matter. Each had its share of adherents, I suppose, and each adherent his or her own spin on the basic tenets, but I couldn't help thinking of the two broad currents as, respectively, the Niacinian and the exuist philosophies of extramarital tinyadventure. Why I did so may of course be readily apparent to those of you who recollect the couple's divergent approaches to the RL dimensions of their torrid affair, but for the rest of you I'll recap: Niacin, remember, told the woman he lived with nothing about his virtual escapades; exu told her husband, Kropotkin, everything that could be told without seeming to be cruel. Niacin tried his futile best to keep the VR and RL regions of his heart from spilling over into one another; exu tried her forthright best to keep the lines of negotiation and accommodation open with Kropotkin (who, I should add, was also more or less openly engaged in a MOO affair of his own). Niacin rather quickly caved in to the pressures of his psychic split, and bailed; exu presumably might have carried on in comparative stability for months, as previously she had with HortonWho.

On Niacin's side of the ledger, in other words, lay psychic schism and moral queasiness; on exu's side were relative resilience and what seemed to me an admirable honesty. And you might think, therefore, that it would have been a simple matter for me to opt for exu's strategy. You might also think, I imagine, that Jessica's own openness about her ongoing affair had in any case already made the decision for me.

But I thought other things. I thought, for instance, about a certain night in July soon after my visit from the purple guest—and long after exu had moved on from both Horton and Niacin to a third MOO love, with Kropotkin also well into his second—when I'd sat in the hot tub juggling two or three mindless conversations with the usual assortment of chatterheads while at the same time keeping one eye on a trickle of laconic pages coming from the Crossroads, from exu, informing me that also at the very same time, in real life, her husband was storming out of the house in an unprecedented rage, a rage I understood to be in some way related to the aforementioned processes of negotiation and accommodation. I thought about how I'd paged her asking if she was all right, and gotten only a stoic *exu will survive* in answer. I thought about how I'd tried at that point to steer things back to our usual irony-tinged banter ("Oh I'm sure he will survive," I'd grinned, for exu happened to be gendered male at the time, "but will he get thru the nite w/o thinking dark thoughts about the ultimate possibilities for human relationship?") and about how little irony I'd detected in her reply (*exu is thinking them now, actually. But has most of his life. Had a few years of rest is all*).

I thought about the wave of empathy that had swept through me then (*DrBombay squeezes your hand,* I had typed, the words flying out from the hot tub to the Crossroads to the spare bedroom in a quiet Seattle neighborhood where exu sat before her computer, thinking dark thoughts), and about the understanding I had acquired along with that empathy, so that from then on I could no longer fondly imagine that exu's RL honesty about her VR relationships guaranteed her any less emotionally battering a love life than Niacin's secrecy did him.

But more to the point, perhaps, I thought it possibly a little premature of me to think that in the end I'd have to choose between the two of them at all. My adventure with Solanas was still not much more than a notion, let's remember, and now that my close call amid the bug zappers and the leathery thumps had alerted me to where that notion was headed, I wasn't very sure I cared to follow. True, I might find it easier said than done to stop myself from going there. Already I could feel that I had gone a sort of rudderless—as if some structural, guiding part of me had snapped when Jessica broke the news to me that morning. And whether the force impelling me from then on toward a virtual entanglement was just an itch to even the RL score, or whether it was something not as simple—some suddenly unshackled urge, say, to have a fuller taste of that unique blend of intimacy and distance that had always been (why not confess it now?) the thing that most appealed to me about MOOish relationships—I didn't get the sense that my will alone would be strong enough to resist it.

I only knew that there were other forces pushing in the opposite direction. I knew that despite what Jessica had done, was doing, and despite my own confused reaction to it, I longed more than I longed for almost anything to live in loving peace with her, and with myself. We'd both done enough hurting by then—we'd hurt each other, and we had just plain hurt—and I wanted not to do any more of it. And though there may be some among you who don't see what could have been the harm in trading textual fantasies with a pseudonym whose owner lived 3,000 miles from me, I saw it clearly enough. I'd traded every shot I'd ever had at real love, after all, for fantasies of one kind or another.

And so for now the balance of forces remained in equilibrium, and I was able to delay a while longer having to decide whether I was at heart an exuist or a Niacinian. I told Jessica nothing about that night in Serpentella's café, and strictly speaking I hid nothing from her either. I hoped as well, and very much, that I might go on having nothing to hide.

Two weeks later, on a Friday afternoon, Jessica informed me that Eduardo had returned from Mexico City and that she would be seeing him on Sunday night.

I took the news in stride. I had decided by then that we'd get through this all right, that Jessica just needed to explore her feelings, find her bearings, sow some wild oats or whatever it was she was going through, and that I would wait the whole thing out with patience and, as always, with ambivalence. Besides, I had my MOOish life to keep me occupied in the meantime, and it was going well. A few days before, I'd filled in the last details on the Garden and posted a note on the refrigerator in the kitchen announcing that my creation was open to the public. Already I was getting rave reviews from perfect strangers, and quota donations too, and what with all the gratification these responses gave me, the thought of complicating my life with tinysexual liaisons of any sort lost much of its appeal. I had begun, curiously enough, to feel happier than I had in a long time.

That night, though, after Jessica and I had gone to bed, I lay awake in the grip of a kind of heartache, a yearning for someone or something that I couldn't quite identify. And then a name rose to my lips and settled there, unspoken.

It was exu's.

In the morning I logged on right after breakfast, but exu wasn't to be found. I remembered then that she and Kropotkin were spending most of the weekend out seeing the bands at Lollapalooza's Seattle stopover—with Solanas, in fact, and with Alva, who were both down visiting from Vancouver. There wasn't really anybody else around all day, and in the night I couldn't sleep again, and exu's name was on my tongue again, and the same yearning, again, was in my heart. But now there was a bitterness inside me too. I thought about how Jessica would be out with Eduardo the next evening, and then with a kind of grim satisfaction I thought, "Let's go on now as Shayla and let's just see if anyone will fuck me."

So I did. I got up in the dark and went upstairs to Jessica's computer and while she slept I woke up Shayla. A male player by the name of Mordecai-Q paged me almost immediately, having peeked at my description. "You look interesting," he said, and he invited me to join him in his room (which he called the Singles Den, if you can believe it). I looked at his description then and found myself unable to return his compliment. *Hi there Shayla howya doing?* it began, and the programmed personal reference wasn't bad, but things went downhill from there: *Well here I am.21 years old, 5'5", 126 pounds, sandy-blond hair, brown eyes. I study Electronic Engineering in Fullerton, California. If you want to get to know me better just page or if your in the same room talk to me. Thanks for being interested in me and maybe I will hear from you soon.*

I joined him anyway. He turned out to be every bit as dull as his description promised. And awkward, too. He hugged me suddenly, unbidden, with no explanation and no follow-through. I tousled his sandy-blond hair a bit while our tedious chat dragged on, and this seemed to draw him out some. *Mordecai-Q shyly takes you by the hand and leads you in a slowdance that seems to last forever*, he emoted—and that might have been nice if it hadn't so obviously been just the output of some modified bonker program somebody else had written. He apologized for not asking first before taking my hand, and when I jokingly replied "Help! Help! I've been date-raped!" he asked:

"Are we on a date?"

I was getting depressed.

I played on gamely, though: "Hugs—dancing—hanging out in the 'Singles Den'—I'd say it qualifies. Why not?"

"Well," said Mordecai-Q, "I've never been on a date before."

I had to leave. I was starting to feel sorry for Mordecai-Q, and guilty for toying with him like this. He was asking for my RL mailing address now, but I begged off, telling him it was my policy not to mix the real world with the virtual.

"Come on," he said, "I'm not some weird guy or something."

I smiled at him then, although I didn't feel very happy, and I said, "Honey, relax. Life is complicated enuff around here without adding extra layers. That's my approach. If yours is different, that's cool, but it isn't mine."

And then I said good night and went home.

But before I logged off altogether I slipped over into my Dr. Bombay account and left a message for exu. There were two sentences in it, one in the subject line and one in the body, and they went:

Subject: "I miss you."

Body: "I really do."

In the morning I woke up regretting that message. Why in the world, I asked myself, did I have to go stirring things up on that front when it was still tricky enough keeping my feelings about Solanas in some sort of manageable perspective? I had no answer. I spent the day drinking too much coffee, and mostly on the edge of tears.

By the time the evening arrived I was missing exu again pretty bad. Jessica left the house around ten for her rendezvous with Eduardo, and by eleven I was logged on and quietly thrilled to see that exu was back. I understood a little better now why my crush on her had so pangfully returned, and the main reason didn't seem all that tricky after all: I was miserable, simply, about Jessica of course, and pining for a shoulder to rest my miserable head on. And exu's happened to be the softest, most inviting shoulder I knew just then.

But pouring out my heartache to her proved to be a moderately challenging proposition that night. She had a lot of social catching up to do after her weekend away, it seemed, and so I was obliged to unburden myself through intermittent pages and whispers as we multiMOOed together, moving back and forth between the Lambda and Interzone scenes and trying to keep up with the usual flurry of aimless witticisms. She seemed impatient with me, I thought, and though in fact she was giving me a rather heroic chunk of her time, considering the distractions, and though she furthermore explained that any weirdnesses in her tone were probably due to a nasty, teeth-grinding batch of "herbal Ecstacy" she'd taken at Lollapalooza earlier in the day, I began to worry that I'd alienated her irrevocably with the needy subtext of my MOO-mail message.

And then, around one in the morning, Jessica returned and came downstairs and gave me a distant smile. She looked flushed, a little, though whether with alcohol or pleasure I didn't care to guess, and as she eyed the lines of text scrolling up my screen, she rested one hand on my shoulder and leaned a little lazily on me.

You feel the ghost of Ecco hanging around, I typed for exu's benefit (inserting the event into the ambient wordscape with a program known as the "God" feature), and exu asked with sudden animation "Is she really there???"—for she had often told me how much she missed Ecco's presence on the MOO. And I nodded and said "Yeah, she sez hi," and then exu said a hearty hello back, and then, just like that, Jessica was sitting in my lap and typing on my keyboard, so that Dr. Bombay was her now, and I was only me, with my arms folded quietly around the softness of her belly and my eyes peering out from behind her back to watch the two women carry on their chatty, bubbling reunion. I watched and said nothing, feeling displaced and a little forlorn, feeling shut out from the warmth of both of them and not sure which of the two to feel more jealous of, and wanting nothing more right then than just to go to bed.

Which we did, Jessica and I, soon thereafter.

The next evening Solanas was back in Vancouver and on the MOO again, and I sensed that I was no longer really even trying to keep my feelings about her in manageable perspective. We met in the living room, which seemed especially talkative that night, and there amid the manic, undirected chat of at least a dozen oversocialized undergraduates I threw my arms around her, giving her a big welcome-home kiss. When she returned the greeting with a polite peck on the cheek, I pouted ostentatiously, and only half-jokingly. She smirked, then she embraced me and gave me a long, passionate kiss, but it was only a preprogrammed one, like Mordecai-Q's slow dance. I staggered around in my best pantomime of an amorous daze, and I rolled around at her feet like a love-struck puppy dog, but I didn't actually care much for this game. That familiar tang of male-adolescent frustration was welling up beneath its playful surface, and threatening to leech the fun out of it entirely.

So I morphed into Samantha, and suddenly, subtly, the fun seemed to shift to another level. I felt pretty again, and in this context pretty felt powerful—as if I had permission now to be not only allured, but alluring as well. My self-mocking, supplicant Bombayishness fell away and I became, as much as I was capable of becoming, the self-possessed and sharp-tongued charmer I imagined Samantha to be.

We played some new games then. I alluded mysteriously to the few details about her RL body I had picked up from exu—the color of her eyes, for instance, the curious tattoo. This seemed to fluster her a little, and to intrigue her, and she invited me to leave the living room with her for the relative quiet of the entrance hall, where for no particular reason we began to improvise a larky scene of dueling femmes fatales: I spat bitter, noirish melodrama at her while her lower lip trembled in faux-distress; she switched into her überwomanly Wanda La Rouge morph (a FabulousHotBabe in red bustier and microminiskirt with a half-smoked cigarette dangling from her ruby red lips) and advanced on me with sultry menace as I did some trembling of my own; there was even applause from an onlooking guest or two when it was all over.

"I'm tired of being in public," Solanas whispered to me then. "I'm going home. Come and hang out if you'd like."

I did. Her home, as I've mentioned, was a bead of seawater floating somewhere in the unlinked regions of LambdaMOO. It was a warm and private place, though not so private as to shut out a volley of artless come-ons being paged at me just then from someone named "Fawn," in "The Lesbian Palace." I mentioned the distraction to Solanas, who laughed and said, "You must be convincing in that body."

"It's a type," I replied, flashing that perky-edgy, Elizabeth-Montgomery-on-half-a-gram smile that more or less defined Samantha for me. "You go for it or you don't. But if you do . . . look out."

"Dangerous, hm?" she asked.

I thought about that one for a bit, then I said:

"Oh, not moi per se—it's the attraction that's dangerous. You know?"

And then I changed the subject. I sensed a mood of steadily intensifying possibility inside that bead of seawater, and I was enjoying it far too much to want to try and actually make something of it. Solanas seemed to be enjoying herself as well. We kept on talking for another hour or so, still play-acting some, still making wisecracks, but mostly, and really for the first time since the day we met, just talking.

It felt surprisingly easy to do.

In fact, it felt intoxicatingly easy to do.

And yes, to be honest, it also felt more than a little bit dangerous.

"Well, darling," she said at last, around 3:45 A.M. my time, "I have to get up for work at 8. So fly off on your coke spoon and let me get to bed. Quit being interesting already."

I flew off. Jessica had been asleep for four hours by then.

The next day began amusingly and ended in a purgatory of RL rage and tears. The amusing part was much too short, as it always is, but it had enough to do with the hellish part to merit some retelling here:

It happened shortly after I logged on in the early afternoon. I saw no sign of Solanas that day, nor any of exu, but Niacin was there—in his Ishmael morph—and I thought I'd page him for a visit. Instead, though, and I'm not sure why, I took a remote peek at his description first, and what I saw made me think again: Ishmael was naked from head to toe, his manhood (*large, thick, and nicely shaped*) aloft in the virtual breeze, and his attention evidently on other things than idle conversation, for I noticed too that he was not alone, and that his visitor (one Bionica) was also in the buff and in a graphic if somewhat prosaically rendered state of arousal (*It looks as though there is some moisture between her legs*). I'd thought Finn would have built more privacy than this into his nakedware, but what the hell, the result was kind of fun from where I sat—a mild, cheesy turn-on not dissimilar, I imagined, to watching two lovers go at it in silhouette behind a drawn window blind. And after all, I thought, they'd never know.

But I was definitely mistaken about that. "Bad boy!" Bionica paged me, almost instantly, and almost as quickly I remembered how easy it was to program a player object to alert its owner any time someone else accessed its description file. I felt embarrassed, certainly, but not as much as I felt entertained: MOOish social technology in all its constantly evolving imperfection was forever serving up such moments of unintended comic relief, but I hadn't experienced many quite as rich as this one. I chuckled IRL, then I remote-emoted *DrBombay turns the color of tomato soup* back at Bionica, and then I forgot about the incident for the rest of the afternoon.

Out at dinner that evening, however, with Jessica and her best friend Hillary, I was inspired by the effects of gin, vermouth, and a certain glum tension hanging over our table to recount the story in some detail, thinking at first that it might lighten things up—and only gradually thinking better of it. Hillary listened with a glassy simulacrum of amusement while both of us watched the storm gather in Jessica's eyes. It hung there until I'd finished with the anecdote, and it hung on all through dinner, and it finally broke the moment Jessica and I stepped alone into our apartment. She said then, with quiet vehemence, that she wasn't sure she could stand it anymore. She said that frankly she could care less if I was getting my rocks off spying on virtual people having virtual sex, that wasn't the point. She said the story just reminded her again, that's all, of what a voyeur I was at heart, of how incapable I was of making love, real love, with all of me not just my cock, to a real person who was really there and not locked safely up inside some image or some fantasy or some goddamned possibility et fucking cetera.

I didn't take the critique very well, I have to say. I fought back bitterly, and we kept at it long and hard, well into the night and all through the next morning. We fought with a violence that stopped just short of being physical (but only just), and we fought with a desperation that reduced us both at various times to cringing, pleading parodies of wounded animals, our faces slick with tears and snot. We fought, I guess, because we didn't know what else to do.

And when we couldn't fight anymore, and after we'd been human again for a couple hours, Jessica told me she thought it might be best if she spent the coming weekend over at Hillary's, just to chill out for a while and get some time to think. And I agreed.

I was logged on again by the middle of the afternoon, though the MOO and its weightless complications seemed a frivolous distraction to me after what I'd just been through. I ended up in Club Doome, where a crowd of seminotable old-timers had collected serendipitously: exu was there, and Doome himself, and MaoTseHedgehog and Wooga, not to mention the very old and quota-wealthy Mailstrom, who had lately donated 50K to my garden and thereby elevated himself to near-divinity in my eyes. I thought I might glean some pearls of historical wisdom from this rare gathering, but aside from an underlying mood of auld lang syne the chat turned out to be the standard MOOish fare: the usual pointless puns, the usual oblique references to current events both in VR and out of it, and of course the usual disputatiousness concerning Minnie (whose unsettling saga was just then building toward a particularly unsettling new chapter).

In the midst of this, Solanas paged me and we flirted back and forth a bit, but my heart wasn't in it. It was the first time we'd spoken since my visit to the bead of seawater, and when she alluded admiringly to the aura of dangerousness I'd wrapped myself in that night, a kind of exhaustion overcame me. I felt powerless to live up to the persona I'd been inventing then, and not very much inclined to try.

"Ah, that was just Samantha talking," I paged, and I wasn't really kidding. "But thank you anyway."

"Oh dear," she replied, "and me already ten mins. late to work on account of a boy who turns out to be utterly safe. If I'd known, I'd not have stuck around so long."

She wasn't quite kidding either, I got the feeling. At any rate she said good-bye immediately, and disconnected.

But then, when I logged on the next evening, I got a friendly page from a morph of hers called Shelley, a spivak, who said to join em in eir bead of seawater when I got a moment, because e had something e wanted to give me. And when I got a moment I joined em, and e handed me an object whose description read, in part, A *delicate silver hoop, designed to adorn a pierced eyebrow.* It was a gag of sorts—a playful reference to the age gap between us, which was too small to matter much but big enough to make Shelley (or Solanas, or whoever) feel a little more proprietary than me about such Generation X accoutrements as piercings and tattoos—and e'd attached a wee but angst-ridden figurine of Gen-X pop idol Trent Reznor to it for an added laugh. But I was touched, for real. I morphed into Samantha, typed the command *don hoop*, and admired the bangle now seamlessly integrated into my description. Shelley had a look at it too and clapped eir hands in delight, and I hugged em, and thanked em.

But I didn't hang around for long. It was Jessica's last night at home before she went away to Hillary's, and I wanted to be sure we went to bed together: I wanted to hold her warm, solid, gently breathing body in my arms as she fell asleep.

The next morning Jessica packed some things and left the house, and once or twice that afternoon I caught myself on the verge of thinking I would never see her again. It was a foolish thought, of course, and easy to shrug off.

Less easily dismissed, though, was my growing conviction that the fractured state of my emotional affairs had finally made tinysex of any kind a complete impossibility for me. I spent most of the afternoon, in fact, resigning myself to this development, talking it over with my friend Elsa on the front porch of her sunny cottage in the Lambda woods somewhere. She knew something of my RL troubles already and she learned now, in broad and unspecific outlines, about my virtual frustrations: I told her about my inability to abandon myself to anonymous MOOsex with the Mordecai-Qs of the world, and about the fruitlessly oscillating approach-withdrawal pattern I had fallen into with Solanas/Shelley. I told her I was still curious about tinysex, though, and since I remembered her telling me once that a former MOO lover had given her the collected logs of their more memorable netsexual encounters, I asked her if she might let me have a look at one or two of them some time.

The request must have seemed a pathetic one, and I suppose it was, but her rejection of it was polite enough, and it came with a sort of consolation offer: "Would you like me to take my clothes off instead? I love showing people, and wouldn't mind that."

So I watched as my friend Elsa removed her clothes, one layer at a time, and I could see then why she enjoyed showing off her virtual nakedness. It was lovely: nothing overheated or prurient, just the clean lines of a moderately appealing body described with affection and honesty, right down to the artificial leg that Elsa said she also wore in real life, and that she took off last of all, revealing a limb amputated above the knee, with an impressive scar on the front of the thigh. I thanked her as she dressed again, and I complimented her on her work and joked a bit about the mild lather her display of it had gotten me into.

But if anything, I now felt even sadder than I had before. I felt as if the most scathing of Jessica's accusations stood at last irrevocably confirmed: I was a voyeur through and through, and even in the allegedly liberating context of a world without material bodies, I could never be anything more.

It was, therefore, with my expectations of adventure lowered pretty much as far as they would go that I encountered Shelley at 4:30 on the following afternoon and initiated a chat that was to continue more or less uninterrupted until approximately 8 o'clock the next morning, by which time it would have gone a very adventurous distance indeed beyond the bounds of what is normally considered polite conversation.

I had stayed away from LambdaMOO the night before, depressed by the scene with Elsa and by the emptiness of my apartment. There'd been a Beavis and Butt-head marathon on MTV and I'd decided to watch that instead. Then after a while I'd started flipping between the MTV and the porno channels. Then eventually I'd locked in on the porn and proceeded to masturbate myself into a thoughtless stupor that had ended, finally, in a dreamless sleep around 4 A.M.

And in the morning I had felt about as wholesome and desirable as you might imagine I would.

But now, as I said, it was late in the afternoon, and I (in the hot tub) was paging pleasantly with Shelley (in the bead of seawater), and things didn't seem quite so dreary anymore. There was a casual velocity to our interactions today, a steady, just-perceptible acceleration toward increasingly self-revelatory ground. "You're welcome to come hang out here, you know," Shelley paged me finally, and so I came, and pretty soon e was—she was—giving me a brief tour of all the selves that she had been on LambdaMOO, at one time or another. Shelley and Solanas I knew, of course, and Wanda La Rouge as well, but now for the first time and in quick succession I met Soren (a bony, flaxen-haired teenage boy with sunken, moody eyes), and Annelise (a winking portrait of late-Victorian neurasthenic girlhood, her face shimmering with the ethereal pallor of future suicide), and selenaea (her earliest morph, a purring, female werecat with teeth that cut like razors). And as I met them all, her already cluttered image in my head grew yet more crowded and confused, while at the same time I sensed with increasing clarity the presence of a single, shapeless, seventh character who moved beneath the play of surfaces, who did the others' talking for them, who had no name unless it was perhaps that one simuous letter that almost always persisted when the surface changed.

It was this person that I wanted to know better now: it was S*. I started pressing her for more—for stories, for confessions—and predictably enough I focused my interrogation on the subject of her experiences with tinysex. *DrBombay has this pathetic pre-Foucauldian notion that knowing details about a person's sex life is somehow the key to knowing their true self,* I emoted. *Indulge him, wouldja?*

And she did. But it turned out there wasn't much for me to know. "Let's see," she said. "Two experiences with actual fucking. Both resulting from casual flirtation in the Hot Tub as I recall. One of the guys took me to a beach somewhere. I thought it was terribly silly both times. Wandered around the apartment, got a beer, played with the cat. Returned to the computer to moan now and then.

"Didn't do much for me at all," she added, as if she needed to. But then we moved on to more ambiguous categories of sexual interaction, and as we did the material got a little richer, and the interrogation became something more like a conversation again. I told her, without naming any names, about the variety of erotic feelings MOOish people had inspired in me—about my tinycrushes on exu, on Ashley-Melissa, on her. She said, "Yes, I think there's something about this place that kind of fosters crushes," and she described two "intense relationships" with men in VR that had both fizzled once she met them IRL. I talked a little bit then about my own intense relationship, the RL one with Jessica, and about its current difficulties. She said she was sorry to hear things were going badly, and she seemed to mean it. She said she didn't know much about being in a couple, though. She said in real life she had only ever had "affairs." She said that was pretty much the way she liked it.

And then she said, "Oh yeah. I just remembered another experience that probably counts as netsex, although in a rather nontraditional way." She said that once, as selenaea the werecat, she had "pounced" on a MOOish acquaintance, had pinned this person to the ground, and had spent a leisurely while playing with em as if with captured prey, raking claws and teeth across the surface of eir skin while e trembled in terror.

"Yow," I said. "That sounds, um, pretty intense to me."

I wasn't lying.

She had morphed into selenaea by that point, and as she stood there radiating feline grace and menace, she eyed me with a speculative grin. I cowered expectantly and, I hoped, invitingly. But I cowered in vain: some unseen distraction seemed to draw her off, a page from somewhere in the MOO perhaps, or a phone call IRL, and I felt suddenly exposed, ridiculous. I needed to get out of there, to get some dinner, and I told her so.

"OK, happy feeding," she said after a bit, almost as if the menacing and cowering of just a moment before had never happened. Almost: except that as she said it she extended a forepaw and rested it on my neck, just under my ear, then pulled it lightly across my throat, *four razor-claws drawing parallel reddish lines* in Dr. Bombay's skin. I took a sharp breath IRL when she did that, and not in terror either. Not exactly.

I logged off then, dizzy with hunger and uncertainty. I ordered Chinese takeout, watched MTV for a little while, and wondered whether it would really be such a hot idea for me to go back onto the MOO.

Of course I did, though, before too long.

Of course: S* was still there (Shelley again), and I joined her almost immediately. The lag on Lambda had gotten pretty bad by then, so I opened up a second connection to Interzone and made my way to Serpentella's café, where she sat waiting for me on the dilapidated couch. She showed me some new things she was working on—a candy machine, for instance, that dispensed chocolates with live spiders inside them. We played with that one for a while, and I suggested an enhancement or two, and then we sat back down on the couch and got to talking again. I proposed we gossip, and we did: about exu and her new MOOlover, the famous Doome; about Niacin and the stormy, extended romance he had lately carried on for several months with Alva; about HortonWho and other likable pains in the ass. S* mentioned in the midst of this that she was pouring herself a glass of wine out there in her apartment in Vancouver, and I said "excellent idea" and "brb" (for "be right back") and went upstairs to pour myself a shot of rum.

"To gossip," I said upon my return, and *DrBenway raises his glass.*

Serpentella clinks her screen came back at me, and it wasn't long thereafter that I started feeling tipsy. We both began to commit a lot of typos then and I to get a little mushy. I found myself reminiscing about the day we met, and confessing what I'd had in mind the last time I'd been sitting on this couch, in this café, with her. "I don't believe a word of it," she said, and grinned, and told me she was pouring herself another glass of wine.

The constant popping of the café's bug zappers had lost its charm by then and I didn't mind saying it, so S* suggested we retire to her Interzone home. I followed her out of the café, into the adjoining freak show, past a silver lamé curtain and up into the large glass tank that Serpentella lived in, surrounded by red velvet and her comic-book collection. We settled into a comfortable chaise longue there, and she mentioned she had music on now, out there in her apartment in Vancouver. I begged her to put on *Exile in Guyville*, by the young and prematurely world-weary indie-rock sensation Liz Phair, and sing the lyrics for me, for I had lost my only copy of the record somehow and missed it sorely, and I knew from our predinner conversation that S* was also a fan. I suppose the fact that all the songs on the record seemed to be about either ill-considered affairs or terminally damaged relationships might have influenced my choice as well, but I don't remember thinking about it much, and S* seemed happy to oblige.

Serpentella [sings]: I woke up alarmed. I didn't know where I was at first . . . Just that I woke up in your arms, and almost immediately I felt sorry . . .

I smiled: the song was "Fuck and Run," and one of my favorites. S* kept feeding lines to me intermittently as we talked on into the early-morning hours, and I sang back now and then, hearing the music only in my head. It made a good soundtrack. We were retracing all the main threads of the day's conversation now: the complications of other people's tinysex lives, the injuries and regrets of our own RL relationships. As well, we both talked now with increasing ease about the long meandering path of flirtation that had brought us to this room together, comparing notes and trading recollections the way new lovers often do once the threshold of physical intimacy has been crossed and the veils of everyday politeness have been lifted. The only difference being, of course, that no such intimacy had occurred. We were not lovers, and as far as I could tell we were not going to be: we both seemed to want something more than conversation to happen now, but either we didn't want it badly enough, or we didn't quite know what it was.

Serpentella sang: *I can feel it in my bo-ones . . .*

And Dr. Benway finished the line: *. . . I'm gonna spend my whole life alone.*

I smiled then and gave her a big kiss. She smiled back, leaned sloppily against me. But there was no momentum there: the two gestures scrolled slowly up our screens, followed only by further lines of playful, probing, but increasingly languid dialogue. We'd been together for nine hours straight, not counting my dinner break, and it was plain now that the acceleration that had taken us this far had cut out finally, and left us coasting. I began making noises about logging off. I began, too, to prepare myself for the emptiness I would inevitably feel when I did—the familiar, ashy awareness of having stepped up to the brink of intimacy and pulled away again without making the leap. It was nice to know that this time at least my pulling away was in some sort of loose accord with my better judgment, but it still seemed a little too much like every other anxious getaway I'd ever made for me to feel very good about it.

All the same, I stretched my arms and made as if to go.

S* grinned. "Bored, darling?"

"Not bored, my dear. Dead tired."

She hm'd and poked me in the ribs, to test. I jumped, though only sluggishly. "You wouldn't happen to be ticklish, would you?" she asked. I denied it, lying, and asked her the same.

"Oh god. Horribly, horribly so," she replied. Expectantly? Invitingly? I couldn't be sure, but I did know this: suddenly I didn't feel so tired anymore.

I flashed a wicked grin and held my fingers up over her, like Bela Lugosi.

She fled to the other end of the chaise longue.

I followed.

She cowered.

I tickled her mercilessly then: ribs, armpits, belly, back of knees, whatever she exposed in trying to cover up whatever else I'd been tickling. She shrieked and squirmed and said at last, "What, am I supposed to say uncle or something?"

She grinned.

"Ah shaddap," I said, and I grinned too. Then I bent down and kissed her again—only this time I made it long and hard.

She didn't respond.

I kissed her some more.

And still nothing happened.

I sat there watching my computer screen for signs of life. It seemed like I watched for a good long time. And then I saw this:

Serpentella raises an eyebrow. She wraps her arms around your neck, and kisses you back.

I let out a long breath, IRL. And then I wrote:

DrBenway sighs deeply and melts into your arms, pressing his body against yours.

The anxious pause again, but not so long this time:

Serpentella tangles her fingers in your hair and grazes her teeth across your lower lip.

And I:

DrBenway touches the back of your neck lightly, nibbles at your ear. . . .

And after that, there were no more anxious pauses.

In fact, there were no more interruptions of any kind, really, until two hours later, when at last I shut my computer down and padded off into the dim morning sunlight of my empty bedroom, not feeling so empty after all, myself.

Not feeling so empty after all.

How very nice, I hear you say, but just what was our Dr. Benway/Bombay feeling at that moment then? What exactly was he thinking as he pulled the sheets up over himself and drifted off to sleep? And more to the point, what precisely had he been feeling, and thinking, and for God's sake doing in those two conspicuously undocumented hours between the nibbling of Serpentella's ear and the turning off of his computer?

Dear reader: Please don't misunderstand me when I say that now and then your curiosity gets a little burdensome. For what I mean by this is only that I don't by any means take lightly my authorial obligation to satisfy that curiosity—and that I recognize the need, however onerous, at times to sacrifice my own sense of personal decorum to this responsibility.

I understand, moreover, that the last few years of winking public discourse on the subject of online eroticism may have raised the level of your inquisitiveness beyond what it might otherwise be, and I am also not unconscious of the fact that vast portions of that discourse have been liberally salted with distortions and miscomprehensions of one sort or another. I am willing to admit, therefore, that in my haste to draw a veil over what was (after all) a very private moment in the MOOish lives of S* and myself, I may have left certain legitimately pressing questions unanswered. And if for no other reason, finally, than a lingering attachment to the fiction that my virtual experiences bore some possible resemblance to a level-headed investigation into the curious late-twentieth-century technocultural phenomenon of tinysex, I am prepared now to address at least a few of those questions.

To start with then: All that stuff you've heard about "one-handed typing"? Forget it. Or rather, try and look at it from where I sat, that early morning: my eyes riveted on the screen, my fingers tense on the keyboard, my body caught up in a rhythm that was not the taut, sustained excitement of RL sex but a series of intermittent, gusty arousals, each cued to the appearance of a new emote from S*, each soon dispersed amid the hardly trivial work of composing a follow-up line that both made physical sense and didn't take too long to finish. Do you suppose then that in the midst of all this rapid-fire reading, writing, and spatial reasoning (which by the way produced well over a hundred separate and often fairly complicated emotes in the ninety minutes or so it took to reach our virtual finale) I managed also to attend to the subtle biomechanics of bringing myself to a real-life climax?

I did not. And frankly, though my hat is off to the mighty Finn and all those other tinysexual pentathletes who claim their every orgasm in VR has its simultaneous counterpart in RL, I don't know that I would have availed myself of their techniques that morning even if I could have figured them out. Oh, my loins were engaged, no doubt about it—but I can't say the thrill that thrilled me most was a genital one. I wouldn't even say it was sexual, necessarily. I'm not sure just what category of thrill I'd put it in, to be honest, but I can pretty much tell you what I'd call it:

Lucidity.

I never felt more lucidly embodied in VR than I did during those ninety minutes with S*, is what it was. Together, in the concentrated attention we turned on one anothers' virtual bodies and our own, we conjured up a MOOspace that surpassed in clarity even my most vivid memories of early visits, when the sights and sensations of VR had still been fresh to me and striking to my imagination. And while it's true that in itself this cocreative process wasn't what you'd quite call sex (indeed, it seemed at times a little more like comedy, as when Dr. Benway's description forced us to reckon with the fact that I was wearing diapers throughout the proceedings), there was definitely something sexy about it. It was as if we'd stumbled onto the secret source of all the free-floating libidinal energy in the MOO—and it turned out to be the simple possibility that sometimes the act of representation itself can be erotic.

Ah yes: I see your crap detector flashing even now, quite properly advising you that anyone who mentions representation and the erotic in the same sentence most likely just means smut. But honestly, I don't. In fact, if anything sets my crap detector flashing it's the glib assumption—commoner than it ought to be in the aforementioned winking public discourse—that tinysex and all its online variants are just some new-fangled, propeller-headed form of pornography. And yes, I realize there will be some among you who share this assumption, perhaps not even glibly either; and no, I don't expect to change very many of your minds. But folks, you know me pretty well by now. You have seen me drooling in abject voyeurism before the cathode jigglings of the late-night soft-core cable channels, and if personal decorum didn't stop me from letting you glimpse that pretty scene, it's certainly no obstacle to my telling you now that I have sampled and even devoured porn in many forms besides the televisual: I have stared at the magazines and rented the videos, I have dialed the phone lines and downloaded the image files, I have perused the purloined Victoria's Secret catalogs, I have suspended my disbelief in the "letters from our readers," and I have sat numbly in the postclimactic backwash of all these activities, wondering what in heaven's name it was that had seemed so compelling about them only moments before.

Do you think then, you doubters, that there's any chance you might just take my word for it when I tell you that what I saw and felt and did that morning in the bluish glow of my computer was not in fact pornography?

Beyond that, I won't argue the point. I don't in any case need to convince *myself* about it. Sure, it's true that in the thick of things the question hovered in my mind—and never more than at those moments when I couldn't help noticing the unfortunate influence of all those "letters from our readers" on my tinysexual vocabulary. But from the moment I switched off the monitor, there was no longer any doubt in me about the difference: I could feel it in my bones, and on the surface of my skin, and in my head, my feet, my fingers—a feeling quite unlike the anesthetic aftereffects of porn, and not nearly so familiar to me, no, but instantly recognizable all the same. How could I not have recognized it, after all? Every time I'd ever crossed the line between the possible and the actual, every time I'd gone at last from the cold comfort of wanting to the warm danger of having, every time, in short, that I had first held a woman I desired in my arms—I had come away with this selfsame speedball combination of satiety and lightness coursing through my body.

And so I didn't even have to think about it; I just knew. My body knew. That even though its eyes had seen no one, and its ears heard no one, and its hands touched no one—still it had been held, and closely, by another body, and it had held that body closely in return.

That, then, was what I was feeling as I padded off into the dim morning sunlight, if you really want to know. As for what I was thinking—well. I have told you that I did not feel as empty as my bed, but I knew very well who was missing from it, and who belonged in it. And what I thought, as I pulled the sheets up over me, was that I loved her too much to tell her what had just happened—or to pretend that nothing had.

NEW YORK CITY, SEPTEMBER 1994

The Bedroom
You are at the basement level of an overpriced and
  undersized East Village duplex apartment. It's either
  cramped or cozy down here, depending on your mood.
  The ceiling is low and the walls are never farther
  than a couple arms' lengths away. Pine bookshelves
  cover one wall, three dresser drawers (two black-
  lacquered and one cherry-stained) line another. In
  the northwest corner there's a bed: a waist-high
  platform painted white, a futon mattress also white,
  white sheets, white comforter, two bloodred pillows.
A black metal staircase spirals up to the ceiling. A
  passage to the southeast opens into The_Author's
  Fabulous Office Nook.
Jessica (sleeping) and The_Author (sleeping) lie in the
  bed.
You see 19-Inch Television Set here.
The lights are out and it's pitch black in here.

The_Author is dreaming.

The_Author treads water, in his dream. His head bobs
  just above the surface of a broad seawater cove. High
  red cliffs ring the cove, unclimbable; there are no

beaches anywhere, no visible means of exit from the
water.

The_Author likes it here. The water's warm and he has
company. He can see other heads bobbing in the
distance, spread out across the cove in a sparse
constellation. He converses with them, casually;
sound carries very well here at the water's surface,
and he is on a first-name basis with the others, all
of them: exu, S*, Niacin, Elsa, Kropotkin, Alva . . .

The_Author, in the morning, will catalog this as his
third MOO dream.

The_Author will go over the list in his mind. Dream
One: exu as Kali, making words shake on his computer
screen. Dream Two: The_Author wandering through the
hallways of a dusty, antique mansion, looking for
Finn. Dream Three: this floating in a cove of
distant, bobbing heads.

The_Author will note with interest how the settings
change, how his unconscious seems to struggle with
the task of representing LambdaMOO -- first showing
him the text his eyes see, then showing him the place
his mind's eye sees, then giving him, at last, a
picture of something he has never actually quite
pictured, but always somehow sensed: the abstract
substance of the network, the medium in which the
MOOer floats, warm, weightless.

The_Author will ask himself, someday, which of these
images of the MOO is the truest, and he will find he
doesn't know the answer.

The_Author is not looking for any answers at the
moment, however.

The_Author is dreaming.

The_Author treads water, in his dream. He converses
with the others, casually. He hears a distant
roaring, steady, growing louder. They all know
what it is, that it will be there soon, and that
there will be nothing else to do when it arrives
except to dive, and wait, and hope they come up
breathing after the tidal wave has passed.

VR

8

Toad Minnie

Or TINYLIFE, and How It Ends

Now it came to pass that on the evening after my long night's journey into daybreak with S* (although for reasons having nothing to do with that particular event), Dr. Bombay and his morph Samantha parted ways.

Their parting was a somewhat melancholy affair, but it was ultimately nothing if not businesslike: I morphed into Samantha's shape, I saved a copy of her description to my desktop hard drive for posterity, and then I shifted back to Dr. B and, without a further thought for the matter, deleted the cocaine-addled sorceress-cum-homemaker from my catalog of morphs. That done, I did the same to the dolphin, Faaa, and then methodically I moved on down the list of my remaining morphs, deleting this one, that one, then the next, until, at last, no more remained. There was only me, and I, as I had really always been, was Dr. Bombay—the central self around whom all the others had revolved.

Lord knows, I wouldn't have committed this small massacre if I hadn't had to. As a character, Dr. Bombay felt naked and rather dull to me without his now-deleted companions. But the hard truth was, I simply couldn't afford to keep them around anymore; for I was broke. By which I mean, of course, quota-broke—and no, not really any more so than I'd been at any other moment in the long and irksome quota-bankruptcy into which the Garden of Forking Paths had plunged me. Except that now I could no longer kid myself that this was just a temporary condition, soon to be rectified somehow by the intercession of whatever rudimentary market forces could be said to operate on LambdaMOO. The Quotto scheme had been a delusion from the start, needless to say; but even the flow of contributions from the garden-going public, which for a while had seemed so promising, was slowing down now with a grim finality to less than a trickle. I was still 87,000 bytes over-quota, and it was clear at this point that I would be a very senior MOOer indeed before I ever made that deficit up through private donations. The way I saw it, in other words, I had no choice: I must at long last swallow my pride and make a formal appeal to the crabbed beneficence and exalted judgment of the Architecture Review Board.

Which meant in turn, as exu helpfully explained, that the morphs were toast. There wasn't any way around it: one simply did not go before the ARB and ask for extra disk space without first thoroughly purging oneself of superfluous kiloby-tage—"superfluous" being, apparently, a kind of shorthand for morphs, old MOO-mail, and bonkers. Especially bonkers. Which was unfortunate, I guess, since if I'd had a pile of the latter in my possession, I could have made a great show of sacrificing them and maybe thereby have managed to let my little coterie of morphs survive unnoticed. Not having even a single bonker to my name, how-ever (and never having been much of a MOO-mail hoarder in any case), I found my options pretty well reduced to one: the morphs must go.

And so they went. And I, thus slimmed down to the lean and hungry profile proper to a quota-supplicant, submitted my request for 87K and change.

Two very interesting weeks would pass before I finally got an answer.

Let us now, however, put those weeks on hold, set back the narrative clock a bit, and take a second look at that late-summer afternoon on which, to my chagrin, I was caught spying on the nakedness of Ishmael/Niacin and of his occasional net-sex-pal Bionica. I have already told you nearly everything worth mentioning about that lovely scene, but I must also tell you now that it was not my only memorable encounter on the MOO that day. There was one other, and I think it might be useful, as we navigate the curious course of MOO-historical events to follow, to have heard a little bit about it at this point. So:

About an hour past my debut as a virtual peeping Tom, while I was pleasantly conversing with Sebastiano in his handsome Weaveworld cottage (*The floor is polished hardwood, but the walls and rafters are rough hewn timber which still exudes the smell of fresh cut pine. Large windows with weathered shutters are always opened wide. You see a bookshelf with some curious titles in it, a cluttered desk, and a simple but comfortable futon bed in the corner*), the following inscrutable message appeared on my screen, paged at me from the mansion's coat closet by an unknown guest character:

"Hi. You may, if you wish, connect to 192.168.1.1, where we can talk, from time to time."

What could it mean? The numbers didn't puzzle me—they had to be the address of some MUD somewhere—but why the guest would just assume I'd want to go and meet it there was an enigma.

"You sure that page was for me?" I replied.

A pause.

"Absolutely sure."

I shrugged an RL shrug. "Whee! How mysterious," I paged, not certain I wanted to play this game much longer, but willing to go along with it for now.

"Heh. Not for nothing were Chandler's mysteries set in California, huh? NYakkers are too cautious."

A wheel or two began to turn inside my head. The guest knew where I lived, the Chandler reference rang a certain bell, and then came this:

"Hey, you can bring Sebby along," paged the guest, referring to Sebastiano with a familiarity that pretty much gave the game away. "In fact, I'd enjoy chatting to the both of you, it's been a while. . . . It's simply that I can't chat here."

A broad grin spread across my RL face. "Say . . . what time is it where you are?" I coyly paged. "Would it be somewhere between, oh, Tasmanian Standard Time and Outback Daylight Savings?"

"Precisely, good Dr.," came the reply, and in my mind's ear I heard the gruff and baritone Australian accents I had always imagined for the voice of HortonWho, the sometime geist and full-time newt, the lover of Philip Marlowe mysteries, of post-poststructuralist philosophy, and once upon a time, of my dear friend exu.

I was glad to see him, and he was right: it had been a while. Fifty-six days, to be precise, since his last clandestine visit disguised as the purple guest. It felt like ages, and I was eager to get caught up with him, to find out what he'd been doing with himself in all these weeks of exile.

It didn't take long. I opened a connection to the address the guest had given me, typed my way through a brief login process, and thereupon encountered Anthony—for that was Horton's RL name, and it was what he called himself in this, his very own private MOO, located on a desktop server somewhere in the environs of Melbourne. Sebastiano followed quickly after, hugs and pleasantries were traded all around, and in short order Anthony made plain enough what had been occupying him of late: he was preparing for an all-out, one-man war on LambdaMOO—"a war of strategic intervention," as he put it, whose methods were to consist of a dizzying weave of technological and political attacks, and whose aims were to coalesce around the single, paramount goal of overthrowing Lambda's present system of government, such as it was.

Step one toward this goal, apparently, was the MOO in which we stood—a pristine, lag-free place where Anthony could strategize in undisturbed security. He had built no structures there that I could see; only the room we met in, which he'd given the name "nowhere" and left with its featureless default settings intact. *You see nothing special,* said the description, but in fact I saw the opposite: in its unbounded emptiness the place was strikingly eerie, and I couldn't help picturing it as a sort of ghostly version of Superman's top-secret Fortress of Solitude, the Arctic redoubt to which the Man of Steel sometimes repaired in order to brood upon his lifelong exile from the planet Krypton.

I don't imagine Anthony thought of it in quite those terms, but it was plain he'd been doing a lot of brooding lately, for he was now more bitter than ever about the incursions Laurel and her supporters had made into his real life. "They caused more damage than I can really describe without boring your tits off," he said, though he didn't seem to mind telling us in detail how particularly galling it had been to lose his old university Internet account (thanks, as you'll recall, to Laurel's letter of complaint to his former system administrator). "That link was a strategic resource," lamented Anthony, who claimed he'd lost some 60 megabytes of personal data along with it, confiscated summarily by the sysadmin and never returned. Still, the experience had not been without its uses: if nothing else, it had taught him that he ought no longer to rely on any single access provider for his connection to the Net. He had since made "alternate arrangements," he said—"a triply redundant" set of Internet accounts now linked him and his fortress-MOO to the world, protecting him against any future attempts by his enemies to shut him out of VR again. "When I come back at them (as I surely will)," said Anthony, "it will be a soundly based attack."

And a deviously complicated one as well. I cannot say for certain that I fully understood the details of his plan, but the essence was this: he was going to poke a finger into the heart of LambdaMOO's internal social contradictions, and then he was going to wiggle that finger vigorously until the whole thing fell apart. In more concrete terms, it all had something to do with an as-yet-unrealized invention Anthony was calling "little monsters." These, once perfected, would be LambdaMOO programs endowed with all the usual abilities of normal LambdaMOO player objects, except that in their case, an actual LambdaMOO player account would not be necessary in order to manipulate them. Instead, they would take input from anyone on any MOO (and send the output back from

Lambda) via a network-communications feature that was integral to the database. Strictly speaking, in other words, they would not be players but virtual communication devices, and since HortonWho's almost-historic dispute against the link to aCleanWellLightedMOO had more or less established that such devices were not themselves subject to MOOish discipline, the little monsters would be free to roam the MOO entirely untouchable by Lambda's messy justice system.

Not that the vestigial Power Elite wouldn't do their damnedest to rub them out, of course. But this was evidently also part of Anthony's master plan. As he gleefully observed, the moment anyone tried to bring a dispute against one of his net-puppets, he would straightaway "crank up HortonWho.vs.aCleanWellLighted-MOO again, via proxy," and watch with pleasure as the CWL crowd went into a frenzy of hair-splitting attempts to draw the line between their own communications link and his. He readily conceded that their efforts might in time succed, and that a judgment banning some or even all of the little monsters might at last be won, but in that case his adversaries would then face the even tougher challenge of enforcing such a ban. "If you look at the problem of detecting such players, it's very difficult," said Anthony, explaining that the only way to go about it would involve a lot of labor-intensive close examination of object code. Not an impossible job, to be sure, but then the purpose of his monsters, ultimately, was not to make themselves indestructible—it was to make the existing social system so chaotic and exhausting that eventually nobody in her right mind would even try to make it work. "The point is this, DrB," said Anthony. "Wars are not won by killing people, they are won by economic collapse of the enemy."

I had to laugh. "You're perfectly mad."

"Am I? I suppose it's possible," he granted, and he did a cheerful little mock-Hitlerian strut by way of acting the part ("Heute, der Sudatenland," he declaimed, "morgens LambdaMOO!"). But then he sobered up a bit and added: "Doesn't make me mistaken however."

And no, all things considered, it didn't. In its particulars, I decided, the invasion of the little monsters really *was* just a little too baroque to ever get off the ground; but in its general outlines, Anthony's recipe for revolution made no small amount of sense to me. For one thing, precedent attested to its viability: after all, even in Haakon's depoliticized account of the wizards' long-ago abdication (according to which their withdrawal from the social sphere had been a unilateral and purely administrative decision), it was clear that the increasing amounts of time and effort required to manage the player population had been the deciding factor. And whether or not you believed Anthony's only slightly less credible version of that momentous event—according to which it had been no one else but he (as chief negotiator for the rebel MOO Underground alliance) who finally made the wizards see just how untenable their role as autocrats had become—it wasn't hard to picture him single-handedly plunging the MOO into sufficient chaos to bring down yet another social order. He plainly had the cussedness for it, and besides, as a general rule (which he himself now sagely articulated) "it's easier to make-ungovernable than to govern."

There was, moreover, an additional sort of historical momentum to Anthony's plans. In his tactical retreat to a private MOO, and in his strategic decision to aim his attacks at the boundaries between LambdaMOO and the rest of the Net, he was in a way only anticipating the future that no less a figure than Pavel Curtis foresaw for MUDdish VR: that long-dreamt-of day when "distributed MUD-ding" became a reality, when every MUD would spread out seamlessly across as many internetworked personal computers as it had inhabitants, and every MUD-der would supply the disk space and other hardware necessary to maintain her own MUDly existence. From Pavel's managerial perspective, needless to say, the benefits of such a scenario were substantial: once players didn't have to share the resources of a single computer, such administrative burdens as quota allocation, server security, and Internet bills would largely disperse into thin air, becoming the locally (and easily) managed problems of the players themselves. From Anthony's perspective as a grizzled ancholibertarian warrior, however, the appeal was possibly even greater, and he made no secret of his eagerness to see the collective quandaries of Lambda's virtual democracy someday dissolved into the individual struggles of a thousand interlinked but ultimately autonomous little mini-MOOs. "MOO politics will be different when everyone can run their own," he had declared upon welcoming me into his Spartan hideout. "It becomes less a state thing than a propertarian thing."

Now, let me say this right up front: in my two or three decades as a politically conscious human being, I have never quite decided for myself the relative merits of the "state thing" versus the "propertarian thing." God knows, in any case, I've never been one to advocate the indiscriminate dismantling of governments, especially when the only organizing principle offered in their stead is that of private ownership. This said, however, I must now confess that on that particular late-summer afternoon, my sentiments regarding the state of governmental affairs on LambdaMOO were such that, had the grizzled ancholibertarian warrior known to most of MOOdom as HortonWho marched forth from his fortress of solitude on that very day and forthwith realized his cherished dream of smashing the MOOish state, I don't believe I would have shed so much as a virtual tear.

Now let me tell you why. It's common for the bloom of a young man's political optimism to fade as middle-age and its sundry disillusionments approach, so I won't belabor that ancient story here, except to say that in the warp speed of a MOOish life the tale might naturally be expected to run its course more quickly than usual, and that after two months of daily immersions in VR I had by now been living MOOishly quite long enough to have covered that course almost in its entirety. My early, easy enthusiasms for LambdaMOO's democracy (the birth of which I had, after all, eyewitnessed as an impressionable newbie) had since been steadily worn away at by the often difficult realities of taking part in that democracy—by my frustrations with the ARB, for instance, by my discomfort with the awkward workings of the justice system in the case of HortonWho and others, by the onerous work of keeping up with all the growing plethora of civic mailing lists, and by my occasional suspicions that for all the textual dust kicked up by the more politically minded of my fellow MOOers, the vast majority of virtual citizens could not have possibly cared less about any of this.

Until a certain moment of the day before my visit to Horton's private MOO, however, my native hopefulness about the prospects for Lambda's political health had never entirely deserted me. But then, in that unhappy hour, I had laid eyes on a document entitled, with a blunt but eloquent simplicity, *Toad Minnie*. Or rather: *P:ToadMinnie*. For the document was a petition—an official attempt by citizen Memphistopheles (the very same who had once terrorized me with his threats to report my suspicious quota-transfers to the authorities) to put before the LambdaMOO electorate the question of Minnie's continued presence among us. If vetted by the wizards as technically feasible, the petition would be opened for signing. If signed by enough qualified players, the petition would become a ballot. And if then voted for by twice as many players as voted against, the petition's unambiguous title would be enacted: the character called Minnie would (along with all her virtual possessions) be deleted, and every effort would be made to keep her real-life "typist" from ever logging on to LambdaMOO again.

I'm not quite sure why Memf's request appalled me so. It wasn't as if there'd never been a petition to have a player toaded before. The petition to wipe out Dr. Jest had after all been one of the earliest in the history of Lambdamocracy, and it had hardly seemed unsettling at the time. True, there had been no arbitration then, and nowadays everyone pretty much agreed that disputes were the only proper way to seek social action against individuals. But as Memf correctly pointed out, the individual arbitrators had proven themselves profoundly reluctant to mete out punishments as harsh as toading, so that in practical terms nobody but the entire citizenry could really be asked to toad someone as formidably controversial as Minnie.

All the same, I *was* appalled. Memf's charges were amply documented and they were largely reasonable ("a long history of vindictiveness, paranoia, slander, harassment, lying, and cheating; but especially her compulsive spam"), but as far as I could tell, they amounted to the implication that Minnie was a pain in almost everybody's ass. This, frankly, did not seem to me to be a capital offense. And even if it was, let's face it: Memf's timing was creepy in the extreme. It had not been three weeks since Minnie was hacked; the perpetrator hadn't even been identified yet, let alone punished. And now Memf was proposing to effect through democratic means exactly what Minnie's assailant had attempted via cruder methods. He might just as well have been asking us to award the hacker a medal—and honestly, I think that had he actually proposed as much I wouldn't have found his petition quite so troubling. At least its essential thuggishness would have been more readily transparent to the voting public. As it was, however, I found myself wondering whether *P:ToadMinnie didn't in fact represent the end of MOOish civilization as I knew it—a heavy load with which to tax a simple, embryonic piece of legislation, I know, but like I said, my faith in Lambda-MOO's democratic process was already somewhat sunken. With Memf now opening up the possibility that that process would from here on in be taking its lead from the virtual equivalent of hit men, my faith at last reached bottom.

And so it was that on the following day, as I came away from my curious rendezvous with HortonWho/Anthony, a part of me was positively rooting for the success of his half-baked scheme to wash away the governmental structures of the MOO in a wave of unprecedented social chaos.

It didn't even occur to me, somehow, that the wave was already beginning to break.

No matter: I got the picture soon enough. On the following weekend Minnie launched the opening salvos of a dazzling if typically misfocused counterattack, and the MOOish body politic thereupon commenced displaying symptoms of what I can only think to call a nervous breakdown. More on this later.

In the meantime, let us not forget just how eventful that same weekend was on the smaller scale of my own virtual existence. For we have come back now in our loop-de-looping way to the moment of my long night's journey with S*, and to the evening subsequent thereto in which it came to pass that Dr. Bombay and his morphs Samantha, Faaa, et alia parted ways and that I threw myself, at last, upon the mercy of the quotacrats.

There's not much more to say about the morphs. They were gone and I missed them—though not terribly, since I knew that once I got back under quota there was nothing to stop me from reviving them. Far more worrying, consequently, was the still-uncertain outcome of my quota request, although in fact there isn't presently a lot to say about that subject either, inasmuch as I was to get no answer from the ARB, as I've mentioned, for another couple weeks. We are left, therefore, to consider that personal matter that most preoccupied me in the interval— the aftermath of my date with S*.

About which, frankly, there isn't much I can tell you with any certainty, though I can tell you this: in the moment I awoke that Sunday morning, roused by the sound of Jessica's key turning in the front door as she came back from her strategic hiatus at Hillary's house, I knew for a fact that there would be no more such trysts for S* and me. I had tentatively told her as much upon our parting earlier that morning, but now the queasy, clutching feeling in my stomach as I welcomed Jessica home made it official: I did not want this. Not this strange, intangible confusion of erotic spheres. There was no perfume on the pillows, no excessively rumpled bedding, no lipstick traces on the stemware to bear the record of my infidelity (if that in fact was what it was), but even so I felt its presence in the house as if a mist of it had seeped out of my PC in the night and left its slightly alien residue on everything in sight.

It had no place here. And yet if I proceeded to have my virtual affair with S* there was no other place that it could happen. Sure, the MOO was everywhere and nowhere, all at once, but unless you counted my occasional brief escapes into VR at work, *my* MOO was ultimately nowhere else but in this house: downstairs, to be precise, in the little office space where my computer sat, about ten steps away from the double bed that marked the heart of this, the home that Jessica and I were after all still trying our loving, flailing best to make together. I felt angry with her, it's true, and hurt by her as well, and sorely tempted anyway by the exotic prospect of a MOO romance. But there was no way, in the end, that I could bring myself to go on making half-imagined love to another woman right here under the roof we shared. I would have had to have been an exuist of the bravest sort, or a Niacinian of the most detached, to pull it off—and now I knew, at last, that I was neither. So that was that.

But if I thought, and I suppose I did, that in arriving at this conclusion I had finished grappling with the consequences of the night before, I was mistaken. This grew apparent to me over the next day or two, as that queasy, clutching feeling in my stomach gradually matured into a quiet but imperative sense of guilt, and I began to wrestle with an urge to confess all to Jessica and in confessing win her forgiveness. My wiser nature told me not to bother, but as you may have noticed, ours was not a situation in which anybody's wiser nature was getting much of a hearing. In any case, when Jessica came home on Tuesday evening, in tears and misery, to tell me that it was all over between her and Eduardo and that she wasn't sure, but it might be over between her and me as well, I knew we had hard work ahead of us—work that for better or worse I would never be able to get through if I didn't first clear my heart of its distracting cargo of dishonesty. And so I took a deep breath, suppressed an involuntary mental image of Jessica storming downstairs to smash my computer in a jealous fit, and told her I'd had tinysex with a female MOOer while she was away.

There was no fit, of course. She took the news with calm, and even with a little curiosity, as if the info-age novelty of the liaison outweighed for the moment anything it might happen to have to do with our relationship. She asked me how it had been, and I said, hesitating for a moment first to gauge how much she really wanted to know, that it had been nice. That it had been pretty much as she'd insisted it would be—like sex, not with an image or a fantasy, but with a person. Then she asked me who this person was, and I said nobody she knew, but that I wouldn't say the name in any case. I didn't see the point. And neither did she, I guess. She shrugged her shoulders then, and with the merest trace of acidity she said that, well, the funny thing was that the way she'd spent the weekend anyhow was not, in fact, at Hillary's getting her bearings and sorting things out as per the stated itinerary, but at Eduardo's—filling up on carnal knowledge of the plain old-fashioned sort.

At which point I began to cry, which I suppose I had a right to do. The odd and maybe even slightly ridiculous truth, however, is that it wasn't from the pain of Jessica's revelation that I was crying, or even from my sadness at the generally battered shape our love was in by then. It was relief that made my tears flow, really. Relief at learning, after all my abstract speculations on the possible RL consequences of tinysex, that for now at least my confession had provoked no worse than this, and that our love still stood a chance at all.

Even so, I soon figured out that my coming clean hadn't made life altogether simpler for me. Jessica knew now that a more-than-hypothetical attraction existed between me and someone on the MOO, and I knew too that her initial equanimity wouldn't last long if she thought I was spending much of my MOO time with that particular someone. I had told Jessica I would not be having any more netsex with S*, because I knew myself that it was true—but I had made no promise to stop talking to her. And I don't think that I could have, either, just then.

On the following evening S* and I got our first chance for a real conversation

since Sunday morning. There was much to be discussed, I knew, but as it happened Jessica was sitting just upstairs at the moment, working on her own computer, and I felt too nervous, too constrained to do much more than dance
around the important stuff with cryptically flirtatious small talk. I kept thinking I
heard Jessica's footsteps coming down the stairs, and even though the footsteps
never really came, I finally felt too flustered to continue talking. I told S* (or
Sama, as she was calling herself that night) that I'd have to be going, and I told
her, briefly, why; and she replied that she hoped she wasn't causing problems, and
that she realized this must be "a rather confusing situation" for me.

"Confusing, yup," I said.

But not for her?

It irked me suddenly, and more then I wished it did, to imagine that the events
of Saturday/Sunday last had left her entirely unrattled—safe and untouched
behind that smooth white shell of hers. I had to ask:

"You're not the least confused I trust?"

"The least confused? Or in the least confused? There's a difference, you know."

"In the least," I answered, grinning. "Sheesh."

She grinned back: *Sama corrects papers for a living, you know.* She remained
uncracked. But then:

"No, I'm confused," she admitted. "Processing things."

"That wasn't my usual behaviour," she said.

DrBombay nods. Nor his.

Then I said, "Well."

I said, "I _do_ have to go.

I went.

Predictably, I guess, things only got more complicated after that. S* continued
"processing," and two days later I received a lengthy MOO-letter from her.

"Yes, this IS in fact about What Happened," the letter began, "so if you don't
feel like dealing, please ignore what follows." I swallowed nervously and read on.

"I don't think that we necessarily need to categorize what happened," Sama
wrote, in what turned out to be a mild and perfectly reasonable reproach for the
skittishness I'd been displaying around her ever since our night of tinysin,
"because I personally find definitions of that sort to be taxing to come up
with and ultimately useless. I do, however, need to have some sort of idea of
what's going on in your head. The alternative, as I see it, is to ignore that we
spent the better part of a day together, or perhaps box it away as some sort of

hothouse   intimacy that flourished for a moment, and return to what you called our 'surfacy' relationship. I'm sure   that there are other, and quite possibly better, alternatives, but I'm also quite sure that I can't continue in   this sort of haze of not knowing what the hell is going on.   It doesn't sit well with me, and the more it stretches out, the more inclined I am to throw my hands in the air and say 'fuck it,' which I think would be rather a shame."

Her letter ended with further apologies for bringing up possibly unpleasant matters, and for the strange flurry of extra spaces that had somehow floated into her text. I spent the better part of the next afternoon composing a reply. I didn't know a whole lot better than S* did, frankly, what was going on inside my head, but I managed to pull a few coherent sentiments together. What I hoped for us, I wrote, was that we might be able to remain friends in a way that "honored the intimacy" we had established the week before without, however, entailing any sort of emotional involvement that might remotely be construed as threatening the stability of my RL relationship. It was an awkward formulation, to say the least, and I had to perform a variety of verbal acrobatics to make it sound even remotely credible. Nor had I made the job any easier by informing Jessica the night before, in yet another spasm of compulsive honesty, that I would be taking this time to work on a letter "resolving things" between S* and me. The tension looming in the apartment now—as I sat writing at my computer and as Jessica banged around noisily doing weekend chores—was not exactly conducive to clarity of thought and purpose. I had the distinct impression, in fact, that I was in the process of resolving nothing whatsoever, and that if I actually sent this letter I would only be drawing myself deeper into psychic territory I was ill-equipped to chart.

I typed the *send* command and paused for a moment with my finger on the *enter* key, remembering a conversation I had had with exu three days earlier, after I'd told her about me and S* and how uncomfortable it had suddenly gotten to MOO from home. She had sympathized (*exu knows the squirmy at home feeling*) but pointed out she'd warned me more than once against letting my emotions get mixed up in my netsexual research. "You told me so," I conceded. But I wanted to explain, and gropingly attempted to, that the confusion wasn't just a matter of the awkward overlap between the MOO and my RL. It was more that there was something about VR itself—about the way real lives and bodies melted into it, never quite erased but always shrouded in a liquifying haze of code and text and scarcely checked imagination—that left me powerfully uncertain about the nature of the emotions I'd invested in it.

"Or rather," I groped, "uncertain of their . . . weight?"

I didn't know exactly what I meant, but exu seemed to.

"Yeah, 's like I said before," she answered. "Nothing has any actual size here. "Or border," she added. "Or standard of measure."

Three days later, with a finger poised to send my letter on its way to S*, I thought about those words again, for a moment or two.

And then I pressed the *enter* key.

Meanwhile, back at the sociopolitical level:

*P:ToadMinnie, having been vetted fairly quickly by the wizards, now stood gathering signatures while a more than usually torrid firestorm of debate proceeded to rage around it. Somewhat to my surprise—and not a little to my gratification—the opinions saturating the bandwidth on *social and on the petition's own mailing list appeared to be running heavily against the measure. Memf defended it as stalwartly as he could, and though by far outnumbered, he was ably seconded by the tireless rhetorician Ducko—a well-respected (and well-connected) programmer who, in the course of two bitterly contested disputes with Minnie, had amassed a wealth of meticulous arguments against her right to go on walking the face of the MOO. Ducko and Memf took turns outlining all of Minnie's alleged crimes—her acts of slander, spurious disputes, manipulations of the arbitration system, and other more or less general subversions of the MOO's democratic apparatus—and between them they produced almost as much square footage of text as all their many antagonists put together.

Their heroic output wasn't winning them any popularity contests, though. "Why do I feel like I've just fallen into the middle of a scene from _Lord of the Flies_ when I read this list?," wrote Sartre on *P:ToadMinnie, finding in Memf and Ducko's high-minded arguments nothing but a load of "displaced adolescent aggression." Other comparisons were hardly so kind. "Memf, Hitler would be proud of you," wrote Gretch. And sure, that sort of thing was par for the course in any online set-to, but there was also no denying that this particular debate was stirring up much more than its share of allusions to Nazis, inquisitions, lynchings, and the KKK—or that the bulk of them were aimed at Memphistopheles and his supporters. Even the most cool-headed members of the opposition couldn't resist getting in a subtle ad-hominem here and there. stingaree, for instance, having determined, after long and sharply reasoned consideration, that Memf's arguments "fail to show anything except that minnie has a poor grasp of manners and strong opinions about the way LM should function," added pointedly: "one could claim the same about some of her opponents."

It might have been easy to conclude, at this point, that Minnie was as good as saved. Indeed, with stingaree publicly opposed to her toading (the very same stingaree, remember, who had not shrunk from turning HortonWho into a six-month newt, a sentence still among the harshest in the history of the arbitration system), and with the general direction of the mailing-list traffic tending anyway toward a rout for Memphistopheles and co., what else *could* I conclude?

Well, for one thing, that the mailing lists were not the only place where politics happened on the MOO. After all, you didn't have to be as paranoid as Minnie or Horton to see that power, in this particular virtual society, flowed through all sorts of nooks and crannies on its way to the light of public record. Though I suppose it helped. During my visit to his secret ice castle, as a matter of fact, the former HortonWho had lectured me on this very topic, explaining patiently that the abundance of mailing lists so characteristic of the new MOO democracy ("one per petition, one per dispute") had in fact been more or less intentionally created to provide a smokescreen for the backroom machinations of the MOO's true power brokers. "Pavel's masterstroke," he called it: the fragmentation of public discourse into "an endless proliferation of newsgroups," endlessly dissipating the political energies of the hoi polloi, and much more easily controlled than the anarchic give-and-take of live discussion.

"It's quite . . . ironic . . . ," Anthony observed (dramatic ellipses his own, and no doubt accompanied IRL by a meaningful elevation of at least one eyebrow), "to consider that LambdaMOO's principal value is its realtime interactive text . . . while +all+ of the overt political behaviour is channeled through mailing-lists. . . .

"In fact, of course, all the really important decisions are made in realtime, and then a coherent public image is thrown up on the recording devices."

He paused.

"This, I believe, is what Minnie refers to as the conspiracy," said Anthony. And he believed, furthermore, that strictly speaking she was right to call it that, although he hastened to add that he didn't really think there were any fewer conspiracies, on the MOO, than there were MOOers. Only that some of those conspiracies just happened to have more . . . well, more leverage than others.

His ultimate point being, I gathered, that if some subset of the Power Elite had already decided, in some murky unrecorded conversation somewhere, that Minnie was to be got rid of, then gotten rid of she would be—whether by ballot, by arbitration, or by the return of a certain midnight hacker. And never mind the pseudodemocratic spectacle of the mailing lists or its apparent promise, in this case at least, that decency would prevail. "Minnie's ass is grass," insisted Anthony, "unless something changes."

Myself, I couldn't claim to see things quite so clearly, but I could see in any case that Minnie's fate still rested on more than just the course of rational, open debate. There were 7,000 voters out there, most of whom had never laid eyes on *social or for that matter even heard of Minnie. And while it might be argued (and often was) that this only proved how inappropriate it was to make a MOO-wide referendum out of her case, among certain segments of Memphistopheles's camp the only challenge posed by this great unruffled mass of citizens was how to get them feeling personally threatened by Minnie in as short a time as possible.

It was to this end, evidently, that an anonymous chain letter was launched, insinuating that Minnie's ceaseless, rambling diatribes, posted daily to assorted political newsgroups, were almost single-handedly driving the lag rate up to its presently insufferable levels. The claim was a dubious one, and Memf was swift in disavowing it—but not swift enough, perhaps, to undo the damage it had done. Everyone despised lag, after all—and how many gullible new voters, once introduced to the notion that there was actually some villain they could *blame* their laggy suffering on, might cherish that notion all the way to the ballot box?

Nor did the Minnie-bashers really even have to go to such truth-bending lengths to sway the heedless masses to their side. Ducko, for instance, was presumably only stating the facts when he threatened to quit the MOO for good and take his many useful bits of programming with him unless Minnie's hash was in some way permanently settled. Not that he put it quite that way on *social, of course. There he was at pains to make us understand he was only trying to make a point: i.e., that the choice was not simply between driving Minnie off the MOO and letting her stay, but between driving her off and allowing her to go on driving other, more productive players off with her cantankerous, vindictive ways. "We will either lose nice people or not-nice people," wrote Ducko, summing up what struck me as a chilling but at least coherent line of reasoning.

For the benefit of those who didn't read *social, however, Ducko had a blunter argument to make: he commenced to shut down, one by one, all the fertile objects he had programmed, starting with an especially popular feature object of his called "@honey" (which displayed the name of the user's sweetheart on demand and was a big hit with young lovers of all ages). The shutdown, meant to give us all a grim foretaste of life without Ducko, didn't go over too well among the politically aware ("you sir, are at heart, nothing but an oily blackmailer," wrote Maltese_Falcon on *social, laying it on a bit thick as usual). But out there in the wilds of the living room and the hot tub, where fartbonks, O. J. jokes, and pick-up lines passed for enlightened discourse, who knew what effects Ducko's tactics were having? Who knew, again, how many chat-happy newbies would effectively be choosing, come voting time, between the continued existence of some player nobody really seemed to like much anyway and the continued functionality of their very own handy-dandy @*honey* FO?

In short, for all the fire Minnie's would-be toaders were drawing on the mailing lists, it was still too early to predict their defeat. They had the power of the programmer on their side (as Ducko's none-too-idle threats demonstrated) and they had the advantage of Minnie's abiding unpopularity as well (which, for all the names being flung at them, still far outmatched their own). Perhaps it was even true, as Minnie had so often insinuated, that they had the tacit support of a wizard or two. After all, it was well known that Ducko was great pals with enaJ (she had even entrusted him with certain quasi-wizardly duties on occasion) and furthermore it *was* starting to look just the slightest bit fishy that the wizards' investigation into Minnie's hacking still hadn't turned up anything more conclusive than the Internet site the perp had logged in from. Perhaps, all things considered, Anthony was right, and Minnie had picked a fight with forces that—"unless something changed"—would finally and inevitably crush her.

Perhaps. But rest assured that Minnie was doing her damnedest, as she always had been, to make sure something changed. Her response to Memphistopheles's petition was, as I've mentioned, as effectively disruptive a piece of political intervention as she had yet unleashed upon the MOO. What was possibly the most confounding thing about it, though, was that to all appearances it had nothing to do with Memphistopheles's petition whatsoever. Indeed, against stupefyingly long odds, Minnie had thus far maintained an airtight public silence on the topic. Instead, her daily (and sometimes hourly) missives to **social* in the wake of **P:ToadMinnie*'s appearance were almost wholly devoted, so it seemed to me, to a different sort of proposition altogether: making exu miserable.

Well, yes: so it seemed to me. Though let's be honest here—my perspective on the matter may have been the slightest bit distorted by sentiments of a personal nature. The truth, to put it as objectively as I can, is that Minnie had her sights set on much bigger game than my best MOO friend. She was in fact primarily occupied, as ever, with exposing the unbridled corruption and venality of the MOO's ruling classes, and it was only the luck of a very bad draw that put exu in the way of her reformatory zeal this time around. Well, that, and the backroom machinations of a certain grizzled anarcholibertarian newt.

It happened like this. On the Sunday of that same eventful weekend of the long night's journey, the morphs retired, et cetera and so forth, Minnie posted a small bombshell to **social* and left it there to detonate upon contact. Ostensibly, the message concerned the same thing all her messages had been about of late: the unbridled corruption and venality of Laurel (who by no coincidence happened currently to be disputing Minnie, on charges of barraging players with unwanted political MOO-mail). Specifically, according to Minnie, Laurel's crowning act of malfeasance consisted of her having indulged at least once, under cover of an unregistered second character she called screwball, in the questionable practice of signing a single petition two times. And now, lest anyone take this lapse of integrity on Laurel's part to indicate anything less than a widespread contempt for democratic principles among the MOOish elites (Laurel's membership therein evidently dating from the days of her campaign to criminalize MOO rape, to which Ducko had rallied with particular fervor), Minnie presented the readers of *social with the aforementioned incendiary device. It was a brief message containing evidence of similar double-signing by none other than a duly elected member of the ARB: exu.

Now, serious as this accusation was, it wasn't the charge itself that made Minnie's message so provocative. It was the evidence: twenty-four lines of logged real-time dialogue between the duly elected ARB member Doome and a mysterious interlocutor (identified in the transcript only by the generic "you" with which VR addressed each one of us: *You say . . . , You go . . .*), in which Doome confessed quite off-the-record to knowing that exu had an unregistered spare named Draculetta, whose signature Minnie later found affixed, bold as brass and not too far from exu's, at the bottom of a petition floated a few months before by Doome himself. The conversation was plainly a private one, and plainly recorded by the nameless "you," who also plainly was not Minnie ("you" 's conversational style being too urbane, for one thing). And inasmuch as the ancient VR social crime of nonconsensually publishing private logs still had a far more compelling aura of taboo about it than the novel political one of which exu stood accused (for who among us could not think, with a blush or a grimace or both, of some intimate conversation or two we would much rather not see splashed all over the mailing lists?), it was perhaps no surprise that the swarm of agitated responses generated by Minnie's message circled largely around the identity of the player who had betrayed Doome's confidence:

"Minnie, who is the 'you' in the logs you posted?"

Over and over the question was put, while Minnie steadfastly refused to answer or even address it, until for a while there it got to sounding like the official slogan of the mailing list, repeated every ten messages or so with a vehemence that faded gradually, as the days passed, into weary exasperation:

"Minnie, who is the 'you'?"

The thing is, everybody knew who the "you" was. There was after all no mistaking the cool intensity of "you"'s interest in what, exactly, Doome knew about exu and how, exactly, he knew it (among the more revealing lines: *You ask, "Are you sure you're not boffing exu?"*). And besides, for those not fully up to speed on the soap-operatic details of MOOish history, Doome had named the name almost immediately anyway, in a message posted just a short while after Minnie's: it was HortonWho, of course.

Which explained a lot. Starting with why Minnie would suddenly be picking a fight with exu, of all people (one of the few public officials still willing to say nice things about her in public), and possibly extending to why she was being so baffifingly unwilling to respond to her interrogators, or for that matter to her would-be executioners. Because if Minnie was now in league with HortonWho, who could say what other forms their cooperation was taking? Might he not be feeding her more than just tidbits from his archive of logs? Advice on strategy, perhaps? I remembered Anthony's cheery prediction that "LambdaMOO will collapse of its own internal contradictions :)," and I remembered too his equally cheery plans to hasten that collapse, and I wondered if Minnie wasn't now, in the seeming perversity of her silences, simply taking a page from his book on virtual guerrilla warfare—keeping her hand in things just actively enough to push the right buttons here and there, then stepping back to let the ensuing controversies tear the power structure apart. Who knew? Maybe Anthony had scrapped the "little monsters" scenario altogether and decided to let Minnie be his agent of social chaos instead.

Well, if that was the plan, it definitely appeared to be working. Folks were getting tired of the "Who is the 'you'?" game, which was obviously getting nowhere in its appeal to Minnie's sense of etiquette, and were beginning to turn their attention to the substance of her accusations. Laurel and exu both, in fact, felt sufficiently chastened to post apologies to *social: the double-signings had been unintentional, they swore—acts of carelessness, not of depravity—but they were inexcusable acts all the same, and they would certainly never happen again. This quieted some of the incipient grumbling among the readership, but hardly all of it. And when Laurel challenged her critics, in effect, to haul her into arbitration now or forever hold their peace ("If no one files a dispute in the next 7 days on this issue, I'll consider the matter closed. Thanks"), she quickly got a taker from among the cream of the old-guard Power Elite: Rhay himself, no tool of Minnie's for sure, and apparently in a genuine snit about Laurel's transgression ("This abuse of the ballot system means my voice is worth less because I play by the rules. My proposed resolution to this abuse is to remove voting privileges from Laurel and screwball, and any other known second characters").

exu officially signed on as a codefendant a day or two later, figuring it was only a matter of time before she too was dragged before an arbitrator. "Thought I'd just streamline my martyrdom a bit," she explained on the *D:Rhay.vs.Laurel* list, tongue gamely in cheek, lest any chink appear in the wisecracking, level-headed unflappability that defined her public persona. The private exu, however, was beginning to look pretty well flapped. Between Minnie's singling her out as an icon of nefariousness and HortonWho's gleeful merchandising of her private relationship with Doome, exu was feeling, so she told me, like "there's this two-headed shark with its teeth sunk relentlessly into my leg." She seemed edgier than I'd ever known her to be, and ever so slightly snappish, though I couldn't say I blamed her. Can't say I'd have blamed her, in fact, if she'd lost it altogether and stormed out onto *social hurling great flaming tirades at Minnie and anyone who typed like her.

What exu actually did next, though, wasn't quite so easy to understand: she filed a dispute against Minnie's hacker. Which is to say she filed a dispute against whoever it was who had logged on as the yellow guest on the night of August 17 and trashed Minnie and all her stuff. Which is to say she was quite possibly pissing in the wind. There being no easy way to deduce from an Internet site address alone the identity of the person connecting from it, the yellow guest could in principle have been almost anybody on the MOO or off it. And yet . . . what if the wizards knew more than they were letting on? What if the hacker's identity was, in fact, an open secret, well-known among the old-guard Power Elite but unacknowledged publicly for the simple, double-edged reason that (a) the victim happened to be Minnie and (b) the assailant happened to be one of them? For many a MOOer, these were no idle speculations. They were in fact hardening rapidly into articles of faith (with the wizard Crotchet and a certain fringe-PE bad boy named Yeehah topping the list of suspects), and exu, veteran that she was of the old campaigns to overthrow the wizardocracy, had fallen in among the faithful.

But did that really quite explain why she was going out of her way, at just this moment, to stick her neck out for Minnie?

DrBombay looks at you incredulously, I emoted from across the MOO, the day she told me about the dispute. "Bucking for sainthood are you?"

exu muahahas was her response. There was a method to her kindness, she explained, and it seemed to revolve around the possibility that Minnie, mystified by exu's failure to respond to her provocations in the expected flamethrowing manner, might just decide to leave her alone—and might even desist entirely from letting Anthony pick out any more targets for her. "What better way can you think of to thwart Horton's Master Plan?" exu asked. But ultimately, and this is the part that sort of blew me away, the driving force behind her curious project actually seemed to be a genuine desire to see Minnie's hacker brought to justice—and to see a blow struck, into the bargain, for every second-class MOO citizen who'd ever lacked the right connections to get a fair deal out of this brave MOO democracy of ours. Or as she put it: "I really don't want to see an upper-class whiteboy rapist get away with it."

I grinned back at her in astonishment. "May you never cease to amaze me," I paged, and my admiration was sincere. I think, indeed, that my respect for exu's performance as a MOO-politico—for her common sense and her compassion, for her ability to bare-knuckle it with the best of them without abandoning her sense of humor or her principles—had never been deeper than it was in that moment.

But there was an uneasiness nagging at me, too. What exactly, I found myself wondering, was this upper class to which exu referred? She meant it half in jest, I guessed, but I couldn't help wishing that the phrase still meant something a little more weighty—that it still rang loud and true the way it might have back in exu's days of running with the Underground. I didn't know for sure how much the class equations of the MOO had changed since then or even, frankly, whether they had changed at all. But I knew this much: my brain was coming closer by the day to blowing a circuit from trying to keep track of all the players, factions, and associated agendas swirling twisterlike across the MOO's political landscape, and it would have been a tremendous relief to me just now if I could have suddenly seen the place divided neatly into the Rulers and the Rest of Us. But how could I? The lines of battle seemed to be getting blurrier all the time, and my own best friend, the player whose wisecracking, level-headed commentaries had always managed to make the lines so clear for me, was starting to look pretty blurry herself. Her unquenchable anarchist sympathies, for instance, were sitting more and more incongruously with her own steady ascent into the firmament of MOOish power—a rise that had started with her role as lead performer in the Bungle Affair, had proceeded on through her present tenure on the ARB, and now continued to advance a notch or two with her every well-aimed intervention in the great debates that seemed, these days, to be as much a route to prestige and clout as being friendly with a wizard ever was.

Not that she wasn't, increasingly, friendly with wizards as well. In fact, the terminally cynical might suggest that nothing in her political résumé quite outshone her good luck in having picked a VR lover who, as of just this week, had unexpectedly been inducted into the ranks of the MOO's fallen but not yet fully disempowered technological nobility. Yes: Doome was now a wizard. For as if the general tumult surrounding matters of governance wasn't already enough, Haakon had picked this moment to name three new assistants—Doome, Dif, and (to the sputtering indignation of Finn, who swore he wouldn't have taken the job anyway but wouldn't have minded being *asked,* for heaven's sake) Briar-Wood. But if this turn of events might once have unambiguously confirmed exu's entree into what might once have unambiguously been called the Power Elite, it wasn't clear to me, under the present circumstances, whether exu's relationship with Doome served her political ascent any more than it had served his—or for that matter, whether it served either of them as anything but an agreeable way to keep warm through the virtual night.

In any case, for me, as for the rest of the MOO, the real interest in Doome's (and Dif's and BriarWood's) sudden elevation to the wizardry lay elsewhere. For Haakon didn't often make his archwizardly presence felt these days, and when he did, the MOO took notice, reminded once again that all the scraps of power they were fighting over were as nothing compared to the ultimate sovereignty of He Who Might at Any Minute Pull the Plug on Us All.

And so a tizzy of conjecture and concern swept through the MOO as word of Haakon's latest appointments spread. Questions were raised (though ever so politely) as to the methods and criteria by which the archwizard had made his final choices. A petition was written (though never passed) calling for the right to override by popular ballot any future wizardly nominations. Haakon put in a rare appearance on *social,* where he patiently explained his selection process, and he even let it be known that he would not object in principle to the veto scheme. But none of this quite settled the anxieties he'd set loose. A rumor started circulating to the effect that Haakon was in fact preparing another of his coups d'etat, and that he had already assigned to his new under-wiz Doome the job of scrapping LambdaMOO's hopelessly chaotic system of government and rebuilding it from scratch ("Here we go again!" Sebastiano paged me, certain that the rumor must be true). It turned out Haakon had merely been proposing to overhaul the hopelessly chaotic *arbitration* system, with a view to plugging all those nasty loopholes Minnie had for so long been both criticizing and exploiting. But even this would represent no minor wizardly intrusion into the social sphere, and the very fact that Haakon was considering it at all only served to heighten the prevailing impression that Minnie—and the permanent state of uproar surrounding her—had brought LambdaMOO to the brink of some fundamental, wrenching crisis.

In the middle of all this exu and I snuck away one day, to a quiet little MOO I'd found running on a university server in Portugal somewhere. I'd built myself a little white-washed Iberian country house there and a character called Dr. Bombain, and exu visited as a guest. The lag was almost nonexistent, the privacy luxurious, and we talked at length and at leisure for the first time in too long a while. Predictably enough, we fell to pondering the mess poor LambdaMOO was in, and naturally enough we proceeded to wondering how it had ever gotten there.

So much had changed since the days of Mr. Bungle, exu reflected. The population had boomed, the texture of life had grown more "urbanized"—more cosmopolitan, more brutal, more anonymous. There were a lot more interesting people around, said exu, but at the same time there was a bigger and unrulier mob of them, and she doubted whether the likes of Bungle would have caused much of a stir any more. These days it evidently took the likes of Minnie to throw the whole place into turmoil, and this in itself, we agreed, said something meaningful about what LambdaMOO had become. But what exactly?

The question appeared to have been eating at exu, although perhaps not in quite so abstract a form. "I'm trying to figure out," she said, "why I wanted Bungle toaded, and Horton, but not Minnie? . . . She's certainly caused more grief to more people."

I thought about that. And presently a bit of jargon left over from my one college sociology course came to mind, and it occurred to me that maybe the distinction exu was looking for lay somewhere in the difference between what social theorists sometimes called *Gemeinschaft* and *Gesellschaft*—often translated as "community" and "society." Gemeinschaft, to the best of my recollection, implied a relationship among individuals that was based on fellow feeling, personal obligations, and implicit standards of behavior. It was how very small towns worked, and primitive tribes, and quilting bees. Gesellschaft, on the other hand, bound individuals together under the rule of written law, of abstract institutions and impersonal rights and responsibilities. It was how Sweden worked, and damn little else. The rest of the world's social groupings combined these two modes in varying degrees of relative predominance, not always easily sorted out one from the other. In LambdaMOO's case, however, it seemed safe enough to say (and so I did) that in the wake of Bungle the reigning social paradigm had lurched violently away from the cozier, gemeinschaftlich end of the spectrum and gone careening toward the more abstract gesellschaftlich, And if that was true, then what was Minnie finally guilty of—in all her manic crusades to clean up our democratic institutions—but embracing the new paradigm more wholeheartedly than the rest of us were ready to? "In her kooky fucked up way," I mused, "she's taking LM seriously as a society, but screwing with it as a community in the process."

Curiously enough, this seemed to be just the analysis exu had been angling toward. *Guest likes that,* she emoted. "Do you think maybe you could post something on *soc to that effect?"

I was flattered, but I demurred, pleading dread of controversy. *DrBombain loathes flames,* I told her, and it was true enough. But there was at least one other reason why I wasn't eager to go repeating what I'd just said in front of all the MOO, and that was that I only half believed any of it. In pretty much the same way, actually, that I only half believed exu and I were sitting together in a little whitewashed Iberian country house, I was coming to doubt that sociological analyses of any sort could ever tell the whole truth—or even a wholly satisfying one—about what had become of LambdaMOO. Because if the MOO was in some sense genuinely a society now, it was also, in another sense, still just a bunch of people coming together to pretend they were a society. And seen from that perspective, all my German-inflected theorizing might look pretty silly sitting next to the far more appropriate insight of the exasperated player Sartre, with which I was finding myself more and more in agreement: things were getting way too *Lord of the Flies* around here. Too much of the simple camaraderie and animosity of the playground was getting dressed up in too much of the grown-up language of the polis—of governors and governed, of crime and punishment, of campaigns and conspiracies—and the mismatch was starting to wax just the slightest bit grotesque.

And maybe that was the real reason exu felt compelled to draw a line between Minnie and the MOO-villains of days gone by. I'm pretty sure, at any rate, that it was mine. I knew there were important differences between the grief Minnie was causing and the damage Bungle and Horton had done, but just now, to be honest, it wasn't any of those differences that kept me from wanting to see her toaded. It was the fact that I simply didn't feel like seeing *anybody* toaded anymore. Or rather, to put it more truthfully, that I simply didn't feel like witnessing even one more collectively determined, duly debated, and officially sanctioned social decision enacted on the MOO for as long as I lived. And yes, I'm aware that wasn't the sort of attitude a good MOO citizen should try to cultivate. But what can I say? At the moment I wasn't feeling very much like any sort of MOO citizen at all. I was feeling more like, well, like exu's friend. And wondering what I could do, short of wading personally into the godforsaken morass that was MOOish politics, to help her through this nasty stretch of her MOOish life.

DrBombain hugs you and holds you, I finally offered, *and wants to protect you and honest to gosh feels the most overpowering affection for you sometimes.*

It wasn't much; just a warm, sappy gesture and the certainty of my friendship. But it was how I felt, and I figured it might come as some small comfort to her anyhow, and so it seemed to: exu thanked me for it. We sat then, suddenly both shy, making chitchat and enjoying the quiet of the Portuguese MOO.

Guest supposes it should get a character here.

I nodded.

"It could be our private rendezvous," I said solemnly. "We could start a . . . a CONSPIRACY!"

I stifled a giggle IRL.

The guest just rolled its eyes.

Now: some people liked to say the MOO was only a game, and some people liked to say it was as real as RL itself, and both sets of people, if you ask me, were off the mark. Finn had a better idea, I think: he liked to say the MOO was like a book.

By this, Finn sometimes meant that it was like a particular book, the name of which was *Les Liaisons Dangereuses* and the subject of which—the labyrinthine sexual and political intrigues of eighteenth-century French nobility—reminded him uncannily of social life on LambdaMOO (not that he'd actually gone and *read* this book, you understand, but the movie version gave a pretty good idea of what it was all about, and plus you got to see Uma Thurman pretty much naked). More often, though, what Finn meant by the comparison was something far more general: he meant that we, the people of the MOO, were all characters in a great, multifaceted novel of our own construction. That we were all of us, as we went along, writing our plots and subplots, our dialogues and set pieces, and that the sum of all these was, in essence, a narrative tome of staggering proportions.

Naturally, like any good analogy, Finn's succeeded not so much by being right as by being more right than it was wrong. It captured certain meaningful similarities between literature and VR—two parallel universes of text, each rooted in play but somehow also more (much more) than playful—and yet you didn't have to look too hard to see the differences. There were plenty of them, large and small, and I could spend a good few pages elaborating on them all, if I wanted to. But just now all I want to do is draw your attention to what seems to me the single most important way in which the MOO is not in fact like any book, and that is this: you can hardly ever be sure, in VR, when the story is going to end.

With books, of course, it's easy. Consider, for example, the one you're holding in your hands. No need to stop and count the pages—you can tell with just a glance that there are not too many of them left now. You can tell we've reached that moment in the narrative where plots and subplots should by rights be winding down toward their final resolutions.

But how was I supposed to tell? How could I know with any certainty, at this point, that my tiny life was coming to a close? My MOOish days, unlike these pages, were not numbered, and no final resolutions loomed on their horizon. All I could really say for sure was that it was getting time for me to take a break from LambdaMOO. I had been logging on daily now for all but three of the last ninety days, and for an average, lately, of about twenty-five hours a week. I had set out, maybe you recall, to "glimpse whatever there was of genuine historical novelty in VR's slippery social and philosophical dynamics," and I had glimpsed my share, I think. But now the novelty was wearing off. The MOO no longer felt exotic to me, and there was little left for me to learn from it except, day by day, whatever I might need to know to keep on living in it.

Which was a tough enough assignment in itself, believe me. In particular, my phantom relationship with S* increasingly was taxing my abilities to make heads or tails of it. As I had feared, our awkward attempts at a MOO-mail post mortem had only led us deeper into the same emotional confusion we had meant to escape, its weightless indeterminacy closing steadily in on us as we progressed. We were spending some part of almost every day in conversation now—some days in breezy imitation of a blissfully uncomplicated friendship, some days in dangerous proximity to the edge of that attraction that had made any such friendship impossible from the start, some days in numbing examination and cross-examination of our respective motives and intentions. *Sama wonders if this is going to turn into a race to see who can cut and run first,* she wondered one day. But neither of us ran, and the cuts never went deep enough to force the clarity of any sort of definition on whatever the hell it was we thought we were up to.

Likewise, the course of MOOish politics was looking more and more illegible to me. For a moment there I'd been half-certain that the Minnie troubles would end, and imminently, in some decisive outcome pivotal to the history of the MOO. I don't know why. Maybe it was the precedent of the Bungle crisis that had led me to think so. Maybe it was the earful of apocalyptic theorizing I had gotten during my visit to Anthony/HortonWho's private nowhere. Whatever the reason, it eluded me now, and I began to suspect that the present crisis might in fact go on indefinitely—that Minnie herself might be nothing more than a symptom of irresolvable dilemmas built into the strange project of virtual democracy, and that the wave of discord she appeared to have ushered in might very well go rolling on regardless of the final vote on *P:ToadMinnie. Banish her, and someone else could easily step up to take her place at the center of the storm. HortonWho himself was certainly a likely candidate (his newting was due to be lifted in less than three months), but almost anybody with a bone to pick and a surplus of time and energy would do, and God knows the MOO had no shortage of players who fit that bill.

And so it was with a somewhat diminished sense of the historic that I continued to keep an eye on current events. Memf's petition, I learned one day, had garnered enough signatures to become a ballot, and though I was not thrilled to learn this, I couldn't be bothered to wrestle with the question of what it meant for the soul of LambdaMOO. I simply cast my no vote and moved on to what I now considered the more involving aspects of the controversy—i.e., anything to do with exu. Having resolved that the most useful role I could possibly play in all this was to offer her the occasional word of support or consolation, I kept that role in mind as I went on watching public life unfold on the MOO. I made a point of subscribing to the mailing list of exu's dispute against the mysterious Minnie-hacker, and paid as close attention as I could bear to pay while that particular quest for justice ran aground on technicalities and general indifference. The proceedings against exu and Laurel for their double-signings proved more eventful, ending in a sentence of several weeks' revocation of their voting rights and the curious assignment of Doome himself to write the software that was to do the revoking. I didn't know whether to think of Doome's part in the manacling of his own netlover as a conflict of interest, a noble sacrifice, or just sort of kinky, but I knew that none of this had been very much fun for exu, and I did what I could to make my sympathy felt.

All of which is basically to say, among other things, that I would not be leaving any gaping hole in the fabric of LambdaMOO if I checked out for a week or two. exu would soldier on just fine without my meager assistance; whatever S* and I were playing at showed no signs of coming to a head any time soon; my other friendships, my garden, the giddy realms of the hot tub and the living room (into which I still enjoyed an occasional afternoon foray in the guise of Shayla, for a laugh) would suffer little from my absence—and all would still, in any case, be there when I returned.

And like I said, I was ready for the break. I was ready to take stock of everything I'd experienced and studied and felt over the last three months, and I was ready, too, to take a certain trip I'd been planning for a few weeks now, the final lesson, as I imagined it, of my education in the meaning of VR: I was going to Palo Alto to gaze upon the server. I had already made arrangements with Pavel, and I had bought my airline tickets, and when I came back, I supposed, it would be with some sort of ultimate enlightenment about the MOO in hand. I would be ready then, at last, to leave all pretenses to research behind and let my life on LambdaMOO lead me where it might.

But I never did come back.

Not really. I went to California and a week or so later I returned, and it's true I still made visits to the MOO after that. But the visits were scattered, and brief, and largely for the sentimental purpose of preserving Dr. Bombay from the reaper's scythe. I chose, in the end, not to pursue my MOOish life any further, and though I think I'd just as soon leave it at that, I suppose that after all we've been through together, dear reader, I do owe you some sort of explanation as to why my virtual biography ends here.

All right, then: it was the ARB that drove me off, I'm tempted very much to say. The case could certainly be made. About a week and a half prior to my departure for the West Coast, and precisely two weeks (as promised) from the day I deleted Samantha, the ARB MOO-mailed me its decision on my quota request, and its decision, in a nutshell, was no: we do not love thee, Dr. Bombay.

Thumbs down, in other words. Or rather, three thumbs down to five thumbs up (with one abstention), which in the obscure arithmetic of ARBish rules of order added up to a grand total of Nein, Danke.

Nyet, that is.

Negatory.

Hit the road, Jack.

I was not amused. The ARB members, per procedure, had posted their votes to a restricted but publicly readable mailing list, and I scoured their comments to try and figure out what had gone wrong. By the dates attached to their messages I learned that the first member to cast a "no" had been none other than Memphistopheles, and this of course immediately raised his ranking in my personal list of Most Despicable MOOers to its all-time high. "It is just too profligate," was the little lynch-mobster's oh-so-considered-(yeah-right) opinion of my virtual life's work, and his fellow nay-voter Raimi sourly agreed: "The 200k+ [construction] with its 129 rooms is equivalent to recreating Isengard." *Isengard?* Good God, the indignity! My subtle, artful embodiment of the I Ching's unfathomably profound wisdom equated with a scale model of some *hobbit-castle or something?* How could I not, I ask you, have taken such rejection as a none-too-subtle hint that there was ultimately no place for me on LambdaMOO? How could I not, in seeing my greatest contribution to this vexed community thus spurned, have felt the ties between the MOO and me begin to come irrevocably undone?

Well, I didn't. To be perfectly honest about it, the ARB's verdict didn't upset me nearly as much as I'd thought it might. There *were* more yes votes than no votes, after all, and many of the comments from the yes crowd were glowing ("very original, well thought out . . . beautifully written," that sort of thing). Hell, even Memf confessed, in his comments, to "mixed feelings" about his vote and to admiring the garden itself, in spite of its unforgivable size. And considering that Memf and the other two no-voters were nearing the ends of their terms in office anyway, I knew that if I just waited till after the current round of ARB elections and submitted my request all over again, I could probably count on a favorable judgment soon enough.

In short, there is no way that I can truthfully blame the ARB for my decision to walk away from LambdaMOO. And so I am left, I guess, with no alternative but to tell you what the actual reason was:

I did it for love.

Yes, I know it's cornball. But I'm afraid it's true. Of all the possible motivations I have subsequently sifted through, the only one that really sticks is that I left because my love for Jessica required it. In part, I mean this in a fairly pragmatic sense: if we were going to make any sort of honest effort to patch things up between us, it wouldn't be well served by my continued conversations with S*. I could no longer successfully pretend, either to myself or Jessica, that these were necessary to the process of untangling whatever knot of mutual cathexis our night of tinysex had tied us into, for it was growing all the time more obvious that they only kept the heat between us smoldering indefinitely. Yet neither could I bring myself to put an end to them. I only grew more furtive in my contacts with S*, avoiding extended conversation with her except when Jessica was out of the house or I was MOOing from work. This did my conscience little good, and it hardly kept Jessica from looking daggers at me whenever she passed through my office space on her way to the bathroom and happened to spot so much as a random page from Sama on my screen. (That Jessica now knew any of S*'s names at all was further testament to the near-impossibility of keeping virtual emotional entanglements safely boxed away inside VR—or at any rate to my stupidity in leaving a printout of one of Sama's MOO-letters lying around on my desk one day.)

But ultimately, I think, the distractions I needed most to leave behind were deeper ones. They were the seductions natural to any world built from the stuff of books and maps: the siren song of possibility, the vivid presence of the half-imagined, the freedom of words and thought to fly beyond the here and now and trace the shape of every road not taken. Such are the basic ingredients of the human condition, I know, the spiritual inheritance of an animal uniquely adapted to the strange and wonderful environment of signifiers, yes—but now and then, let's not forget, these gifts can also drive a human being just a little crazy, and so they had done to me. Jessica was here, and now, and beautiful, and I would lose her if I didn't here and now shake off my chronic homesickness for all those half-imagined, siren-singing roads untaken. The MOO hadn't given me that malady, of course, and in a way it may have even helped me move toward getting over it: how could I have spent all that time in the Garden of Forking Paths, after all, and not have sensed that I was somehow trying to teach myself the wisdom of embracing the path my life had put me on? But now fate was daring me to try and finally live that wisdom, and I had the feeling that it wouldn't make the challenge any easier if I went on dividing my home life between the hard-walled place where Jessica and I began and ended every day together and the supremely malleable dream estate of Lambda House.

Thus, anyway, do I explain to myself at this late date my half-unconscious decision to quit the MOO. Nor can I, therefore, claim to look on it with much regret. Because if that choice really was a part of my investment in the possibility of a real-live, lifetime love affair, all I can say is that it's paid me back more richly than I ever dared imagine. I will not bore you with the details of my present happiness, or of the more or less conventional course I followed to it—the messy months of reconciliation, the long and finally futile skirting of the marriage question, the exchange of vows, the honeymoon, and then: the deep and day-to-day surprise of learning how much freer love may flow when it's more tightly bound.

Suffice it to say that I am overjoyed my story ends this way. But I'll confess I wish it wasn't how I was obliged to end this book. For some of you will have already jumped to the conclusion that I intend to make a moral of this ending. And some, no matter how much I protest, will draw that moral anyway. You know the one I mean: that nothing genuine can come of any place so thoroughly infused with unreality as the MOO. That "virtual community" is at best a pleasant oxymoron and at worst a threat to all that makes authentic human connection meaningful and vital. That virtual reality itself—both in its MOOish form and as the mythic end point toward which the simulation-driven technoculture of late modernity converges—finally represents no more than a false escape from what is difficult and scary about living with real people in real life. And that, therefore, the only thing standing between this increasingly mediated society of ours and its wholesale decay into a technological fantasyland may be such small, brave acts of sanity as my own withdrawal from LambdaMOO.

So goes the more elaborate version of the moral, at any rate, encountered usually in lengthy, bookish commentaries on the perils of the Information Age. The cruder and more common version, on the other hand, can sometimes be heard even within the MOO itself, where now and then a random guest or an unassimilated newbie or for that matter a fed-up old-timer may ascend the nearest soap box (as it were) and proclaim to all within shouting distance the standard formulation:

"You people need to get a life!"

In my experience, however, this sentiment is more often muttered at a greater remove, and in the softer tones of pity or bewilderment, by people whose only knowledge of MUDs is based on what they hear from friends, or see in magazines, or read about in books. Yes, books. Like this one. By which I very much do mean that I'm aware how long you may by now have been wondering when I'd get around to addressing those questions that so often pop first thing into the mind of someone newly acquainted with the world of MUDs, such as: Do these people *not* in fact have lives? Can anybody possibly invest such time and energy in such a place and not be in the throes of a miserable, soul-wasting addiction? Ought there to be a law or something against this stuff, lest the best years of our nation's youth be lost to building castles in the digital air? And so forth.

Nor have I left these questions dangling for lack of answers. I could have early on brought up the amply researched findings of MIT psychologist Sherry Turkle, who concluded that in many cases MUDs serve players as a kind of therapeutic environment, allowing them to come to grips with issues of identity and desire that might otherwise go on to hobble them in real life. I could have further noted, per both Turkle's and my own observations, that the intense, forty-hours-a-week-and-up MUD habits that can so alarm outsiders are often transient in nature, coinciding with and easing periods of difficult adjustment in a MUDder's life, and usually subsiding once the RL troubles have been resolved. I could have also pointed out the useful skills and broadening contacts that can be acquired in a place like LambdaMOO, could have told you heart-warming anecdotes about young people whose successful programming careers began literally with building castles in the digital air, or whose escapes from drab, small-town existences were given impetus by otherwise unlikely truck with friends from foreign lands and foreign contexts, with philosophers logging in from London or with research scientists connecting live from Antarctica.

And failing all that, I could have simply reported what any long-time player knows: that barring the occasional exceptions (the tales of academic careers derailed by runaway VR addiction, the case or two of clinical insanity masked by VR's friendly glow), most MOOers lead RLs no more or less well adjusted than the average person's. They mostly hold productive, full-time jobs, or pursue productive, full-time educations; and for what it's worth, they very rarely ever, in the flesh, turn out to be the unbathed, awkward, painfully unattractive, and possibly drooling shut-in geeks of popular imagination.

And yet observe: *DrBombay has refrained, throughout an entire book-length commentary on the MOOish way of life, from making any of these arguments.* Why is this? Can he really think them not worth making? Can it really be that he finds the standard concerns about the quality of MOOers' existences so frivolous as to merit no consideration on his part?

No, friends. It's just that all along I have been hoping the existences thus far considered would be argument enough. I have offered you three hundred pages and more of violent conflict, of loves and lusts, of friendships deep and intricate, of corny jokes and heady debates, of creative labors large and small, of efforts variously sincere, manipulative, misguided, brilliant (and all of the above) to shape a world in which the quirks and passions of eight thousand people at a time might coexist—and I have trusted in these pages to convince you, sooner or later, that MOOers do indeed have lives.

And if you still aren't quite convinced, allow me to offer you one last page from the book of MOOish history. For this, I think, was finally what persuaded me:

On the evening of October 12, 1994, the voting on *B:ToadMinnie came to a close, and the results, made public at 9:36 P.M., showed that the ballot had failed by a margin of 2 to 1. Minnie had been spared; and more than that, her right to remain among us—even as she went on chasing her dark, half-imagined conspiracies and her frantic visions of a shining MOO upon the hill; even as she drove us all quite nearly bonkers in the process—had been resoundingly affirmed.

I read the news while I was still in Palo Alto, logged in briefly to the MOO through a Xerox network terminal just upstairs (and a universe away) from the Lambda server humming in the basement. The strength of the voters' rejection surprised me somewhat, but not as much as my own reaction to it did: I felt proud, almost embarrassingly so. I had thought, by then, that I had given up on LambdaMOO's democracy, and maybe I had. But when I saw how fiercely that same democracy had ultimately clung, in the face of powerful distractions, confusions, and manipulations, to the simple decency of letting Minnie remain a part of it, it made my heart swell. I felt as hopeful for the future of that small society, right then, as I had a year and a half before, when its bold new shape had just emerged from the crucible of the Bungle Affair.

The contrast between the two moments was a stark one, of course. The post-Bungle order had after all been founded on the destruction of a character—on a principled act of exclusion from the still-unformed commonwealth of the MOO—whereas the vote on *B:ToadMinnie had ended in salvation, and with an equally principled act of inclusion by a MOO now well accustomed to thinking of itself as a polity. But the present episode, I suspected, was just as valuable an object lesson in collective self-rule as the first had been. Indeed, it would later occur to me that in an age of waning personal involvement in community and government, it was hard to overvalue the rare, empowering taste of politics in action that so many MOOers had been afforded by the Bungle Affair, the Minnie Mess, and all the minor crises in between. MOO society was, if nothing else, a hands-on political education for its members, and if that education has in the long run contributed even infinitesimally to a greater and wiser level of political participation IRL, then I don't see how any of the other real-life benefits that may accrue from living virtually—the free psychotherapy, the programming experience, the broadened horizons—could possibly surpass that one in importance.

But truth be told, I wasn't caring much about the state of real-world politics as I learned how LambdaMOO had voted that day. The decision not to toad Minnie struck me simply, and movingly, as a watershed in the evolution of my virtual world. The MOO was still an infant society in many ways, and like all infants it had had to learn, at one point, to define itself in opposition to some thing, some principle, someone. That someone had been Mr. Bungle, of course, and without the MOO's rejection of him there might not have been a MOO democracy of which to speak. But a developing self must also learn, once confident in its identity, to accommodate the fears and frictions that inevitably come from living in community; and until the day I read the *B:ToadMinnie* results, I hadn't been sure the MOO would ever reach this second stage.

There could be no doubt about it now, however: The MOO had grown, not just in size but in its soul. And as there is perhaps no more defining feature of a living thing than what might best be thought of as a kind of soulful growth, I knew then something I had hitherto only been able to suspect: that Lambda-MOO itself, somehow, somewhere along the path from its genesis in the mind of Pavel Curtis to its luminescence in the minds of thousands, had gotten a life.

I had gotten one too, by the way, amid the thousands of minds and the months of my immersion. And if you still are wondering what the value of such a life could possibly be, all I can really say is trust me: it didn't take the promise of a healthier mind or a better job or a sharper sense of civic duty or any other conceivable RL dividend to make it feel like a life worth living. Nor did it take a sudden intimation of the perils of the Information Age to make me feel like leaving it.

I left, in the end, because two lives was more than I could handle at the time. That's all.

I left because the tiny one had grown too big for me.

The Living Room
It is very bright, open, and airy here, with large
  plate-glass windows looking southward over the pool
  to the greenery beyond. On the north wall, there is a
  rough stonework fireplace. The east and west walls
  are almost completely covered with large, well-
  stocked bookcases. An exit in the northwest corner
  leads to the kitchen and, in a more northerly
  direction, to the entrance hall. At the south end of
  the east wall, there is a sliding glass door leading
  out onto a wooden deck. There are two sets of
  couches, one clustered around the fireplace and one
  with a view out the windows.
Pavel, Pavel's_Wife, and The_Author are here.

Pavel gestures toward the plate-glass windows to the
  south.

Pavel says, "And out there, as you can see, is The
  Pool. Right where it's supposed to be."

Pavel says, "No broadsword-wielding kobolds lurking
  underneath it, though. As far as I know."

The_Author moves closer to the windows, peers out.

The_Author says, "And _that_, I presume, would be the
  Hot Tub?"

Pavel nods.

The_Author grins.

The_Author is enjoying this little tour. There's
  nothing especially revelatory about it, certainly,
  but after his anticlimactic visit to The Server three
  days ago, he isn't expecting much in the way of
  revelations anyway.

Pavel gestures toward the northerly exit.

Pavel exits to the north.

Pavel's_Wife exits to the north.

The_Author exits to the north.

go north

The Entrance Hall
  This small foyer is the hub of the house. To the
  north are the double doors forming the main entrance
  to the house. There is a mirror at about head height
  on the east wall, just to the right of a corridor
  leading off into the bedroom area. The south wall is
  all rough stonework, the back of the living room
  fireplace; at the west end of the wall is the opening
  leading south into the living room and southwest into
  the kitchen. Finally, to the west is an open archway
  leading into the dining room.
Pavel, Pavel's_Wife, and The_Author are here.

Pavel says, "Entrance Hall."

The_Author smiles, glances around.

Pavel meanders down the corridor to the east.

Pavel's_Wife meanders down the corridor to the east.

The_Author meanders down the corridor to the east.

go east

Corridor
The corridor goes east and west.
There is a door to the north leading to the powder
  room.
Pavel, Pavel's_Wife, and The_Author are here.

Pavel gestures northward.

Pavel says, "The Powder Room. Just a small bathroom
  really."

The_Author peers in through the Powder Room's open
  door. He is surprised to see a room there at all,
  actually. He never paid much attention to the text in
  this part of the corridor.

Pavel wanders down the corridor to the east.

Pavel's_Wife wanders down the corridor to the east.

The_Author wanders down the corridor to the east.

go east

Corridor
The corridor from the west ends here with short flights
  of stairs going up and down to the east. South leads
  to one of the master bedrooms.
Pavel, Pavel's_Wife, and The_Author are here.

Pavel heads south to the bedroom.

Pavel's_Wife heads south to the bedroom.

The_Author heads south to the bedroom.

go south

Master Bedroom
This is the main master bedroom, overlooking the pool
  to the south through a sliding glass door. There are
  louvered doors leading west, and a north exit to the
  corridor.
Pavel, Pavel's_Wife, and The_Author are here.

Pavel spreads his arms wide.

Pavel says, "And this, of course, is the Master
  Bedroom."

The_Author's eyes widen.

The_Author exclaims, "Hey! This is where I first had
  MOOsex!"

The_Author turns -- giddy with the memory, homesick
  suddenly for Jessica and Ecco both -- and grins
  broadly at his hosts.

Pavel does not grin.

Pavel's_Wife also does not grin.

The_Author . o O (What did I say?)

The_Author says, "Um, so . . ."

The_Author says, "Would it be all right if I took some
  pictures?"

Pavel looks at Pavel's_Wife.

Pavel's_Wife looks at Pavel, then at The_Author. She
  smiles politely.

Pavel's_Wife says, "Sure, I don't see why not. If you
  could just, though . . ."

Pavel's_Wife says, "If you could wait till we get back
  to the other parts of the house? I'd kind of like to
  keep this room a little private."

The_Author says, "Oh. Oh, God, yes, of course."

The_Author is quietly kicking himself. He gets it now.
  This is _their_ home. Not his. _Their_ bedroom. Not
  8,000 MOOers'. Of course. And yet . . .

The_Author realizes he can't quite convince himself.
  There is a piece of his mind that knows he has been
  here before -- has lived here before -- and will not
  be persuaded otherwise.

Pavel says, "Shall we?"

Pavel heads out to the corridor.

Pavel's_Wife heads out to the corridor.

The_Author heads out to the corridor.

@join author

The Living Room
It is very bright, open, and airy here, with large
  plate-glass windows looking southward over the pool
  to the greenery beyond. On the north wall, there is a
  rough stonework fireplace. The east and west walls
  are almost completely covered with large, well-
  stocked bookcases. An exit in the northwest corner
  leads to the kitchen and, in a more northerly

direction, to the entrance. At the south end of the
east wall, there is a sliding glass door leading out
onto a wooden deck. There are two sets of couches,
one clustered around the fireplace and one with a
view out the windows.
Pavel, Pavel's_Wife, and The_Author are sitting on the
couches near the windows.

Pavel is telling stories: about MOO politics, about MOO
history.

The_Author is listening, laughing now and then, taking
notes.

The_Author is also not listening. He is looking: past
Pavel at the surfaces of this house, the walls, the
couches, the well-stocked bookcases. His eyes are
telling him it's all real, but there's a piece of his
mind that knows it can't be. Nothing looks exactly as
it ought to. Things are out of place here, rearranged,
as when a memory from waking life becomes a parody of
itself when you're asleep. Becomes a dream.

The_Author is wide awake, of course, but this, in the
end, is how he will remember the house he sits in
now: it is his fourth MOO dream. It is his last.

The_Author rises to go, finally.

The_Author exits to the north.

Pavel exits to the north.

Pavel's_Wife exits to the north.

go north

The Entrance Hall
This small foyer is the hub of the house. To the north
are the double doors forming the main entrance to

the house. There is a mirror at about head height
on the east wall, just to the right of a corridor
leading off into the bedroom area. The south wall is
all rough stonework, the back of the living room
fireplace; at the west end of the wall is the opening
leading south into the living room and southwest into
the kitchen. Finally, to the west is an open archway
leading into the dining room.
You see a globe here.
Pavel, Pavel's_Wife, and The_Author are here.

The_Author stands, taking his leave of Pavel and
   Pavel's_Wife.

The_Author doesn't seem to notice anything remarkable
   about this room. He detects no change in the scenery
   since he last was here.

You do, however.

You see a globe here.

look globe

A Globe
A large globe of planet Earth. It's mostly blue with
   big brown and white splotches. 'Enter globe' to get a
   closer look.

enter globe

You step into the globe . . . .

Earth

A big blue-green planet.
Within Earth you see: Africa, Asia, Australia, Europe,
   North America, South America, and Antarctica.

enter north america

North America, Earth
Home of the (cough) brave where the buffalo used to
  roam. . .
Within North America you see: USA, Canada, Central
  America, Greenland, Caribbean, North Pole, and
  Indian_home.

enter usa

USA, North America
The place where everybody thinks they are better then
  everybody else. And I _DO_ live here so shaddup you
  worthless pile of . . . .
Within USA you see: Georgia, Missouri, Vermont, Maine,
  Massachusetts, Rhode Island, Connecticut, New York,
  New Jersey, Pennsylvania, Maryland, Washington, D.C.,
  Virginia, West Virginia, North Carolina, South
  Carolina, Florida, Ohio, Kentucky, Alabama, Louisiana,
  Arkansas, Illinois, Indiana, Michigan, Wisconsin,
  Minnesota, Iowa, North Dakota, South Dakota, Kansas,
  Oklahoma, Texas, New Mexico, Montana, Idaho, Utah,
  Arizona, Nevada, Washington, Oregon, California,
  Hawaii, Alaska, Nebraska, Colorado, Mississippi,
  Tennessee, Delaware, Wyoming, and New Hampshire.

enter new york

New York, USA
The Empire State!!!
Within New York you see: Albany, North Babylon,
  Oceanside, New York City, Rochester, Bronx, Yonkers,
  Syracuse, Brooklyn, Brewster, Ithaca, Long Island,
  Alfred, Binghamton/Vestal, Larchmont, Medina,
  Gloversville, Jamestown, Flushing, Schuylerville,
  Annandale-on-Hudson, Schenectady, Troy, Deansboro,
  Coxsackie, and Chappaqua.

enter new york city

New York City, New York

New York City, March 1998

The greatest city in the Tri-State area!
Within New York City you see: Tribeca, Manhattan, nyc,
  Staten Island, east village, Center of the World, and
  Silicon Alley.

enter east village

east village, New York City
The place to be. Don't accept any substitutes.
Within east village you see: 13th Street squats, East
  10th Street Between First and A.

enter east 10th street

East 10th Street Between First and A
You are on a block of nicely spruced-up Lower East Side
  tenements running east to west, their heights uneven,
  their faces mostly brick, some painted and some not.
  A smattering of young and struggling ginkgo trees
  dots the sidewalks here. No parking space is left
  untaken.
Places of interest: The Famous Russian Baths of Tenth
  Street, The Building Where The_Author Lives.
The time is 2:35 a.m. EST.
The date is March 31.
The year is 1998.

You brush the dust of three and a half years off your
  sleeves.

enter building

You find the entrance to The Building Where The_Author
  Lives left conveniently ajar, almost as if someone
  were expecting you. . . .
The Building Where The_Author Lives
You are in the first-floor corridor of a nicely spruced
  up Lower East Side tenement. There are many apartment
  doors in here, but only one stands conveniently ajar,
  almost as if someone were expecting you. . . .

enter ajar

The Living/Dining Room
You are at the ground-floor level of an overpriced and
  undersized East Village duplex apartment. A cheap
  Scandinavian loveseat hugs one wall and across from
  it a brickfaced fireplace fills most of another.
Next to the fireplace a black metal staircase spirals
  down into the floor. To the south you see a small
  kitchen area. To the north a plate-glass door looks
  out into a small backyard.

go down

The Bedroom
You are in the basement level of an overpriced and
  undersized East Village duplex apartment. It's either
  cramped or cozy down here, depending on your mood.
  The ceiling is low and the walls are never farther
  than a couple arms' lengths away. In the northwest
  corner there's a bed: a waist-high platform painted
  white, a futon mattress also white, white sheets,
  white comforter, two bloodred pillows.
A black metal staircase spirals up to the ceiling. A
  passage to the southeast opens into The_Author's
  Fabulous Office Nook.
Jessica (sleeping) lies in the bed.
You see 19-inch Television set here.
It's dark down here. A sliver of light shines in from
  The_Author's Fabulous Office Nook.

go nook

The_Author's Fabulous Office Nook
You are in a small space surrounded by crowded
  bookshelves. There is just about room enough in here
  for two people. There is a desk, its white-laminate
  surface barely visible beneath a clutter of papers,
  books, bills, coffee cups . . .
To the south, a bathroom; to the north, a bedroom.

The_Author is seated at the desk.
You see computer, printer, and telephone here.
Halogen light streams down from overhead.

The printer is printing.

The_Author gazes intently at the computer screen, his
  right hand folded across his stomach, his left hand
  slowly rubbing his chin.

The_Author looks up at the ceiling.

The_Author looks back at the screen.

The_Author sighs and swivels slightly in his chair, and
  it is then that something flickers at the corner of
  his eye and causes him to swing around and give a
  little yelp of surprise.

The_Author looks directly at you.

You wonder what The_Author sees. Don't you?

look me

The_Reader
You see a shimmer of anonymous intelligence, a swirling
  barely visible in the air, like heat waves rising
  from midsummer blacktop. Now and then the waves
  almost take on the shape of a face -- The_Author's
  best friend, The_Author's freshman English professor,
  the nice lady who works the counter at The_Author's
  favorite bagel store -- but the image never holds.
It is awake and looks alert.

The_Author blinks, rubs his eyes, looks again straight
  at you -- and sees nothing but the bookshelves that
  surround him.

The printer stops printing.

The_Author shakes his head, turns slowly back to the
  desk and pulls a sheaf of pages from the printer. He
  sits there leafing through them for a moment or two.

The_Author sighs and sets the pages down on the desk
  before him.

The_Author yawns, rises, switches off the light.

The_Author exits to the north.

look

The_Author's Fabulous Office Nook
You are in a small space surrounded by crowded
  bookshelves. There is just about enough room in here
  for two people. There is a desk, its white-laminate
  surface barely visible beneath a clutter of papers,
  books, bills, coffee cups . . .
To the south, a bathroom; to the north, a bedroom.
You see computer, printer, and telephone here.
There is no light but the glow from the computer
  screen.

sit desk

desk
You are seated in an ergonomically designed office
  chair. On the desk before you: a computer, a printer,
  a telephone, a clutter, a sheaf of pages.

get pages

You pick up the sheaf of pages. There appears to be
  some writing on them. There is just enough light in
  here to read the writing.

read pages

You begin reading the sheaf of pages.

* *

EPILOGUE
March 1998

Throughout the fall of 1994, as it grew more and more
obvious to me that I was never going to go back home
to LambdaMOO, there were moments when I wavered,
pausing in the midst of whatever I was doing at my
desk to fire up the modem and open a connection to
the MOO's familiar login screen. "PLEASE NOTE," the
words on the screen would advise me (for the umpteenth
time), "LambdaMOO is a new kind of society, where
thousands of people voluntarily come together from
all over the world. What these people say or do may
not always be to your liking; as when visiting any
international city, it is wise to be careful who you
associate with and what you say. . . ."

Beneath these words was the usual brief disclaimer
absolving Pavel Curtis and the Xerox Corporation
of responsibility for any statements or viewpoints
encountered within the MOO, and this was followed
by an even briefer status report indicating the
approximate length of the lag and the number of
players connected at that moment.

Beneath that line the cursor blinked, waiting for me
to type the word "connect" and then my character name
and password. I rarely did. Sometimes I logged in as
a guest and looked around awhile, incognito; I could
read a few screenfuls of *social that way, or just
drop in on Dr. Bombay and look at him sleeping. Other
times I ran a quick @who command without even logging
in at all, just to see if any of my friends were on.
They often were, of course, but I almost always
convinced myself I was too busy to log in and get
caught up in conversation. The pull of LambdaMOO was
weakening, I could feel it. My odd, lonely geistings

grew more and more infrequent, and I began to wonder
if I really understood anymore, or if I ever had,
what had been the attraction or the meaning of it
all.

But then one day in mid-December I connected to the
login screen and knew again what LambdaMOO had been
about. "The lag is approximately 12 seconds," said
the status report. "There are 248 connected." The
number of players wasn't a whole lot larger than it
usually was, but it was the largest I'd ever seen,
and suddenly the thought of all those people inside
the MOO -- of all the connecting and hassling and
horsing around that was going on right then and there
-- just melted me a little. I logged in as Dr. Bombay
and checked immediately to see who was on, but nobody
there was anyone I knew. So I read mailing lists for
a little while. I took a look at Niacin's latest
character-description, and I looked at exu's and
S*'s, too. I teleported to the living room and
wandered: out through the entrance hall, down the
corridor, into the library. I kept hoping some friend
of mine would show up and page me for a chat. But no
one did. I typed @quit, eventually, and felt the
slightest bit like I was going to cry.

At some point in that same month I upgraded my Internet
connection and for the first time was able to access
a new and, at the time, still relatively unknown
virtual space -- a global library full of brightly
illustrated "pages" of information, each one linked
to another in a free-form mesh that appeared,
potentially at least, to spread forever in every
direction. It was called the World Wide Web, and
though it seemed then not much more than an intriguing
possibility, I have since come to think of it as the
tidal wave I'd dreamt would sweep across the MOO. In
the early months of 1995, the Web burst into popular
consciousness in a flurry of magazine covers, initial
stock offerings, and cocktail-party conversations,

and as its fame and fortune grew it swiftly remade
the Internet in its own vivid image. The Net that
MUDs had flourished in -- a place of unadorned text
and self-contained sites spread out among the
universities and research centers of the world --
gave way to a place of swirling color, sound, and
commerce, a free-flowing sea of information that was
growing so vast so quickly that the great engines of
media hype could barely keep ahead of it in their
rush to exaggerate its importance.

Tucked into an ever-smaller corner of this fast-
evolving picture, the world of MUDs was looking more
and more like a quaint, old-fashioned diversion. That
anyone had ever thought the future of cyberspace
could be glimpsed within that world (and in the year
or two before the Web took off, plenty of intelligent
people had entertained that very thought) began to
seem increasingly implausible. As for the MUD that
I'd called home, it too was fading from the cultural
radar. The nimbus of media attention that had for a
time surrounded LambdaMOO evaporated altogether, and
after a while it grew easy enough for anyone who'd
ever heard talk of the MOO to forget that such a
place had ever existed.

But I remembered, diligently. My MOOing days were done,
but I kept going back to them, poring day after day
and month after month over the notes and transcripts
and official documents that I'd accumulated in my
time on Lambda. I was trying to shape them all into
some kind of order that made sense of what I'd
experienced there; I was trying to turn it all into
the sentences and paragraphs and chapters of a book.
Yet the longer I spent immersed in my memories of
LambdaMOO, the more foreign the place itself became
to me. I geisted in and out from time to time, when I
needed to check some historical or architectural
fact; I made sure I woke up Dr. Bombay often enough
to keep him alive, sometimes indulging in a quick

chat with whatever pal was on when I logged in. But I
no longer felt even the passing twinge of homesickness
for the MOO that I had felt on that mid-December day
in 1994. With every day I sat (through the months,
and then the years) revisiting what I had known of
LambdaMOO, my life there drifted further away from
me, deeper into my past.

* * *

And then one day the book was finished, more or less,
and it occurred to me to wonder what had become of
LambdaMOO in the years that I'd devoted to writing
its portrait. I had some vague notions. Various
rumors of crisis had reached me over the months. I
had heard, for instance, that Pavel Curtis was
declaring an end to the experiment in self-rule and
was bringing back the wizardocracy. I had heard that
Curtis was quitting Xerox and leaving the fate of the
server up for grabs. I had heard that no one could
abide the MOO and its eternal social turmoil
anymore, and that the players were on the brink of
voting to shut it down for good. But every time I'd
happened to pop in for a peek, the MOO had looked to
all appearances as healthy as it ever had. The
landscape, at its core, was still about what I
remembered, and at its edges it was still evolving at
its usual brisk, haphazard pace. There were always a
couple hundred players or so connected when I logged
on, and there were often a couple ballots up for
vote. It was the same old LambdaMOO, as far as I
could tell.

But maybe I couldn't tell. Maybe the years of absence
had dulled my sense of what was what on LambdaMOO. Or
maybe I'd forgotten that nothing there was ever
really what it seemed.

I decided to ask around. My periodic @who checks told
me almost everybody I had known on the MOO still had

an active account there, and I was curious in any
case to find out what had happened with all of them.
So I sent some e-mails, made some phone calls, got in
touch one way or another with the old friends and
acquaintances of my virtual existence. And this is
what they told me:

They said that LambdaMOO has never really been the same
since the days of Minnie's almost-toading.

They said as well that nothing has really changed.

They said that Minnie remains, still actively pursuing
her unique notions of truth and justice, though no
one seems to pay her much attention anymore.

They said that all the wizards, pretty much, are still
around, but that the rumors of their return to power
have been greatly exaggerated.

It turns out, nonetheless, that there was a kernel of
truth to those rumors: in early 1996, the archwizard
Haakon did indeed intervene once more in Lambda's
social affairs, delivering an edict that abruptly
canceled his earlier withdrawal into a realm of
purely technical decision making. It sounded ominous,
but on closer examination it was clear that all the
edict really did was codify something everyone had
already figured out by now: that in a world so
thoroughly dependent on the workings of technology,
there was in fact no such thing as a purely technical
decision. Thenceforth, Haakon proclaimed, the
wizards' fiat power was in full effect -- they
would do whatever they had to do to keep the database
running smoothly, no more or less, and would no
longer sweat the social implications of their actions
overmuch. As far as Haakon was concerned, the purpose
was merely to put an end to a lot of pointless soul-
searching and recrimination that had pushed the job
of wizarding to the brink of thanklessness.

In any case, LambdaMOO appeared to take the announcement in stride. The wizardly fiat was ultimately
never put to any significant use; the democratic
institutions of the MOO -- the ARB, the mediation
system -- soldiered on unimpeded, and the petitions
kept on coming, one or two a month. And yes, the
electorate really was given the opportunity, at one
point, to decide whether to shut down LambdaMOO for
good. The ballot failed more resoundingly than any
other ever has.

Which isn't to say that social peace now reigns in
Lambda's corner of virtual reality or that the
citizenry is uniformly happy with the way things have
turned out there. HortonWho, for instance, never did
forgive the place for sending him into exile, as far
as I can make out. He revived his character as soon
as its six-month newting was up, and he still logs on
nearly every day, still doing so from his home in the
outskirts of Melbourne (or so I presume; he prefers
nowadays to keep the details of his RL to himself).
But the revolutionary fervor of his early MOOing days
has been replaced with what appears to be a permanent
state of melancholic disillusionment, interspersed
with spirited forays onto the mailing lists to make
the case for his dark version of MOO history. As he
told me in a recent e-mail, he's come to think of the
MOO -- and cyberspace in general, I suppose -- as
just the latest in a long, sad saga of new worlds
discovered, conquered, and drained of all their
promise and possibility. The radically liminal nature
of VR, he believes, its irresolvably ambiguous
oscillation between fact and fiction, reality and
imagination, is being flattened out and tidied up to
make the virtual dimension safe for general
consumption. "I've come to believe that this is how
history works," he wrote, "and how the new is
appropriated into the status quo. Ambiguities are
hunted down and exterminated with the same rigorous

intensity as that with which the buffalo were exterminated."

He was somewhat vague about the guilty parties, nominating in no particular order "the state, the comfortable sleeping masses, the will to solutions, corporate reality." But he left no doubt that I and my story-hunting colleagues in the media have also had a part in the snuffing out of VR's once wide-open indeterminacy. "It's not your fault," he said. "But after you came looking for pelts, and traded trinkets with us, the covered wagons of conventional reality followed along the trails we'd blazed. The trails were cut by animals, the animals have been driven out by suburban sprawl. . . . How could it be otherwise?"

Not surprisingly perhaps, Horton's fellow anarch and rabble-rouser Finn is also unimpressed with Lambda's current state of affairs, though his complaints, typically, are a little more down-to-earth. "There's nothing you can sink your teeth into these days," he says, pointing to a general absence of the sort of MOO-engulfing controversies he once thrived on. "Politics I guess is dead. People have settled into the arbitration disputes; they get a kick out of that for a while, but they're mostly frivolous disputes and people just wanting to get attention." Real life, meanwhile, has taken on more interest for Finn. He finally moved out of his parents' basement a couple years ago, setting out for Rochester, New York, to found an Internet software business with some other MUDders he knew, and once he got there, he also ended up in a serious RL relationship with a woman he had previously known only as Aurea on LambdaMOO. Two years down the road, both ventures appear to be going swimmingly. His company isn't the next Netscape or anything, but it's landed some respectable gigs, including a contract to run the official _Sally Jessy Raphael_ chat room; Finn and Aurea remain happily involved. His days as an online Casanova and all-around firebrand are pretty well over, but if he misses them much he doesn't show it. He still MOOs daily, but he mostly just sits idling in Lambda House's smoking room while he goes about his business at work. "I've still got friends on Lambda, and it's still fun," he says. "But it's not as much of a stage where you can play out your political ambitions and real arguments. It's no longer really a metaphor for real life. It's just not as passionate, I suppose."

For the mighty morphing gender-bender Niacin, as well, the passion seems to have gone out of MOOing long ago. At the time I left, he had acquired a stable of approximately fifteen spare characters, with several morphs per spare, and his "social intrigues," he now reports, "were Byzantine in their complexity." Inevitably perhaps, he drew closer to the other great morpher in our circle, S*, and it wasn't long before the two were involved in a serious virtual relationship. Their affair lasted about a year and a half, and when it ended, Niacin writes, "I realized that with her I'd taken the VR love thang about as far as I ever could; I just couldn't picture putting that much energy into any phase of VR life again." Niacin had in the meantime also finally ended his long-rocky relationship with the woman he lived with IRL, a relationship that, "bad as it was (or rather because it was so bad), had heightened the intensity of my MOOing." He'd left his lousy secretarial job as well, his RL in general was gradually getting happier, and the happier it got the less he felt like spending time in virtual reality. "In retrospect," he says, "it's evident to me just how much the misery of my real life (and not my intellectual curiosity, or my gender-role issues, or whatever) was the thing that made VR seem so dazzling back inna the day.

"Then there was also the fact that VR had started to seem tacky," he adds. "By '96 it seemed like every

yutz in the world was on the Internet, 'living the
fantasy.' Whatever elitist pioneer spirit had seemed
to me to permeate Lambda back in '91 or '92 was
completely gone. I missed that, and Interzone was
marginal compensation at best."

And so he just stopped going, basically. He let his
spares die out, reaped one by one as he let them lie,
and he now logs on to Lambda once a month, at most,
to check his MOO-mail. It's enough for him. "I'm
teaching prep-school English and living in Austin
with a woman I really like," he tells me. "My life is
pretty simple now. I feel like I've grown up a lot."

As it happens, S* seems to feel about the same. Her
life is going well, or so she told me in an e-mail a
few weeks ago, though she didn't tell me much in the
way of details. I didn't ask. I mainly wanted to know
about her relationship to VR, and she confirmed what
my @who queries had already told me over the last
year or so: "I don't go there much any more." She
also gave me some reasons why she doesn't, as best
she could figure them out: "Perhaps it's because my
life there was largely about drama, & I find myself
less & less attracted to drama these days. Also
perhaps because I am increasingly cynical about
the power of words to change much of anything. . . .
Mostly, though, it's just that I'm doing other
things these days, & they're more interesting to
me than VR."

I took her word for it. We hadn't spoken in years,
except to exchange a few brief, somewhat formal
e-mail messages concerning what I might or might not
end up quoting from our time together in my book. And
not surprisingly, I guess, her sessions on the MOO
somehow had never coincided with my occasional visits
over the years. She's been a phantom for me, like
the others -- Horton, Finn, Niacin, and the rest:
Sebastiano, Elsa, Minnie, enaJ, dunkirk . . . They have

gone on living lives invisible to me, moving on, growing up, while I have sat surrounded with the ghosts they left behind on my hard drive and sometimes watched for traces of their living selves in the vapor trails of the @who command.

As for exu, I haven't seen even that much of her in over a year. The cold, hard, technical truth, you see, is that the player object #50981, formerly known as exu, is no more: the acrimony of MOOish politics finally got to be too much for her, and she committed MOOicide in July of 1996. As Lambda funeral customs dictate, the player's name and recycled object number were passed on to friends. Doome got the number, and I am told he made a charming little memorial puppet out of the new object it defined. As for the name, it went to a MOOer who loved her more than he had ever thought he could love a name on a computer screen: "exu" is now among the several aliases attached to player object #53475, also known as Faaa, and also known as Samantha, and also, mainly, known as Dr. Bombay. I wear the alias with pride and in the fond hope that, someday, the woman who created and destroyed exu will decide the time has come to revive the character and reclaim the name.

But I doubt she will. The woman in question is getting along just fine without her old identity, if I'm in any position to judge, and I think I am. For she alone, of all the people I encountered on LambdaMOO, has remained a living presence for me ever since, and over the course of many e-mail messages and the odd phone call I have kept up, from afar, with the rich unfolding of her real and virtual existences. I have followed with amusement, with anxiety, sometimes with sympathetic sadness, and often with pride the adventures and vicissitudes of her personal life, which I have seen her manage with the same openhearted but self-preserving aplomb I had always

admired in her virtual dealings. I can't tell you the
best parts, but what I can say is that she's led a
full life in the years since I knew her as exu: she
set to work again in earnest on her dissertation; she
started teaching undergrads and going to conferences
to present her papers; she bought a motorcycle and
took it on thousand-mile road trips.

And through it all she MOOed, and she is MOOing still.
The late, untimely passing of exu certainly didn't
stop her -- she had a little-known second character
on Lambda waiting in reserve, and she has kept it
very much alive. I won't reveal the character's name,
not even under cover of a pseudo-pseudonym, because
the former exu's MOO life is a lot quieter now and I
believe she'd like to keep it that way. She has cut
back somewhat on the frequency of her visits to
LambdaMOO, and on their length, and she has nothing
to do with public affairs there if she can help it.
"I spend most of my time on Interzone," she says,
"with a similarly weary group of oldtimers. . . . We
read each other's writing. We play, we listen to each
other's rants, or we spend hours at a time not saying
anything at all, the way you can with old friends."

Weary though she may be, however, she doesn't regret
her involvement in the political debates that
ultimately exhausted her. "I'm way beyond sick of
theorizing about cyberspace," she says, "and have
become completely anti-utopian about VR, but all in
all the experience has been good for me. It's made me
a much better writer . . . encouraged me to go out and
get myself published. It's also given me a social
presence IRL in a way I never used to think I had.
After all the practice I got taking stands, making
points, influencing audiences who were sometimes
incredibly hostile, grad student seminars, for
instance, came to seem comparatively amazingly easy
places to formulate and express arguments."

I know: I said once that to look for RL benefits from
MOOing was to miss the point entirely. But now I must
confess that nonetheless it gratifies me to my soul
to learn how tangibly my good friend's life on
LambdaMOO has come to help her prosper elsewhere. I'm
not sure why. Perhaps it's because, in spite of
myself, I can't help wishing I too had a ready answer
when people ask me what real good, other than a book
deal, ever came of my own months wandering the halls
of LambdaMOO. And perhaps, also, it's because the
only remotely serviceable reply I can ever think of
is to point to this enduring friendship, and to the
friend it's given me, who was exu when I knew her
first but who need never be exu again as far as my
affections are concerned. Her well-being will always
gratify me, I imagine, no matter how she arrives at
it, and her place in my heart remains assured no
matter what name I know her by.

One last confession, though: I still miss exu,
sometimes.

I really do.

* * *

And LambdaMOO? I miss it also, in an abstract and
uncertain sort of way. The problem, really, is that
it's hard for me to know exactly what it is I'm
missing anymore. On this point I'm afraid my informal
survey of surviving users has been inconclusive. The
common thread of postlapsarian disenchantment that
runs in varying degrees through all their responses --
from HortonWho's darkling meditations on the tragic
shape of history through the sober, morning-after cool
of Niacin and S* to the sated shrug of Finn and the
mellow exhaustion of exu -- could indicate a number
of different things, not all of them especially
informative about the current state of LambdaMOO. It

could simply mean, for instance, that there is a
natural limit to the length of virtual lives, and
that my virtual-world-weary friends have all reached
or anyway are rapidly approaching it. It could also
mean that the initial charm of cyberspace, not just
for this handful of MOOers but for society in
general, is dissipating swiftly as its novelty
dissolves into the status quo. Or it could mean,
finally, just what on its surface it appears to mean:
that LambdaMOO just isn't what it used to be. That
the age of golden ages there is over, and that my
former virtual abode is now in a state of terminal
cultural decline.

I wouldn't bet on that one, though. Difficult as it may
be for me to figure out exactly what is going on with
LambdaMOO these days, I think it's safe to say the
place is not in any imminent danger of fading away.
Lambda is still one of the most populous and complex
MUDs around, and the world of MUDs itself, though
dwarfed now by the fast-expanding universe of the
Web, is bigger and more diverse than it ever was. VR
as MUDs define it -- text-based, slow-moving, socially
intricate -- will probably never have the same mass
appeal as 3-D, Technicolor virtual realities like
Doom and Quake and similarly immersive networked
games, and it will surely never become the seamlessly
distributed, universal network interface that Pavel
Curtis once dreamed of transforming it into. But
these days even Curtis recognizes that the defining
virtue of MUDs lies elsewhere -- that their appeal
has nothing to do with high-tech spectacle or
practical utility, and everything to do with the
unique pleasures of "textual repartee and prose-based
reality," as he puts it -- with language cherished for
its own sake. Delivering those pleasures is what MUDs
do best as a medium, Curtis believes, and he's
convinced that for the purposes of what they do best,
MUDs will never be replaced.

"In the same way that books haven't gotten any better
technologically for hundreds of years, MUDs are
already perfect," he insists. "I don't think they
will die, and I don't think they will get hugely more
popular. Doom, Quake, they'll always have more
attraction to a mass audience. But to the
intellectual, or just the one who appreciates
language -- the reader -- I think there's going to be
a strong attraction to MUDs sort of forever. And
there's something really charming about that. What
could you do to improve on it? Nothing. You're
already there."

As for his own attempts at Xerox PARC to "improve" the
MOOish interface, to turn it into a Net-wide tool for
"serious" collaborative enterprise, Curtis put that
all behind him long ago. True to the rumors, he left
Xerox several months back, cofounding a software
company called Placeware, whose high-bandwidth,
multimedia collaborative networking products have
little to do with the wordy, quirky architecture of
MUDs. But there was never any question of abandoning
LambdaMOO. The server came with him to Placeware's
offices in Mountain View, where it still resides,
officially the property of Stanford University, but
otherwise entirely in the care and possession of the
man who brought the MOO into existence seven years
ago.

"I'm still the archwizard," Curtis informs me. "And I'm
still the one with his finger on the power button."

But aside from drily noting this perennially momentous
fact -- the great hard-wired conundrum of Lambda's
democratic experiment and still the ultimate source,
I can only assume, of all that is both interesting
and maddening about MOOish politics -- Pavel Curtis
makes no great claims to any responsibility for what
goes on within the world whose fate his index finger
controls. Nor could he, in good conscience. By all

reports, including his own, the archwizard Haakon
spends almost as little time in LambdaMOO these days
as I do. For that matter, he has had nearly nothing
to do with MOOish governance in the five years since
he introduced the petition system; and in the seven
years since he laid down the basic floor plan of
Lambda House, he has had even less to do with the
shaping of MOOish architecture. The MOO was his
creation once, but that was very long ago: it's his
no more.

And he is therefore no more qualified to tell me what's
become of LambdaMOO, I think, than any of the others
in my hardly scientific sample. Which leaves me
finally with no other choice, if I would really know
the state of affairs in the place that I once thought
of as my second home, than to go back and make it my
home again, if only for a little while -- to expose
myself once more to the currents of its history, the
seductions of its geography, and the wit, invention,
fear, lust, anger, warmth, and banality of its
citizens.

I think I'll pass. Once was enough, God knows. Besides,
I'd probably feel obliged to write another book about
it all, and frankly, you've already heard about as
much of LambdaMOO's saga as you need to hear from me.
If you really want to find out how the rest of the
story goes, well, it's still out there-- somewhere
vaguely to the west of me, somewhere between reality
and imagination, somewhere that I would say is more
or less where all the stories of the world have ever
been told. And didn't Haakon say the MOO is for
readers? What then, dear reader, are you waiting
for?

* *

(You finish reading.)

You are seated in an ergonomically designed office
  chair. On the desk before you : a computer, a
  printer, a telephone, a clutter. On the computer: a
  screen. On the screen: a square of light, and
  floating in it lines of words you've seen before:
  "PLEASE NOTE: LambdaMOO is a new kind of society,
  where thousands of people voluntarily come together
  from all over the world. . . ."

You lay down the sheaf of pages.

You rest your hands on the desk before you.

You stretch your fingers out to touch the computer's
  keyboard.

You type a word. The word is "connect."

Acknowledgments

This book owes its life above all to the many lives that make up LambdaMOO. By the time my sojourn there was done, at least ten thousand players had passed through the place, some leaving visible traces on its surfaces, some leaving only memories, but all contributing in one way or another to the remarkable collective work of culture and imagination they inhabited (and in many cases continue to inhabit). They are writers all, and I feel slightly awkward getting paid to write about the world that they have written into being for the sheer love, fun, and hell of it. I would gladly acknowledge my debt to each and every one of them by name if I had the space, but since I don't, I'll limit my thanks to the pseudonyms of those who helped me most directly with this project.

BriarWood, Kerrit, Margaret, Minnie, Miseria, Moondreamer, Ople, Rhay, Sebastiano, stingaree, Wooga, and all the oldtimers at aCleanWellLightedMOO granted me extensive interviews, some on-line, most face-to-face. Haakon, enaJ, Kropotkin, glynn, and TomTraceback gave me more than interviews; their generosity with their time, resources, and attention was heartening. Niacin, Horton-Who, S*, Elsa, and Finn allowed me to print far more about their personal lives than I had any right to expect. And exu gave me all of the above and the MOO itself: she taught me how to see it. Any other MOOers who came to my aid and whom I have failed to mention should know that the failure was not intentional. In any case, you know who you are, all of you, and much better than I ever could.

Acknowledgments

My debts to people outside the MOO, of course, are also numerous. The work of Elizabeth Reid introduced me to MUDs and made my first forays into MUD-dish VR less baffling than they might have been. Other writers who have oriented me along the way include Howard Rheingold (whose book *The Virtual Community* supplied me with much of the early history of networks and MUDding recounted in chapter two), Richard Bartle (MUD pioneer and likewise an invaluable MUD historian), Lynn Cherny (sharp-eyed analyst of MOO politics and culture), Kathaleen Amende (chronicler of the Schmoo Wars), and Shannon McRae (ethnographer of MOOish sex and gender).

Lisa Kennedy, at *The Village Voice,* saw a feature article in the Mr. Bungle story when I was still only thinking of it as a curious anecdote, and Jeff Salamon, another keen-eyed *Voice* editor, helped inestimably to make the article happen and to give it shape. Mark Kelley, my agent, gave me the kindly kick in the ass without which I would never have turned the article into a book proposal. Ben Ratliff, Jonathan Landreth, and Elise Proulx, my editors at Henry Holt, oversaw the transformation from book proposal to book with exemplary trustworthiness and savvy.

Erik Davis, Joe Levy, Kit Reed, Jeff Salamon (again), and Sherry Turkle each took the time to read the manuscript and offer feedback, all of which was thoughtful and some of which was crucial. To the students of Beth Loffreda at Rutgers University, of Tom Keenan and Tom Levine at Princeton and Johns Hopkins, of Robert Christgau and of Stacy Horn at New York University, and of Josh Quittner at Columbia, who responded both challengingly and enthusiastically to readings of some of the chapters, and to the many readers of "A Rape in Cyberspace" who have e-mailed me criticisms and appreciations over the years, I am also grateful.

Assistance with the beastly job itself, the writing of the thing, came from a number of quarters. When the work was at its loneliest and most maddening, the Writer's Room was an oasis of camaraderie and calm. When inspiration flagged, the prose of Herman Melville, Salman Rushdie, and Cormac McCarthy (to say nothing of the grande lattes of the Starbucks Corporation) supplied it in abundance. And very often, as she has always been, my mother, Jane Dibbell, was on hand with moral and material support.

But if anyone put as much effort into bringing these pages to the light of day as I did, it was Jessica Chalmers. I said it before and I will say it now, again: this book is hers.